Praise for
DOUGLAS MUIR ★ ★ ★ ★

RED STAR RUN

"THIS ONE TAKES OFF LIKE A DRAG RACER AND NEVER DECELERATES. HIS MOSCOW SCENES RIVAL *GORKY PARK* IN THEIR AUTHENTICITY."

> —Oakley Hall
> author of *The Downhill Racer*

". . . A BOOK THAT WILL KEEP YOU NAILED TO YOUR CHAIR. MOVE OVER, TOM CLANCY!"

> —Paul Gillette
> author of *Play Misty for Me*

TIDES OF WAR

"FAST-PACED . . . IT STARTS WITH A BANG AND CHARGES HEADLONG TO A SURPRISING CONCLUSION."

> —T. Jefferson Parker
> author of *Laguna Heat*

AMERICAN REICH

"A HUMDINGER OF A THRILLER."

> —Channel 7 Eyewitness News
> (Seattle)

"FAST-PACED . . . MUIR PULLS IT OFF WITH CONSIDERABLE APLOMB."

> —*Los Angeles Times*

RED STAR RUN

DOUGLAS MUIR

CHARTER BOOKS, NEW YORK

RED STAR RUN

A Charter Book/published by arrangement with
the author

PRINTING HISTORY
Charter edition/July 1988

ISBN: 1-55773-067-9

Charter Books are published by The Berkley Publishing Group,
200 Madison Avenue, New York, New York 10016.
The name "CHARTER" and the "C" logo
are trademarks belonging to Charter Communications, Inc.

PRINTED IN THE UNITED STATES OF AMERICA

10 9 8 7 6 5 4 3 2 1

ACKNOWLEDGMENTS

The author extends special thanks for the assistance of the following individuals: Ed Breslin, Vicki Duncan, Paul Gillette, Oakley Hall, Marilyn Rose, Samuel Taylor, Richard Walter, and Cynthia Whitcomb. My gratitude also to the Fictionaires, Incentive Associates of Laguna Hills, the American Ballet Theatre, and the UCI Russian Institute.

I will take a walk in the meadow
Strolling underneath the leafy branches,
Loolee, loolee, in the meadow,
Loolee, loolee, in the meadow.

Now I choose three twigs from the birch tree,
And from them make three silver whistles,
Loolee, loolee, silver whistles,
Loolee, loolee, silver whistles.

Now a balalaika from a fourth twig,
I shall sing and play my balalaika,
Loolee, loolee, balalaika,
Loolee, loolee, balalaika.

—Ancient Russian folk melody used by
Tchaikovsky in his Fourth Symphony

1

WIND. ABNORMALLY HIGH TIDES. The rain, the heaviest in
thirty years, had been torrential. The night before, storm-
driven swells battered southern California, damaging the
celebrity homes precariously perched along Malibu Beach.
Just before dawn the sea calmed, and now only a gentle drizzle
fell from the overcast November sky.

Actress Tina Conner's home wasn't an estate by any means,
but it was a stunning architectural statement and exquisitely
furnished. Set on reinforced concrete pilings several feet
higher than the neighboring beachfront, the superstar's house
had weathered the storm without a scratch.

The contract man was a slender-framed, expensively attired
individual with a pockmarked, olive-complexion face, disdain-
ful lips, wiry black eyebrows, and a pathetic black toupee. He
was part French, part Algerian, but one-hundred percent
professional killer. Since first light the assassin had been
slumped in the seat of his rented Mercedes 450SL, parked on
the bluff, monitoring the scene below. The vantage provided a

bird's eye view of Tina Conner's home and the adjoining beach.

His passport read Najeeb Ahmed, but he preferred to be known only by the name Khamsin—after the hot, violent desert wind. Khamsin prided himself on detail and infinite patience. Gazing through ten-by-seventy Zeiss binoculars, his eyes gave a chronic twitch as he once more printed on his mind the shape of the place below. He slowly shook his head. Until the storm debris was bulldozed away and the utilities fully restored, the area seemed an unlikely place for the celebrity actress and her Russian lover to end up their vacation. Khamsin idly wondered why the athletic Nuri Baranov had turned from gymnastics and pursued a career in dancing. The career really no longer mattered; the young defector was marked for death. As long as Khamsin was paid handsomely, he would follow the instructions from Moscow without asking questions.

Initially the KGB had expressed reservations over whether he could complete the assignment alone. In other major terrorist operations, Khamsin Ahmed had headed a team. In this one, however, it was better to travel alone—quietly, quickly, and without encumbrances. Indeed, he was anxious to get this and one other assassination completed so he could return quickly to Paris. Home to Danielle, the wild mulatto woman who took such splendid care of him!

Lowering the high-power glasses, Khamsin checked his watch. Very soon his quarry should come out to walk the dog. Reaching into the roadster's glove compartment, Khamsin withdrew the box of blunt-nose .30 caliber rifle shells he'd purchased the day before.

Nuri Baranov never slept well in strange beds, a definite inconvenience considering his upcoming travel schedule with the U.S. Dance Company. The managing director had allowed him only eight days leave away from New York, and Nuri had already spent five of them in Puerto Vallarta. He'd played in the sun and still managed to squeeze in a few hours on his exposé book manuscript, *The Kremlin Sword*. Most important, there'd been privacy and ample time to make love to Tina Conner.

Never would it have occurred to him that during these final vacation days at his actress-friend's Malibu beach cottage that he'd be up most of the night, helping neighbors shovel sandbags to protect their homes against the raging surf. He'd worked up a sweat, retired exhausted, and gone to sleep immediately. Not a moment's insomnia.

In deep repose, Nuri's imagination—never lacking for vividness—ran unleashed. Again there are the thundering Pacific waves, but now he finds himself running along the beach nude. He's being pursued by Ivan the Terrible's dreaded Oprichnik warriors astride sweating black stallions. The sinister men are dressed entirely in black and have brooms and dog's heads dangling from their saddles.

Nuri stumbles and falls and the horsemen rage around him. He covers his head, exhausted. As the incoming surf rolls over him, a distant echo, memorized long ago in school, comes back to him. *Like a mountain eagle, soaring above the storm, so Ivan breasts the raging tide of human breakers.* Nuri remembers the words are from Sergei Eisenstein's famous screenplay. The water pushes him up the beach. More words from *Ivan the Terrible: The song of the azure sea, the Russian sea, rings high in the dome.*

Again wetness on his face, followed by a gentle whimper. Both seemed to be a part of the dream, or were they real? The sound seemed familiar. Nuri opened his eyes. Licking his chin and nuzzling against his tousled blond hair was Tina's playful Afghan hound. He grunted with annoyance and shoved the dog away.

Awake now, Nuri stretched his nude, six-foot muscular frame and rolled over to wrap his arms around Tina. But she was gone, the pale blue Italian linen sheets on the opposite side of the bed empty and cold to the touch. He glanced at his watch and sat up slowly. Beside him the dog cocked its head and turned its slender nose toward the kitchen. Nuri, too, sniffed the air and savored the aroma of baked muffins and freshly-brewed coffee. "Tina!" he called, a bit too brusquely. "Come in here, please."

There was a clatter of dishes and a mumbled response from the far end of the house, but she seemed to be taking her time joining him. He kept his silence, remembering how the actress had insisted that his impetuous, demanding nature was a burr in their relationship that had to be polished away. *Before* they took the big step of marriage.

Tina finally swept into the room, dressed in a champagne-colored silk robe that clung to her figure. She wiped her hands on a tea towel. "Learning to be the homemaker," she said, beaming. "The maid's on vacation."

When he took her in a little too lustfully, she frowned. Tina's light brown shoulder-length hair, gently waved, was already combed and her serious hazel eyes looked into his with an intensity he liked. She wore no makeup on her smooth, narrow face. She seldom needed it. But he hated her for her top-of-the-morning cheerfulness. He wasn't totally awake. Not yet.

Tina's effervescence continued: "Considering your Herculean efforts last night, you still feel like taking in the Getty Museum this afternoon?"

He didn't want to go, but he'd promised. "When I come out to Hollywood, you're the hostess. I'm 'putty in your hands'— is that how you say it?"

Tina looked at him askance and came closer. "But willful enough, I trust, to make a breakfast decision? Orange, guava, or kumquat juice?"

Nuri scowled. Abruptly, the Afghan hound jumped up on the bed between them. He gently booted the animal off the sheets and pulled Tina toward him. "Mmmmmm. Breakfast can wait. Come back to bed."

Eased back in the seat of the small Mercedes, Khamsin Ahmed had nearly dozed off. Almost an hour had passed. The rain had stopped, and now two figures emerged from the waterfront cottage below. The assassin sat up quickly, brushed back the sides of his toupee with his palms, and once more raised the binoculars.

The couple was easily recognizable. Khamsin's keen eyes watched as, hand in hand, Nuri Baranov and Tina Conner strolled up the beach, dodging the litter and the pools left in the sand by the storm. Chasing a tossed stick, a gangly white Afghan skittered before them.

Khamsin smiled with anticipation as he rolled down the driver's side window and sharpened the focus on the glasses. He watched the dancer pause to playfully tease the dog. Beside Nuri, Tina Conner folded her arms and shivered in her light windbreaker. Even without film makeup the young woman looked devastatingly beautiful. It was unfortunate the actress would have to bear witness to what was about to happen.

As Khamsin continued to observe, Tina turned to her fair-haired companion and draped both arms loosely around his neck. In response, the muscular Russian pulled her nearer, trying to ignore the barking animal at his heels. Nuri finally turned, and with a glower of impatience, flung a stick of driftwood as far as he could. While the Afghan raced off, Nuri wrapped Tina in his arms, smiled down at her, and carefully parted her windblown hair. They kissed passionately, Nuri's hands sliding down her waist and buttocks.

Khamsin swallowed hard. He stared a while longer, then stiffened in his resolve. Placing the binoculars aside, he reached for the telescopic-sight Browning .30-.30 rifle beside him and slammed several blunt-nose bullets into the magazine.

A shout from down on the beach distracted him. Khamsin glanced up, his steely eyes once more menacing the sand. Like an antelope at a waterhole, his target stood perfectly still. Suddenly alert, Nuri Baranov appeared to be focusing on the bluff—on Khamsin's car. Beside the wary Russian, Tina Conner appeared confused. The gamboling dog made divots in the sand as it skidded to a halt. Wiry tail raised slightly, its Sphinxlike hunter's eyes scanned the hillside.

Khamsin winced in irritation as the Afghan began barking. The actress touched Nuri's shoulder and pointed toward the bluff. The couple exchanged brief words, turned, and ran back up the beach. They were met by a man in a business suit who suddenly appeared from behind Tina's house.

Staring at the scene, Khamsin hesitated, unsure if he should raise the rifle. His heart was like a trip hammer; he could feel his face turning florid with anger. The bodyguard was unexpected. *Another witness!* Khamsin could get off three shots and kill them all, but there was still the escape factor. *Merde!*

The adrenaline was working; it would be difficult to back off now. He was about to bring up the Browning and get on with it when two teenagers on a dirt bike came roaring over the hill behind him. They parked nearby to take in the view. Khamsin cursed again under his breath. People, everywhere in southern California there were people. It seemed impossible to get away from them. Stashing the rifle under the dash, he reluctantly started the engine and backed the Mercedes away from the vantage point.

Khamsin gritted his teeth. Fuck the KGB *residentura* and his erroneous information! Young Baranov was not supposed to

have government protection any longer, certainly not here at
Malibu! Khamsin would be forced to come up with an
alternative plan; he'd have to be more imaginative.

They found the Getty Museum uncrowded. Tina had
reminded Nuri that it was a weekday and off-season. The
dancer was pleased; he hated crowds. It was well past noon,
but after a late, lingering breakfast, neither of them was
hungry. Nuri was still edgy over the stranger with the
binoculars on the bluff, but he wasn't about to let the incident
spoil his day with Tina. *False alarms*—there had been too
many of them—New York, Puerto Vallarta, now here.

They'd let FBI agent Paul McGinnis drive them the short
distance down the coast to the hillside re-creation of a
Herculaneum villa that was oil tycoon Paul Getty's gift to art
connoisseurs.

Lingering on one side of the gallery, Nuri observed Tina,
surprised by her keen interest in Renaissance and Baroque art.
Her attention alternated between a Masaccio tempera of St.
Andrew and a guidebook in her hand. She finally looked up,
smiling. "Your watchdog didn't mind waiting outside."

"He'll survive the snub. I think Paul McGinnis is a little
intimidated by your demands for privacy."

"Good."

Nuri smiled at her. "You're brave and I like it."

They were alone in the gallery. Tina's footsteps on the pink
marble floor echoed as she came up to him. Her hand moved
soothingly along the side of his face, then stroked his hair. She
said, "No. In reality, I'm terrified."

He searched her eyes and saw the truth. The valor was a
facade; she was very much afraid.

"Nuri . . ." She looked at him seriously, but her voice had
the ring of a childlike pledge. "I want it to work between us,
but for my sake, I'd like . . ." She hesitated. "For *our sake* I
insist you forget helping the others. I mean, the defection."

"The *escape*, Tina."

"All the more perilous sounding." She lowered her eyes.
"I've fought you on the underground book and admit defeat,
but this other crazy dream—" She didn't finish, for his fingers
gently closed her lips. Tina pouted and looked away.

He said quietly but firmly, "A little over a month from now
the Bolshoi begins its road company tour in Vienna. KGB or
no KGB, I want to be there at the same time. Quietly,

unobserved. If I can't expect your support, I trust you'll at least keep my confidence." He gave her a quick kiss.

Tina didn't reply, but when she finally looked back at him, the hostility had disappeared. She tried, unsuccessfully, to smile. It didn't matter. Nuri saw the familiar things he liked: Compassion. Intelligence. A virtual kaleidoscope of talent. Beauty in a special, imperfect way. And as always, the irresistible sexiness.

Giving an irritated sigh, Tina resumed her stroll through the museum. Again Nuri knew the enchantment that had drawn him to this woman. The tanned, mobile face, the gently upraised chin, the slightly turned-up nose and sensuous lips. There was the dime-sized birthmark on the side of her neck, which she tried desperately to keep covered with makeup. They'd been dating for almost a year, but Tina Conner looked even more enticing and adventurous now than that first night they'd made love on a deserted beach on France's Cote d'Azur.

Nuri recalled their first meeting, the St. Tropez bookshop where they'd both been browsing. He had collided with Tina as she came strolling absentmindedly around a counter, perusing a book on Renaissance puppetry. He'd enjoyed the intimate contact with her, but promptly apologized. Tina had recognized him immediately, as he did her, and she'd been surprised by his urbane English. They'd stared at each other then, as they still often did.

On reflection, it was fireworks at first sight, and the excitement had not abated since that Riviera meeting. And beyond the two-way current that flowed between them—the passionate, reciprocated heat—there was the challenge to his mind. There was also Tina's own talent and staggering success. He was hooked, not by any trace of feminine weakness or dependence, but by this woman's matching talent and strength.

They were together, *except* for his Bolshoi plans. She was afraid for him and let it show. He'd have to work on her opposition.

Khamsin Ahmed turned off Santa Monica Boulevard and headed into the Century City complex. He noted the digital clock on the Mercedes dashboard; it was just past noon. Despite his setback at Malibu, Khamsin had no intention of returning to the beach today. He would take care of Nuri's demise tomorrow. Right now there was another, equally important task to perform.

Khamsin gritted his teeth. Too damned much to do in a short time. The KGB was taking advantage of his stay in Los Angeles; he would make a note to charge them overtime. *Coûte que coûte!*

Parking the car in the cavernous subterranean garage of the ABC Entertainment Center, Khamsin took the escalator to the upper plaza. His hand sweated slightly as it gripped the Samsonite briefcase that closely matched his Italian knit suit. Tan; it was his favorite color. Passing Harry's American Bar he was tempted to stop in for a quick fortifier, but decided against it. Too close by and bartenders remembered faces, especially his kind of face.

At the end of the plaza two sharply-planed, triangular skyscrapers soared overhead. He knew the executive offices of L. Brian Beck's publishing empire were in the northernmost tower.

Khamsin waited in the lobby until it was quiet and an empty car was available; out of habit he preferred being alone in elevators, with plenty of elbow room. He whistled "The Lullaby of Birdland" as the lift made a rapid ascent to the top of the forty-four story building.

Khamsin paused in the corridor outside the elevators and checked his Rolex. It was twelve-thirty, exactly. Good. If his information were correct, Tangerine Hamilton would be alone in the shipping room with a brown-bag lunch. Khamsin located the stairwell entrance without difficulty. He'd use it later for his departure, descending three floors as a precaution before summoning the elevator.

Before him stood an imposing pair of oak doors with raised bronze letters: BECK PUBLISHING CORPORATION. Along the corridor were a half-dozen gold-framed enlargements of magazine covers. Khamsin recognized all of them. Two were popular American publications, the other four he'd seen in Europe. Executive offices here, not what he was after. He wanted Overseas Film Distribution Service, one of entrepreneur Beck's subsidiaries purportedly located on the same floor.

Khamsin stepped quickly down the hall and found the suite he was looking for. He avoided the reception entry, choosing instead a second door marked SHIPPING—NO ADMITTANCE. Calmly he slipped on his goatskin driving gloves and turned the handle. The door was unlocked and he went inside.

She was there, appearing just like the photograph he carried in his pocket: a young black woman in her mid-thirties, definitely attractive, with a look of self-assurance. She sat at a metal desk, perusing one of publisher Beck's supermarket tabloids and nibbling on a chocolate-chip cookie. Khamsin felt a kind of mock sorrow. Home in Paris he'd come to favor black women, particularly those like this one, with voluptuous bodies and steamy eyes. She had yet to say a word, but already he was excited. No, not now, he scolded himself. Stick to the business at hand. You're a professional.

Khamsin looked around the office. Behind Tangerine Hamilton was a Formica-covered editing table; along the far wall a closed door framed on each side with ceiling-high racks of film. Near the desk on the floor a pair of octagon-shaped cans, hinged open and empty.

Khamsin turned his feral gaze back on the woman, who stared at him with an annoyed look. "Yes?" She was appalled by his scarred face and tried not to let it show. Khamsin had seen that look too many times before to be offended.

"Tangerine?" he asked. His every movement was well thought out; he had to be absolutely sure of her identity. *Details.* "You are the friend of Nuri Baranov?"

She nodded, managing a trace of a smile. Her eyes gleamed as bright as the topaz bauble on her sweater.

Khamsin slowly opened his briefcase. Calmly, wordlessly, he withdrew the Desert Eagle .357 magnum, aimed it under the pin over the woman's heart, and fired. The sound-suppressor muffled the blast.

Tangerine, her mouth frozen half open in surprise, was propelled backward in her chair. Her body seemed to teeter interminably, then slowly, with barely a sound, she slumped to the floor. Her head thudded on the lip of a large film can, and her bovine eyes, ringed full with white, stared blankly up at him.

"Compte rendu, mademoiselle," he whispered. "An account rendered, yes? One down, one to go." Khamsin smiled to himself as he stared down at Tangerine Hamilton. Finally annoyed by the woman's grotesque gaze, he grabbed the hinged lid of the film can and slammed it down over her head. Then he shoved the gun back in the tan briefcase and slipped quietly out of the office.

2

PAUL MCGINNIS readily admitted to being a no-nonsense beer and baloney type. Stocky, barrel-chested, brown hair gone slightly bald, at forty-one he was the oldest man on the Nuri Baranov protection roster. The FBI agent had learned a good deal in eighteen years of undercover work—first with the National Security Agency, more recently with the Bureau.

The Getty Art Museum meant nothing to McGinnis, and he'd remained outside. The single-access, cobblestoned road-way that wound up from the Coast Highway made his surveillance of other arriving visitors a piece of cake. A guard station at the foot of the drive admitted only guests with advance reservations. Nuri and Tina would be safe enough.

McGinnis wondered if his alertness any longer mattered. Two more days and the Bureau, in agreement with the State Department, would wash its hands of the Russian defector's file. A year had lapsed and the operation had cost the taxpayers a bundle. McGinnis and his three relief men were looking forward to the end of the boring vigil and moving on to other assignments.

10

McGinnis looked up as a white Nissan 240ZX arrived at the top of the driveway and parked in a prohibited zone. The car and its lone male occupant were expected. The man's name was Saarto, and he was to be the Bureau's one-man *replacement*, of sorts. From what McGinnis had learned earlier, Saarto was a private detective-turned-bodyguard who was leaving the employment of infamous publisher L. Brian Beck to go to work for Tina Conner—paid for, of course, by her film studio.

Generally, McGinnis disliked hired guns from the private sector. Watching Saarto slip out of the car, smooth his hair in the rearview mirror, and swagger forward only confirmed his reservations. On first appearance alone, the man had obviously read too much Raymond Chandler and John MacDonald. Frowning in concentration, McGinnis tried desperately to remember Saarto's first name. *Was it John or Jim?* McGinnis had been up half the night with Nuri and Tina at Malibu and his mind felt woolly; he should have listened more carefully on the phone. *Shit.*

The newcomer sported a dark, even tan made even more pronounced by his turquoise eyes. *Too bright,* McGinnis thought, wondering if they were a pair of those new fashion contacts. Saarto was tall, his frame posture perfect; he had light brown wavy hair, a narrow nose, and a pronounced jawline. McGinnis figured he'd easily fit the part of an oarsman in a Kirk Douglas Viking movie.

McGinnis leaned against his own car, chewing on a toothpick as the new man approached. A half-assed soldier-of-fortune type, McGinnis reflected. Might even have a little mercenary experience. He'd seen the image too often in southern California—one more self-centered young cocker, more brawn than brains. Probably doubling in brass as a film extra and would-be stunt man.

"I'm Paul McGinnis. We talked on the phone." He extended a paw and Saarto shook it. Firmly enough.

The private detective gestured toward the museum entry. "They're inside?"

"You got it."

"Good. We can talk privately."

McGinnis ventured a smile. "Understand the studio set you up. They figure a Bureau man is an easy replacement?" It was more of a hard-edged statement than a query. McGinnis had gone without lunch and invariably had a choleric disposition when he was hungry. He began again, "Look, Jim—"

"The name's *Johann* Saarto. My friends call me Jon. I spell it J-O-N." The clarification was restrained, as grave and uncomfortable as a prison uniform.

"Sure. I'll get it straight."

"What do you have in mind, McGinnis?"

"Figured you might have a few questions before I leave town." McGinnis smiled. "The big takeover."

"Takeover? I'm not *replacing* anybody. Come Wednesday I'm being paid to protect Tina, not the Russian."

McGinnis shrugged. "He's being set up to become an *American*. And the latest word is that they plan to marry. Nice-looking couple."

"You don't say." Jon Saarto smiled for the first time, revealing a white, even bite as perfect as the rest of his face. McGinnis figured the teeth were capped.

"You'll find Tina skittish." McGinnis pointed in the direction of Malibu. "Insisted there was a possible incident this morning at the beach house. Hundred goddamn false alarms a week, but still, just one of them might—"

Saarto interjected, "I'd think with time the political danger would pass."

"That's the official U.S. government line, not mine." McGinnis took out a handkerchief and rubbed vigorously at a smashed insect on the car windshield. Without looking up, he confessed, "I've been on this assignment too long, Saarto. I'm bushed. You'll find that keeping up with that talented bastard burns you out. He moves like lightning and with just as much energy."

The private detective nodded. "In my book he's still a dandy in leotards. If he's smart, he'll drop out of the limelight and go low profile."

McGinnis had to smile at that; he'd heard it all before. "Fat chance. With all that explosive talent and fucking ego? Not to mention that powerful father of his in the Kremlin?" McGinnis shook his head and lowered his voice. *Go ahead, rub the new man's nose in all of it.* "Not enough the kid makes good on the New York dance scene. He opts to hang out with a big-name Hollywood star and write anti-Soviet literature—some kind of exposé on the KGB. Tell me, Mr. Saarto. You sure your film studio boss has the guts, persistence, and megabucks to follow through with this? Like how much coin is a celebrity like Tina Conner worth?"

Jon Saarto's wide-set, turquoise eyes blazed back at him. "Plenty."

"Next question. Mind if I ask how much First Consolidated Studios offered to lure you away from that millionaire porno publisher?"

"That's proprietary information."

Frowning, McGinnis decided to back down a little. "You'll be a facade of protection at best. I'll give you a tip, Saarto. Despite our government's stated line, I think the heat's still on. Nuri's in trouble."

"Be specific."

"I'd like to, but the FBI gets only so much superficial double-talk. International eyesore to the Soviet nation, the usual defection shit. My guess is there's more hidden here."

"Whatever, Tina Conner's a part of the picture. My part." Saarto looked up, his eyes vacantly following a pelican soaring toward the beach. Finally he shot McGinnis an indifferent gaze. "I can handle it. Alone, or if necessary, with additional paid help." Saarto withdrew a package of sugar-free gum, calmly unwrapped a stick and shoved it in his mouth. He extended the package, but McGinnis declined.

A moment's awkward silence passed. McGinnis let out an uncomfortable sigh. "Mind if I ask what a former L.A. private eye knows about the Soviets?"

Saarto looked at him sharply. "My father's from Finland and my mother was born in Russia. Both came here from Helsinki after the war. I speak both languages well enough. And you?"

"Sorry, I'm not that talented." McGinnis paused, studying his adversary with newfound respect. *Not such a dimwit after all.* He decided to give Saarto the works. "You want to be filled in with what I have?"

Saarto shrugged. "I didn't drive out here to look at Roman art."

"Okay, from the top. Nuri Baranov's part Latvian, part Ukrainian. One of his grandmothers was Jewish, hence the name Nuri. Like his father, the revisionist Soviet chairman, he's outspoken, completely unafraid, and a little vain. Also stubborn. A chip off the old block." McGinnis paused to give weight to his next statement. "In my book, Saarto, fearless people are prone to blunder. Big shots eventually make big mistakes. Especially under stress."

The new bodyguard grew more attentive. "Keep talking."

"The 'old block' may be combined Chairman and Premier, but he has internal enemies."

"I read the papers, Mr. McGinnis. The Soviets are always squabbling with each other. What's the big deal?"

"There's a rumor that all hell's about to break loose in the Kremlin. Baranov's son's defecting to the West only compounds the matter. It's an embarrassment to the Soviet Politburo and Presidium, not to mention a fucking bone in the throat of the KGB."

"You really think the stakes are that high?"

"Maybe higher." McGinnis hesitated. "You think it's your kind of scene, Saarto? Swapping the glitter of Hollywood, instead playing Russian Roulette while chugging straight vodka?"

Saarto glanced at his watch. "You finished, or is there more?"

McGinnis thought for a moment. "One more thing. There's some scuttlebutt that our government's interest in Nuri is a two-way street. Rumors that the dancer is in reality a double agent, and that's the real reason the FBI kept tabs on him."

"Only scuttlebutt? No substance?"

"From where I sit, rumors, nothing more. I say it's CIA-inspired bullshit. So far Nuri's clean. Harmless enough, except for his big mouth. A confused-artist type with a *determined desideratum*. He lusts for the stars, you know what I mean?

Nuri hovered in a telephone booth near the Getty's entrance vestibule. He shook his head in disbelief, suddenly feeling dizzy and sick to his stomach. Placing a hand against the wall to steady himself, he slowly, as if in a trance, replaced the receiver on the hook. He'd managed to slip away from Tina for a few seconds to telephone Overseas Film Distribution Service only to discover that his contact there was dead!

Initially the switchboard operator claimed the shipping clerk was unable to come to the phone, but then a homicide detective had picked up the line and asked Nuri his name and a battery of questions. At last came the shocking truth: Tangerine, the young black woman who smuggled his messages and other material into the USSR, had been brutally murdered.

Nuri had good reason to doubt that the homicide was a
"crime of passion" as the police suspected. He stared at the
phone for a full minute, trying to calm himself. He didn't want
Tina to know he was upset, not now. Nor did he need her to
panic. Tina knew he was smuggling manuscript pages into
Moscow by microfilm, but she didn't know how the underground network functioned, *who* was assisting him. Nor was
the actress aware that he was waiting for more information
from Marina Pleskova, data on the Bolshoi's upcoming tour
outside the Soviet Union. Information that was to have been
transmitted through two-way film shipments by Tangerine
Hamilton. He needed to know more about the tragedy at
Century City, but he'd have to tend to it later, when he was
alone. Possibly Paul McGinnis could assist. For once the FBI
agent might be more of a help than a hindrance.

Nuri waited until the erratic stirrings in his mind subsided,
then took a deep breath and headed back to the Hall of
Aphrodite, where he'd left Tina.

In Moscow the sprawling stone complex that was KGB
Headquarters occupied the entire northeast end of Dzerzhinsky
Square. Lubyanka Prison, located to the rear, had a connecting
stone courtyard providing KGB functionaries convenient access to the interrogation and detention facilities. The entire
complex was an area most Soviet citizens discussed in
whispers and avoided if they could help it. Actually, most of
Lubyanka had been remodeled to make room for KGB office
expansion, and the dirtiest of interrogations as well as the
abrupt disappearance of captives were now handled elsewhere
in the city. For the sake of convenience, however, two rooms in
Lubyanka's basement had been retained for the more *sedate*
forms of questioning.

Behind a riveted steel door in one of these chambers, a blue-
jeaned, broken-faced youth from Moscow State University sat
rigidly in a wooden chair. His soiled shirt was ringed with
sweat and unbuttoned, his arms and legs bound behind him.
The student's face bled from a cut beneath one eye. A pair of
steel-framed eyeglasses lay twisted and shattered at his feet.

The interrogation room was no more than an elongated
cubicle of peeled paint and damp walls that smelled of mildew.
In Moscow, with its lacework underground rivers, basements
were notorious for weeping all winter. The prisoner, too, was

tearful. An improvised spotlight blinded him, while in the shadows a pair of ill-tempered officers from the KGB's notorious Fifth Directorate conversed in hushed tones. Both interrogators were women. The tall one in charge, who bore the rank of lieutenant colonel, stepped back into the light.

She said to the prisoner, "Your copying machine has been confiscated, my friend. Your secretive printing days are over."

The young man drew back slightly. Despite an earlier pummeling, he stifled an absurd compulsion to smile at his interrogator's appearance. The woman before him, apparently in her early forties, had introduced herself as Colonel Bruna Kloski. By any measure she was a character study in the grotesque. She was Amazon-tall with gangly arms and a pasty, heavily powdered face; her mouth was small with pouting goldfish lips and her gleaming, collar-length blond hair looked as if it might have been lifted from a display mannequin at GUM. The woman's KGB uniform was ill-fitting, her blue epaulets askew; the drab khaki stockings covering her muscular, bowed legs were wrinkled, their seams uneven. The small medals pinned over her dumpy breasts gleamed as she came closer. Kloski's face twisted in a deadly smile as she put on a glove of black kid leather. Her fist came at him in a blur.

The prisoner winced, temporarily blinded by the numbing blow to the side of his face. The high-ranking woman colonel was as strong as an ape.

Despite the pain, he bravely murmured, "Gorillas and other simians use their knuckles to walk. It's a shame you haven't learned to be equally productive, Colonel."

She struck him again, harder, then stood back and gloated, "Now, citizen, I suspect you are ready to talk, yes?" She peeled off the glove and studied her watch. "The scopolamine should have taken effect. Excellent. I thoroughly dislike violence. Now then, who are your accomplices? Most important, what do you know of this *konspiratsia* of dancer Nuri Baranov's?"

He lowered his head, trying to avoid the vile woman's eyes, but she roughly jerked his chin back up and rasped in his ear, "The dancer conspires to have other Soviet artists defect, yes? Who, besides yourself, are the other dissidents who support him?"

He stared at her through fogged eyes as a stack of paper was waved in his face.

"And there is this traitorous document." In a gravelly voice she read from the cover page. "*The Kremlin Sword*, by one Nuri Baranov. Chapter six, correct? Ah! In your eyes you recognize it!" Colonel Kloski was so close he could smell her breath. She reeked of smoked herring and pepper vodka. Kloski continued, "I am sorry for you, my young friend. If you wish to pursue a printing career, you will do it in prison. Your other distribution contacts will be apprehended as well. But today you will tell me where you obtained this slanderous manuscript, and *where*." Spittle spewed from her mouth as her voice became a shriek. "Do you hear me, citizen? Who is your contact?"

The student stiffened. He resolutely shook his head and closed his eyes.

"Then it is most regrettable," she sneered. "The KGB has the most sophisticated electronic persuasion devices, but my associate here has no patience with them. You must forgive her for ignoring modern technology and resorting to old-fashioned measures."

The prisoner watched Kloski signal her dour-faced, equally unattractive assistant, who stepped quickly forward with a pair of blunt-nosed pliers. Behind his back he felt his fingers being forcefully extended.

An instant later his scream reverberated around the chamber.

Bruna Kloski didn't look away, nor did she bat an eyelash. "One fingernail at a time," she said dully. "We will cease when you speak up with the truth. Who provides you with these manuscript pages? Over how long a period?"

"Stop!" he cried, hysterical with pain. "The Bolshoi! Comrade Marina Pleskova. The ballerina gives them to me monthly."

3

A SMALL BLAZE crackled in the fireplace of the Oval Office. The President's dog, an arthritic schnauzer, got up from its place on the hearth and hobbled over to sniff the alligator-hide briefcase of the diplomat who had just entered the room.

Gregory Hewett rarely smiled; when he did, his lips were as thin as the lines on his Neiman-Marcus pinstripe. The sober-minded Ambassador was a bald, portly somatotype with a moon-shaped face and deep-set, wistful eyes. A long-time friend of the President, Hewett had only recently been appointed to head the U.S. legation in Moscow. This was his first visit back to the States since accepting appointment.

The President shook his hand. Hewett straightened his English silk tie and stood attentively. He asked in a hesitant voice, "The Secretary of State asked me to drop everything, Mr. President. I take it the matter is urgent?"

"Indeed, it is." The Chief Executive, a lanky, good-natured type with a creased, liver-spotted face and twinkling eyes, waved Hewett toward a wingback chair then sat down himself in a tired suede rocker. Ignoring ceremony, the President

18

propped his rancher boots on the corner of his desk and ran both hands repeatedly over a mane of hair the color of an owl's wing.

Gregory Hewett, too, settled back, once more studying the nation's leader opposite him. The President looked troubled. Hewett waited patiently, confident that whatever woes his usually easygoing friend anguished over wouldn't be suppressed for long.

The President seemed to be studying him. "I won't keep you from missing your plane, Greg. Hardly appropriate for our Ambassador to miss that annual military parade in Moscow. Your first opportunity to sit in the Red Square dignitary box?"

Hewett hunched his shoulders and nodded. "My predecessors tell me it's not much of a show. Same weaponry, same endless lines of jackboots and smug *chinovniki*." Hewett quickly translated, "That's *bureaucrats*, Mr. President. Do you mind if I smoke?"

"Your cigars or mine?" The Chief Executive grinned and gestured toward a handsome sandalwood humidor.

Hewett shook his head. He withdrew a half-dozen Havanas from his pocket and nudged them across the broad, scrupulously neat desk. "Castro's contraband, but in this case it's legal enough. A 'welcome wagon' gift from Chairman Baranov when I first arrived on station."

"Good. The Russians must like you, Ambassador."

Hewett chortled. "Other than the Soviet leader himself, I'm as welcome around the Kremlin as crabgrass on your putting green."

The President seized a cigar, unwrapped it, and sniffed the delicate fragrance. Despite the taut mood, both men smiled with pleasure and lit up. The President settled back and savored the smoke, but Hewett puffed nervously, remaining attentive and erect on the edge of his chair. He finally asked, "Sir, do I sense trouble? Matters aside from those in the diplomatic pouch?"

"You do indeed. Since the State Department forwarded your report from Moscow, events have accelerated. Certain KGB personnel appear to be getting restless. Under the circumstances, Ambassador, perhaps you can tell me who's really at the Soviet helm?"

"Sir, I hesitate to predict—"

"Hesitate, my ass. It's a part of the job. In the months

ahead, if I'm to square off against an adversary with lead in his glove, I at least want to know whose hand it's in. And equally important, whether my opponent leads with a right or a left."

Hewett shrugged with impatience. "In the Soviet dictatorship today it's the triumvirate that counts. We may have to learn to negotiate with three individuals—a damnable interlocking threesome."

The President frowned. "I prefer to deal with one man—Baranov."

"Frankly, so would I. But in reality what we have is like the Russian's proverbial troika—a highly-trained, three-horse team." Hewett puffed his cigar. "The Chairman of the Soviet Politburo, the leader of the Red Army, and the head of the KGB make an invincible trio, I'm afraid. Or so the *Bolsheviki* are led to believe."

The President shook his head and said quickly, "Until last month I had this Pavlin Baranov in a decent gentleman's standoff. Cautious, stubborn, willing to listen, and when the mood struck him, at least willing to do a little horse trading. A tank for a tank, a sub for a sub, a missile for a missile. We made progress at our summit. But now my initiatives meet with committee double-talk, bullshit, and *nyets* before they're even out of the briefcase!"

Hewett nodded. Feeling a growing discomfort, he kept his silence.

"Ambassador, there's a profile that's missing, a 'matter of intent.' And I'm full-up with well-meaning but faulty CIA intelligence. I studied your official report as well, but now I'd like your candid, off-the-record thoughts. Some off-the-cuff, over-the-backyard-fence observations."

The mahogany Westminster clock on the fireplace mantel chimed the hour. Hewett waved for it to finish, then said, "Backyards are one of our *imperialist* luxuries, Mr. President. They do without them in Moscow." Hewett started to take a pull on his cigar but changed his mind and set it on a nearby ashtray. Still not sure whether he was on the hot seat or not, he thought for a moment before proceeding. "We've examined the profiles, sir, but sometimes it's difficult to comprehend the Soviet's virulent strain of paranoia. Among our many disagreements with them, perhaps we were imprudent in laughing off Pavlin Baranov's recent offer to trade certain dissident 'personalities.' His so-called small token of good faith to improved relations."

The President's cigar halted halfway to his mouth. Hurtling forward in his chair, he snapped, "The Soviet Chairman's proposal was inhumane, illegal, and preposterous on any count. Any insinuation of our CIA involvement in trading the defecting dancer and physics professor for General Shaeffer in Lubyanka Prison was, and still is, out of the question." The President hesitated, then continued in a calmer voice. "Incidentally, you may have missed the obituary notice in the papers. Professor Penkovsky died of a heart attack in Boston three weeks ago."

Hewett nodded gravely. "I'm aware of that. But we still have the Chairman's son, young Nuri. And I understand he's making sensational headlines. Not only on the dance scene, but he's glittering under the sordid Hollywood spotlight as well. A bit too brazenly, I might suggest. For a defector, he talks too much, and in remarkably articulate English. Moreover, the word in Moscow is that Nuri's working on some kind of blasphemous book. Not only about his own escape to the West, but an exposé on Fiodor Talik and his KGB."

The tension in the office increased perceptibly.

The President exhaled sharply and shook his head. "Nuri Baranov was granted political asylum. He intends to apply for citizenship. Do I detect, Ambassador, the same discomforting clamor coming from you as I hear from my outspoken, reactionary Defense secretary?"

"No, sir. I'm a diplomatic appointee, not a military think-tank type or an espionage professional."

"Defense Secretary Fleming is hardly a spy."

Hewett flushed. "I'm sorry, Mr. President. I'm forgetting Fleming is also a personal friend of yours. But you must admit the man is often outspoken and takes unprecedented liberties."

The skin on the Chief Executive's face tightened as he looked at Hewett stonily. "The secretary is under my personal orders to cool his heels. He and this General Shaeffer may be close, but the point is, this former military attaché made some blundering mistakes in Moscow. And we've no one else to swap, even if such an arrangement with the Soviets appealed to me."

Hewett clasped his hands and lowered his eyes; avoiding the

President's scrutiny, he asked, "You're inclined to let an American rot in a Soviet prison?"

"Hardly likely. The Russians will treat Shaeffer fairly enough, realizing he's a trump card. U-2 pilot Gary Powers came back to us none the worse for wear. And I'm not that sympathetic to Shaeffer. Once his diplomatic tour in Moscow was over, he had no business going back on his own, without diplomatic immunity, and taking *inappropriate* photographs."

Hewett was surprised, and let it show. "That was before my tenure in the Soviet Union began, but the official record indicates the KGB trumped up the charges."

The President went on accusingly. "Shaeffer was on a mission for U.S. Army Intelligence. He might as well have been on a fool's errand, everything considered. Our CIA people uncovered the ill-conceived scheme."

"You're going over all this for a reason, Mr. President?"

"I am. And what I have to say must remain outside official channels. That includes State, CIA, and the Defense Department. *Particularly* Fleming and his Army friends at the Pentagon."

Hewett nodded.

The President sucked several times on his cigar before continuing. "I've learned a certain military aide of Chairman Baranov, a Soviet Army marshal, sent out a feeler to his counterpart here in Washington. I suspect one of our Undersecretaries of Defense is involved but I can't prove it. The Soviets, apparently, still want their Bolshoi Ballet star back, and they're willing to negotiate. This time, however, it won't be with me."

"Some gall. They still want to trade for General Shaeffer?"

The President's lips curled in a half smile. "The Soviet Chairman wants his son returned alive, of course. KGB General Fiodor Talik, it appears, wants no part of his overture. Our intelligence has determined that the KGB wants the dancer dead. Wherever, however. Outside Lincoln Center, the East River, poison, you name it."

"Why?" Hewett shifted uncomfortably in his seat. "For twenty years now we've protected former KGB personnel, Soviet military officers, and other controversial defectors who fled to the West. None of them yet have incurred the KGB's reprisal by liquidation."

The President's eyes narrowed. "Their death sentences stand. The KGB's failure results from new identities, financial support, and often enough, U.S. government protection. Nuri Baranov is a performer with an eye for publicity. He's high profile, headstrong, and in a dangerous position.''

"Mr. President, about this trade—"

"No, my friend. I'm not ready to play the ghoul by agreeing to a swap. A barter of this ilk would never stand up to international opinion. Nor could I live with my own conscience.''

"May I ask how this unauthorized, behind-the-scene negotiating is supposed to come about, Mr. President?''

"I suspect the Russians would do the dirty work themselves, once we relax our vigilance and look the other way. Nuri Baranov could be seized in New York or during his upcoming European tour.''

Hewett mumbled, "Back to Moscow and God knows what fate. Undoubtedly a showcase trial and minimal punishment if his father retains control. But if the KGB dictates the rules, it's a different matter.''

Once more anger seemed to cross the President's face. "Of course, I'll refuse to cooperate, but I'll need your help. When you return to Moscow, try to influence the Soviet leader. If possible, meet with him *privately*. Explain my position regarding his son. The facts are, instead of pulling out our FBI bodyguards this week as planned, they'll remain on duty, alerted and strengthened in numbers.''

Hewett thought for a moment. "Earlier this year you expressed concern that the defecting dancer might be a clever plant—a Soviet spy. Are you convinced otherwise now?''

"I'm confident Nuri's bona fide. Our security people, paranoid as usual, aren't so sure. They're still quietly investigating.''

"Perhaps, Mr. President, we as well as the Soviets have placed too much significance on young Baranov's defection.''

"It would have been better had the ballet star gone to England, or to France, like Nureyev. Think for a moment, Ambassador. What would have happened if Stalin's daughter had defected to the U.S. while *her father* was still alive?''

Hewett watched the tall Chief Executive rise to his feet, grumble to himself, and go to the windows overlooking the south lawn. The President stared out at the twinkling headlights moving slowly along Constitution Avenue. Another half hour, Hewett reflected, and the homeward rush would be over for the fortunate federal workers in Washington, while he still had a dozen flying hours ahead of him before returning to the embassy compound in Moscow and a decent night's sleep. Hewett hated jet lag with a passion. It was always worse on the eastbound leg.

The President turned to face him. "I have the feeling Chairman Baranov's son is only the tip of the iceberg. A precursor of some yet-to-be-identified threat. General Talik, I'm afraid, is more ruthless than Stalin's notorious Beria. Supposing Talik forces Baranov out of office?"

Hewett stiffened. "There was a similar hypothesis in the London press this morning. For the Soviets, it would mean the end of *glasnost*. For us . . ."

"Go on, Ambassador. I'm listening."

Hewett loosened his tie. "Mr. President, if the KGB minister can make a mockery of Chairman Baranov and discredit him, he will. But as long as the Red Army supports Baranov, Talik will probably be held in check."

The President studied Hewett. "Short of an assassination attempt."

Hewett grimaced. "Fiodor Talik is an opportunistic, rapacious hawk, but I doubt if he's that adventurous."

"So you hope." The President digested Hewett's remarks, put out his cigar, and picked up the phone. "Get me Lindsay at the Bureau." Checking his watch, he added, "If he's already left the office, try his mobile line and put it on the scramble."

Hewett waited, trying to remain calm.

The President covered the phone's mouthpiece and turned back to him. "One way or another, Ambassador, I intend to maintain a working relationship—however tenuous—with Chairman Baranov. I'll need your help in Moscow."

"I'll give it my best effort, Mr. President, but containing a perverse madman like Fiodor Talik won't be easy."

The White House operator made a swift connection with the FBI director. The end of the mobile phone conversation Hewett could overhear was terse and to the point. "Nothing's impossible for you, Lindsay," the President insisted. "Find a pretense, but get that Russkie dancer down from New York for a meeting. Three, four days hence. What's that? Well, round him up as soon as he returns from the west coast. Wait. Use my name with Harry Kaufmann, Tina Conner's boss at First Consolidated. No, I don't care what you use for a reason! My wife and I will organize a dinner for the performing arts if need be. A recital, why the hell not? I know I'm not a ballet fan, but I'll learn, dammit. Good night, Lindsay."

The President replaced the telephone receiver and faced Hewett. "Forget that Red Square parade and postpone your travel plans for a few days, Ambassador. I want you to talk to Baranov's talented son before you leave." The President drummed his desk. "What's the prognosis, Hewett? How the hell do we avoid another *Ten Days that Shook the World*? Or worse?"

4

THE MOSCOW NIGHT was cold. Blowing across Sverdlov Square and carrying with it the season's first snowfall, the wind whooped around the pillars of the Bolshoi's pseudo-Greek facade. Nearby, the serrated walls of the Kremlin, the Spassky Tower, and onion-domed St. Basil's Cathedral looked down on the city like brooding, disgruntled beasts. The limousines, one a Ziv and the other a Chaika, were parked diagonally in front of the State Theatre's entrance, their drivers and several green-uniformed KGB guards huddled to one side, stomping their feet and slapping their hands.

A white Moskvitch pulled up and two civilian men in woollen greatcoats emerged. They went up to the KGB guards and spoke briefly. The pair went back to the Moskvitch, checked the immediate area to make sure they were unobserved, then withdrew from the trunk a large coil of rope. They headed quickly around the side of the theatre to the stage door.

The sullen pair passed through the entry easily, having arranged earlier to have the doorman temporarily replaced with one of their KGB own. Now the two men separated, the one

26

with the rope avoiding the stage hands as he deftly climbed a ladder into the flying scenery, there to disappear among the tree props that would be used in *Giselle*. The second man slipped downstairs and waited until the lead ballerinas and sundry attendants left their shared dressing room. Entering and moving swiftly to the place he knew belonged to Marina Pleskova, he removed from his pocket a small, sealed envelope and propped it up before her mirror.

In Moscow the gray, barren winter and the State Theatre season began at the same time. Though the night outside the Bolshoi was bleak, inside the brilliantly lit red and gold baroque auditorium it was comfortably warm, the audience expectant.

The two most powerful men in the Soviet Union stepped into the balcony box reserved for dignitaries. Pavlin Baranov and Fiodor Talik wore similar hand-tailored Italian suits; their lapel medals glinted under the lights of the massive crystal chandelier overhead. A pair of austerely dressed, slightly overweight women joined them, smiling benignly down on the vast semicircle of assembled citizens and privileged tourists fortunate enough to obtain tickets for the Bolshoi's seasonal opening. The two Russian leaders surveyed the audience, nodding to acknowledge the spontaneous applause.

The chunky, beetle-browed minister who headed the KGB, General Fiodor Talik, waited for the Chairman-Premier beside him to take his seat, then he, too, sat down. By personal preference Talik did not wear his KGB officer's uniform to the theatre. The State Security minister smiled with smugness as he glanced around the auditorium.

Studying the crowd, Talik mused that this was the same theatre where only seventy years earlier a satin-sashed, diamond-studded aristocracy often outshone the performers up front. Now the grandeur, the tradition, the heroic proportions—any remnants of ostentation or individuality—were confined to the stage, where they rightfully belonged. *Like museum pieces!* Indeed, what a stage, reflected Talik, continuing to absorb the scene with keen satisfaction. Opening nights never failed to stir him.

The KGB head turned to the Soviet leader next to him. Chairman Pavlin Baranov, a widower, had chosen to escort his sister to the theatre. It was the first time Talik had attended a ballet at the same time as Pavlin Baranov, whom he secretly detested. The Chairman-Premier's presence was like a proximity fuse that set off Talik's smoldering hate. Pavlin Baranov was a dangerous revisionist, an obnoxious elitist, and despite his youthful vigor, an artifact of some past romantic era. His commitment to Lenin lacked totality. No matter, soon he would be so much USSR history. Pavlin Baranov and *glasnost* were both doomed. It would only be a matter of days before Talik would make his move.

Masking his contempt, Talik nudged Baranov's shoulder and pointed to the elaborately printed program. The roster of talent, the season's brilliant repertoire, the rigorous domestic and international schedule—all denied the image of a wounded ballet corps that just last season had lost its most talented *premier danseur*.

Talik watched the head of the Soviet world—a man ten years younger than himself and far better looking—slip on his fashionable Italian eyeglasses and examine the program. Pavlin Baranov finally looked up and dourly gave a nod of approval. Talik remembered that it had been almost a year since Baranov's son had defected to the West. The bitterness and shame still showed on the Chairman's face, particularly in the wide-set, revealing blue eyes. Talik smiled to himself as Baranov abruptly turned away from him and resumed polite conversation with the two women.

Fiodor Talik not only took pride in running the KGB, but as a board member of the State Theatre Artistic Committee, he considered himself a knowledgeable, and somewhat fussy balletomane. Once more Talik critically examined the printed program, running a finger down the list of performers the Bolshoi management had assembled for both the Moscow and road companies. The talent was in alphabetical order, with no name larger than the others. Excellent, he thought. Ballet master Pyotr Maryinsky was suppressing the cult of personality, just as he, Talik, had earlier suggested. *Or had he demanded?* Talik couldn't remember the tone of the directive, but it didn't matter. The seasonal repertoire and advanced publicity was stressing a fine collective look. And *numbers*, he noted. The performance roster was also greater in size. Good! All soviet citizens respect numbers.

Folding his arms before him, Talik looked around the plush, multilevel auditorium, reflecting that all most Russians want before they die—regardless of their collective—is their own small moment on stage. He wondered if this were so different from the longings of the average American. Why hadn't the ambitious, star-struck Nuri Baranov comprehended this? "Artistic freedom," the dancer had cried to the exploitive Western press at the time of his defection. Such *lies*! Nuri's motive was greed; the dancer's vented egocentrism poisoned the ideology of the entire corps de ballet.

Talik's wife said something to him, but he ignored her, preferring instead to indulge his angry thoughts. In only moments the heavy red velvet and gold brocade curtain would part and Mother Rus would again prove to the world that she could easily spare the likes of Nureyev, Barishnikov, Godunov, and now, most recently, the defection of the Chairman's own son, Nuri.

No, thought Talik. Young Baranov was not just a shameful defector, but a *traitor*! His recently discovered writings, of which Nuri's father was still ignorant, were seditious, unforgivable; a major crime against the regime. The dancer was a turncoat to his peers and an enemy of the Soviet peoples. No matter. The nonconformist young man who had chosen to join a foreign ballet company and live his life as an American Imperialist had not heard the last from the KGB. Far from it! Talik was determined, and had the undercover resources at his disposal to accomplish the perfect retribution. A retribution directed at *both* Baranovs! Perhaps, at this very moment, the termination of young Nuri had already been accomplished by the enterprising Khamsin Ahmed.

Bolshoi Artistic Director Pyotr Maryinsky, his critical emerald-green eyes as cool as plaques of ice, stood alone in the stage wings, surveying his realm. Maryinsky pushed his mop of graying, curly red hair away from his eyes and permitted his lips to curl in a petulant frown as he leafed through several papers on a clipboard. At thirty-nine the handsome, unusually narrow-faced Russian was the youngest ballet master in the State Theatre's history. His dancers called him Maestro, a title often reserved for a senior instructor or music conductor. Maryinsky glanced up at the illuminated clock above the computer-controlled lighting console. Tonight's performances would be *Le Festin* and *Giselle*, and Maryinsky was both puzzled and annoyed by the sudden disappearance of prima ballerina Marina Pleskova. She had been in her dressing room moments earlier, but now appeared to be missing from the ranks. Marina would not be needed for the Rimsky-Korsakov opening march or "Lesghinka," but she did have the lead role in *Giselle*.

"Timur!" Maryinsky called to a nearby male dancer.

Timur Malovik, an almond-eyed youth with jet black hair and the high cheekbones of a Tartar, stepped briskly up to him. "Yes, Comrade Maryinsky?

"Are you still sharing a flat with Marina Pleskova?"

"Of course." Timur looked at him curiously. "Is something wrong?"

Maryinsky thought for a moment, rubbing his chin. "You must tell me. When I talked with her yesterday she appeared tearful and dejected. Another letter from Nuri?"

Timur shrugged, a hand on his hip. "She'll recover quickly enough. Her art will prevail. I know Marina well."

Maryinsky scowled. "This continuing correspondence. Is it true? Nuri cannot be serious about the actress?"

Timur laughed and said quickly, "The affair does not surprise Marina. For her, Nuri was unrequited love then, and impossible love now. She knows this, Maestro. Do not worry yourself unnecessarily."

Maryinsky slowly shook his head and growled, "The publicity is unprecedented. Hollywood! Such decadence. You're positive Marina's taking all this well?"

"I'm sure, Maestro." Timur turned as behind him the asbestos barrier whispered upward into the loft. The red curtain parted and the orchestra swept into the furious strains of the *Coq d'Or*. A troupe of two dozen dancers in folk costume stormed out on the stage. Quickly, Timur joined the second rank, leaving the ballet master alone in the wing.

Despite Timur Malovik's assurances, Marinsky felt uneasy. He turned away from the stage and pressed into one of the theatre's back hallways. He finally found Marina with the wardrobe mistress and Natasha Chernyskaya, a film director from Mosfilm Studios who was interviewing Bolshoi personnel for a planned documentary. While she answered the Chernyskaya woman's questions, the ballerina was undergoing some last minute repairs to her flowered hairpiece. She looked up at Maryinsky. "Yes, Maestro?"

Maryinsky smiled back at her. Since he now felt no need to

interrupt, he backed out of the doorway. Marina Pleskova didn't appear depressed, that was all that mattered. He was satisfied. Maryinsky hurried back to the stage to supervise the performance.

The excerpts from *Le Festin* went smoothly and quickly, and Maryinsky was pleased. At intermission he went out to the lobby to greet the dignitaries in the audience, as was his custom. It wasn't often that the Soviet Chairman and the minister for State Security attended the theatre on the same evening. There were other important individuals to acknowledge, and Maryinsky was late in getting backstage for the first act of *Giselle*. Marina Pleskova and Timur Malovik looked stunning on stage, and Maryinsky smiled. The extra rehearsal this morning had been a wise decision.

Now Timur danced alone while Marina retreated to the opposite wing, climbed up on the mobile crane, and prepared to take her place in the tree foliage. Maryinsky squinted into the flies, hopeful the stage hand above would work quickly with her harness, preparing Marina for the pixielike movements she would make among the branches. The overhead lights were too bright and Maryinsky couldn't see beyond the first row of scenery.

The music hit on her cues, but still no Marina.

Maryinsky stepped swiftly to the lighting control console, picked up a communications headset, and spoke irritably to the crane operator. "I can't see the ballerina. Lower the crane a full meter."

Marina Pleskova came partially into view. Marinsky frowned. She still hadn't begun to move and flutter about. Why was she delaying? The harness? Had she attached it wrong? He cursed softly.

Marinsky heard a muffled shout from one of the stage hands. He turned to see a workman point and leap at the same time, trying to reach the tie-off for a rectangular iron weight used to counterbalance flying scenery. The weight was a light one, only seventy-five kilos, but now, unexpectedly, it shot upward into the flies. Maryinsky knew that at the other end, beyond the pulley rigging, a stage trimming or unit of scenery would be making an unscheduled, possibly dangerous descent.

Puzzled, he looked out on the stage. Something was definitely wrong with the performance.

Beyond the footlights the conductor's baton cut horizontally through the air and dropped to the floor. The music died, an inattentive French horn and bassoon trailing off into a disquieting, eerie silence. A horrific gasp came from the audience.

At stage center Timur Malovik seemed to freeze in place, as if caught up in a sudden Lapland storm. Seeing the conductor's chalk-white face and gaping mouth, Malovik slowly looked up.

As did Pyotr Marinsky from his place in the wings.

Marina! In full view of the audience, her frail figure hung suspended below the tree. Not from a harness, but by a rope around the throat! The improvised hangman's noose bit tighter and tighter into her skin, stretching her neck and distorting her once pretty features. Her body twitched violently.

Maryinsky stared, his heart thudding. Above him the young ballerina's face turned ghastly blue. Goldfishlike eyes bulged from their sockets.

The awkward silence was finally shattered as several women in the audience began to wail. Marina Pleskova's grisly *danse macabre* lasted only seven seconds, but it seemed a hellish eternity for Pyotr Marinsky. At last he was able to get a tight grip on his emotions and order the curtain closed.

5

TINA CONNER was well aware that she was the hottest property in Hollywood. She admitted to being notoriously spoiled. It wasn't the earthshaking misfortunes that made her petulant, but the minor inconveniences. Like the converted mobile home serving as her temporary dressing room near Soundstage Seven, where Universal's tour trams passed by at twenty-minute intervals. Twice she'd asked to have the trailer moved to a quieter area. Both times her requests had been ignored by the studio brass. Supernova star status or not, she was still a guest on the lot. Tina Conner's basic contract was with First Consolidated, across town. The Hollywood term for working on another studio's project was "loan out."

Tourists! One more day, Tina thought, and she could say good-bye to bug-eyed, autograph-crazy women, screaming kids, and paunchy men who wore camera equipment as if it were costume jewelry.

Today had been a short shooting session and she'd finished early. It was already two-thirty, and Nuri had insisted on coming in from the beach to pick her up.

33

Tina gazed into the light-framed mirror over the vanity. Withdrawing the rhinestone barrettes from her upswept hair, she let the locks fall back on her shoulders, then reached for the cleansing cream. Edging closer to the mirror in what had become a weekly ritual, she searched for crow's feet and chin wrinkles. There were a few hairlines, but nothing prominent. Her skin was soft and pliant; there wasn't a blemish on the cheeks or her gently turned up, small nose. Once more, out of nervous habit, she rose and checked her body profile from both sides. The bustline, aerobic thighs, and rear were up to snuff. Her diet was working, but it was an effort.

Plenty of time left, she mused. Thank God. Ambition and talent were beside the point. Tina Conner was one actress who didn't look forward to character roles in her forties and fifties— or like Bette Davis, beyond that. In a way, she'd had her fill of the limelight already. Early retirement and obscurity looked better after every picture. Tina was comfortable in the special industry niche she'd carved out for herself, and the financial reward was satisfying. She was determined to make it while she could, putting away a nest egg for marriage or leaner days. All this, provided challenging roles kept turning up like magic. If not, she'd take a hiatus and escape to Switzerland, finding solitude beneath the Jungfrau or along Lake Léman.

So far the press had been kind to her. Only this morning *Variety* had captioned an article FUTURE BRIGHT FOR TINA CONNER. Success seemed to be breeding success. If anything, Hollywood kept her too busy. Before meeting Nuri, and the frequent weekend trips to New York, she'd cherished getting away, even briefly, to the ranch out in California's Owens Valley, where her parents had recently retired.

Tina thought of the ranch again, then her childhood home in Pasadena. *Growing up*. It seemed like eons ago, but it was only yesterday. Back then her name had been Tina Bomberg. Her first Hollywood agent changed the name. Tina smiled at the memory. Hired initially as a contract player, her first two pictures were box-office bombs, and thankfully no one remembered her few lines. Recalling them now, she was ashamed. It was her third film effort in a supporting role at MGM that won her national acclaim as an actress. The trades were ecstatic. *Newsweek* and *Penthouse* both claimed she was "something special"—far more than a pretty face and body. The critics at

Cannes raved, and audiences thronged to the box office. Not only in the U.S., but around the world.

The dressing room's door chime jarred Tina back to the present. Closing her makeup case, she hastily pulled on a royal-blue, Thai silk robe and padded to the entry. She hoped the guard outside was following instructions. Uninvited visitors were not to approach her dressing room.

Tina opened the door and Nuri immediately strode inside, his trim frame rising three inches above her. He wore stylish, tight-fitting black leather pants and a matching jacket—not the usual heavy motorcycle attire, but smartly-tailored coordinates she'd helped him pick out on Rodeo Drive. From his windblown hair she knew he'd arrived on the Kawasaki 900 he rented just the day before. It annoyed her that he wouldn't wear a helmet.

Nuri surveyed her, his blue eyes dancing. "Your highness, my steed awaits outside to carry you away from this capitalist sweatshop."

She smiled. From the day they'd met in St. Tropez, the young Russian's English was near perfect, though slightly accented. His vocabulary was extraordinary. Tina would have expected no less from a privileged Soviet leader's son whose country dacha was amply staffed not only by servants, but private language tutors. There was also the expensive speech and drama coaching in New York over the past year. Nuri had admitted to her that because of his book project, perfecting his idiomatic English and polishing up on colloquialisms had become an obsession.

As Nuri came toward her, she heard an odd humming sound emanating from his jacket pocket. He looked momentarily startled and the smile disappeared from his face. Withdrawing from his jacket a slender black case the size of a Hershey bar, he listened, then hesitantly pointed it around the dressing room. He ignored Tina and stepped closer to the mirrored dressing table.

"Nuri, what is it?"

He held a finger to her mouth, gesturing for silence, and she understood. The anti-bug warning device Nuri held in his hand increased in pitch as he guided it across her clutter of makeup gear. After a moment he held it still over a plastic powder box left on the table earlier by her makeup artist, a young Korean woman Tina knew only as Kim. Nuri's face was a mask of annoyance as he picked the container up and examined the bottom.

Tina watched him quickly remove the small, adhesive-mounted transmitter disk and go into the bathroom. She heard the toilet flush.

"The powder box," he asked sharply on his return. "Where did you get it?"

Tina, too, felt angry. Her thoughts were in complete disarray as she sat down at the dressing table. She didn't know the makeup artist at all, but had assumed the woman could be trusted. Was Kim in reality a *North* Korean? And did it matter at all? Tina had said nothing in her presence about Nuri. Still, there was a lesson in this. They were being watched, and she could assume nothing, trust no stranger. Sighing with resignation, she said to Nuri, "My new makeup girl brought it to me this morning."

"You'll demand her replacement, of course?"

"Yes, but I doubt if it's a studio problem. Probably a bad egg in the union with influence. Or she was bribed. Money talks in this town."

Nuri's expression softened as he came up to her. "Even without this kind of trouble, your film career has drawbacks. Like leaving for work at an ungodly hour." He smiled. "The dog and I both missed you this morning."

"Likewise." Tina rose to face him, and they kissed for a long time. Finally she had to pull away to breathe. "Nuri, why did you bring the Kawasaki? And where's your FBI friend?"

"I like motorcycles, you prefer chauffeurs." Nuri shook his head, his blond eyebrows arching mischievously. "I lost McGinnis in traffic back at the beach."

Tina stiffened. "Sorry, but I refuse to ride back to Malibu through L.A.'s gridlock traffic on a bike. In the American vernacular, I'm chickenshit."

Despite her sustained frown, he laughed recklessly. "Relax. We'll take the scenic route. Mulholland Drive through the Santa Monica Mountains."

She had to grin. Her emigré friend had come to understand southern California geography and traffic better than most locals. "Nuri, it's not just the bike. It's the *high visibility*. By riding in a limousine with tinted windows, we maintain a reasonably low profile. The press still hasn't caught on that you've returned to Los Angeles with me following Mexico. Let them assume you've returned to New York.''

"You worry too much."

Turning to the dressing table, Tina picked up the morning's *Los Angeles Times* and held it up for Nuri to read the banner headline: KREMLIN SHAKE-UP RUMORED. "Well?" she asked seriously. "You don't want to read the story?"

"I've already seen it." His voice bit of impatience.

"The media will be after you for comment."

"Tina, listen please. My father has made his bed at the Politburo. However tidy or unruly, he must sleep in it. In Russia, leaders must be forever vigilant. It is dangerous to *pochivat na lavrakh*—rest on one's laurels." Nuri hesitated, studying her. "I have no comment for reporters on anything but ballet. But when my book is complete and released in Russia, it will be a different matter." He looked at her seriously. "I'm sorry. I have my fate, my father has his."

"Fate, my love, is what we make of it."

Nuri shook his head. "*Nyet*. Not always. Unfortunately, my future may depend on *others*. For me to upset the Soviet chairman is one thing, but crossing the KGB is a different matter. I have met this General Talik. He is Russia's angel of official vengeance."

"You know him personally?"

"Everyone at the Bolshoi knows him. Fiodor Talik is not only the Soviet Security minister, but a ballet benefactor as well. Unfortunately, a rather corrupt one. He and a few others like him have made me a fatalist, Tina."

She said eagerly, "I want to help. A letter, a telegram. A reconciliation with your father. Why not a new beginning?"

"Impossible," he replied in a tremulo of anger. "In Russia we have a popular saying: 'Do not attempt to sit between two chairs.' Do you understand? I forbid you to interfere. Please leave it alone, Tina."

She stared at him, stunned by the sudden, pugnacious turn. "No. You've made your defection incident seem worse than it is."

"Listen to me." Nuri spelled it out. "It isn't my father who sets these harassment policies. As for artistic shackling, Nijinsky and Spessivtseva found respite only in madness. Other dancers fared worse under intimidation from the KGB or its predecessors. Wait! Don't interrupt me. In 1924 ballerina

Ivanova—who was George Balanchine's partner—drowned, and it was suspected the incident involved the secret police. And Yuri Soloviev, known for his soaring leaps and portrayal of *Blue Bird* and *Spectre de la Rose*, committed a surprise suicide with no apparent motive in 1977. The incidents go on—"

Tina held up her hand. "Please Nuri, change the subject. You recite dance history as if it were religion."

"Ballet is my religion." Folding his arms, he smiled with softness. "Though now there's a rival goddess who's entered my life."

Tina returned his smile. She watched him saunter over to the gold velvet couch along the far wall and fall back on it. Propping his Gucci boots carelessly on the coffee table, Nuri winked and waggled his tongue like a Neapolitan gigolo. He shrugged. "I'm practicing a new slang word today. *Horny*. Come join me and I'll demonstrate, yes?"

Tina shot him a critical look. "I'm unimpressed." She didn't mean it, not at all. *Damn those brooding, intense Russian eyes of his!* She found something secretive, mystical in their depths—an aloofness and intensity that was indescribable. In the motion picture business Tina Conner was deferential to no one, but when it came to Nuri, especially in matters of sex, it was a different matter. Around him she literally floated, hung suspended in joy. She liked his sensitivity, but she also enjoyed his masculine manner and strong decisiveness.

Nuri beckoned again with his finger. "So I'll try another approach. I'm *not* horny, but simply in love and desperately in need of substance."

"*Sustenance*. Let's go home and we'll discuss it there."

Shaking his head, Nuri sent her a Rasputinlike glare. "Now. Your czar has commanded."

"Don't be a sexist ass." Tina paused to laugh. "With your blond hair, you could hardly make it playing Ivan the Terrible. His half-wit cousin Vladimir I might believe."

Nuri grinned sagely and raised his hand. "Ah, but Vladimir would have become czar but for some boyar lackey with a knife. Whatever, I'm impressed that Tina Conner understands Russian cinema."

"I've done my homework." She paused to examine a broken fingernail. An elusive thought took hold. "Supposing Tina Conner wasn't a successful Hollywood actress? The same face, but an unknown, some bimbo off the beach. Would you then have given her a tumble back on the Riviera?" She watched him stare at the ceiling, pretending to work it out in his brain.

Finally he shrugged and waved a hand. "Depends on how attractive and how pushy. I've done my share of rejecting, but unfortunately if I ignore women, they assume I'm a 'golden boy.'"

She was puzzled and let it show.

Nuri smiled. "In the Soviet Union homosexuals are called golden boys. Rejected American women can be neurotic; they jump to conclusions, yes? How do I convince them that I'm merely the world's most *spoiled* heterosexual?"

Tina shook her head. "Hell hath no fury like a woman scorned."

"The English dramatist Congreve. Am I correct? *The Mourning Bride.*"

"I'm impressed with Soviet education, but if I accomplish one thing, Nuri love, it's to cure you of your insufferable narcissism."

He laughed and peeled off his jacket, revealing a black T-shirt with a Dallas Opera Company logo. Extending both hands, he said softly, "Fine. Supposing you begin curing me now."

She shook her head. "I may be crazy about you, but we've as much privacy in this dressing room as a jar of guppies at a hobby show."

Nuri rose and came to where she stood by the dressing table. She watched him in the mirror as he gently held the side of her face and looked at the long, silky brown hair that shined from the light in the window. Abruptly he stepped away, going over and closing the Levolor blinds. "And would puppies care one iota or go about their business?" he asked.

Her exasperated reply was a whisper. "I said 'guppies,' Nuri. Another word to look up in your English-Russian dictionary."

Nuri locked the dressing room's door, came back to her, and gently removed the silk robe. He smelled of the new bar of Aramis soap she'd placed in the shower at the Malibu house. He grabbed her hands firmly, holding her, then gradually reduced the pressure and slowly, softly traced his fingers up and down her neck. Breathing heavily, his slender hands explored again, gently but determined, until they reached her peaking nipples.

Tina's hands, too, began to move sensuously, and it took only seconds for her rising libido to find itself in terse whispers. They kissed again, more passionately. She said softly, "Mmmmm. I give in. You're irresistible."

While they put their passion together on the white plush carpet, the Universal tram operator's voice outside droned, "To your left is the dressing room of talented Tina Conner, Hollywood's favorite. She's reportedly in that trailer this afternoon and we know you'd like to see her, but notice the Pinkerton man guarding the door. Production schedules what they are, I suspect she's diligently studying a script. Now across the way in bungalow number three . . ."

Tina and Nuri heard the tram accelerate and the tour conductor's voice trail off.

The Bel Air mansion was one of those pseudo-Spanish, white stucco castles popular in Los Angeles during the early thirties. Obscured by a high hedgerow and surrounded by an electric fence, approaching it was more difficult than gaining entry to one of beautiful downtown Burbank's sound stages. The dazzling estate belonged to L. Brian Beck, the controversial, outspoken publisher of the weekly supermarket tabloid *Street*, as well as the more controversial girlie slicks *Voyeur* and *Snatch*.

The gossip-and-porno king led a thorny, controversial life. Among a multitude of vexations, Beck had an artificial right foot, his lower leg having been purposely shattered by mobsters several years earlier. Since that incident, guard dogs and bodyguards clearly outnumbered the flouncing honey pots so much a part of the estate's tableau.

Parked just inside the compound's ornate iron gate, Jon Saarto sat in his Nissan and waited for Beck's limousine to return and head up the estate driveway. The bodyguard was pleased that this would be his last day heading up L. Brian Beck's security crew.

Saarto grew restless. Glancing in the rearview mirror, he examined his cleanly-shaved upper lip. Saarto had decided to modify his image with the change in jobs, and the moustache was the first to go. He felt naked without it, though a couple of women had complimented him, insisting he looked like a young Warren Beatty. Saarto didn't want to look like Beatty, or any actor for that matter. Since taking on Beck's bodyguard job, he'd had his fill of Hollywood celebrities. Unfortunately, protecting Tina Conner and Nuri Baranov, there would still be plenty of glitz.

Today was the first time Saarto had not accompanied the multimillionaire publisher out of the compound. Beck was piqued by his resignation and had left him behind to guard the grounds. Another member of the protective staff had already taken over Saarto's favored role.

Saarto heard the gate open.

Beck's light blue stretchout Lincoln came up the drive and edged to a stop beside the Nissan. The dark-tinted, bulletproof window rolled down with a soft hiss, and Saarto knew that his employer wanted him. He dutifully stepped out of his car and approached Beck's limo.

The slump-shouldered, thirty-six-year old publisher, with his unruly shock of albino white hair, hollow cheeks, and red-lined eyes, looked hung over. Beck's palsied right hand was accentuated by the silver Napoleon Eagle handle of the walking cane he tapped on the limo's window frame. "Saarto, come closer. I have a question."

Saarto leaned forward and gazed into the back of the vehicle. He was surprised to see that Beck had company. A wiry, well-dressed individual with a pockmarked, unfriendly face. The man, who appeared to be an Arab, wore a cheap hairpiece that looked as if it were on backward. Saarto had never seen him before, and the publisher made no attempt at an introduction.

Beck said quietly, "I've read your resignation, Jon. Extremely short notice. Supposing I refuse to let you go?"

Saarto stiffened. "You've no choice in the matter. I signed no contract and it's still a free country."

Pursing his thin, almost colorless lips, Beck scoffed, "True. But supposing I offered you two bills more a week?"

Saarto firmly shook his head. "A thoughtful gesture, but the answer's still no."

Two other bodyguards stood idly beside the gate, surveying the scene. Both men carried .303 Lee Enfields equipped with infrared image intensifiers, a rifle favored by military snipers.

Saarto preferred a shoulder-holstered .38 and a shotgun. He liked to work in close quarters.

Beck looked at him narrowly. "Why the fool? First Consolidated Studios hires and fires at the drop of a hat." Beck paused, wrinkling his nose. "As for performing arts like ballet, you're fucking tone deaf. You'll feel as out of place as an Amish farmer at Mardi Gras. Wise up, Saarto. Stop being the hard-headed Finn. What's so important about Tina Conner and her fag friend from New York?"

"Still the fucking homophobe, Brian? Tina's bed partner is as straight as you are." Saarto smiled thinly. "Or pretend to be."

Beck flinched, then said quickly in a reedlike voice, "Supposing Nuri Baranov turns out to be more than a defector? Possibly a goddamned spy? Your professional reputation— what there is of it—would be finished."

"I'll take that gamble. Besides needing a change, let's say I'm in this for the money. Like you, L.B., I'm greedy."

"Whatever they've offered, I'll raise it. You're my right hand and I need you."

Saarto shook his head. "Sorry Beck, it's time to move on."

The publisher nervously lit a cigarette and studied him through a cloud of smoke. "Tina Conner's a bitch, you know that, don't you?" Beck paused, slowly shaking his head and grimacing. "You'll be working for the most difficult broad in Hollywood to reach, write about, or for that matter, even *invent* news about. Miss Privacy with a capital C—for cunt." Squinting at Saarto, he added, "Let's hope this liaison with the Russian dancer will change all that."

"You're fishing, Mr. Beck. For what?"

"Go ahead, work for Tina for a month. Come back to me then with an inside line. A story—an *exposé*, right? I'll make it well worth your while. Megabucks like you've never seen before, Saarto."

"Forget it. You'd blackmail your own mother to fatten your wallet."

Beck glared at him hatefully. "Cocksucking bastard! Your final check is up at the house. Forget the rest of the day and get your ass off the estate." Beck snapped his fingers at the driver and rolled up the window.

Saarto watched the limousine proceed up the driveway.

* * *

Khamsin Ahmed had remained silent, listening to the man beside him long enough. "You let him go so easily?"

Beck growled, "I have no choice. If and when my temper cools, I'll again try to raise the ante. Mr. Ahmed, I'm curious. Are you French or Algerian?"

"A little of both. Don't change the subject. This Jon Saarto may know too much."

"About my lifestyle and personal habits, unfortunately yes. But about our business arrangement, absolutely nothing."

Khamsin nodded. "No matter. If events go well for me in the next twenty-four hours, this bodyguard will have one less client to protect."

Beck looked at him sharply. "Meaning?"

"I have other business here in Los Angeles. *Nuri Baranov*. I did not come solely to check up on you, Monsieur Beck." Khamsin shrugged. "However, I am curious. Is the L before your name purely an affectation, or does it represent an embarrassing name?"

"*Lysander*. And it's none of your affair."

. "As you wish. Just as my other mission is none of your affair. Let's address ourselves to the concussion-bomb data, yes? I'm sorry, but our financial arrangement will be ended unless your contact comes through with the remainder of the guidance plans. *Immediately*."

Beck was perspiring, but his voice remained calm and determined. "Don't threaten me, Khamsin. I'm being as persuasive as I can with my friend at the Naval Weapons Center. Unfortunately, with your indiscretion yesterday in my shipping office, I'll have to be doubly cautious. I could be watched day and night during the investigation. It was impetuous of you, a foolish act."

"Hardly." Khamsin exhaled slowly. "It was an *imperative* act. You were a fool in not suspecting earlier that this Tangerine was a clever plant. It is unfortunate that the bitch also worked for the CIA. The KGB has no mercy for double agents."

"You've compromised my position," Beck said doggedly.

"Not at all. I plan in meticulous detail. The civil authorities will undoubtedly consider Tangerine's death a crime of passion. I was most thorough at her apartment, making it appear a madman in a jealouos rage had visited the place. Lipstick-smeared insults, breaking the frame of her boyfriend's photo and tearing it to bits, yes? Homicide will have its hands full; the loose ends will remain for months."

"The CIA won't be fooled."

"Only warned, then. But what can they do? It was tit for tat, *Monsieur* Beck. I assure you, the Agency understands tit for tat perfectly."

6

LOCATED IN Moscow's Lenin Hills, Mosfilm Studios was a virtual city in itself. The workday had already ended, but in the basement of one of the post-production buildings a young employee continued to labor over one of the latest Italian editing machines.

Dimitri Kollontai's job as an assistant editor was to assemble, catalog, and distribute motion picture footage. In mute testimony to his workload, beside him were ceiling-high racks filled with thousands of feet of film. The racks were painted green. A door at one end of the cutting room led to a projection facility and storage space for yet more celluloid. The work area was spotless and painted a monotonous surgical green.

Dimitri glanced up at the digital clock over his editing table. The numerals glowed green. He would have much preferred to work on the building's first floor, where the color scheme was primarily beige. The second floor was done in shades of blue. Dimitri disliked green.

It was a little after six-thirty, and he'd already worked— quite unofficially—an hour beyond normal Mosfilm quitting time. At last it was safe to assume that the other editors had left the building and he would be alone with little chance of being disturbed. To make sure, he would lock the door. But as he was about to throw the bolt, he heard a hesitant knock.

Dimitri opened the door and was confronted by a familiar but unexpected face. It was his good friend Natasha Chernyskaya, one of several film directors who had an office on the top floor. He smiled at her, but she seemed in a sullen mood.

She quickly entered the editing room without being invited. To Dimitri, Natasha was one of the best-looking women on the lot, the actress pool not excepted. She also had plenty of talent going for her—the international awards testified to that. As always, she excited Dimitri, and he had to work hard not to let it show. Tonight Natasha's long brown hair was braided back in a bun, and though she smelled of perfume, her charcoal eyes and usually shiny face looked tired and agitated. Dimitri wondered what she was doing in the building so late.

Natasha said quietly, "I can't stay, but I thought you should know everything now, before it comes out in *Pravda*."

"I don't understand."

She looked at him and placed a hand on his arm. "There's bad news for your friend Nuri Baranov. Sad news for all of us. Last night at the theatre. Marina Pleskova committed suicide. Her official obituary is to be released tomorrow morning." Natasha hesitated. "Under the circumstances, you must be especially careful."

Dimitri's spirits sagged. Desperate for more details, he waited for the woman director to elaborate.

Natasha edged back to the entry and looked up and down the hallway. She spoke in a diminutive voice. "I'm sorry. I'd like to tell you more, but I can't risk being seen here."

He extended his hand. "Natasha . . ."

"I will try to call you later. Good night, Dimitri. Good luck."

He watched her go, then closed and locked the door. Backed up against it, he blew out a long breath of air. Dimitri suddenly felt empty, alone, and afraid, for he knew in his heart the ballerina could not possibly have committed suicide. He stood there for a moment until his mind cleared, then went to work.

Dimitri found the American feature film he needed and brought projection-reel number three back to his editing bench. After what he'd just learned, it would be difficult to concentrate, but he had to get on with it. If not for Marina Pleskova's sake, for Nuri's. A film shipment was scheduled to leave in the morning and he was determined to use it to get a message out to the dancer.

He gave the customs documents affixed to the film can his usual dubious glance. On the surface everything was in order. Overseas Film Distribution Service in Los Angeles sent over three dozen pictures a year to Moscow, each to be reviewed for possible distribution in the USSR. It was a futile gesture, for to date less than three percent of that number managed to pass Soviet censorship. Even so, the wishful thinking American producers submitted their prints. While waiting for elusive state approval, most films were kept on the Mosfilm lot, here in this room. It was Dimitri's job to inventory the prints and prepare them for projection. At the conclusion of the official preview, he sent them back out of the country, always with precisely the same number of frames per reel as had been admitted. It was a convenient arrangement for Dimitri Kollontai at one end and Tangerine Hamilton at the other. They had both exploited it to the fullest.

Trying to put his depression aside, Dimitri hunched over the editing table and began rolling through the reel of a feature called *War Song*. Near the end of the footage, just beyond the metallic tab that activated the projectors to change from one reel to another, he braked the rewind. With a magnifier he checked each frame of the end leader until he found what he was looking for. The usual material from Brian Beck and his assistant Tangerine was there, as expected: microfilmed data secreted away from the Naval Weapons Test Center in California—espionage material Dimitri would dutifully pass on to the KGB.

Little did the KGB realize that he would first carefully document the dates and microfilmed drawing numbers in his own personal notebook, this information to be passed on as quickly as possible to the proper CIA contact in Moscow. It was a vicious circle of counterespionage, and Dimitri was beginning to have misgivings over his participation. Nuri had promised to help him defect, but when, and how?

Dimitri carefully removed the secret American weaponry information, placing these dozen frames in the usual envelope provided by the KGB. He locked them away in a security drawer until he could arrange to have them picked up in the

morning. Next he removed the sequence Nuri Baranov had
arranged for Tangerine to hide in the reel, carefully exchanging
these frame for frame with the film Marina Pleskova had
brought to him three days earlier. When the splicing was
complete, Dimitri replaced the reel in its proper can and
returned the film to its storage place.

Now that he was finished with his work, Dimitri decided to
go to the apartment Marina had shared with Timur Malovik and
express condolences to the male dancer. He was also determined to find out the truth—what happened last night at the
Bolshoi Theatre.

Dimitri secured the editing room, but before he could grab
his coat, the door rattled from the outside. Then there was a
loud pounding, followed by his name being shouted.

"Dimitri Kollontai?" It was a thick, woman's voice, and it
was familiar.

Stashing the small plastic can containing Nuri's microfilm
into a pants pocket, Dimitri gingerly opened the door. Staring
back at him were two uniformed KGB personnel, one a tall,
cold-eyed woman colonel, the other an armed sergeant in spit-
shined jackboots.

Dimitri took a deep breath and managed a smile. "You work
late, Comrade Colonel Kloski. I'm honored. You don't trust
the morning courier and have come for the documents yourself?" Immediately he went to the editing table and worked the
combination on the security drawer. Opening it, he wordlessly
handed over the manila envelope containing the film frames
from the American spy Brian Beck.

Bruna Kloski passed the envelope on to her assistant without
comment, then withdrew a photograph from her tunic and
thrust it before Dimitri. "This is the ballerina Marina Pleskova—with you. Ice skating in Gorky Park, yes? She apparently knows you well. Am I correct, citizen?"

Dimitri felt a growing qualm. He looked at the picture,
aware that it had been taken just the previous week, at a time
when he and the ballerina had exchanged several documents.
He shrugged his shoulders.

The KBG woman colonel spoke to him again, her voice
more strident. "You are a double agent and a traitor, Citizen
Kollontai. By mandate of the Fifth Directorate I place you
under house arrest. You will come with us for questioning."

Panic consumed Dimitri. *Interrogation, torture.* He wasn't

so much afraid of either, but Nuri Baranov's incriminating film was in his pocket! The end of the hallway—the toilet. He needed to get there, flush it away. Dear God, could he fake being sick? He leaned against the wall, pretending to breathe with difficulty. "Comrade Colonel," he gasped, "I will gladly come with you to resolve this misunderstanding, but I haven't been well today. Will you wait, please? I fear I'm going to be sick again." Dimitri stumbled, then ran down the long hallway.

Without waiting for orders, the zealous KGB sergeant leveled his automatic rifle and expertly fired a short burst of bullets before the assistant film editor could push open the lavatory door.

Red-faced, Bruna Kloski turned to her assistant. "You stupid, impetuous fool."

Clawing at his back, Dimitri Kollantai slid to the floor. He kicked twice, then lay perfectly still.

The KGB sergeant apologized. "I'm sorry, Comrade Colonel, but he tried to escape."

"Into a lavatory without windows? I needed to interrogate him." Sighing with defeat, she thought for a moment, then strode down the hall toward the sprawled form. "Perhaps he had good reason to seek out the commode. Search the body carefully."

In Los Angeles it was a little before seven in the morning. Tina and Nuri had an informal agreement: whoever left the beach house last prepared breakfast. The size of the meal being optional, Nuri decided to whip up blueberry bran muffins and coffee, let it go at that. He checked his watch. Tina had told him she was due at Universal City at eight for a voice-over recording session. Nuri was glad for the decent hour of Tina's call. No predawn departure for early makeup today.

Nuri hovered over the kitchen bar, clad only in a pair of gray flannel sweat pants and an old red, white, and blue tank shirt that was a holdover from the Los Angeles Olympics. He sipped coffee while perusing a copy of the *DAR Citizenship Manual for Prospective Citizens*.

At last fully dressed, Tina entered the room.

Nuri sniffed. The scent of Joy cologne replaced the lingering aroma of freshly ground Kona coffee. He said to her, "Stunning and provocative, as usual."

"Sorry, I'm running late. The studio limo's outside. Okay if I just wrap a muffin and take it along?"

Nuri nodded. "How many justices on the Supreme Court?"

She looked at him askance. "Nine."

"Very good. You ready for another? Who wrote the words to the patriotic song 'America'?"

She grabbed her purse and muffin and headed toward the door. "Francis Scott—"

Nuri quickly blocked her way. "Not so fast. I didn't say 'Star Spangled Banner.'" He read from the pamphlet. "Reverend Samuel Smith, 1832."

Tina shook her head. "For God's sake, *what* are you reading?"

"*Studying.*" He held up the title. "Courtesy of the National Society of the Daughters of the American Revolution."

"Five years to naturalization and the oath of citizenship and you're cramming now?"

"Why not? Productive research for my book." He smiled at her. "As a child I did especially well in a dialectical materialism, scientific communism, and history of the party. Now I need to understand history from the capitalist viewpoint."

Tina glanced at the booklet in his hand. "The *women's* viewpoint at that. Excellent." She kissed him on both cheeks, then the lips. "For effort. I'll meet you later at the studio. Don't be late. Harry Kaufmann's a stickler for on-time appointments."

Walking her to the door, Nuri picked up an engraved invitation from the hallway sideboard. "Have you seen this?" he asked enthusiastically. "From last week's mail."

Tina scanned the engraved invitation, handed it back to him, and walked on outside. Gazing up at the overcast beach sky, she said, "Forget it, Nuri. I know your eyes light up at the thought of a spectacular Hollywood party. Especially the kind thrown at publisher L. Brian Beck's Bel Air Castle. But the answer's no. I've been putting down that rich 'good old boy' for years, and I fully intend to continue avoiding him. And his tabloids."

Nuri grabbed her arm. "There's something you should understand. A shipping clerk who helped me smuggle my writing into Moscow worked for Beck. In a curious way, I may be indebted to your redneck friend."

"Does he know what you're doing?"

"No." Nuri hesitated. He was ready to tell Tina about Tangerine's ugly death, then decided against it. He'd explain later, when there was more time.

"Nuri, what's your point?"

"Curiosity. I'd like to meet the man."

"Or some of the well-stacked bimbos around him?"

Nuri grew taut.

Tina continued, "Look, love, do yourself a favor and look again at the date. Saturday night you'll be in New York and I'll be en route to Europe. Enough said?" Hurrying off, Tina greeted the driver and climbed in the back of the limo. She blew Nuri a kiss and closed the door.

Managing a sorrowful shrug, Nuri turned and shuffled back into the house. He tore the L. Brian Beck invitation in half, disappointed they'd miss a super event. Hollywood parties were different than parties in Moscow, and he needed to know more. *Research for the book.* The sexily attired, exotic ladies reputed to frequent the publisher's soirees had nothing to do with it, he repeated to himself.

7

SEVEN A.M. LOS ANGELES TIME was mid-afternoon in Moscow.

Standing at the window of his thirty-floor Arsenal Building office, the combined Chairman and Premier of the Soviet Union gazed pensively out over the Kremlin. At the opposite side of his ornately carved wooden desk, the artistic director of the Bolshoi State Theatre, Pyotr Maryinsky, waited anxiously. A short distance away a secretary poised in readiness with a note pad. A sepulchral quiet hung over the chamber.

At fifty-one Pavlin Aleksandrovich Baranov was tall, collected, and strikingly handsome. His lean, sharply-drawn features were unlike the fleshy peasant faces of many of his contemporaries, and there was only a trace of gray in his light brown wavy hair. But today the Soviet leader's face was pale and he appeared strangely withdrawn; there were noticeable pockets under his Baltic blue eyes, and his usually erect shoulders seemed slumped forward in exhaustion.

Baranov finally turned away from the bulletproof window

and looked at Maryinsky. "None of this would have happened had my son become a world-class gymnast."

Pyotr Maryinsky looked away. "Hindsight is comforting, but unproductive, Comrade Chairman."

Pavlin Baranov changed the subject. "When will a full report on the ballerina's death be available?"

"The Civil Militia is still investigating. They take their time."

Baranov slowly patted his stomach. "My digestive system behaves like an alarm clock. These days my body tells me things before my brain."

Maryinsky shifted uncomfortably in his seat as the Soviet leader retreated into silence and stared out the window. Once more Maryinsky surveyed the room with its high ceilings, tapestries, and tired wood paneling that had been installed in the Stalin era. Only two pictures hung on the walls: behind the Chairman's desk a large portrait of Lenin, and on the opposite side of the room an oversize sepia photograph of a steam locomotive with railroad workers, beneath it in cursive lettering, *The Great Siberian Railway in 1900*.

Maryinsky sighed audibly. It was getting late. They had discussed all the parameters of Baranov's plan, and Maryinsky several times had dared to voice his disagreement. He was having a difficult time getting through to Baranov about the morale of his dancers, and more important, his own deep-rooted fear of Fiodor Talik and repeated KGB interference at the Bolshoi.

"Comrade Chairman, what you've proposed is well and good on *paper*. Whether or not short-term State psychiatric treatment or any other clinical approach to rehabilitation into Soviet life is workable would remain to be seen. It's all hypothetical at best. There's no doubt in my mind that the Russian peoples would demand Nuri's eventual if not immediate return to the stage."

"And would you immediately accept him?" Baranov gave Maryinsky a keen glance from the window.

"I suspect the Bolshoi would have no choice in the matter. But as far as his fellow dancers, the party oligarchy, and the KGB—"

Baranov gave a sharp wave of his hand and returned behind his desk to sit. "I understand."

Maryinsky said quietly, "In America Nuri has turned to fluff pieces. Experimental dance that is cute but hardly inspiring. Unsuited to his physical, masculine stature, yes? He rightfully belongs in *classical dance* at the Bolshoi." Reasoning that he'd said enough for today, Maryinsky changed the subject. Hesitantly, he asked, "Comrade Chairman, will you reconsider and lift the travel restrictions on our road company?"

"It's been discussed by party committees. I'm sorry, but in the present hostile climate, you'll not be permitted to visit the United States or pro-West European countries. Until we can resume détente, your tour must be limited to Austria, Egypt, and the Balkan countries."

Maryinsky said swiftly, "Which brings me to another sore wound. With your permission, Comrade Chairman. Must the head of the KGB's Fifth Directorate herself accompany the Bolshoi to Vienna? It is an insult to both our artistic and political integrity."

Baranov shrugged. "I've no control over these security matters. General Talik insists that a high-level KGB officer accompany you. I take it you have a personal dislike of Colonel Kloski?"

Maryinsky glowered but didn't pursue his point. He glanced at the secretary, a haughty older woman who scribbled constantly without looking up. Her bony wrist glittered with jewelry. Judging from her copious notes, Maryinsky gathered she was much like his own bureaucratic assistant, writing annoyingly long reports when shorter ones would suffice.

As if sensing Maryinsky's displeasure with the secretary's presence, Pavlin Baranov turned to her. "Refreshments," he ordered.

The woman nodded, set aside her note pad, and treaded softly across the red and green Turkoman carpet to the door.

The Chairman waited until she was out of earshot before continuing. "You may say your mind in this office, Comrade Maryinsky. It is safe, I assure you. Having spent my own apprenticeship in the KGB's First Directorate, I'm intimately familiar with effective countermeasures for electronic surveillance."

The blue telephone rang on Baranov's desk. Maryinsky knew that blue telephones in the Kremlin were for top-level army and defense communication, red ones for KGB matters. Routine business with the various ministries was handled on the white phone with its maze of push buttons.

Baranov picked up the blue receiver, identified himself, and listened. He sat back in his chair, responding with a yes more times than he did no for what seemed to Maryinsky a full five minutes.

"Thank you, Comrade Marshal," Baranov said into the line before finally hanging up and gazing back across his desk. He then said slowly, "Pyotr, my friend, it appears there are complications. The United States military establishment, I've just learned, is most eager to have their 'knight-errant,' this General Shaeffer, returned. The American President, however, is in disagreement and most adamantly opposes our proposal." Baranov drummed his fingers on the desk and thought for a moment. "That will be his loss. The trade arrangement will proceed without knowledge of the White House." The usual silkiness was missing from Baranov's voice as he added, uncomfortably, "I have no choice, lest Nuri suffers more sinister complications."

Like the Chairman, Maryinsky suspected there was a mounting urgency, a grave consequence developing over the young dancer's defection. Maryinsky felt deprived of information, but he wasn't about to ask for more now; in due time the Soviet leader would include him in his plans.

The Chairman's secretary returned with a tray containing tea, mineral water, and a napkin-covered plate. Maryinsky indicated that he would have tea with lemon. Baranov helped himself to the water and lifted the napkin from the plate. "*Yoblochnaya*, Comrade Maryinsky?"

Maryinsky stared for a moment at the appetizing apple pastries with their delicate crust and rich apricot sauce. He took two.

The secretary went up to Baranov and said quietly, "Comrade Chairman, the film director—Natasha Chernyskaya. She has telephoned twice and would like you to return her call as soon as possible."

"Yes, yes. Later." Baranov frowned. Ignoring the food, he sipped his mineral water, then said in a stern tone to Maryinsky, "My loyal Soviet Army friends will deliver Nuri into our hands, Maestro."

Maryinsky nodded and cleared his throat of pastry. "Alive and well, I trust."

Baranov didn't flinch. He asked stonily, "Who do you

believe holds the most power in the Kremlin, my friend?
General Talik, or me?"

Maryinsky placed aside his *yoblochnaya* and managed a
lame smile. "You, Comrade Chairman, of course. But while
we are on the subject, may I speak frankly about the KGB
leader?"

Baranov nodded.

"General Talik's being a ballet connoisseur and a member of
the State Theatre's directorate or not, his influence at the
Bolshoi is becoming increasingly meddlesome." Maryinsky
hesitated, staring into his teacup. "If you'll pardon the
familiarity, many of us in the company feel that Fiodor
Borisovich is a victim of *la manie de grandeur*—power going
to his head." Maryinsky swallowed hard and waited for the
axe to fall. It didn't. He was relieved to see the Soviet leader
smile.

"You don't appear to be finished, Maestro. Proceed."

Maryinsky was feeling unusually brave today. He fired the
other barrel. "To hear Fiodor Talik speak, it is as if he alone
were the discoverer, benefactor, and protector of our talented
dancers. And now, with Nuri's situation, apparently the judge,
incarcerator, and would-be *eliminator* as well. The comrade
general forgets too quickly that your son and the other
performers are the product of Russia and its art, with centuries
of *tradition* behind it. Tradition is a treasure to be protected."

Baranov listened, then said querulously, "The arts would be
nowhere today—nor would you be anywhere, comrade—
without collectives and the benevolence of the proletariat."

Maryinsky bristled, but spoke softly. "Your son may have
been our *premier danseur*, but he would have been nothing
without the heritage from the old Imperial School." Pyotr
paused, carefully weighing his words. "I am a loyal socialist,
Comrade Chairman, but I have much experience in the theatre.
Nuri is impetuous and curious, like so many of the new
generation. It is a confused dichotomy. Perhaps he asks, a bit
too loudly, what the revolution has done for him."

The secretary, reseated beside the desk, had resumed her
notations on the meeting. Her frozen Byzantine face looked at
Maryinsky with disdain.

Baranov stiffened. Hands gripping the arms of his chair, he
suddenly rose to his feet. "What if we were to ask, Comrade
Artistic Director, what ballet has done for the Soviet peoples?

A foolish question, yes? Artists, be they *my own offspring* or otherwise, must not ask what the revolution has done for them!" Baranov hesitated, his blue eyes narrowing. "According to Lenin, revolution is simply an icon to be defended."

The room took on a chill. Maryinsky sipped his tea and watched the Chairman return to the window as if resuming a vigil.

Pavlin Baranov said in a subdued voice, "I will have Nuri back in Moscow. *Alive.*"

At the Bonaventure Hotel in downtown Los Angeles, Khamsin Ahmed had breakfast brought up to his room. He'd risen early, showered and shaved, and already spent a half hour listening to cassettes of bugged phone conversations from the previous day. Khamsin knew both Tina Conner's and Nuri Baranov's schedule for the next dozen hours—provided they made no last-minute, arbitrary changes. Khamsin was determined to take care of the dancer today.

As for the other business, publisher Beck had procrastinated, asking for forty-eight hours to come up with the remainder of the concussion-bomb weaponry data. Khamsin had to wait for these before leaving for Paris. He would make sure Beck delivered as promised.

Finishing the toast and espresso coffee, Khamsin unlocked his attaché case. He pulled out the false bottom and carefully withdrew the two sticks of dynamite from the swaddling of foam rubber. The detonator cap was in his suitcase, still wrapped in a pair of rolled stockings. All he needed now to finish a simple but highly effective bomb were several innocent components—copper wire, tape, clothespins, and a battery. These could be purchased from a local hardware.

If he were to pass as an electrical repairman, he'd need workman's clothing. Khamsin would purchase these, along with a small kit of electrician's tools, at a surplus store he'd spotted earlier on West Seventh Street.

It was just after eight-thirty when he left the hotel to begin his errands. Khamsin hurried, for he intended to be ready and waiting when Nuri arrived at First Consolidated Studios.

8

KGB COLONEL BRUNA KLOSKI had been kept waiting in General Talik's reception area for twenty minutes. Impatient and restless, she rose from her chair, hitched her wrinkled skirt, and wandered over to examine a nearby glass display case. Inside was a magnificent steel saber, burnished and heavily ornamented with gold and ivory. As Bruna gazed at the collector's piece, the pulse of concentration in her temples quickened. Weapons of any kind fascinated her. The priceless sword brought to mind an ancient oath of the czar's troops.

> To shed throughout Rus the blood of the guilty
> To burn out treason with fire
> To cut out treachery with the sword
> Not self nor others sparing
> For the sake of the great Russian realm!

Go forward, she reminded herself. Traitors to our *Soviet cause*, likewise, must die. Dangerous, outspoken dissidents like Nuri Baranov must be marked for death. Damn the dancer's father and other squeamish party bureaucrats afraid of their own shadows, men who failed to act with resolve. Bruna Kloski hated weak men. Ruthless, determined men made far better Leninists.

She moved closer, squinting into the case to read the inscription on the saber. VARNA, SEPTEMBER 28, 1928.

The KGB lieutenant seated at General Talik's reception desk watched her. "Made by the Zlatoust Armory, one talented craftsman, Ivan Bushuyev. You, too, admire it, Comrade Colonel?"

Stiffly, she turned. "Of course. I was surprised to find it here at KGB Command." She softened her stance and smiled at the young, curly-haired officer. He had an innocent, pretty face that she liked.

The lieutenant grinned unabashedly and explained, "The glass case is secure enough. General Talik borrows from the treasures in the Armory Museum when it suits his pleasure."

Kloski gave a grunt of approval and stepped away from the display. With a grim smile she conceded, "Rank has its privileges. How much longer, Lieutenant, is it proposed that I be kept waiting?"

He looked up from his desk, surprised by her boldness. "Not much longer, Comrade Colonel. The general is engaged in an important meeting. He does insist that you wait. Wouldn't you prefer to sit and be more comfortable?"

She looked around her. The reception chamber displayed a strikingly contemporary air, with only a blue metal-and-chrome desk, a chair for the handsome duty man, several modern files, and the long white sofa. The furnishings were either Danish or Swedish, Kloski wasn't sure which. Restless and having no intention of sitting, she stepped back over to the floor-to-ceiling window. Outside, the sky was a heavy gray, and her reflection bounced back at her in the tinted glass.

Kloski straightened both her hair and the collar of her tunic, then looked out on the complex that Fiodor Talik preferred over the main KGB facility in Moscow's Dzerzhinsky Square.

For some reason the head of the KGB felt compelled to put some distance between himself and the infamous ghosts of the Kremlin. When this new annex had been built ten miles southwest of Moscow, Talik was commander of the First Chief Directorate here. After becoming top man in the KGB, he'd elected not to return to the austere Gothic structure in Moscow.

Possibly, Kloski mused, it was because this facility was nearer his country dacha. Or perhaps he was closer to the sophisticated computers and massive file of dossiers kept downstairs in the annex basement. She doubted whether it was because Talik preferred to be near her own Fifth Directorate several floors below, a division often despised by most KGB officers because of its methods.

Mokrie dela—wet affairs—was the ugly KGB euphemism that had been given to her dissident and ideological affairs operation. No one could say Bruna Kloski didn't take immense pride in her work. Very few in the KGB had such a phlegmatic nature and the detached emotional bearing required for her specialized work; she was the very essence of coldness, and proud of it. Inflicting pain meant nothing. The words good and bad had no meaning whatsoever when it came to achieving the will of State Security. Over the years Kloski had learned that any cretin could terminate a life, given simple resources. But it took imagination and professionalism to do the job properly, at the same time destroying the adversary's character. That was really what this requisite business was all about; putting the sword not only to the victim, but more important, destroying his or her reputation.

Kloski surveyed the courtyard below and, beyond it, the concentric outer circles of barbed wire, chain-link fencing, and guard-dog patrols. The seventh floor, which accommodated Fiodor Talik's reception room and office, allowed a splendid view of the countryside. The building, designed by Finnish architects and in the shape of a three-pointed star, was covered with aluminum, glass, and blue stone.

Hearing a door open behind her, Kloski turned. General Talik stood at the entry to his office, pumping the hands of two KGB officers who were leaving. The pair wore *papakhas*, distinctive caps worn only by generals and full colonels, like herself. She'd never seen the officers before. In the last five years, to keep pace with the CIA, the security service had expanded at an unprecedented rate, bringing about new faces and promotions everywhere. She watched with impatience as Fiodor Talik kept up a spirited conversation with his departing visitors. Bootlickers, she reflected. She disliked their truckling manner.

Once more she studied the chunky figure across the room—this KGB general named Fiodor Borisovich Talik, who, like the infamous Stalin and Beria, had no qualms about employing a spiked steel fist. Talik's ruthless, amoral nature had its advantages. Someone had to stand up to *glasnost*. Tyrannical as he might be, the general was ideologically correct and had an enviable record of serving the Leninist State. A veteran of service in the KGB progenitors—the MGB, the NKVD, and even the Cheka—Fiodor Talik as a young man had been inspirational in the kidnapping of German scientists in 1944, a forced deportation that gave Russia its great technical jump forward after the war. The three rows of ribbons on Talik's chest evidenced his impressive achievements: two Orders of Lenin, the Order of Alexander Nevsky, an Order of the Red Banner, and the Twenty-Five Year Service Medal. Above these hung the gold star of a Hero of the Soviet Union.

Like many well-educated Russians, Talik spoke passable English. He'd also become well-known as a benefactor of the performing arts, particularly the ballet. Despite this artistic bent, among KGB personnel it was commonly whispered that their top superior was impatient with intellectuals and distrusted them. Talik had wide-ranging power, for he not only headed the KGB, but was also minister of Internal Affairs and, of course, a member of the Politburo.

Kloski made no pretense at being a judge of pulchritude, not with what little she had to offer; but even she knew an ugly, coarse man when she saw one. Talik had bushy gray hair and a wide, toadlike face with small, deep-set brown eyes surmounting a bulbous nose. Today he had a woollen scarf around his squat neck and appeared to be suffering from bronchitis. Kloski watched him dismiss the two officers and finally turn in her direction. His malicious, ferretlike eyes settled on her, but as always, she held his gaze, unafraid. With a sweep of his hand and a slight bow, Talik ushered her into his private sanctum.

Furnished in contemporary chrome and glass with expensive crimson fabrics, the office was spacious and strikingly extravagant compared to the austerity of other ministerial-level offices.

Talik had never liked this Bruna Kloski woman, but was determined, as usual, not to let it show. Retreating behind the desk, he folded his hands on its transparent surface and gestured that she should sit opposite him. "I'm sorry you had

to wait, Comrade Colonel, but reprimands to good field men
take time, and above all, diplomacy."

She looked back at him with indifference. "May I smoke,
Comrade General?"

Already out of habit she'd withdrawn a package of English
Players from her tunic and extended them, but Talik shook his
head, pointing to the scarf around his throat. "Enjoy your
smoke. Today I must decline." He hesitated. "The officers you
saw are old friends, but they've been drinking on duty, despite
the new directives."

Colonel Kloski pushed out her chin and said airily, "In the
twelfth century St. Vladimir wrote, 'It is Russia's joy to drink.
We cannot do without it.'"

Watching her light a cigarette, Talik smiled. "True, I
suspect. Slavic suffering and spirits seem to go hand in hand."

Kloski lowered her eyes. "Stalin's man Beria taught my
father to endure suffering without vodka in the gulags,
Comrade General."

Talik frowned and shifted uncomfortably in his seat. It was
time to end the roundabout dialogue, for the woman colonel
was notorious for her windy party monologues and irrelevant,
ill-timed quotations. She was almost as bad as the dissident
Pentecostals who took refuge in the American embassy. With
them, it was screaming "Jesus Saves." Kloski had a habit of
calling out *"Lenin zhivyot"*—Lenin lives! Talik looked at her
narrowly as she took a long drag on the unfiltered Player,
corrupting her throat and lungs with smoke.

Talik opened a brown *papka* before him, scanned the first
page inside, and said to her, "Please read this, Comrade
Colonel. Examine the preamble, General Kersky's and my own
notations, and the satellite wire immediately, but save the
computer printouts to go over in your office later."

While she perused the documents, Talik covered his mouth
and coughed. He was certain the bronchial hack made him
sound like a wheezing old dog. Pulling the scarf tighter around
his neck and placing a codeine lozenge in his mouth, he sat
back in his chair. Again Talik thought about this gross woman
who sat before him. He detested her, but at this moment she
had more value to him than the Diamond Crown of Peter the
Great. He watched her read rapidly through the *papka*,
occasionally nodding with pleasure.

Bruna Kloski's index finger bore an ugly nicotine stain; her eyes, very nearly the same shade of yellow, like a cat's, were intensely direct, stabbing rather than seeing. Her lips were wet and blubbery and her hair looked like an unkempt wig. Worst of all, Kloski's uniform looked slept in, her stomach rolling over a tightly-clenched uniform belt.

Talik was fastidious about his own personal appearance. This tall woman officer was one of the most competent members of his staff, but her grooming left everything to be desired. Talik shivered at the thought of opening the green folder of her *zapiska* and having to make a detailed report on her private habits. So far he'd managed to avoid this.

When she'd finished with the material, Kloski leaned forward and stubbed out her cigarette in Talik's carved amber ashtray. "You honor me with this high-level, proprietary information, Comrade General."

Talik nodded. "To prepare you for the challenge ahead." He patted another stack of papers on the glass desk. "The printouts from the film you obtained for us, Colonel. The beginnings of Nuri Baranov's manuscript, *The Kremlin Sword*. The young man has a vile imagination. Your undercover work is commendable." Talik hesitated. "However, there's still some distaste in my mouth following the sordid incident at the Bolshoi Theatre."

Kloski hitched her skirt and rose to her feet. "Distaste, Comrade General? You did suggest some international publicity was in order. When former KGB leader Andropov created an entirely new directorate, the Fifth, we were given specific objectives. My responsibilities were clearly defined. They included harassing religious believers, particularly the Jews, and to eliminate *underground publishing*." She started to circle the room, arms folded behind her back. "Comrade General, our purge against ideological heresy has been extremely effective. You've given me encouragement at every occasion to continue this policy. Now, because of Nuri Baranov's parental status, do I detect a softening of this resolve?"

"No, you do not. But there are times when good taste must outweigh expediency."

Eyes flashing, the colonel persisted. "I suggest good taste is a minor detail. The ballerina, like Nuri Baranov, was an enemy of the State. Article Seventy. Better her termination in an apparent suicide than to waste valuable rubles sending her to the camps. How else might our former *premier danseur* be given an immediate object lesson?"

"Sit down, Colonel Kloski. You're abusing my Turkoman carpet—as well as my nerves." Talik glanced at the new Strela wristwatch his wife had given him two days earlier for his birthday. "To go on. You've read of these developments—there are those in Washington, D.C., who want their general back quite badly. And our ill-advised Chairman is foolishly considering these overtures. Outrageous, if not treasonable conduct. The scheme will be halted, of course."

"Quickly, I trust. Our hour to move draws near at hand."

Talik nodded and said irritably, "There's one problem—the matter of the Soviet Army's own intelligence arm. I must determine how much support it will give the chairman. You, Comrade Colonel, will take care of this."

Talik watched Bruna Kloski sit forward on the edge of her seat, expectant. He smiled to himself, musing that the woman might pass for a Jewish grandmother at a Bar Mitzvah were it not for those menacing, reptilian eyes. Good; she would strike as swiftly and surely as a viper.

"General, your instructions?" she asked thickly.

"The usual investigative drill, but expand your scope. I'm placing you directly in charge of the situation, Colonel Kloski. You will not report to General Nikolay at North American Affairs on the matter, but rather, directly to me. It is a matter of top priority. All opposition to the KGB and my leadership must be quickly eradicated. Do I have your unflinching support?"

She nodded.

"As for young Nuri, proceed with the original plan. He must be eliminated before others succeed in dragging him back to Soviet soil."

She said somberly, "I submit the latter would be difficult without KGB knowledge."

"When one is Chairman of the Soviet Union, nothing is impossible. Pavlin Baranov is a stubborn man. He is my enemy, Colonel. And your enemy."

Bruna Kloski gave him an icy smile. "Then let Nuri be traded and forcibly returned. You wish an even *stronger case* against the Chairman, yes? Give me an hour in the Lubyanka basement with this dissident dancer and I will have him confessing he is Peter the Great."

It was Talik's turn to smile. "Unnecessary. You'll make

certain this one called Khamsin does not fail. And you'll also ensure that the genial American, General Shaeffer, remains in our custody. He may prove a valuable hostage."

Kloski's yellow eyes stared at him pointedly. "You offer me a bouquet of contradictions, Comrade General."

Talik cleared his throat and continued in a quiet, controlled voice. "I offer you a possible promotion, Colonel Kloski. Return to your office and study these documents carefully. Pay particular attention to the specific dates in New York, Paris, and Stockholm. Find this contract assassin immediately. I demand an updated report, as well as copies of your own directives, within twenty-four hours."

She said quickly, "The matter will go forward. You need not concern yourself with the distasteful details."

"It's a very special party, Comrade Colonel. Invite only your very best people."

"*Lenin zhivyot!* And good day, Comrade General." She saluted stiffly and stepped to the door.

After Bruna Kloski had disappeared, Talik began coughing again. The bastard bronchitis was getting him down and he felt like hell; it was a miserable time to worry over Soviet consolidation of power. When it came down to it, Talik knew he had secured his position well. Americans didn't comprehend this maneuvering; power struggles in the Soviet Union were complex, and only Russians really understood them. Talik had almost reached the zenith of power and planned no retreat. He was immune to censured discipline and sufficiently placed to protect his backside against any but the most formidable party attack. The only additional achievement would be his extraordinary election to the combined offices: First Secretary, Chairman, and Premier—like Pavlin Baranov.

Each time Talik savored the thought, the dream came into sharper focus. Closer, much closer, almost within reach. Controlling the Red Army would be the key. Talik would achieve his goals, if necessary, without the party electoral process. Chairman Baranov was a bone in the KGB's throat. His own throat, Talik thought. He started to cough again.

Reaching into a small cabinet behind him, Talik brought out a 500-gram bottle of Ukrainian pepper vodka and a glass that he poured half full. He toasted both the framed picture of his wife on the corner of the desk and the portrait of Lenin on the wall, then, swallowed the liquid quickly. Into Dante's *Inferno*, he reflected.

Already his throat felt better. Talik could think of nothing more exhilarating than to sit in the dignitary box before Lenin's tomb and see huge portraits of himself paraded across Red Square. Television cameras and satellites would bring the glorious scene to the entire world!

He thought once more about Bruna Kloski—a gruesome individual with a grating name. The colonel was capable, hardworking, cunning, but she made Talik's skin crawl. Within this beast's eyes was a veiled inscrutability that had too often bothered him. Was Kloski hiding something? More times than he could recount he'd examined her files. A KGB officer in her position might conceivably alter documents, especially her own. But why? He secretly wished there was another individual he could entrust in the days ahead, even an intermediary. No, this wasn't possible. Not enough time, and events had come too far. After he was finished with Bruna Kloski, Talik would consider having her liquidated.

He turned to the small cabinet behind him, withdrawing from the top drawer three color photos of Bolshoi ballerinas. Talik smiled to himself. One of the photographs was of a smiling Marina Pleskova. He fanned the other pictures in his hand and idly compared the young lovelies to the fat cow that was his wife—the unsmiling woman who imperiously stared back at him from the silver-framed portrait on his desk.

Talik frowned as he methodically tore Marina's likeness into small pieces and deposited it in a nearby wastebasket. This done, he returned his attention to the other two photos, turning them over and studying his notations on the back, including each ballerina's personal telephone number. More time would be needed, he mused. He had the power; all that was needed now was time and gentle persuasion. Possibly the enticement of promotion to principal dancer status. He would work on their egos. First the carrot, then his stick.

9

NURI TIGHTENED HIS GRIP on the motorcycle's handlebars. Glancing at his watch, he saw that it was already going on ten. It was one of those dismal, smoggy days in Los Angeles with no trace of a breeze. Despite the air pollution and his sensitive eyes, Nuri was determined to ride the Kawasaki into the city for his dance practice and later rendezvous with Tina. There was plenty of time, but still he gunned the bike, letting it out on the Sunset Boulevard curves.

The congested traffic and smog were petty inconveniences, for Nuri had taken eagerly to America—the good and the bad—from the moment of his arrival. Moscow might be noted for clean air, but it had its dispiriting gray skies and monotonous cold. No city was perfect. He liked the way this country looked and smelled, especially the way Times Square at rush hour sounded. He felt in tune with both New York and Los Angeles, their vigor and directness. Most of all he loved the way people moved—the electricity in their bodies, the lightness of their step and the way they talked, freely and openly, without the threat of censorship or gulags.

Most of all he loved the smooth-skinned, tan and trim girls he'd seen on the local beaches, their hairless armpits and scant bikinis. If Hollywood were in fact a tinsel town, he wasn't opposed to learning a little more about glitter. But not today, for while Tina finished up at Universal, he needed to get in some overdue dance practice.

Behind him the navy-blue BMW sedan with FBI agent Paul McGinnis at the wheel had difficulty keeping up. Nuri smiled and accelerated the bike again. He circled UCLA and took Westwood Boulevard down to Pico. Waiting for a crowded intersection light to turn, he felt relief that no one recognized him. In Russia he'd have been mobbed by well-wishing fans.

The rehearsal room the film studio made available to him—through Tina's influence—was in a small, two-story annex across the street from First Consolidated's back gate. Most of the building was rented out to musicians for practice rooms, the remaining offices given over to an overflow of sound-department personnel from the main lot.

Parking the Kawasaki in a space behind the building, Nuri grabbed his tote bag and hurried through the courtyard to the stairway. He ignored agent McGinnis, who parked at the front curb and remained in the car, apparently content with his view of the stairs and long balcony fronting the practice rooms.

As Nuri approached, a coverall-clad electrician glanced up from a fuse box he was servicing at the foot of the staircase. The man smiled at him from a narrow, dark-complexioned face that was a horror movie of pockmarked flesh. Nodding politely, Nuri fought a sudden urge to recoil at the individual's appearance. To make matters worse, the maintenance man wore a botchy black rug of a hairpiece. Nuri smiled inwardly, amused by the incongruity of such bad cosmetics in Holly-wood, of all places! He took the stairs to the second level two at a time. The door to room 11, the dance rehearsal studio, was open and he went inside.

The mirror-lined chamber, as long as a boxcar and a half-dozen feet wider, was empty except for a piano and folding chair. Nuri removed his top and bottom sweats, tossed them in a corner, and put on his rehearsal shoes. He noted that it was time for replacements again—his ninth pair of Capezios this year. As usual, his maroon tights were baggy at the knees and crotch and a glaring mismatch to the bright turquoise leg-warmers. During workouts he could care less; he'd be alone and the practice gear was chosen for comfort, not appearance. In Moscow practice and rehearsals were a little more formal. He'd often showed off, tying his hair back with fancy silk scarves. Today he used a folded, red paisley kerchief to soak up the sweat on his forehead. Just like Stallone in the Rambo films.

Savoring the pleasant moment of solitude, Nuri looked long and hard in the mirror. His memory triggered a cluster of images. Like most serious male dancers, he prided himself in maintaining a perfectly proportioned, athletic body with a weight that seldom varied above one hundred sixty-five pounds. His arms and legs were taut—they had to be. Muscular cords rippled when he lifted his dance partners as if the women were mere straw dolls. Nuri took intense pride in his ability to leap as if he were weightless and seemingly float for a second in midair, stupefying audiences. And the entrechat whirls—he did eight easily—made even the so-called experts catch their breath.

Nuri was convinced that for him dancing was as rudimentary as breathing; he could be sensitive when required, but his movements—austere, in the masculine sense—were in total harmony whether playing the role of a hardened Tartar chieftain or bringing out the essence of Slavic languor in *Les Sylphides*. He was best known, however, for aggressive, physical roles.

He had good reason to feel self-confident. Even in the Soviet sphere, where the cult of the individual was so often repressed, there'd been no disagreement. Nuri Pavlinovich Baranov had reached the top of the heap. If he had lived three quarters of a century earlier, he would have been soloist to the Czar.

Nuri's mind suddenly flashed backward, like the rerun of an old movie. He saw his childhood and once more felt the pains of growing up. His father had wanted him to pursue gymnastics, for at the age of fifteen Nuri had been outstanding at both the compulsory and optional routines. His coach had called him a natural. But Nuri's love for music had drawn him instead to ballet.

A pampered upbringing in dance school and being the son of a Politburo member had isolated the boy Nuri Baranov from the ruts of ordinary Soviet existence. His wonderful mother Larissa, of Ukrainian origin, died of cancer the day before his nineteenth birthday. All Soviet officialdom had mourned the

family loss. His grandmother had been part Jewish; she'd been
the one to suggest Larissa call her son Nuri, which meant
"fire" in Hebrew. His mother had obliged the older woman,
believing the name, like the proverbial "Phoenix rising,"
would be a good-luck omen for long life and immortality. His
attractive, outgoing mother had been a superstitious woman,
fascinated with longevity. But she'd died young.

Nuri thought about his father, who had never remarried.
Pavlin Baranov was Latvian-born and had spent most of his life
in Kiev and Moscow, slowly and steadily working his way up
the party ladder. Nuri didn't know much about those early days
under Bulganin, Malenkov, Khrushchev. In the closed society
of communism, many of the details of his father's spectacular
rise through the ranks had been kept not only from Nuri, but
the public as well.

Despite their strong differences and current estrangement,
Nuri admired his father. He, too, possessed talent—of another
kind. It was well-known that the senior Baranov, like other
clever Soviet leaders since Stalin, had come to power by
careful compromise and avoiding mistakes.

Mistakes, Nuri reflected, beginning his warm-ups at the
barre. The only way to avoid them was by constant practice.

Khamsin glanced at his watch. The rest of the day was going
to be a hot one, he thought. He could feel the perspiration
forming under his toupee as he completed his circle of the
building and stepped out of the sun. Long before becoming a
highly-paid contract killer—he found the words "assassin"
and "executioner" distasteful—Khamsin had served as a
journeyman electrician in both Marseilles and Otan. It was a
convenient disguise that worked superbly for him in his new
profession.

Now it was time to put the special detonator system and
dynamite to work. Before, he'd used similar devices to fit
below an automobile's steering column, where it would
explode when the driver turned the wheel a few degrees in
either direction. Nuri Baranov had not accommodated him by
driving a car in from Malibu. Not that it mattered. The nearly
invisible clip-on wires and triggering mechanism would work
equally well attached to wheel spokes on the dancer's motorcycle. The bomb would be hidden under the seat, right over the
gas tank.

Khamsin enjoyed his work. He knew he'd be paid well for this job, extremely well. The Fifth Directorate and Colonel Kloski, who apparently was the enforcement edge of the KGB knife, would again reward him generously. *If he were unsuccessful, it would be a different matter*. But failure was beyond consideration. Khamsin was an expert.

Arching his dark, caterpillar eyebrows, he once more surveyed the area in front of the building. Across the way two delivery trucks rolled past the guard shack and through First Consolidated's back gate. Traffic on the street itself was light. The dark blue FBI sedan was still parked at the curb. Behind the wheel the driver, like a duty-bound Doberman, sat motionless, his eyes fixed on the stairway leading to Nuri's practice room.

Khamsin could care less if Nuri Baranov were talented or untalented, dangerous or completely harmless. The fact that the Soviet KGB called the dancer a seditious scum meant absolutely nothing to him. All that mattered was Nuri's death, to be achieved as expeditiously as possible.

Gazing in the practice-room mirror, Nuri's thoughts continued to be drawn back to his youth. He half smiled as he remembered his early schooling. He'd been shy then, a fast learner, though often unruly. Excellent at several sports but indifferent to team participation, he preferred to draw, play the piano, and dance. When the fog of adolescence lifted and with it his shyness, he'd seen himself and his goals more vividly— just as clearly as the image in the mirror now.

Nuri had been precocious in a score of ways. He'd passed the entrance examinations for the Bolshoi Choreographic Institute at the age of sixteen, coming under the tutelage of the outstanding instructor Yaraslovenko, who had once coached Ulanova.

Traditions at the State Dance Academy were strong. From the beginning Nuri accepted the heavy-handed controls in order to master the Russian Classical technique. But eventually his exceptional creative nature, sensitivity, and unrestrained enthusiasm came into conflict with the discipline of the party machinery. His father's status in the Politburo had not helped matters.

At the conclusion of his training and acceptance into the Bolshoi performing ranks, the aging Yaraslovenko had taken

him aside and said, "You are the most gifted talent to leave my
classes. Your career will be unparalleled, provided you do not
stumble along the way and make enemies."

Nuri recalled his fist two seasons at the famous Bolshoi State
Theatre. After being selected as a principal, it was commonly
agreed that he'd left memorable interpretations on some of the
most difficult productions in the company repertory. But he
hadn't heeded Yaraslovenko. Nuri had indeed made enemies.

On one occasion, at a birthday party, he'd made a self-
appointed speech complaining about conformity being the
death of art. It drew glowers of disapproval. To Pyotr
Maryinsky, the Bolshoi's ballet master, Nuri had admitted to
reading and admiring Solzhenitsyn. There were other incidents, like disagreements over costumes and unauthorized
choreographic experimentation. Nuri had neglected his French
lessons, the real language of ballet, and concentrated on
perfecting his English, insisting there was only so much time to
study. The disfavor had mounted.

Despite Nuri's growing acclaim, Maryinsky had intimidated
him with repeated warnings. When Pavlin Baranov sent him
stern admonitions, the father-son relationship became increasingly abrasive. In spite of minor recriminations from fellow
dancers who were zealous party members, Nuri managed to
survive one international tour and two more years of domestic
performances.

He continued his warm-ups, making an effort to put the
Bolshoi difficulties out of his mind.

Khamsin Ahmed once more checked the car at the curb. The
FBI agent named McGinnis appeared settled in, not about to
wander. Good. Picking up the tool box, Khamsin slipped
around to the back of the building, where Nuri had parked his
motorcycle. Khamsin had chosen the bomb over the telescopic-sight Browning for two reasons: he could be out of the
vicinity when the incident took place, and the KGB had
insisted that the dancer's eradication be as newsworthy as
possible. In fact, after the job had been satisfactorily accomplished, Khamsin would call the press with the KGB-proposed
lie. The "terrorist" attack on Nuri Baranov would be blamed
on the Free Ukrainian Front, a publicity-eager group hateful of
Moscow and particularly contemptuous of Chairman Pavlin
Baranov, who, despite his deceased wife being Ukrainian, had

at one time ruthlessly persecuted some four hundred Kiev dissidents opposed to Russification.

Khamsin worked rapidly with pliers and tape. His expert hands were steady enough, but his heart thumped and his throat felt dry. The sun was too hot, and he worried about the small adhesive tabs that held his toupee in place.

Unlike most dancers, Nuri preferred a fast warm-up. Continuing at the barre, he did a dozen each plié, *tendu, ronds-de-jambe à terre, adagio,* and *grand battement.*

The rehearsal room was depressingly quiet. The solitude, for some inexplicable reason, brought back memories of his defection scene in New York. When the final decision to flee had been made in his hotel room, he'd tossed and turned for hours. He'd been determined for months, but at the last minute became suddenly afraid; fearful not only for himself, but also for tarnishing the reputation of his powerful father in Moscow. There had been others in the company who had planned to defect with him, including prima ballerina Marina Pleskova.

Unfortunately, the Bolshoi's guest appearance at New York's Lincoln Center had concerned the KGB from the outset, and at night Nuri had been separated from his friends. The suites at the Regency Hotel had been shared, each by four or five other members of the company. The *committee* approach, as a precaution; the odds were good that one in the group could be counted on to inform. On top of this, around-the-clock, alert KGB escorts sat in the reception lobby below, logging the dancers in and out of the hotel. Nuri, by reason of rank or possibly his father's position, was assigned only two roommates, one his long-time friend dancer Timur Malovik, the other a cellist from the orchestra named Gregor.

Nuri smiled to himself, once more recalling the incident. The young Tartar Timur was a loyal friend and had also planned to defect, but at the last moment became frightened and backed off. Gregor was the ballet company's most active party member, but he was also a closet homosexual, and unknown to the KGB, one of the hotel's room waiters had caught his eye. At four in the morning Gregor, assuming Nuri and Timur were asleep, had conveniently left the room for a prearranged tryst.

Nuri had been forced to move quickly. There wasn't time to cajole or beg Timur or reconnoiter with the others who

wanted to flee. Their only chance for escape was to make their
moves individually—when, where, and however they could.
Guilt-ridden but determined, Nuri grabbed his own opportunity.

Clad only in what clothes he could toss quickly into a small
duffel, he'd taken the freight elevator to the hotel's basement
and service entrance. Twenty minutes later he was in a New
York police precinct asking for political asylum. *Freedom*,
he'd repeatedly stressed to the perplexed duty sergeant. Nuri
tried to explain everything, telling the man in blue that it was
more than the suffocating, all-pervading Soviet bureaucracy,
that it was his *art* that really mattered. He'd explained that he
needed freedom to grow, to freely explore the modern dance
idioms. The sergeant with the bulldog face behind the desk
didn't understand what *premier danseur* meant or little else
about the ballet world, but he'd made the necessary phone
calls.

Recalling the awkward moment, Nuri looked in the mirror
and smiled. He had come to America to practice his art, but by
his association with Tina he'd become a celebrity—an easy
prey for magazine covers and TV talk shows, neither of which
he really needed. He'd become a show business favorite, a
star, but also a gossip piece! Soon, if all went well, he'd also
be known as an author; he liked the ring of that better.

Nuri had mixed emotions about the words "star" and
"celebrity"—their capitalist significance. Everything in the
United States was so temporary! Make it while you can. Here
the name of the game was not the perfection of classical
tradition, but rather catching the fever and holding on.

He put his smile away as he recalled how Marina Pleskova
and the others had been unable to make a break for freedom.
Stepping away from the barre, he began his floor work, but his
thoughts remained on those who had been left behind. As
dangerous as the ploy might be, he was determined to help
them get out of the Soviet Union. No matter how long it took.
He was more committed than ever.

10

AT LAST KHAMSIN was finished with the booby trap. The delicate copper wires leading to the spoked wheel were nearly invisible and the TNT was securely in place under the seat. There was no evidence whatsoever of his tampering, unless one were to examine the motorbike in detail. Khamsin stepped away from his work, satisfied. Already he felt the flush of success. The KGB woman in Moscow would once more be pleased with his performance.

Khamsin wiped the sweat off his forehead. He would now retreat in confidence to the air-conditioned cocktail lounge he'd staked out earlier, waiting there in comfort over an iced tea or lemonade. The explosive charge was larger than necessary and he'd have no trouble hearing it a mile away.

Having worked up a decent warm-up sweat, Nuri removed a small tape player and several cassettes from his tote bag. He quickly flipped through the tapes. Finding the music for the final scene of Tchaikovsky's *Sleeping Beauty*, he slipped it on the player. It was a piano accompanist's interpretation of the

"Classical Pas de Deux" for Aurora and Prince Desire. Nuri
stepped back to the barre and waited for the finish of the Tom
Thumb sequence and the final romantic adagio to begin. The
tape had a way to go.

The practice room was lonely by its emptiness; no fellow
dancers rehearsing, no accompanist, only an upright piano
with a padlocked keyboard. Nuri grinned; even in America
artistry could be shackled.

He thought about his fellow dancers back in New York, the
big rehearsal hall just down the street from Lincoln Center.
Again he felt an obsessive curiosity over what might be
happening during his absence. Aware that it was the end of the
day, when rehearsal schedules for upcoming ballets were
finalized and information tape-recorded, he would call New
York and listen to find out who was being cast for roles.
Checking the tape the last thing before going to sleep was a
way of life—no matter how much stature a dancer had with the
company. Even during his stay in Malibu he'd continued to
make the calls before retiring.

Tchaikovsky's brilliant six/eight entrance began and Nuri
danced the thirty-two bars flawlessly. He did the same with the
"Variation," and felt exhilarated. Rehearsing without a partner
never hampered him.

When the tape was concluded, he played it again. And
again.

A chunky-armed woman and two small girls in red dancing
tights stepped hesitantly into the room. Nuri ignored them until
he had finished the final coda. At the conclusion of the number,
the woman politely applauded. The two girls, no more than
seven or eight years old, did the same, then sat on the floor to
put on their ballet shoes.

The beaming, flustered woman had recognized him immediately. She apologized, "I'm sorry, Mr. Baranov. It appears
we've arrived early. I didn't expect the room to be occupied."

Nuri removed a towel from his tote and wiped his face.
"No. It's all right. I've worked long enough." Continuing with
some cool-down movements, he smiled at the girls. He asked
the woman, "You're their mother or the accompanist?" He
watched her go to the piano and remove the padlock.

"I'm both," she replied eagerly, nodding toward her
daughters. "They're very talented. This is Celia and there's
Tess."

The girls jumped up, finally recognizing Nuri. Starry-eyed and expectant, they came boldly up to him, each holding out a shoe. "Mr. Baranov, will you sign my slipper?" said the tallest.

Nuri shrugged. "I didn't bring a pen."

The mother dug feverishly through her purse and supplied one. "Voilà," she purred.

He signed their practice Capezios with a flourish and patted both girls on their shoulders. "You've seen me work, now I will watch you, yes?" He gestured with his hand. "Let me see an *épaule derriere*."

The girls eagerly obliged, adding a pirouette.

Nuri grinned. "See how loose and flexible your young legs are! Excellent!" Nuri grabbed his muscular calf, beckoning the children to come closer. "Feel here. It is tight, yes? For me, everything goes into the supported adagios and leaps. I have to warm up for long periods to stretch my legs so they will be pliant like yours!"

"Nuri!" The shout came from the doorway.

He turned to face an agitated Paul McGinnis. The bureau man held up his arm, displaying a black diver's watch. "I suggest you shag ass if we're to meet Tina and Harry Kaufmann on time."

Shag ass. Nuri frowned, annoyed once more with McGinnis for acting more like a manager than a government watchdog. The ever-present FBI and occasional CIA shadowing constantly reminded him of his fragile status. Paul McGinnis and the other spooks stabbed at a small, unhealed sore, that minor part of him that would forever wonder if he'd made a mistake running to the West.

Grumbling, but without gazing up at the agent, he gathered up his things. The mother and her two daughters continued to look on as if touched by God. At the doorway Nuri paused and looked back at them. He asked the children, "What are your plans for the future?"

The first girl replied, "I want to teach dancing."

The second: "I can't decide whether I want to dance or be a mother."

Nuri laughed good-naturedly. "Any woman can have a baby. But not every woman can become a pretty ballerina." He winked and left the room.

On the staircase McGinnis looked back at him. "Do I detect
a soft spot in that frigid Russian heart of yours?"

"Hot ice, wet fire, Mr. McGinnis."

"Screw your Slavic symbolism. You planning on wearing
those tights on your motorcycle on the way to the gym?"

"Gym? There's no shower here?" Nuri felt annoyed.

"No. I've made arrangements to get you into the Bel Air
Sports Club. Five minutes down the road." McGinnis looked
at him sourly and jerked a thumb toward his car at the curb.
"Throw on your sweats and get in. You want me to play
nursemaid too?"

"What about my Kawasaki?"

"Relax. You can pick it up later."

Slumped in a booth in the cocktail lounge, Khamsin once
more examined his watch. Still no explosion. He wondered if
there were logistics he hadn't considered. Until now he hadn't
reasoned that Nuri might leave the bike and merely stroll
across the street and enter the film studio's rear gate on foot.
Growing more restless with each passing minute, Khamsin
decided to leave the bar.

He drove swiftly back to the studio, wondering now whether
he should have used the telescopic-sight rifle after all. No, the
neighborhood was too congested with traffic; a clean getaway
would have been chancy.

He swore when he saw the motorcycle undisturbed, parked
in the lot where the dancer had left it. Khamsin debated what to
do. He'd forgotten that it was lunch time.

Figuring he could do nothing about the delay and feeling a
little hungry, Khamsin drove down the street to grab a fast
sandwich at McDonald's. He was on edge and ate quickly, all
the time keeping his ears attentive. He tried to read a
newspaper, but he was overcome with impatience and couldn't
concentrate. Another half hour elapsed, and still there was no
resounding blast.

Nuri stared in amazement. The chief executive's office at
First Consolidated Studios was a stunning, 1900s art nouveau
fantasy. Stepping quickly across the plush, indigo-blue carpet,
he shook hands with studio head Harry Kaufmann.

"Glad to meet you, kid. Sit down." Kaufmann's suntanned

face crinkled in a wry smile. "It's a pleasure meeting a male dancer to whom attractive women aren't a nuisance."

Wincing at Kaufmann's sarcasm, Nuri took a seat in front of an impressive five-by-nine foot koa wood desk that was the focal point of the room. He was pleased that Paul McGinnis had agreed to wait outside in the reception area. The FBI shadow was making him increasingly nervous and irritable.

Kaufmann's secretary had told Nuri that Tina would be a half hour late, so he decided to use the time promoting his manuscript to the studio boss. *The Kremlin Sword* would make as fine a motion picture as it would a book, but without some preliminary contacts, it might not see the light of day in either medium. Tina had insisted that Harry Kaufmann's blessing might help the project along.

The introductions out of the way, Nuri withdrew the partial manuscript from his tote bag and tossed it on the desk. He watched the studio chief remove his cashmere jacket and toss it carelessly over a chair. Kaufmann remained standing as he leafed through several pages of copy. The film executive was in his late forties—short, lean, and vain, with a florid face, perfect white teeth, and cunning brown eyes. His fingernails were varnished and he wore stylish eyeglasses rimmed in Florentine gold which he nervously took on and off. Gathering up Nuri's material, Kaufmann sat on the corner of his desk, Gucci loafers off, his Dior monogrammed tie loosened. "This is it?" he asked sharply, "the whole ball of wax?"

Nuri frowned. "Only the beginning."

Glancing randomly through several pages, Kaufmann waved a finger with a diamond-studded ring. "Relax, already," he admonished. "I'm a slow reader."

Nuri sighed with impatience. Kaufmann's agitated manner made him uncomfortable. Though the film company's top banana wasn't a big man, he had a commanding presence. Nuri guessed the massive wooden desk had something to do with it. Harry Kaufmann's personality also screamed from the credenza and wall behind him: there were a couple of Oscars, numerous accolades, framed magazine covers, photos with celebrities, and poses of himself hang-gliding, white-water rafting, and deep-sea fishing.

Nuri looked around him. The rest of the office was just as brassy—and big. It had turn-of-the-century class, but in a vulgar sort of way. Nuri smiled, suddenly remembering the new colloquialism Tina had taught him—*high tack*. Kaufmann's executive suite reminded him of a French movie he'd once seen at the University of Moscow Historical Film Exposition. The office's zigzagging, bas-relief ceilings, ornate furniture, and art nouveau accessories were a potpourri of Frank Lloyd Wright, Toulouse Lautrec, and Gauguin.

"Jesus," Kaufmann grunted, shaking his head. "This isn't fiction. You really intend to drop this bomb while your old man's in office? For that matter, even alive?"

"Bomb?" Nuri winced. "Time permitting, yes. And it's not a family matter. The best is yet to come."

"Like what?"

Nuri shrugged. He met Kaufmann's inquiring gaze. "I plan to test reality. With my friends back at the Bolshoi. I intend to help three of them escape from the Soviet Union." He hesitated. "Time permitting, of course, and if I can afford it. My dancing comes first, and there's the matter of a decent compensation to make the literary sweat worthwhile."

"Already the new immigrant sounds like a capitalist." Kaufmann cocked his head and stared at Nuri through the blended bifocals. "You've been here just under a year. Sure that's time enough to understand the other side of the coin?"

Nuri felt put upon. Smiling with impatience, he said, "Tina taught me a simplified way to comprehend capitalism. An evening playing the American game of Monopoly, yes? *Park Place*, *Broadway*. Myself, I prefer a corner on the utilities and railroads."

"Your English. It's damned good. And call me Harry."

Nuri grinned. "It should be. A quarter of my salary goes to my speech coach in New York. I've even forgotten how to tell Russian immigrant jokes in fractured English." Nuri wanted to get back to the subject of economics. "One question, *Harry*. What does capitalism mean to you?"

It was Kaufmann's turn to frown. He said flatly, "A line a block long, an hour early, for the opening of a new Tina Conner picture."

"For you, so simple, then. No concern for the class struggle?"

"Not at this studio, friend. *Grapes of Wrath* tearjerkers came in and out in the thirties, again in the late sixties. Give us another thirty-year breather before the next rerun." Kaufmann regarded him curiously. "Easy, easy. I can read your mind from here. You think I'm riding the poop of a slave galley, cracking a cat-o'-nine-tails? Bullshit. It's your charming lady friend, her expensive contracts, and her fans that have me by the nuts, pal, and don't forget it."

Nuri wasn't listening. He was staring at one of the chrome-framed blowups on the far wall. It was of Shirley Temple in a scene from *Little Miss Marker*. Without looking back at Kaufmann, he asked softly, "The book manuscript, Harry, does the concept have merit or not?"

"Easy, not so fast." Kaufmann glanced at his watch. "Where the hell is Tina?"

11

TWELVE MILES across town in one of the dubbing rooms at Universal Studios, Tina Conner sat at a felt-covered table and spoke her lines into a microphone. The screen up front went dark as the sound crew finally shut down the projector. Tina prayed the director would buy the looping effort and call it a day. She'd fluffed a few times and it was running late; it was difficult concentrating on the script when Nuri Baranov was in town, for he filled her mind like a giant in a Grimm's fairy tale.

"That's a wrap!" The dismissal came from the control console at the back of the room. The recording studio lights came up.

Closing her script, Tina stretched like a cat and climbed to her feet. She hated looping. The recording of voice-over to go with previously-shot scenes always seemed awkward and unreal. She never failed to be surprised how well the sequences turned out. The Italians, she knew, made entire films this way, with half the actor's time spent in the dubbing room.

The bearded film director called out to her. "A boffo

performance, Tina. First Consolidated should be less possessive and loan you out more often."

She picked up her St. Croix shoulder bag and winked. "Guest slots on TV sitcoms usually aren't my thing, genius director. Only when the script and price are right."

He went with her to the exit and pushed open the heavy soundproof door. "Money's not everything," he quipped.

"Yes, but it comes in handy when I'm conducting a transcontinental romance. Air fares between here and New York add up."

They walked out onto the Universal lot. Tina could almost taste the smog hovering low over the San Fernando Valley.

The director escorted her to a waiting limousine. "Another blockbuster like *Transgressions* and you'll be able to buy a Learjet."

Tina looked at him and smiled. Jerry Nathan was one of Hollywood's new whiz kids, oozing with talent, and a good-looking hunk to boot. Tina had enjoyed working with him. "Sorry you're not coming to the Stockholm Festival, Jerry. You'll miss the fun."

"I save my hard-earned coins for Cannes. One party a year is enough for me."

Tina climbed in the back of the silver-gray Cadillac and winked at the filmmaker. "Take care, Jerry." She signaled the driver to take off, noting that for the first time her new bodyguard sat up front beside him.

The limo accelerated and she settled back in the corner of the suede leather seat. Tina had been up since seven, and all she'd eaten was Nuri's hard-as-a-rock muffin. Famished as she was, lunch was still three quarters of an hour away.

Tina wondered why Harry Kaufmann had insisted she bring Nuri into the studio. She hoped it wasn't another of First Consolidated's cheap publicity shots. Leaning forward, she ignored the built-in TV and flicked the dial of the FM receiver, searching for one of the wall-to-wall euphoria stations. She settled on KJOI; elevator music didn't turn her on, but it did allow a little elbow room, time to think.

With the government watchdogs being called off, Tina was worried about Nuri. Actually, she had mixed emotions, unable to decide whether to be pleased or upset that the surveillance was ending. It seemed unbelievable that the Russians would try to harm Nuri, or any dissident for that matter, but she was no expert in these affairs.

Thoughts ran through her mind in disarray—out of focus fragments, vividly sharp recollections—a few of them uncomfortable. The white car parked high on the bluff overlooking the beach house—the man inside with the binoculars; most likely a gawking fan, but why at that hour in the morning? The frightened look on Nuri's face when he'd returned from the pay phone at the Getty Art Museum; his subsequent secretive manner. Tina thought about her upcoming trip to Svenska Filmo, now wondering if she should possibly cancel out, instead accompanying Nuri on his Paris, Nice, and Milan ballet tour. God, the flap that would generate at the studio!

Tina glanced through the glass partition at the back of Jon Saarto's head. The matter of the new private bodyguard—it was still a bone of contention with Harry Kaufmann. He'd agreed to pay only half of the private detective's salary and expenses; Tina was to pay the rest. "It's deductible," Kaufmann kept insisting.

On impulse she pushed the button lowering the limo's glass divider. Jon Saarto turned with an inquisitive look.

Tina poured on the charm. "We met so briefly yesterday, I didn't have a chance to welcome you aboard, Mr. Saarto. Harry Kaufmann recommends you highly. As did my last fortune cookie."

Smiling thinly, he studied her. "The Chinese connection. What did it reveal?"

She laughed. "That a tall strong man with brown wavy hair would come to my rescue."

"That let's out Nuri."

"I trust your intention is to protect *both* of us. But beware Mr. Saarto, you may be sticking your neck out. Isn't there an old Chinese quote, 'Save a person's life and you are responsible for them forever'?"

The bodyguard smiled and turned back toward the front of the vehicle. "Harry Kaufmann should have warned you, Ms. Conner. I'm a cold-hearted, pragmatic realist, here for the salary. When the job's over, we all go our own way."

"You might call me Tina."

He shrugged. "I like the name. About the fortune cookies— in my book, they aren't good for anything but eating."

Tina winced at the bodyguard's abruptness. She pushed the

electric button and the divider glass thudded back into place. Turning up the radio volume, she put Jon Saarto out of her mind. In resignation, she thought how sweet it would be without enemies she didn't understand—like private or government watchdogs, the intrusive press, studio publicity arrangements, unruly fans, and the devil knew what other reruns. Her enormous reservoir of energy was being slowly depleted and the drain had to stop. It needed to be redirected toward Nuri.

She flashed on the affair and the way it was going. Nuri's wit and intelligence were new and refreshing in her life, though his emotionality was unpredictable and occasionally frightening. The relationship was exciting, continually changing. There would be much to expand on, for she was convinced that successful partnerships ceased to be successful when they stopped growing and exploring.

For the past month Tina had dated no one else. She wasn't sure about Nuri. As complex and creative as he was, in the future he'd require plenty of leash, she was sure of that; he was simply too restless a tiger to be held closely or contained. Tina also suspected he was an incipient psychic, capable of reading her every thought. Early on she'd learned never to exaggerate or tell him little fibs, not even the well-meaning white-lie variety that made a clumsy stab at avoiding embarrassment. It had become obvious that Tina Conner would have to find other ways to have a pinch of privacy for herself, for her revealing face, to Nuri, was an open book.

Tina felt a slight headache beginning. In a daze she stared out the limousine window. The traffic was only a blur, for her mind focused on the final hours she and Nuri would have together before flying off in different directions. They would be separated two weeks. Part of the job or not, she dreaded the cacophony in store for her in Stockholm. She didn't feel like hustling Hollywood product at Svenska Filmo at all. But it was a part of her contract. The time would be better spent consolidating her affair with the dancer.

At Fairfax the long Cadillac turned onto Sunset Boulevard, with its ranks of expensive billboards promoting new films and recordings. The fifteen-by-fifty foot sign advertising her own latest picture towered over the La Cienega intersection like some promoter's wet dream. Tina shuddered. Again her eyes tried to avoid it. She was convinced the billboard artist had made her look cross-eyed, and twice she'd mentioned it to the studio advertising manager without results.

When it came down to it, the Hollywood hype game had become a bore. She was no longer interested in having the most important people in town fall all over themselves to please her. Nuri just didn't understood about publisher Brian Beck and his airhead parties.

Perhaps part of it was that she was ready to settle down, that she'd been denying some domestic need or biological imperative for too long. Possibly she was ready for the business of marriage. Would it be Nuri Baranov or someone equally talented and volatile? Whatever, for the present the Russian dancer was her idol, and she was prepared to share his talent with the world.

The midday sun coming through the angled overhead glass was only slightly diffused. Under it, L. Brian Beck's impeccable linen suit shone as white as his hair. One of the publisher's hands leaned on his cane, while the other held a cordless extension phone. He was expecting it to ring at any moment.

The publisher's small arboretum was located behind the estate's quadruple garage. Beck's full-time Japanese gardener called the greenhouse "the glass lean-to." It had come with the Bel Air property, and though Beck himself had no green thumb, he occasionally enjoyed its diversion, especially the exotic orchids and the collection of insect-devouring plants he'd brought back from Paraguay. Most of all he relished the arboretum's solitude and privacy, though the humidity precluded visits when the sun was highest. Like at this very moment.

This time he had no choice in the matter, for it was the only place for meeting guests he wished to keep separated for any number of reasons from the mélange in the main house. Especially visitors like Seymour Wallich, the middle-aged, bespectacled telemetry- and weapons-control designer from the Naval Weapons Center at China Lake.

L. Brian Beck despised losers, and the individual before him was definitely a loser. The weapons engineer was brilliant enough, but he was deep in debt, a chronic gambler seduced by martinis and an extramarital affair. Wallich was a failure clinging to hope, a man who knew painfully well the meaning of the word "mistake." Indeed, for the past three years Seymour Wallich's life had been little else. Beck prided himself on capitalizing on other men's mistakes. It took losers to make winners.

The graying, thin-haired Wallich was short of stature and had twinkling, Ichabod Crane eyes with brows that gave off a chronic twitch. His body moved with fast little gestures, and his pudding face quivered slightly when he spoke. Wallich reminded Beck of a temperamental toy poodle.

Beck asked him, "You brought the documents, I trust?"

Wallich looked at him apprehensively, then nodded.

The remote telephone in the publisher's hand buzzed softly. Beck pushed back his sleeve and checked his Cartier watch. "Ah! Ten minutes late, but I suspect this is the call from our mutual friend." He put the handset to his ear.

"Yes? Where are you calling from?" Beck asked. The voice on the line was Khamsin's, and he was calling from a pay phone outside a restaurant. "I have propitious news, my dear Khamsin. Our man is with me now and he's cooperating. You may come by this evening to pick up the material. No, we won't disappoint you. *Au contraire.* Good-bye." Beck slid the telephone receiver into the waist pocket of his suit jacket.

The weapons-guidance designer looked at Beck speculatively. "If I appear frightened, I'm sorry. What bothers me is the control over the documents when they are being transmitted. Your Overseas Film Distribution link and the woman Tangerine—I've never met her."

Beck said quickly, "And never will. She's dead, an accident. From now on your material will be hand carried into the Soviet Union. Trust my judgment."

A ghostly smile crossed Wallich's face. "Your extortionate manner does not invite trust, Mr. Beck. With your videotapes of my indiscretions, do I have a choice?"

"Indiscretions? I'd say it was your degenerate behavior that turned one of my more pleasant soirees into a bacchanal worthy of Caligula or the Marquis de Sade."

"I was drunk and temporarily out of control."

"And me with my weakness for keeping videotape records of everything."

Wallich avoided Beck's scrutiny. "And making six-figure deals at the expense of loyalty and patriotism."

"The latter are affectations only fools can afford." Beck wiped his forehead with a pale green silk handkerchief that matched his tie. "It's unbearably muggy in here. Let's finish this. Do you want the income to continue or not? And my protection?" Taking no pity with his victim's angst, Beck headed for the exit, leaning heavily on the cane.

His guest, walking alongside, was sweating profusely too. Wallich sighed, wordlessly reached inside his jacket pocket and withdrew a white business envelope. "The film negatives are all here," he said in a barely audible voice, hands trembling as he handed the envelope over.

"Good," Beck said dully. "When I am remunerated, you'll be paid in turn; the usual anonymous deposit to your savings account. Stop fretting, Mr. Wallich. My machinations are well-planned, completely foolproof. You're dealing with an entrepreneurial genius, not some backwoods con artist." Beck was annoyed. He could tell that Seymour Wallich was more hesitant and cautious than usual.

The man's not only emotionally dispossessed, thought Beck, but he's becoming *desperate*. Wallich needed reassurance if he were to continue to cooperate and not panic. Beck didn't dare flesh out the entire plan to the engineer, just a part of it. Slowly, he said, "Your safety is my safety, my friend. We must protect each other."

"I understand, Mr. Beck."

"Do you? We're *partners*, Mr. Wallich. The finger will never be pointed at either of us. At the proper time duplicates of less-important microfilms will be planted on the defector Nuri Baranov. Documents that will incriminate others in your office. There will also be evidence that the dancer had been using my employee Tangerine to transmit these materials into the Soviet Union."

Beck ended it there. He wouldn't elaborate on Nuri's ultimate fate—how Khamsin had told of the dancer's impending liquidation. Wallich might not be able to stomach the concept of assassination. Beck had no qualms himself. If U.S. government investigators could be led to believe the dancer was assisting the KGB and was being punished for failure, all the better. Nuri Baranov was expendable; anything to draw the fire away from Overseas Film Distribution Service, Seymour Wallich, and himself.

It was the perfect plan, Beck thought. Fix the blame on Nuri. Plenty of circumstantial evidence for the FBI, including photographs. In the end more than enough material to sensationalize the front page of his weekly tabloid, *Street*. Even indecencies, perhaps, if his talented reporters put their collective minds to it. Beck studied the glum-faced weaponry designer beside him. "Do you read my publications, Mr. Wallich?"

The engineer lowered his head. "I'm sorry, no. Mr. Beck, may I ask how much more you expect of me?"

Beck reached the door of the arboretum and pushed it open with his cane. "Future? The future's an abstraction. I live for the reality of the present." Smiling, he added in a dull monotone, "You should do likewise."

There were only three people in the cork-walled gun practice range in the KGB basement: General Fiodor Talik, Politburo member Vassily Mishkin, and Colonel Bruna Kloski, who stood off to one side.

Talik again pointed his gun at the target. Mishkin was ashen-faced as he put his hands over his ears and cringed reflexively. He slipped to Talik's left while the KGB general fired a clip from his 9mm Tokarev automatic. The ejected shells kicked out to the right.

Fiodor Talik pushed a control button and the cardboard target came forward on its track. The long, narrow room was quiet again as Talik turned to the head of the Central Committee Party Organization. He said to Mishkin, "The charges, Comrade Minister; I suggest you and the others commit them to memory. Arbitrary scheming, heresy against the teaching of Lenin." Talik slipped another cartridge into the automatic but didn't resume his firing stance. His bronchitis was much better, and he continued to address Mishkin in an even voice, "Adventurism; acting without the approval of the Presidium; aiding and abetting the welfare of traitors to the Soviet State; and self-aggrandizement. More of a revisionist than Khrushchev! Have I said enough, Comrade?"

An introspective frown creased the Party Organization minister's face. "Comrade General Talik, if you are to receive majority Politburo support, you must move more quickly. There are others who vacillate. These ministers, from fear alone, could take a position either way. Shverchenko, Kamenev, and Voroburov are unduly concerned over how the adolescent-minded Americans might react to your usurping of Soviet power. These ministers still lean—albeit weakly— toward the army and Chairman Baranov."

Talik sent a sage wink to Colonel Kloski, then scoffed to Mishkin, "Our American enemies are the most predictable people on this earth. We merely continue a policy of taking one step forward with a smile, two backward with a scowl."

Vassily Mishkin thought for a moment. "And what about our great Red Army?"

Talik laughed. "I suspect they'll have greater respect for the KGB and my own enterprise when I unfold before them the secret plans for the new American concussion weaponry. I have friends in the southern California aerospace industry, Comrade Minister. And now, if you'll excuse me, I must return to my pistol practice. My leadership plans are firm enough, but my hand is not as steady as when I was younger."

"Good day, General. I will do my best to persuade the others."

Talik was glad that the party minister had left the chamber. The smell of gunpowder had not entirely obliterated Mishkin's annoying smell of onions and sweat.

Talik had planned for months to make his stand before the collective leaders of the Soviet Union and place Pavlin Baranov in the penal seat. He'd intended to hold both the High Presidium and Politburo breathless while reciting a litany of accusations against his rival. He hated Pavlin Baranov the moderate, and until the past year had tolerated his revisionist activities. Now matters would change; it was time to act forcefully.

The original plan to call for an examination and criticism of the Chairman-Premier and demand his expulsion would take too much time, even though recent events had abetted the KGB's course. Talik flashed on the incidents: Bolshoi dancer Nuri fleeing to the West; the failure of farm quotas on Baranov's three-year agriculture plan; leniency with the Soviet press; the Chairman's usurping of certain KGB functions; and a softening of the Jewish emigré policy. On top of all this there was Baranov's outlandish scheme to trade an important American military prisoner for the return of his son. Talik could make the list as long as he wanted.

No, he would not wait for the indecisive Politburo or the High Presidium. He would move on his own, immediately. Talik had been a part of the Soviet struggle for nearly forty years and he'd learned well enough that *survival* was all that counted. Now he was on the threshold of opportunity—a chance for personal glory unknown in Russia since the time of Stalin, the real hero of the nation.

Summoning the tall woman colonel to his side, Talik handed her his automatic and gestured toward the target at the end of the room.

Bruna Kloski calmly aimed the weapon and fired repeatedly until the cartridge was expended. Each shot was expertly placed, more accurately than Talik's. She turned to him. "Comrade General, I sense that the Party Organization minister tries your patience."

"In times of crisis I prefer acolytes to Leninites, Colonel. The sacred Soviet proletariat is dedicated with honesty of purpose, but a strong, hard-line leader is needed to focus this energy. To generate cataclysmic events that shape history!"

She nodded and handed back his automatic.

Talik patted the weapon affectionately. "Excuse my immodesty, Comrade Colonel, but if the others can show me a more resolute, energetic—yes, brilliant—Soviet leader, I'll step aside." Having said his piece, he waited for her reaction.

Bruna Kloski's shoulders stiffened and her eyes flashed. She said ponderously, "You have the support of my entire directorate, of course. Death is the best prescription for those who violate socialist morality."

He turned the gun over in his hands, considering it. "I have an assignment for your people, Colonel. A timely accident."

She looked puzzled.

Coldly, without a trace of emotion, Talik said, "I want Chairman Baranov's chauffeur terminated."

"May I be so bold as to ask the reason, Comrade General?"

"The driver was our most reliable informant regarding the Chairman's plans, but now he suddenly refuses to cooperate with the KGB. I believe he compromises us."

"He would dare to be so brazen?"

Talik nodded. "The chauffeur saw your men take a rope into the Bolshoi theatre the night of the ballerina's hanging."

Kloski's eyebrows arched sharply, her lips twisting in a pale, false smile.

Talik shrugged. "Make it look like an accident, and have our own medical staff cover any post-death investigation. Keep the Civil Militia out of it. I'll leave the details to your capable imagination, but I want Pavlin Baranov's personal chauffeur liquidated within twenty-four hours."

"As you command, Comrade General."

"Afterward—his wife and family. Cancel their Moscow housing permit and move them southwest—as far as expedient."

12

WHILE HARRY KAUFMANN examined the partial manuscript for *The Kremlin Sword*, Nuri gazed at the numerous photographs and awards lining the wall. Impressed, he wondered about the convolutions of Hollywood wheeling and dealing, his girlfriend Tina included. There was a large photograph of Kaufmann at poolside with two buxom brunettes, one on each knee. Nuri speculated on whether they were his daughters. "Taken at your home?" he asked curiously.

The studio executive looked up in annoyance. "Last summer."

"Who are the exotic young ladies?"

"On the left, my wife. Julia Shields, the *Precinct Seventeen* show. Tuesdays on NBC. You don't watch the tube at night?"

"Seldom. If I'm not dancing or writing, I like to make love. And who's the other woman?"

"You disappoint me, Nuri. You fail to recognize the Soviet Union's most promising film director?" Nuri looked closer. Of course. It was Natasha Chernyskaya of Mosfilm Studios fame. One of the few fortunate Soviet hero artists permitted to travel the world, virtually at will. Nuri's eyes continued to roam over the wall. He saw a picture of Kaufmann chatting with the President in the White House rose garden, and there were countless celebrity shots, too many to count.

Nuri almost tripped over a box on the floor. No, it was an American Arilines shipping container for pets. He stared at it curiously.

Kaufmann put the manuscript aside, smiled, and scuttled around the desk. "You want a pet? A Yukon muskrat. Temperamental, ornery creature we used as a set prop. The film crew gave it to me yesterday, wrapped in a big red bow. I suppose there's a goddamn message in their sick humor."

Nuri had seen mink, sable, and beaver in Russia, but never a live muskrat. Inquisitively, he bent over, trying to see through the wire-mesh door. It was dark inside but he could make out a large ball of fur that appeared to be sleeping.

Kaufmann hovered over the container. "Keep your fingers away from the opening," he warned.

The dancer was curious; he liked animals. The creature looked big, very big. As Nuri looked closer, the door swung open. A mass of brown fur hurtled toward his face! Heart tripping, he fell backward, clawing frantically, trying to push the animal away.

Nuri heard laughter. Male and *female* laughter. He saw that the muskrat wasn't an angry, sharp-fanged terror at all, but a pair of limp raccoon caps fastened to a curved length of spring steel. He cursed under his breath. Damn these prank-loving Americans. Always, there was time for humor; so unlike Russians, who took themselves so seriously. Shaking his head, Nuri grinned and climbed to his feet. Tina Conner had entered the office in time to enjoy the entire scene. Nuri watched as Kaufmann magisterially went up to Tina and gave her a decorous kiss on the cheek.

She frowned in exasperation. "Harry's pulled that cheap gag on everyone in town. Hardly thought you'd fall for it, love."

"You're late," Nuri replied, smiling with effort. He gestured toward the manuscript on the desk. "I was doing a little snooping while Mr. Kaufmann examined my book." Turning to the studio head, who was in the process of slipping on his Guccis with a scrimshaw shoehorn, Nuri asked, "What's the decision? You'll read all of it?"

Kaufmann glanced at Tina. "You put him up to this?"

She shrugged.

Nuri hoped what he'd written wouldn't be thought of as injustice collecting, one more idiosyncratic outcry over abuses suffered in the Soviet Union. That wasn't what he had in mind. The project, initially, had been a lark, a pastime to wile away the first lonely months in the West. At first he'd been convinced that freedom itself was an illusion, that he had to prove its truths, but experience had taught him he knew better. The story was based on what he could tell the world about corruption in the Soviet hierarchy, the machinations of his father's enemy—the cunning, cruel Fiodor Talik. He had changed the KGB minister's name, of course, but the Soviet people would know. And the rest of the world must understand as well.

Tina interrupted his thoughts. "The beginning of the manuscript is good, Nuri. The rest of it will be even better." She turned to Kaufmann. "Take it home, Harry. Read it carefully."

The film executive pulled on his earlobe meditatively. His eyes darted from Tina to Nuri. "Strong, cutting stuff. I take it you're not planning to go back and visit the USSR in the next light-year?"

Nuri shrugged. "Persona non grata is the least of my problems."

Kaufmann grunted unintelligibly as he pushed the manuscript across the desk. "I'm hooked but not ready to be reeled in. When the project's further along, I'll read it carefully and we talk business." He took off his glasses, flicking them aside. "In the meantime, there's a more important matter to discuss." Kaufmann gestured for Nuri to sit down.

The dancer took his place beside Tina on the handsome sofa. It was fashioned of carved rosewood and upholstered in silk with gold flowers. Tina snuggled up to him, and he kissed her repeatedly behind the earlobe until a polite cough brought them back to attentiveness.

Kaufmann inclined his head. Allowing sarcasm to overcome his unease, he murmured, "Later, kids. You don't mind?"

Tina quipped, "You're not very romantic, Harry."

"Me? I'm plenty romantic—a surplus of imagination in that department."

Tina laughed. "I forgot all the purple scripts coming through your 'story department.'"

Nuri grinned, smugly adding, "*Pravda* insists Hollywood is a modern Sodom and Gomorrah."

Kaufmann was only mildly amused. "Come now, Mr. Baranov. Don't tell us about the purported Babylonian captivity of Hollywood. I've been reading about the sexual excesses of Moscow. Like the notorious groping, even outright anonymous sex on crowded subways and buses."

Nuri felt slightly embarrassed but managed a lame smile. Kaufmann was right; the incidents were on the verge of becoming a pastime and civic scandal. "Possibly the exchange of names and introducing oneself take the adventure out of it," he gibed. "Russian women are very proud," he added with a smile.

Kaufmann grinned. "You mean kinky."

"Nuri!" Tina snapped, before he could elaborate further. She turned to Kaufmann. "Please, Harry. Get on with it so we can go to lunch. Why the summons?"

He said quickly, "You're both invited to the White House for dinner on Friday night. Let's say it's more than an invitation. A *command performance.*"

Nuri looked at Tina. Her eyes were bright with excitement, her mouth half open in surprise.

"Hold it." Kaufmann waved his hand airily. "I know, the invitation is a surprise and why the goddamn short notice. Especially with the two of you about to leave for Europe."

"Harry . . ." Tina began.

He cut her off. "Just agree to the President's party and we'll delay your Stockholm appearance and travel arrangements." Kaufmann turned to Nuri. "Not only do you do the President a favor, but you'll get an extra couple of days to romance your lady friend here."

Nuri shifted uncomfortably, searching for words. "The President of the United States?" He stared at Tina, who was still in her own element of surprise and unable to help him.

She pondered for a moment, then asked, "Why so sudden, Harry? What's the occasion?"

Kaufmann shrugged. "I was only the California state chairman on the big man's campaign. We're friends, but he doesn't tell me everything."

"*What did* he tell you?" she asked, insistent.

"It's a small reception, nondiplomatic. A dozen guests in the East Room. Nuri's been asked to entertain. Nothing fancy, a couple of numbers. The President apologizes for the short notice, but insists there's good reason for it. He wants a meeting afterward regarding Nuri's protection and immigration status."

"Please," Nuri interrupted. "I'm expected in Manhattan early Saturday morning to continue rehearsals for the tour. It's a tight schedule."

"Already arranged," Kaufmann replied. "Your choreographer's agreed, in light of the special circumstances, to send your accompanist down to assist at the White House."

"Your usual panache of efficiency, Harry," Tina said softly.

The studio head continued, "There's another side to this. You may owe it to the Oval Office. As of this morning the President has asked the State Department and FBI to extend your protection for another six months. What's more, the CIA's agreed to lend a hand during the European tour."

Nuri gazed at Kaufmann with sharp suspicion. "Deals, deals." Growing pensive, he turned to Tina and saw her expressive face grow somber. The tension was building, and any earlier accord disappeared from her eyes. She looked acutely miserable.

Her lips quivered as she said, "Oh, God, Nuri, do we need them? More damned government interference in our affairs? Harry's already arranged for a *private bodyguard*. And didn't you brag about disappearing at will, unrecognized, on the streets of Manhattan? Not once has anyone bothered you yet."

Nuri nodded sagely. He said to Kaufmann, "She's right. I don't blame her for being upset."

Tina added, "I'm tired of having other people decide what hotel we stay in, which restaurants we patronize, when and where. And I dislike strangers parading in and out of the guest bathroom and my kitchen at Malibu!"

Kaufmann grimaced. "So what do we do? Tell the President, the FBI, and the CIA to take a walk?"

Tina's hazel eyes—not so pretty now—flashed. "Yes. Why not?"

Kaufmann stiffened slightly. He scribbled big letters on a sheet of paper and held it up. "How'd you like this for a press release?"

SUPERCHARGED STAR ANGRY WITH BOTH
RUSSIANS AND FED SLEUTHS—TELLS
THEM TO KISS OFF.

She glared at Kaufmann. "Your studio publicity mill can kiss off, Harry. Gossip rags like the *Enquirer* and *Street* do well enough without help from your boiler-plate news plants."

The executive wasn't about to be put down. "Like it or not, my so-called 'publicity mill' will get an inside track during your White House visit. Guest appearances like this bonanza are definitely covered in your contract. We're in this together, Tina, or have you forgotten?"

Publicity mill. At first Nuri was unfamiliar with the American idiom. He thought about Tina's objections for several seconds and finally understood. Harry Kaufmann looked flushed with pleasure—why? How far would the studio go? Favorable public relations impressed Nuri, but he'd be damned if he or Tina would become First Consolidated's patsies for the latest and juiciest gossip. Before he could speak up on the uncontrolled insanity that was Hollywood, there was a sharp knock at the office entry.

"We're busy," Kaufmann called out.

The door was flung open and Paul McGinnis strode inside, nudging aside a redhead secretary trying to run interference. The agitated FBI agent hesitated in the center of the room; his face looked like he'd just eaten a lemon. Kaufmann signaled for the duty-bound secretary to withdraw.

McGinnis cleared his throat. "Sorry, but a minute ago I received a phone call from Washington." He looked seriously at Nuri, then continued in an agitated voice, "A tragedy at the Bolshoi Theatre. According to *Izvestia* sources, prima ballerina Marina Pleskova hanged herself." McGinnis paused again. "In plain view of an audience of State dignitaries, including Nuri's father."

Nuri shot to his feet. Adrenaline coursed through his body as he stared at the FBI man in disbelief. It took only seconds for the implication to sink in. Feeling weak and dizzy, he slowly sat back down and felt the comfort of Tina's hand on his shoulder.

Paul McGinnis extrapolated: "The official line from Moscow is that Marina was despondent over correspondence from the defector Nuri Baranov. Sorry, pal. Looks like they're making you up to be a heel as well as a traitor."

Nuri didn't hear. Thunderstruck, his thoughts were several thousand miles away. Suicide was impossible! Something was very wrong. He thought about his earlier relationship with the beautiful, talented Marina Pleskova—how they'd understood each other so well. Or had they? Nuri's mind whirled. Could it be remotely possible? What had gone wrong in the past? No, it had to be *her past*, he reflected, selfishly. The terrible *possessiveness*. Possibly it was Marina's mother who had made the ballerina so frigid, demanding, and clutching.

From the beginning any possible "affair" between Nuri and Marina had been doomed to failure. Though they were of the same age, she'd been like a prying little sister to him, though always they'd been friends. Their individual destinies did not lie beyond a caring friendship and being professional dance partners. Marina should have known that. Or had he expected too much of her?

Nuri remembered how he'd often used excuses to slip away from the ballerina for his nocturnal wandering on the streets of Moscow. Along Kutuzovsky Prospect he'd gazed up at the towering concrete State housing and seen women alone at the windows. Mentally he'd undressed them, sure that they, too, were unhappy, lonely, and hungry for intimacy. In Moscow Nuri had been the sad one, not the talkative, gregarious Marina. Suicide? She was too strong to have done this awful thing.

"No! Impossible!" he shouted, voice breaking.

McGinnis shifted uncomfortably on his feet. "Sorry, there's more. There's something peculiar about the timing of the death announcement. The story was dated thirty-six hours after the incident happened."

Nuri sighed. "Information moves slowly in Moscow."

"Not that slowly. The CIA suspects there was a reason. No Americans were in the Bolshoi Theatre that night, but our embassy personnel became aware of the suicide yesterday. They picked it up from a friendly Italian diplomat who'd been in the audience."

Nuri trembled spasmodically. She'd been *discovered*, then eliminated because of him! And now there would be others. Had the entire Soviet publishing underground been penetrated? Fiodor Talik's stooges were responsible for this perverted act.

Nuri prickled with an anger he'd never felt before. For the first time he began to take seriously the headlines and rumors he'd heard. Perhaps his father's position wasn't so secure. Was Pavlin Baranov, too, about to come under Talik's axe?

He looked around the room at the others. Tina, Kaufmann, and McGinnis were silent, watching him, waiting. *Marina dead.* Reality and nightmare, to Nuri, had become one, fused together, and in his torture he was unable to differentiate between them. He knew, instinctively, that he had to do something; he needed a plan!

The studio head replaced his glasses and looked at Tina and McGinnis. "The press will be badgering Nuri for a comment. God knows what fool questions they'll have."

Nuri didn't hear Kaufmann. Sick with grief, he slumped back down beside Tina. Only she seemed capable of nudging him away from his anger of retribution.

Vaguely he heard McGinnis say, "The media will assume he's already returned to New York."

Tina shook her head. "Fat chance. The more enterprising among them will be on us by morning."

Paul McGinnis said to her, "There's more news. The President is extending Nuri's protection."

"Mr. Kaufmann's already told us." Tina looked at the others in turn. "What do we do about Jon Saarto?"

McGinnis replied crisply, "Keep him on the payroll. You'll need all the help you can get."

Kaufmann grimly interjected, "Any *good* news today, Mr. McGinnis?"

"Sorry. I'll get out of your hair. I'm heading back to the beach to nose around. Your friend Saarto can take over here. He's waiting outside."

Tina said to the FBI agent, "Do me a favor? Take Nuri's motorcycle back to Malibu. We'll bring your car."

McGinnis swore under his breath. "Whatever makes you happy."

"I don't like the scene," said Nuri forlornly.

Harry Kaufmann winced. "Neither do I, but it's the only script we have."

13

THE PASTRAMI SANDWICH Paul McGinnis had wolfed down at one of the studio's lunch wagons hadn't set well in his stomach. Fumbling in his pocket, he found a package of Rolaids and tossed two in his mouth. He was relieved to get away from Harry Kaufmann's office and all the film-biz hype. In McGinnis's book, Tina Conner was being sent to a film festival at the wrong time. The hell with it. If she chose to get fucked over by First Consolidated's publicity department, she deserved the lousy screw.

As for Nuri, McGinnis knew that if he were in the dancer's shoes, he'd clear out fast, go low profile and head for the hills. Find a farm, ranch, go fishing in Alaska, anything. Forget the tossed bouquets at curtain calls, rave reviews, and whatever else turned on a dancer. All so much theatrical bullshit, McGinnis reflected, smiling to himself. The annoying thing about esthetic types like Nuri Baranov was that real men like himself wound up being contaminated by their delicacy.

A year earlier the State Department and CIA security specialists assigned to the young defector's case had warned

McGinnis that Russians were the most difficult exiles in the world, that they were moody, often inconsolable; it was in their blood. Especially *talented* Russian artists. Nuri proved no exception, even before this latest trauma over Marina Pleskova's death. As a U.S. taxpayer, McGinnis felt annoyed. The FBI had better things to do than serve as bodyguards for CIA or State Department causes. Still, he knew better than to make waves. A comfortable though not cushiony retirement was only six years away.

McGinnis nodded to the friendly guard as he passed through the film lot's back gate. McGinnis waited at the curb for the traffic to clear, then strolled across the street to the annex building. He found the bike around back, where Nuri had left it. He stared for a long time at the gleaming red Kawasaki. McGinnis's mind flashed over the half-dozen motorcycles he'd owned before joining up with the government and being required to wear a suit every day. He threw a leg over the handsome bike and said to himself, *Damn, I feel like a fucking kid again*. McGinnis fumbled in his pocket and pulled out the keys Nuri had given him.

Khamsin Ahmed returned to the cocktail lounge he'd been in earlier, this time ordering plain Perrier water with a twist of lemon. The lounge was nearly empty. Two swarthy, heavily madeup women, obviously prostitutes, watched him from their place at the end of the bar. They laughed and chatted noisily and periodically looked his way. Khamsin ignored them, staring into his drink and occasionally dipping into a nearby bowl of peanuts.

He thought about actress Tina Conner, who wasn't a part of his bloody contract. She was too pretty to die, and would live if she didn't get in the way. Khamsin's KGB employers had no quarrel with the talented young actress. Suddenly it occurred to him: she was due to meet Nuri at the film studio, and it was entirely possible she might ride back to the beach with him. Whoever rode that iron steed was doomed to wind up as hamburger. *N'importe, ma chère*, he reflected. It would be one of those things; so much rotten timing for her.

The whores at the end of the counter were looking Khamsin's way again, this time giggling. He wondered if they were mocking his appearance, possibly making jokes about his hairpiece. *Coarse Americans!* He shot them a look of contempt, sorely tempted to show them the unsightly burn scars the toupee concealed.

Irritably, he once more looked at his watch. Nuri Baranov couldn't stay on the studio lot forever. Hunkering closer over the bar, Khamsin rolled his half-empty Perrier glass between nervous fingers. Suddenly the drink chattered away from him, across the countertop. Along the mirrored back wall glassware rattled as the whump of a distant explosion shook the building. The bartender and prostitutes looked up, startled.

Khamsin buried an urge to smile. Arching his wiry eyebrows, he continued to stare dully into his glass of sparkling water. He could see in his mind the results of the detonation: the smoking, tangled heap of motorcycle, or what was left of it. The stench of cordite, the charred, bloodied body—if any parts of it were recognizable. He had to fight back a strong urge to return to the scene of the crime, check it out. *No, absolutely no.* After all his terrorist work in London, Tel Aviv, and Beirut, he'd learned that avoiding the target area afterward was essential. The job was concluded, that was enough. *Par excellence!* Khamsin put Nuri Baranov's carnage out of his mind. All that Khamsin had to do now was to pick up the documents L. Brian Beck had waiting for him.

Khamsin looked forward to returning home to France. His suitcase was ready as always, stuffed with contingency cash, credit cards, fake passports and driver's licenses. Before turning in his rental car, he would dispose of the rifle and pistol, for they were expendable. He had virtual arsenals hidden away in Chicago and New York storage facilities, and there would be plenty of money to buy more weapons when necessary. Colonel Kloski would be pleased, and the funds she would supply would tide him over for several months. He and Danielle could continue to live as lavishly as they pleased in Paris.

Khamsin felt better than he had in a long time. Tipping the bartender liberally, he slid off the stool and left the lounge. On the street, already there were several wailing sirens, and the sound pleased him.

Nuri followed Tina, Harry Kaufmann, and the private detective Jon Saarto out of the studio commissary. After the bad news from Moscow, the luncheon only compounded Nuri's misery. Sensing his displeasure, Kaufmann had cut his own

meal short. Despite her earlier hunger, Tina only picked at her
food, and Nuri had ordered just a bowl of soup. Only Saarto
ate with gusto.

As they strolled back toward the studio's administration
building, the new bodyguard fell in behind them like a faceless
satellite. Nuri, determined to know this individual who would
be spending so much time with Tina, had insisted that Saarto
join them for lunch. The tall Finnish-American, however,
seemed caught up in his own peculiar sangfroid, and had been
uncommunicative and silent. The mood at the commissary
table had been heavy, with Harry Kaufmann doing most of the
talking. Nuri's dislike of the studio executive had intensified.

Glancing back over his shoulder, Kaufmann beckoned to the
new bodyguard. "Don't lag behind, Saarto, I dislike shouting.
Brian Beck called me this morning, threatening to run a story
on First Consolidated. Heavy exposé stuff in *Street* magazine—unless I forgot about hiring you. The bastard claimed
Tina and I were playing dirty pool pirating you away."

Saarto replied shortly, "Maybe you are. Did he convince
you to up the ante?"

"No. Our deal sticks. I'll fight off Beck my own way. You
remain a part of the family. That okay with you, Nuri? Can't
have jealous courtiers pouting in the wings."

Nuri glowered back at Kaufmann but kept an annoyed
silence.

An explosion, close by, suddenly rocked the ground. Nuri
jumped. His nerves, after the silly muskrat incident and the
shocking news from Moscow, were honed to the edge.

Kaufmann smiled. "Don't panic," he said irritably. "It's the
special-effects crew on the back lot. Overly ambitious with the
TNT again. Fucking overkill like that not only plays hell with a
picture's budget, but lights up the studio switchboard for the
rest of the day." Dismissing the blast as if it were only a cherry
bomb tossed by a teenager, Kaufmann faced Nuri. "The
President wants your act scaled down, something that will fit
into the East Room. Think you can arrange it?"

"What?" Nuri, still shaken by the explosion, collected
himself. "Yes, of course. I'll call New York and take care of it
this afternoon."

Kaufmann added, "The White House aide said to remind
you, a performance everyone can *understand*. Like minimal
program explanations. Possible?"

Tina frowned at the studio head. "Explanations for what, Harry? Signposts for the guests to find their way out of a cultural wasteland?"

Nuri said swiftly, "The White House, Mr. Kaufmann, might do well to remember the words of the late George Balanchine. He said, 'When you have a garden of beautiful flowers, do you demand of them, What do you mean? No, you just enjoy them. It is the same with dance.'"

Kaufmann shook his head, unimpressed. To Tina, he prompted, "Take care of the consummate artist here, will you? Try to keep him from quoting Dostoevsky, Chekhov, or God knows who else to the capital press." To Nuri, he firmly added, "In Washington, D.C., for Tina at least, lots of smiles and tender caresses before the cameras. The public will eat it up. And don't forget to mention Tina's latest picture. You understand the drift?"

Nuri fought hard to control his anger. Tina sensed his distress and fired off a salvo of her own. "Harry, why me? Why not find yourself another star? A big, busty blonde?"

"Cute blondes I no longer need."

Jon Saarto spoke up. "He's right. In this town they're the price of a Greyhound ticket from any hamlet in the midwest."

Kaufmann grinned. "Let 'em hang around the boulevard of broken dreams for six months and they're a glut on the market. They'll either work for free or screw for a fee." Kaufmann's eyes met Nuri's directly. "Don't worry. Tina's not one of those bimbos, pal. She's a class actress, you know what I mean? Most important, she has a one-third financial interest in her next picture. So don't get any crazy ideas about her retiring early."

Nuri made up his mind. Capacious, comfortable, or whatever the attraction, he didn't need the bosom of First Consolidated Studios. This would be his last visit with Harry Kaufmann. The manuscript—good or bad—would remain in New York, go to an agent there when it was ready.

They were halfway up the steps of the administration building when Nuri heard agitated voices and a shout of alarm.

An overweight security guard, puffing like a steam locomotive, came running up to Kaufmann. "An explosion, sir! Jesus Christ, the mess!" The man choked out the words, pointing an unsteady finger toward the rear of the lot. "Just outside the gate!"

Nuri tensed. Turning quickly with the others, he saw an ugly black column of smoke cannonading into the air. At the same moment, he heard the wail of approaching sirens. All around him people were running toward the back lot. Nuri held Tina's arm and swiftly followed behind Harry Kaufmann, the badly-shaken security guard, and Saarto.

It took them four minutes to reach the rear gate but only four seconds for Tina to be sick from the gore they saw scattered over the street and desecrating the pale blue studio walls. Harry Kaufmann's face grew wan and shadowed.

Glancing inside the broken window of the guard shack, Nuri saw that the watchman there had been injured by a projectile. It appeared to be a section of handlebar—*from Nuri's rented motorcycle*. Studio first-aid personnel rushed in to assist the stricken man.

Everywhere the stench of burnt cordite was overwhelming. Nuri needed no prompting to realize that an assassin was involved, one with a sadistic streak at that; the bomb was obviously far larger than necessary. The only thing recognizable from Paul McGinnis's dismembered, scattered corpse was a tattered section of his tan suit jacket.

Nuri's heart quailed and his strong legs turned to rubber. Slowly shaking his head in disbelief, he sat down on the curb to avoid having vertigo topple him like a rag doll. But bodyguard Saarto, alarmed by what he found on the scene, wouldn't let him catch his breath. Immediately he strong-armed Nuri and Tina back into the confines of the studio lot.

14

PANDEMONIUM GRIPPED the area around the studio's back gate. Both ends of the street were blockaded as FBI personnel, local police, and firemen swarmed over the scene of the explosion like fire ants. No one in the vicinity escaped questioning, and a wretched hour elapsed before Tina and Nuri could break away from the lot in Harry Kaufmann's personal limousine.

Nuri felt as if he'd reached a new juncture in his life. *The bomb had been meant for him, not Paul McGinnis*. The incident rushed back into focus Tangerine's grisly death as well. It was hard to fathom how the KGB could act so flagrantly here in the United States. McGinnis had warned him, and Nuri had scoffed at the possible danger. And now the FBI agent was *dead*—instead of himself.

The chauffeur drove them back to the beach. Jon Saarto rode with him up front, while a new bureau agent who seemed to appear on the scene from nowhere followed them in another vehicle. Nuri sat in the rear of the limo with Tina nestled against his shoulder. Eyes misted over, she was oddly quiet, though he, too, didn't feel much like talking. McGinnis wasn't family, but he'd grown close to them, a man to be trusted. Nuri would check to see if the agent had a family in Los Angeles. Life in America, for macho individuals like Paul McGinnis, had seemed so wondrously uncomplicated—but now, unfortunately, fatal.

Tina started to sob again. Nuri wiped the tears away from her cheeks and held her tighter. Gently, he kissed her eyelids. She ended her crying and looked up at him. "I'm sorry, Nuri. I need your strength."

He made an effort to smile. "Perhaps I'm jaded, more used to sudden tragedy, the sharp changes from joy to sorrow. It's my Eastern blood." When she looked at him quizzically, he wondered if she'd once more accuse him of being too theatrical. It didn't matter; Americans seldom understood the emotional ambivalence of Russians. What Nuri Baranov said and what he felt were often two different things; at this moment he felt weak, in disrepair, his uneasiness masked by a terrible anger. Up until now his craving for dramatic conflict had been confined to the stage, the seeming endless repertoire of dance. Now there was a new kind of confrontation—a real one, where the stakes weren't tokens of applause, but matters of life and death.

Tina spoke to him again. "We're in trouble, Nuri, and I'm petrified. What happens now? You spend the rest of your life running, looking back over your shoulder?"

"The two-headed eagle was a symbol of the czars. We Russians have a heritage of looking both ways at once." He shrugged, barely managing a grin. "Over the centuries we've learned to live with extremes of loyalty and treachery, success and failure."

Tina pleaded. "I think we should quietly disappear for a few months. Forget everything else. I have enough money for expenses. We could get lost in Europe, possibly Spain or Switzerland."

"For a celebrity it would be impossible." He looked at her, not sure whether to express anguish, dispassion, or rage. He decided to be tough like his Chairman-father. Bite back any cries of anguish with self-control, curb the tears with Soviet style heroics and stubbornness. He said to her, "No. We can't run away."

Tina grabbed his wrist. "It's not a matter of running away. Just *letting go* for a while. Marina's dead; let the others who wish to defect fend for themselves. And your book—is it worth it? You don't need to fire broadsides at Fiodor Talik to make a living! And you don't need to self-destruct."

"I'm sorry, Tina. On this you can't interfere. I'm going to fight them. And I have to do it my way." His voice softened. "Please, we'll talk about it later."

Any accord disappeared from Tina's face. She turned away and gazed vacantly out the limo's window.

Nuri lowered the glass divider up front and called to the detective-bodyguard. "What's in this for you, Mr. Saarto? You a glutton for punishment?"

Saarto turned and smiled. His blue eyes were as clear as trout pools. "A comfortable living. Aimed at saving enough for early retirement."

Nuri held his glance. "Having second thoughts now? It's not too late to back out."

"The going gets tough, I dig in my heels, work harder. That's what the bonus pay is all about."

Nuri winced. "I'm not sure I appreciate mercenaries, Mr. Saarto. If there's a way to strain money out of shit, they usually find it."

"Call me Jon. And I suggest you forget my motives and start thinking in terms of results. Your FBI friends are obviously prone to miscalculate and make mistakes. Paul McGinnis just made one."

Tina stared at Saarto. "For what it's worth, he tried."

The bodyguard grunted back, "It's the final score that counts."

Nuri looked hard at Saarto and risked a smile. "You're an American, Jon. Perhaps you shouldn't be playing Russian roulette with the KGB. It may not be to your temperament. Soviets savor deadly games. The Fifth Directorate, as you've just seen, takes life and death very lightly."

"Obviously so," Tina hastily interjected.

Saarto pushed out his chin. "Do I look frightened? The KGB made a mistake this afternoon, in more ways than one."

While Nuri thought momentarily, Tina pulled away from him to turn on the television. He said to the bodyguard, "Some fool in the Soviet bureaucracy or an incompetent local operative may have made a mistake, but not Fiodor Talik. The KGB general is a cunning professional—a trifle psychotic, but not the type to blunder."

Tina flicked through several TV channels. A late afternoon local newscast had just begun on one of them. Nuri grimaced, for to his dismay the TV newscast began with a grotesque replay of events at First Consolidated Studios.

Up front Jon Saarto signaled the driver to pull over. He then turned to Tina and asked solicitously, "Mind if I join you in back? I'd like to see that news coverage."

She nodded in approval. Nuri pulled her across the seat and Saarto climbed in on the other side. The vehicle edged back out into traffic.

Nuri wondered about the private detective-bodyguard. Such a profession was virtually unknown in Moscow. Saarto looked too smug, too self-confident; a lifetime of violence had apparently hardened him for his job. When Nuri had talked with him at lunch, Saarto had admitted to doing a little prize fighting early on, even training a few boxers himself. He'd also said something about military commando training, a dozen ways to kill a man without sophisticated weapons. Nuri had been fascinated. Yet all this, and he'd worked for a lowbrow gossip and porno publisher? Jon Saarto's dollar-hungry ambitions grated, as did his slick macho manner, glib speech, and kicked-back southern California lifestyle. But what bothered Nuri most were the revealing eyes that lingered longer than necessary on Tina.

Unable to resist the small TV screen before him, Nuri once more saw the news reporters gather around Harry Kaufmann. Like a queen bee, the film studio president seemed to revel in their pandering. Nuri winced at the replay of the afternoon's violence—the bloodstains on the wall and street had screamed loudly enough earlier. Kaufmann's obnoxious re-creation of the incident was too much. Nuri looked away, out the window at the deserted beach, as the limo emerged from the Santa Monica tunnel and proceeded up the Coast Highway. Staring out over the calm, blue-gray Pacific, he tried desperately to refocus his mind.

Detaching himself from the violence on the TV, he thought of his new language, English—the additional effort needed on his vocabulary. Nuri flashed on some odd new words he'd picked up at lunchtime. Terms the talkative, annoying film executive had muttered to associates at an adjoining commissary table. Nuri needed to know the difference—if any—between shnook, shlump, and shlep.

* * *

The eight in the evening arrival of the Secretary of Defense at Andrews Air Force Base was covered by the national press. Hillary Fleming was exhausted. His U.S. delegation had won several rounds in Brussels at the NATO Military Maneuvers Conference, but the Pentagon had been forced to work long hours and make an uncomfortable number of concessions. The long flight back to the capital in Air Force Three had made the Defense chief thin-skinned and irritable.

Sallow-complexioned with steel-gray hair combed straight back, the most powerful member of the President's cabinet was known as a humorless, introspective hard-liner. His detractors claimed Fleming was a paranoid red-baiter.

Fleming answered the questions put forward by the phalanx of reporters as swiftly as possible. Sooner and more brusquely than the TV news crews anticipated, however, the short-mannered Defense secretary abandoned their microphones. Turning his back to the media, Fleming clasped hands with General Frank McCulloch, the Army Chief of Staff, who had unexpectedly come out to greet him. Together they stepped briskly toward a waiting limousine, but before they could reach the vehicle, McCulloch pulled Fleming aside, into the shadows beneath the wing of Air Force Three, where they could talk privately.

The Defense chief sensed McCulloch's distress. "Something of a panic nature, General, that couldn't wait until morning at my office?"

Frank McCulloch said in a firm, bass voice, "Sir, the Army needs Austin Shaeffer out of that Moscow prison."

Fleming groaned, "So what else is new?"

"Plenty. I've always figured the Russian dancer smelled of duplicity. As if we don't have problems enough, some professional tried to wipe Nuri Baranov out this afternoon in Los Angeles."

"He's safe?"

"Apparently for now."

Fleming frowned and said quietly, "The dancer's enemies may be wise to us. Thank God the kid's still alive. Let's trust the Bureau can keep him that way long enough until your own undercover people can drag him out of the country. Then it's the Soviet Chairman's problem."

"Money, I need more of it," McCulloch said quickly. "As

of today I've put a half-dozen Army Q-9 intelligence specialists on the job. All men who won't be recognized if they
encounter CIA or FBI personnel. Mr. Secretary, you wanted
total secrecy. Fine, but how do I keep their personnel transfer
quiet, away from the scrutiny of the Bureau of the Budget or
the GAO?"

Hillary Fleming mulled over the question. He glanced at the
waiting limousine nearby, distracted by a movement in the
back. "There's a woman inside. Do I know her?"

McCulloch replied, "You will shortly. You haven't answered
my question, Mr. Secretary."

Fleming shifted on his feet. "Look, General, I enjoy my
job. I want our mutual friend Shaeffer out of Lubyanka Prison
as much as you do. Unfortunately, if the White House smells
my participation or tacit knowledge in the trade, I'll be out on
the street faster than shit runs through a goose."

"You're not going soft on us?"

"No, I'll support you when I can, but *off the playing field*.
That's always been the arrangement."

McCulloch smiled. "Fine. I've got the ball, Mr. Secretary,
and I fully intend to run with it. This is one game Army's going
to win."

"Good. You can count on me cheering from the sidelines.
Sorry I can't participate."

McCulloch reached inside his tunic and withdrew a box of
pencil-thin Dutch cigars. "Your favorite brand, if I recall."

Fleming smiled. They both lit up Schimmelpennicks.

"About the funding?" McCulloch asked through a cloud of
smoke.

The Defense secretary rolled his cigar between his fingers
and brooded. "I'll see General Lanier tomorrow. He'll find a
way to bury the expenses. Just make damned sure you cover
your own ass." He pointed his Schimmelpennick toward the
limo. "Now can we get inside? It's been a long day."

The chauffeur was instantly at the door. Hillary Fleming
crawled inside and sat next to a young woman who looked
vaguely familiar. She had long black hair, a voluptuous figure,
and distinct Mediterranean facial features which were more
arresting than beautiful. Her eyes gleamed at him. Fleming felt
sure he'd seen her somewhere before in Washington.

McCulloch made the introduction. "Mr. Secretary, I'd like
to introduce Diana Vespucci from the CIA."

Fleming took her hand, smiled, then warily looked back to McCulloch, who had settled in the jump seat before them.

The general explained. "Shall we say Ms. Vespucci's a special friend? She's agreed to help me with the swap."

Fleming noted that McCulloch's hand rested, ever so briefly, on the woman's knee.

McCulloch prompted, "Go ahead, Diana. Tell him what you know."

She sat forward and said in a soft, even voice, "I suspect the CIA director is dragging his heels, probably on the President's orders. We can't prove a thing, and as usual the FBI's not going overboard sharing what they have. Still, a few of us suspect Nuri Baranov's playing a double-agent role. The KGB attempts on his life might even be a sham, or possibly he's working for some other Soviet agency." She paused to crack the window. "Gentlemen, your smoke is killing me. Do you mind?"

Fleming mumbled an apology and put out his cigar. McCulloch, his face stony and blank, as if to say fuck yourself, kept his in his mouth.

Diana Vespucci continued: "Interesting form of gall, if that's what the situation amounts to. The liberated Russian defector preparing for American citizenship, all the while passing information back to Moscow. If not compromising us now, he would later—what we call a KGB sleeper."

The Defense secretary made a face. "Nuri Baranov? I doubt it. Can the agency back up these half-assed theories?"

She hedged. "Sorry, still too many loose ends. Checking them all out takes time and plenty of mindless legwork. We're spread pretty thin. You're not alone in your doubts; from the beginning the President was convinced Nuri was bona fide."

"Your position, then?"

She shrugged. "Tenuous, at best."

Fleming frowned. "A rather feckless response, Ms. Vespucci." He thought for a moment. "It doesn't make sense. Why would the Soviets want Nuri back, be willing to horse trade, if this were true?"

McCulloch puffed on his cigar and looked at Fleming gravely. He replied, "Testing—a facade of protest to make Nuri look good. I say it's all irrelevant. We move fast, trade the damned dancer for Shaeffer. If the kid's bogus, the Russians will probably deliberately slip up somewhere and he'll be back in the West soon enough. There'll be plenty of time for labels like spy, sleeper, or scapegoat later. Right now, I want to get our own man out of Russia."

The photo gallery was actually an extension of publisher L. Brian Beck's bedroom. A sliding shoji screen of expensive rice paper separated it from the main sleeping area. The gallery walls were lined with photographs, most of them nude centerfolds from some of Beck's earlier publications. Many were from a time when he himself had sweated over color separations, layouts, mechanical deadlines, and editorial acquisitions.

Beck's concern over production detail was a thing of the past now. Circulation of the girlie magazines had slumped in the past two years, and most of his energy was now directed toward the moneymaking supermarket tabloid. Even there Beck had cut back. At the Century City office he had a competent staff of professionals who ran the show for him, and Beck seldom became involved in production drudgery.

Beck sat down in the white upholstered rocker in the center of the room and picked up a tray of slides from the table beside him. On the far wall was a large screen with a silver rectilinear surface. Beside Beck were two Carousel projectors, mounted in tandem with special lenses suited for split-screen effects and dissolves.

From a frosted pitcher Beck poured a double martini into a stemmed crystal glass. He added three olives, eased back, and pressed the remote button dimming the room's track lighting. He'd already placed a compact disc of Bach's *Brandenburg Concerto* on the stereo unit. The servants had been warned not to disturb him except for a call from Khamsin Ahmed. The KGB go-between from Paris had yet to make specific arrangements for picking up the vital microfilms, and Beck was anxious to consummate delivery before retiring.

He sipped the cold martini, then examined two slides of actress Tina Conner that the photo lab had specially retouched for him this morning. Both shots were carefully cropped from the neck down and perfectly matched the scale he'd requested.

Excellent. He wondered if the elusive bitch had decided to attend his party two days hence. Hollywood was notorious for late responses to an RSVP invitation. It didn't matter. Beck would have his pleasure now.

He chose the most sultry shot of Tina's face and inserted that slide into the top projector. Sorting through several slides of nude women in compromising frontal positions, Beck found a promiscuous dominatrix in a studded black bra who had posed for his November 1983 issue of *Voyeur*. Placing it—minus the head—in the lower projector, he lined the two slides up, adjusting the focus on the two people until they overlapped perfectly—at the neck.

Tina's new image! Beck smiled to himself as he felt his pulse quicken. His cane slipped off the edge of the rocker and fell to the floor, but he ignored it. It didn't matter. Nothing ever mattered when he was caught up in the ecstasy of masturbating.

15

IT WAS ONE of those glorious sunsets at Malibu Beach. The offshore wind had diminished to a soft, barely noticeable breeze, while the weather forecast indicated increased hazy cloudiness, probably fog later in the evening.

Dining on Szechuan takeout food at a table by the picture window, Tina and Nuri picked unenthusiastically at the last of their spiced beef and steamed rice. Nuri avoided the carved Chinese chopsticks she'd placed on the table, eating with a fork. Fewer than a dozen words had been exchanged during the meal. The day had been a miserable one, and Nuri was glad that it was ending. When they'd both finished eating, Tina cleared the table and came back from the kitchen with green tea in Ming porcelain cups.

Nuri remained silent for a long time, staring out over the surf. The brilliant sky, seeded with orange and pink puffs, faded quickly; already here and there through the clouds stars could be seen. The couple sipped their tea, savoring the twilight solitude.

The beach house was growing cool. Nuri finally rose from

the table, went across the adjacent room to the massive lava
stone fireplace and lit the gas. Artificial logs were clean and
convenient; they were popular in southern California, Tina had
told him. He stared at the flames briefly, then shuffled back
toward her. On the coffee table a copy of the news tabloid
Street caught his eyes and he paused, staring at it with
contempt. He and Tina were on the cover, a photograph
surreptitiously taken in New York a few weeks earlier. He said
to her, "You told me you wouldn't pick up any more gossip
magazines."

"I didn't. Our new bodyguard handed it to me. Courtesy of
his former employer." She slowly sipped her tea.

"Tell Mr. Saarto not to be so considerate," Nuri said
brusquely, and crossed the room again, tossing the magazine in
the fireplace. "I won't read them and I dislike being taunted by
my face on the cover."

"You, a would-be author, a book burner?"

Ignoring her, he went to the window, staring out at the ocean
and darkening sky. Nuri reflected that the problem now was
keeping not only the book project from being washed out to
sea, but himself as well. The ugly German word "kaput" kept
banging around in his mind.

Tina asked quietly, "Would they leave you alone if you gave
up the writing?"

"You don't understand. Without it, back home I am
misunderstood, to some a traitor. I'll be forever ostracized by
millions of Soviets. Many former friends turn against me, yes?
I'm admired only by the handful who dare not speak out on my
behalf. Americans and Russians alike need to know the truth.
Someone must tell the story of this evil personage who heads
the KGB."

"But why not someone else?"

Nuri shook his head and began pacing the floor. Tina's dog
sat up and watched him with interest. Nuri said sharply,
"There's also the matter of *artistic truth*. The success and
happiness I've found in the West is not a myth, as some Soviets
would believe. In Russia the new breed of self-published,
unofficial writer is called the *samizdat*; it is the literature of the
Moscow underground. I'm going to join their ranks. My work
must go on, regardless." He paused, studying Tina's expression with concern. "Ah! I'm too serious, I see it in your eyes."
Measuring out a smile, he spread his arms and bent his knees in

a demi-plié. For the moment playing the smartass, he grandly invoked, "I am the speech of forgotten lips."

Tina laughed, the first time since the incident with the phony muskrat in Kaufmann's office. "Exquisite. You're an actor as well as a dancer. Dare I ask whose celebrated line?"

"Boris Pasternak's." Turning somber, Nuri sat back down at the table. Her soft hand gripped his.

"I saw the film *Dr. Zhivago* three times. It was beautiful."

Nuri looked at her with admiration. "We, too, in the Soviet Union, especially the students, are moved by the Russia of the past—the rustic simplicity of our villages, rolling farmland, and onion-domed churches." He sighed. "The world you know from *Dr. Zhivago*."

Tina smiled. "Speaking of old-fashioned ways, the dish-washer's broken and the maid's still gone." She started to gather up the cups and saucers. "Mind joining me in the kitchen?"

Nuri affected a jauntiness he didn't feel. "Try keeping me out."

Khamsin's anger with himself for his bad luck earlier had finally dissipated. More determined now than ever, he waited patiently a short distance down the sand from Tina's home. The heavy fog rolling in from the ocean would make the job easier. To get inside the Malibu colony it had been necessary to approach from the south, hiking over a mile up the beach from the public access. Though preferring his Browning telescopic rifle, it would have been too conspicuous to carry along the beach. Too many joggers and residents walking their pets. Khamsin would rely on the silencer-equipped .357 magnum handgun beneath his jacket.

Under cover of darkness and from behind an outcropping of rocks, Khamsin had kept watch for half an hour, his eyes finally adapting to the moonless night. Now he observed the beach house with all the patience of a tiger crouching in the grass, fully aware its nocturnal hunger was about to be sated.

Once more he thought about the miscarriage at the film studio, his *rotten luck*. As a professional he was unaccustomed to slipshod results, and the thought of failure never entered his mind. The KGB would be furious with him, for he'd failed earlier in the afternoon and there was no possible way to disguise the fact. Already in Moscow the news would have been picked off the satellite and relayed to the Fifth Directorate's operations center. Khamsin tried not think about the wrath of Bruna Kloski.

Feeling a maverick breeze, from nervous habit Khamsin tucked at the edge of his hairpiece. From his jacket pocket he withdrew a folded, blue knit seaman's cap and carefully pulled it over his head. Then he focused again on Tina Conner's beach house, studying the layout. He checked his watch. The luminous hands and numerals were faded from age, making it difficult to read in the dark, but he could just make out that it was nine-thirty.

Khamsin thought about what lay ahead: it would be dangerous, the escape back down the beach uncertain, but he had absolutely no choice in the matter. It was better to face a known, visible enemy than an invisible one like a reprisal-minded KGB.

The two cars parked in front of the Tina Conner home—one a sheriff's deputy, the other an apparent FBI agent—didn't unduly concern him, though the third individual outside, who alternated between sitting on the oceanfront bulkhead, circumnavigating the house, and patrolling short distances up and down the beach, could mean trouble. There wasn't a discernible pattern to this bodyguard's movements. This restless individual was called Saarto; twice the men at the front of the house had called out his name.

Khamsin figured that eluding this Saarto would be difficult. He might have to be eliminated. The fog was thickening. *Tant mieux!* All the better. From his earlier Malibu stakeout, Khamsin had a good feel for Tina Conner's routines. Soon, he suspected, the big glass slider would open and someone would let out the dog. Even if Nuri, Tina, or the maid didn't stroll with it on the beach, the animal would be let out to do its duties. Khamsin would try to time his strike when the dog returned and the glass door reopened. The brilliant mercury-vapor floodlight illuminating the deck and adjacent beach would be no obstacle, for he'd planned ahead and brought along wire nips with insulated plastic handles.

Saarto's black, steel-encased flashlight was just over a foot long, the heavyweight kind that neatly doubled as a billy club. Slapping it against his palm, the detective-bodyguard thought about what might lie ahead. He sensed impending trouble; it was one of those instinctual things he couldn't explain, least of all to the stubborn FBI agent who had replaced McGinnis and returned with them to Malibu. The plan was for the new man to set up watch at the front of the house while Saarto minded the beach side.

It would be a long night, and Saarto would be glad when daylight arrived. Tomorrow Tina and Nuri would be away from here. Quietly, they'd all go up into the nearby mountains, to the Lake Arrowhead hideaway Harry Kaufmann was to make available to them.

Saarto wasn't sure that he could count on the new FBI stereotype out front. There was also a one-man patrol car from the L.A. County Sheriff's force, but the officer in it appeared kicked back and had ventured down to the beach only once. There would be three of them in all. Saarto knew that combined surveillance work was hairy business. The fed out front was still mourning Paul McGinnis's demise, and Saarto couldn't be sure of the quality of thinking and clearheadedness of anyone motivated by retribution.

The official U.S. government reaction was still to come. Misdirected bomb or not, from the standpoint of international relations the Soviet-inspired elimination of an FBI agent was a dangerously provocative act. Saarto wasn't really concerned about the political aspect; his immediate and primary worry was the personal protection of Tina and Nuri.

He went over to the white Chevrolet sedan parked across the street from Tina's front door. Behind the wheel the newly assigned Bureau man, Niles Donnell, a muscular black man with a pleasant-featured but taut face, puffed on a cigarette. Saarto spoke briefly with Donnell then checked in the opposite direction, making sure the Sheriff's Department vehicle was still parked a short distance away in the cul-de-sac. Satisfied, he headed back around the side of the house, descending the wooden steps and walkway leading to the beach.

Saarto hesitated at the corner of the house, suddenly wary. The beachfront floodlight was extinguished, the deck ominously dark. He was sure he'd made a specific point of asking the couple inside to leave the light on. *Damn their forgetfulness.*

A Kimball grand dominated one corner of the living room. Assuming that a piano at the beach would be forever out of tune, Nuri had ignored it before. He disliked off-key music as much as he hated a sloppy arabesque, but possibly tonight it didn't matter. Sensing his heavy mood, Tina had left him alone, retreating to the bedroom with a script she intended to study.

Nuri looked hard at the piano, then slowly walked over to it. He sat down and flexed his fingers. Breathing deeply, he surrendered himself to the keyboard. He played the sultry, shimmering "Afternoon of a Faun," Debussy's tone poem that had been Marina Pleskova's favorite ballet. Nuri gently fingered the keys, thinking about the music, how it had been destined to have three movements, but Debussy only finished the prelude.

Marina, too, never finished her life's work. She was a fine ballerina, iridescent on stage, delicate but strong, light as a nymph. She was gone, and the Bolshoi scene wouldn't be the same. He played more softly as he thought what it might have been like for her had he helped her escape from Soviet shackles.

Nuri was suddenly conscious of Tina's presence. She'd strolled silently back into the room and was gazing at him in amazement. Skipping over several bars of music, he smiled at her through his sadness. Tina's being there warmed him. He gestured toward the piano, explaining, "My mother's influence. No, I should say *insistence*. I've played very little since her death." He looked back at the keyboard, randomly tapping several notes. "It needs tuning."

"I've given up on it. Off-key or not, you were magnificent."

He tossed her a kiss. "I always wanted to play American music, to indulge myself in your rock and roll, even punk rock. Unfortunately that music—though sometimes available in the black markets—was not permitted in our household. I had to be satisfied with Louis Armstrong or George Gershwin."

Nuri played from memory, his favorite section of "Rhapsody in Blue."

Tina didn't interrupt, but edged closer, admiration filling her eyes. Finishing the piece, he reached over and pulled her to him. She would have applauded had he not held her wrists. Before he could speak, she softly asked, "Why didn't it work between you and Marina?"

Nuri smiled. At the moment she looked so small and breakable. He replied, "Possibly it wasn't love. A youthful, misdirected infatuation, an awkward companionship that even in our dance partnering proved wrong."

"I've heard that you looked splendid together."

"Marina is a fine dancer, but she was light—like a goose feather. I prefer to feel a ballerina's opposition and weight. The interaction is a physical as well as a sensual one. It must be—how do you say it in English—*dynamic*? Yield and resist. Repeatedly yield and resist."

The Afghan hound wandered into the room and poked its slender nose between them. Nuri playfully pushed it away.

Tina padded to the bar at the end of the room, returning with two snifters and a bottle of dry Amontillado. "After what's happened today I could use a nightcap. You'll join me?"

Nuri nodded, holding the glasses while she poured the fragrant sherry. "*You have to forget*, Tina. Put it out of your mind. Let me worry about it."

"The police car outside, how can I?"

He glared at her. "You will. Our lives will go on."

Apprehensively, she raised her glass to his.

Nuri elevated her chin. "That's better."

Over the rim of the drink her lips whispered, "To your opening night in Paris. *L'Opéra*."

"To Svenska Filmo, and the festival appearance of my favorite star in the galaxy. *When she smiles*."

Putting away the troubled look, Tina flipped her hair back over the shoulders and strolled over to the fireplace. She lowered her eyes and murmured, "You know what's best about getting to the top of the heap?"

Nuri considered for a moment. "I'm afraid to ask."

Leaning against the fireplace mantel, she sipped from the snifter, then replied, "On the way up I averaged two propositions a day." She paused, held Nuri's gaze, and smiled impishly. "Now I get to make the overtures. Let's go to bed."

Saarto had given up on the mercury-vapor floodlight. The igniter was probably burned out.

Outside the air was damp and wisps of fog had settled over the beach. He stepped quietly up on the redwood deck that ran the entire waterfront length of the house, once more checking the floor-to-ceiling glass sliders that provided ocean vistas from the large living room and master bedroom. With the night masking his presence, the best view of all was the illuminated bedroom interior—until the dancer remembered the draperies and hastily pulled the drawcord. But only after Tina had already slipped out of her dressing gown and stepped nude into the adjoining master bath.

Saarto let out a lungful of air and swallowed hard. Thankfully, Nuri hadn't seen the bodyguard's unabashed, open-mouthed stare as he stood outside by the balcony rail. Tina's body was far more enticing in the flesh than on the two occasions when Saarto had seen it in films. *Sexuality to spare.* He felt a little light-headed. Saarto had seen plenty of splendidly posed women in the company of publisher Brian Beck, and he'd dated a few himself. But on or off the screen, Tina Conner, with her large eyes and special smile, had a magnetism that surpassed them all; the curves, too, were in all the right places. Saarto was a womanizer, an incurable sexist, and readily admitted it. Were it not for the glass slider, he might almost have reached out and touched Tina's bare ass, she'd seemed so close.

Saarto stepped back in the shadows as the dancer slid open the window and pushed the Afghan outside for its nightly constitutional. Remaining in the bedroom, Nuri closed the door while the dog scurried by the bodyguard, pausing briefly to sniff him before descending the steps to the sand.

Saarto heard Tina reenter the bedroom. *The draperies*—Nuri had inadvertently left them open just a crack at the end of the slider. Heart thudding, Saarto fought back a temptation to edge closer. He turned away from the window, disgusted with the voyeur bubbling up inside him. For several seconds he stood at the deck rail, watching the ghostlike, phosphorescent glimmer of the surf and the patchy, fickle fog. But the light from the master bedroom slanted oblique and narrow across the dark-ened balcony, a beacon of lust, summoning him. Unable to resist the temptation, he slowly, very quietly, treaded back to the window.

Propped against two pillows with the satin sheet pulled over his nude body, Nuri sat on the bed and waited for her.

Tina returned from the bathroom and stood before him, nude and shimmering. Nuri stared, allowing himself to be drugged by her sexy stance. While their eyes held, Nuri thought about their compatibility, the way they were drawn together. Didn't the Greeks have a word for it—beauty of mind and spirit, as well as body? Nuri flashed on the electric moment when a dancer and choreographer were in synchrony, when ideas and intent are perfectly clear. He was determined to find and sustain that lucid moment in his relationship with Tina. They'd grow on this emotional logic, make it a continuous, splendid creative act.

She hesitated before the bed. Nuri smiled, at the same time gesturing to the mound beneath the light blue sheet, which was his masculinity stirring. He said to her, "Under the greenwood tree, who loves to lie with me?"

Tina smiled. "Shakespeare's *As You Like It*?"

He nodded, reminding himself Tina was not one to test when it came to the theatre.

Smiling, she slithered across the bed and came up to him. Taking hold of her breasts, she presented them to him like a pair of jewelled chalices. Nuri sensed her excitement; already the nipples were signaling desire. Like so many Russians, he sometimes liked to be reckless in bed, and was glad that Tina reciprocated.

Gently, with a featherlike touch, he stroked her breasts, the erogenous zones beneath her arms, her neck, behind her ears. His toes drew repeated circles around her tiny ankles while his knees slid firmly but sensuously over the insides of her thighs.

The day's tragic events suddenly seemed erased. It was as if the fog that surrounded the house had oddly insulated them from the truth. Nuri eased Tina back on the bed and they kissed in boundless fury, rolling from side to side.

Arms twined around his back, her nipples hard and pressing against his muscular chest, the odor of sweat and sex played havoc with Nuri's senses. In a sustained thrust, his aching desire penetrated—slowly at first, then in forceful, rhythmic movements. They literally took turns possessing each other, and again and again Nuri found himself on the edge of euphoric climax. *Wait*, he told himself. *Padazheetye!* His eyes clenched in passion as he felt Tina's muscles contracting and milking his deeply-embedded flesh. She whimpered to him, pleading for more, and he cried out joyously, *"Kha-rasho!"* Then, in English, "Good, good!" The vortex of pleasure drew them both deeper and deeper until finally his seed was devoured by her matching orgasm.

16

BEADS OF SWEAT covered the bodyguard's forehead. Never had Saarto seen such a passionate, wonderfully responsive woman. Loathing his sleazy manners, he finally stepped away from the window. *You're a voyeur with a fried brain, Johann, old boy,* he said to himself. *Ready for the padded room for perverts!*

The noise of the surf diminished momentarily and Saarto heard a slight noise from beneath the balcony. The sound jarred him back to reality. Cursing his inattentiveness, he moved with stealth along the redwood decking to the corner of the house. Saarto listened again. The noise could have been his imagination. No, he'd forgotten the prowling dog. What the fuck was its name? Saarto whistled.

Leaning over the balcony rail, he probed with his flashlight beam in both directions. The fog had thickened, and the farthest he could penetrate up the beach was forty feet. The Afghan hound had disappeared. Saarto whistled again.

He heard another sound—scraping wood or metal. Then a high-pitched squeal. *The dog?* Suddenly there was a dull thud beneath the house, somewhere among the pilings. He heard a soft whimper, then nothing but the roar of surf. Saarto doused the flashlight. *Damn this fog.* Withdrawing his Smith & Wesson automatic from his shoulder holster, he cautiously inched his way down the wooden staircase that led to the sand. At the bottom of the steps he hesitated, then moved guardedly under the house between the pilings.

Suddenly there was a sharp click, a flash in the darkness. *A silenced gun!* Hot lead burned and splintered its way into one of the thick pilings just inches from his head.

Saarto threw himself on the sand in a rolling body tuck that carried him behind a nearby concrete bulkhead. He was lucky. It was darker here, much darker. Saarto tried to listen, to get his enemy's bearing, but the surf boomed louder than before.

Several seconds passed. Saarto blinked in the darkness. Around him in three directions were pilings, any one of which in their creosote blackness might be a man. Saarto moved guardedly, first on his knees, then on his feet, staying close to the bulkhead. Suddenly a hand shot out of the darkness, grabbing his gun hand. Saarto's trigger finger was steady enough and the weapon in his hand didn't discharge; despite the pressure, he managed to hold on to it.

Saarto's heart raced. Sweat coursed down his face as he wrestled with his assailant. The man, who wore a stocking cap, hissed as he tried to bring his own gun to bear, the long, silenced muzzle just inches from Saarto's head.

His opponent was surprisingly wiry and tough for his size, but not strong enough. Saarto broke free, feinted to one side, and whirled in the sand. He drove his knee sharply into the man's genitals, causing him to topple forward with an agonizing outcry. The light was better here between the front pilings and Saarto could see well enough for a well-aimed kick at his disabled opponent's gun hand. His foot struck home and the dislodged magnum skittered across the sand. Saarto drove in again, this time with a fist to the man's solar plexus. He paused, catching his own breath while waiting for his adversary's next move.

Dimly silhouetted beneath the overhanging deck, the bent-over, would-be assassin clutched his groin and gasped for air. He looked up, slowly shaking his head.

Calmer now, Saarto leveled his gun and barked, "Who the hell are you? Who let out the contract, and why?"

The cornered opponent didn't respond. Ignoring the gun in

his face, he struggled to his feet and tried to break away. Saarto moved quickly, but was only able to snatch him by the hair. A toupee came off in Saarto's hand along with the knit cap. His opponent swore, feinted like a boxer, and doggedly came back to Saarto again, this time diving for the legs.

Saarto grabbed for an arm, at the same time bringing the barrel of the Smith & Wesson down hard on the bald head. The assassin grunted with pain, but it was only a glancing blow. Agile and quick, he easily stepped away and from out of nowhere drew a knife. Hearing the click of the automatic blade, Saarto leaped backward, barely avoiding the skillful, straightforward thrust. His assailant was a pro.

Saarto grimaced. He wanted to take the man alive, not dead, and force him to talk. But now his slippery adversary, instead of pressing in with the knife, managed to edge back several feet into the darkness. Saarto could see the dim outline, crouched, ready to strike, the knife bared and held out to one side. Saarto held his gun steady with one hand and reached with the other into his jacket pocket for the flashlight. He pointed it at the shadowy figure.

The face was familiar! Even without the hairpiece Saarto recognized the pockmarked, gaunt visage angrily glaring back at him. It was the same face he'd seen in the backseat of Brian Beck's limo just the day before! The man's bald head, incredibly knotted with scar tissue, momentarily mesmerized Saarto. As if deliberately defying him to fire the Smith & Wesson, the assassin, cursing in French, stepped slowly forward with his knife.

"Suicidal madman," Saarto said aloud, carefully aiming his automatic at the hand with the knife. The bullet missed his opponent's fingers but struck the long blade, deflecting the weapon into the sand.

The assassin dodged behind a nearby piling, he hesitated just briefly, then fled into the fog. Saarto flashed his light, too late. He fired his automatic twice, both times for keeps, but the bullets were expended into nothingness.

Saarto heard voices from the side of the house; the others would be coming to take up the chase. No. It would be futile in the fog. With his handkerchief he picked up the would-be killer's .357 silencer-equipped magnum and examined it.

Tiredly, Saarto shook his head. *Identification, motivation.* What was the tie-in with publisher Beck? Facts he'd never know unless the would-be assassin were apprehended. The fog was too thick. The scar-faced individual who apparently spoke fluent French had to be a professional, far too savvy to stick around without weapons. He'd make a run for it now, lick his wounds and replenish his arsenal. Maybe even pick up a goddamn hairpiece. But this man would undoubtedly try again. Contract killers never give up until they were paid. Saarto spit in the sand, disgusted that he'd let the bastard get away.

At the sound of gunshots, Nuri bolted upright in bed. Heart tripping, he turned to Tina. She looked paralyzed with fear. At first neither of them was able to speak; all they could do was hold each other, afraid to move, benumbed and uncertain.

Nuri made up his mind. They couldn't stay where they were and just wait. He gathered up his courage, and resigned to the worst, slid out of bed and turned out the nightstand lamps. Not bothering to dress, he walked nude with measured steps through the darkened room to the window.

Tina called out in searing protest, "Don't open the drapery, Nuri. Please, don't even look."

From outside, Nuri heard shouts and footsteps pounding along the wooden walkway from the front of the house. A familiar voice called out his name from the deck beyond the big window. Holding his breath, Nuri eased up to the glass slider and cautiously parted the draperies an inch at a time.

He saw Jon Saarto hovering outside, white-lipped and grim. In his arms the bodyguard held the lifeless form of Tina's Afghan hound. The dog's silky blond hair was matted with blood, its sharp hunter's eyes glazed over in death.

17

THE WHITE HOUSE guests were asked to arrive at six-thirty. The President had sent one of the Secret Service limos to pick Nuri, Tina, and Saarto up. Tina was dressed in a full-length, shimmering beige dress and a lynx coat, while Nuri and Saarto wore tuxedos.

Tina smiled at the bodyguard. "Sorry you didn't get a place at the dinner table. I tried."

Saarto self-consciously straightened his black bow tie. "I'm used to getting a doggie bag or eating in the kitchen with the help. It goes with the job."

Nuri laughed. "And your exhorbitant pay."

"He deserves better," Tina added.

"Thanks, boss lady." Saarto stared at her a trifle too admiringly, as though he were undressing her.

Nuri tried to hide his annoyance. "I'll trade places with you gladly. The White House hired help is probably more interesting than the stuffy guest list." He looked at Tina and said in afterthought, "So what does Jon deserve, then?"

"A medal, or whatever they give hard-working bodyguards who go beyond the call of duty."

Nuri couldn't disagree with that. He thought again of the long hours Saarto had put in for two nights in a row, then during the day getting them moved quietly from the beach up to Harry Kaufmann's mountain retreat. The brief escape to Lake Arrowhead, after the horrors in Los Angeles, had done wonders for Nuri's morale as well as Tina's. Saarto had then booked them a last-minute flight to Washington, D.C., under assumed names, again in absolute secrecy; this followed by tough security measures during their current stay at the Four Seasons Hotel in Georgetown. Saarto had been so efficient and private over all the arrangements that often the FBI crew had difficulty keeping up. Nuri was beginning to feel obligated, and his animosity toward the bodyguard had eased up a bit.

The limo pulled into the circular drive leading to the White House North Portico. Eyeing the waiting reporters and their cameras, Nuri said to Tina, "Ready to run the gauntlet?"

"As prepared as I'll ever be."

"You looked relaxed tonight. Feeling better?"

"Feeling safe," she replied, gesturing toward the ring of Secret Service personnel hovering around the limousine. "It won't be easy to put McGinnis, the dead dog, and the assassin out of my mind, but I'll try."

Nuri agreed. The President's command performance and dinner afterward were ill-timed. Or was it deliberate, a part of some plan? His eyes remained on Tina as he helped her out of the limo.

Together they faced the press.

Nuri answered most of the questions with his usual contrived smile and thinly-veiled impatience. Too many of the queries were about the attempts on his life—the explosion back in Los Angeles and the second incident at Malibu. They endured the flashing cameras for a couple of minutes, then hastened inside, away from the furor.

Before they could enter the Blue Room and meet the other guests, the President asked for permission to take Nuri aside for a moment. Tina agreed and proceeded on ahead with the First Lady.

"I'm grieved over the death of a capable FBI agent," the President announced when he had Nuri alone. "And equally concerned over your future welfare. Thus your extended protection. But in return, the U.S. government needs your cooperation."

Nuri felt uncomfortable. "I've not asked for protection, sir."

The President ignored that. "Our intelligence indicates that your father's position becomes increasingly perilous."

"I'm a dancer, Mr. President, not a politician." Nuri lowered his head and shifted on his feet. "I'm concerned about my father, of course. Still, your advisors may be misleading you, Mr. President. Much of what you hear is part of a conspiracy to get me back in the Soviet Union—at any cost. A conspiracy of deliberate misinformation I beg you to ignore."

"I'm not so sure about that. With an outstanding dance career going for you, is it absolutely imperative that you write this accusatory manuscript—I believe you call it *The Kremlin Sword*—at this time?"

Nuri felt affronted. *Was there a better time?* Archly, he replied, "Yes, Mr. President. For complex reasons."

"Would you object to telling me those reasons?"

Nuri squirmed. After what happened in Moscow and Los Angeles, clearly a book or helping others to escape would not be enough to slake his fury. Nuri knew now that he had to go for the yoke itself, the man within it. And he couldn't reveal his ultimate plans to anyone, not yet. Not even the President of the United States.

"Permit me to explain, Mr. President. My book and Soviet underground contacts are very important. Despite experiments with *glasnost* in the Soviet Union, our youth still veer hard to Marxism. University students in Russia are more rigid than their American counterparts, less willing to experiment with new ideas. It's my belief, Mr. President, that many of them now accept communism as a preordained, set existence." Nuri paused as a White House waiter came up and asked for his cocktail preference. As usual, Nuri abstained. Any kind of liquor before a performance was one of his taboos.

Nuri looked at the President. "Do you really wish for me to speak my mind?"

The Chief Executive nodded.

"In the USSR the ideals of the past as represented by Solzhenitsyn, Sakarov, Bukovsky, and the other outspoken writers seem of another era completely; sufferings and thought

prompted by an alien society. The Soviet way, Mr. President, is
difficult, but young people are hardened to it. *The dog loves its
leash*. Young Russians tend not to listen to the older voices of
experience, but rather, to those of their own age. I understand
Soviet youth. I will communicate with them in *The Kremlin
Sword*." Nuri hesitated, noting the President's grave face.
"I'm sorry, sir, to be so outspoken. I was carried away."

"After you perform tonight, I want you to relax with my
guests. I must warn you, I did invite Soviet Ambassador
Chekor to attend."

Nuri balked.

"Don't be offended. If all goes well, he'll take a message
from the two of us back to your father. Perhaps, after dinner,
we can meet briefly in the Oval Office. You, Ambassador
Chekor, our own Ambassador to Moscow, and myself. The
session will be brief."

"Whatever you say, Mr. President."

He took Nuri by the elbow. "Let's join the others. I look
forward to your performance. My wife tells me you objected to
doing an excerpt from *Swan Lake* with one of the local
company's ballerinas."

Nuri felt embarrassed. The President was unaware that *Swan
Lake* was primarily a performance for women dancers. He
fabricated, "I didn't mean to criticize the National Ballet, sir.
There just wasn't time to properly rehearse. I will dance alone,
a *pas seul*. The final variation from *Constantia*. Do you like
Chopin's concertos?"

"Excellent. Whatever you select, we're honored."

"As for *Swan Lake*, after one has seen it danced a hundred
times, there is a tendency to nod off."

The President laughed. "The public's classical favorite
bores you?"

Nuri smiled. "It is like the women in the Swiss chocolate
factories who are allowed to eat as much as they like. After a
couple of days they are sick of chocolate and never touch it
again."

"I will acquire a cautious taste, then, for *Constantia*," the
President responded with a grin.

The lobby of the Four Seasons Hotel in Washington's
Georgetown district was unusually crowded. Three gray-suited
serious-faced linebacker types drew no notice as they strong-

armed one of the bellhops into an empty elevator. One of the men pushed the emergency button, stopping the lift between floors.

"The dancer and the actress," barked the tallest, who appeared to be the leader. He glared at the bellman. "You took the luggage upstairs. Which room?"

The young man guardedly looked at the trio surrounding him. The giant spoke again, his voice more subdued. "Relax, pal, this isn't a heist. We're just running a security check and we arrived late. All we need is the fucking room number, okay?"

"I don't know what you're talking about. And they need me in the lobby."

A strong hand grabbed the epaulet on his uniform. "We'll try again. We're referring to Nuri Baranov and Tina Conner. That refresh your memory?"

One of the others pushed forward a twenty dollar bill. The tall one shook his head and smiled thickly. "You insult the kid. This is a classy place, can't you see that?" He withdrew a fifty from a money clip, added it to the proffered twenty, and crammed both bills firmly into the bellhop's pocket. Smiling, he oozed, "Now that your memory's refreshed, we'll begin again."

Soviet Chairman Pavlin Baranov felt disquieted and couldn't sleep. Instead of retiring to his country dacha near Kuntsevo, where he usually went each Friday afternoon to spend the weekend, Baranov had worked in his office until after midnight then gone to his small apartment in the Arsenal Building. After a leisurely bath he'd poured a cup of hot milk and taken it to the bedroom, settling down with the family photo scrapbook. The scenes of his long-gone wife and his recently run-off son once more stirred him. When he'd finally turned off the light and tried for sleep, the images continued to linger.

After an hour of churning emotions and staring at the ceiling, Baranov tossed the bedding aside, put on a robe, and went to the window. He opened the sash another six inches, sniffed the cold night, and stared out into the dismally quiet square. It had stopped snowing several hours earlier. Off in the distance the illuminated clock on the Spassky Tower read almost two-thirty.

Again Baranov thought about ballerina Marina Pleskova's

ghastly death at the Boshoi State Theatre. He wondered if Nuri knew about the incident, and if so, how his son had reacted. Going to the brown leather sofa opposite his bed, Baranov sat and lit a cigarette. Savoring the smoke, he thought again about the strange disappearance of his personal chauffeur this afternoon. The KGB had agreed to investigate, but Baranov had good reason to distrust their effort.

Not only because of his ongoing differences with Fiodor Talik. It had been the woman director from Mosfilm Studios, and not the KGB, who had supplied Baranov with the file of photographs and news clippings of the American actress Tina Conner. The *papka* Natasha had brought in stared back from a nearby table. Again his hands were drawn to it.

He opened the folder and once more thumbed through the documents. Baranov already knew its contents intimately, and wondered if Tina Conner knew as much about him as he did her. It didn't matter. For several minutes he read again the translations beside several of the news articles, then reached for the phone. Despite the late hour, he needed to talk with Natasha Chernyskaya.

On one hand Nuri was impressed; the East Room was a virtual museum of historical American antiques. But on the other he was appalled by the size of his allotted dance area. He was used to a minimum stage of forty-by-thirty feet. Even with improvisation and eliminating the grand jetés, he would be pinched for space.

Waiting outside in the corridor, Nuri brushed the lint off his forest-green tights and flexed his feet in the new Capezios which were still only partially broken in. Considering the informal circumstances and the intimacy of the room, he'd chosen to dance without stage makeup.

At his side stood his accompanist, Madame Dulac, who had flown down from New York. She was still put out by the inconvenience, not the least awed by the White House invitation. Nuri liked the old woman. She had fiery, dilated eyes and a pinched, wrinkled face that was capable of freezing with an ironic smile any unsolicited suggestion or criticism from those unversed in music. For Nuri, Marguerite Dulac was like a second right hand. He said to her, "Nijinsky was given fifteen thousand gold francs to dance four minutes before the

Royal Household. I have a long way to go, performing for free, yes?"

She shrugged. "Perhaps they'll throw coins when you are finished, *ma chère*."

Behind Nuri—inevitably, he reflected—hung the new family watchdog, Jon Saarto. Ignoring the bodyguard, Nuri peeked around the doorway, again taking in the end of the East Room that had been cleared for his solo. The President's guests were being seated at the opposite end of the chamber, with Tina up front beside the First Lady. An electric candelabrum with red parchment shades illuminated Madame Dulac's piano keyboard, and a traveling spotlight had been brought in to enhance the effect of his performance. Still unhappy with the setting, Nuri frowned and repeatedly struck a fist in his palm.

Saarto asked him, "Something wrong?"

Nuri nodded. "It's terrible. Proper distance and sophisticated lighting are a must for optimum ballet. You've not heard of *kinesthetic echo*?"

The bodyguard looked puzzled and a little embarrassed. A foreigner with an English vocabulary surpassing his own? He asked, "What kind of echo?"

Nuri purposely ignored him.

Madame Dulac looked up at Saarto, quickly explaining, "*Eh bien, monsieur.* It is minuscule movement of a spectator's muscles, yes? In sympathy with the larger movements of the dancer." She ended it there.

Nuri finally took pity on Saarto. He explained, "You'd probably understand better, Jon, if you thought of yourself drinking beer, waving or jerking a can with every blow you witnessed on a televised prize fight. Are you a connoisseur of boxing?"

Saarto flinched and said quietly, "Thanks, asshole."

They still weren't ready in the other room. For the umpteenth time Nuri sized up the detective-bodyguard. "Whether you and I see eye to eye or not, Mr. Saarto, you seem to know how to get things done. I understand you speak fluent Russian."

Saarto nodded.

"Have you been to Moscow?"

"*Nyet.* Why do you ask?"

Nuri shrugged. "Perhaps I'll need some assistance that will appeal to your fighter's *instincts*. How about Austria? Have you ever visited Vienna, the purported spy capital of Europe?"

Saarto·glowered. "No."

Nuri thought for a moment, wondering how far he could trust the bodyguard. *Don't push your luck, not yet.* Before he could continue the dialogue, a white-gloved aide emerged from the East Room, signaling that all was in readiness. Madame Dulac touched Nuri's arm and wished him *"Merde."* It was *shit* in French, the traditional stage blessing superstitious dance folk used in place of "good luck." The older woman hurried into the room and her spot at the piano. The overhead lights dimmed.

Nuri took a deep breath. The last time he'd done a command performance was with the Bolshoi before the Queen in London. Then it had been the pas de deux from *Sleeping Beauty.* That partnering with Marina Pleskova once more touched him with melancholy.

Marguerite Dulac's piano called out to him—the music of Frederic Chopin, the final variation from Concerto Number Two in F Minor. Sweeping into the darkened room, Nuri was once more caught up in his own atmosphere. The spotlight followed him. He moved lightly, easily, but with long-legged, masculine self-assurance.

Fuck yourself, Saarto reflected, turning away from the East Room entry. The dancer was obviously no pansy, but he did come off as a testy, egotistical prick. While Nuri performed before the President's guests, Saarto had work to do. He stepped briskly down the hall and slipped into the improvised dressing room where Nuri had left his clothes. Making sure he was alone, Saarto closed the door and began to methodically probe through the dancer's belongings.

Inside an alligator hide wallet he found a couple of snapshots of Nuri and Tina together as well as pictures of Marina Pleskova and several dancers Saarto didn't recognize. They looked Russian. Quickly he scanned through several business cards, a laundry receipt, a Visa card made out to Tina, and a folded piece of paper.

Nothing interested him but the paper that contained a familiar name, Tangerine. Beneath it, a telephone number. Saarto withdrew his own book of phone numbers and compared it with a list of confidential exchanges used by Brian Beck. As he suspected, one of the numbers matched. He made a small check beside it.

Saarto put the dancer's tuxedo and other belongings back as he found them and left the room.

The President's guests were so close Nuri could feel their emotion. He knew they were held spellbound. The music, as always, inspired and drove him; in this sense it was no different from being a rock and roll performer. The classical stances and disciplines he'd learned in Moscow asked his muscles to behave differently from the steps he now enthusiastically practiced in America, but he enjoyed this new freedom and faster style. It matched what his critics called his "animal vitality" and "raw magnetism."

The applause at the conclusion of *Constantia* was spontaneous, not the polite patter usually given by dignitary or benefit groups. For an encore his accompanist had come prepared with an excerpt from Mendelssohn's *Les Elfes*. Performed by a lesser dancer, the solo would have been commonplace and dull, but Nuri was determined to give it extraordinary passion and insight.

He succeeded. Acknowledging the applause with a deep bow, he tossed the First Lady a kiss and exited into the White House main corridor, there to sit on the marble floor, his back to the wall. Knees drawn up and arms clasped around him, Nuri held his head back while his mouth took in lungfuls of air. His face and neck ran with sweat. He sat there for several seconds until Saarto came up to him.

"Here, chum," the bodyguard quipped, tossing him a towel. Saarto smiled and said in fluent Russian, *"Remember me? I not only enjoy watching prize fighters, I used to train them. There's a shower down the hall. The porter will show you the way."*

Nuri was surprised and let it show. He replied in English, "Despite your accent, you speak Russian very well. With a phonetics coach you would pass very well for a Soviet citizen—a Leningrad dock worker, perhaps."

"I doubt whether I'll ever have the need."

Nuri got to his feet. He had to get moving before muscle cramps set in. "Nor do I ever expect to play the lead in *Death of a Salesman* or *Night of the Iguana*. For me the correct intonation of English, the analysis of sounds, is fascinating. A matter of doing something right."

"Or a damned egotistical obsession, maybe? Come off it, Nuri. Some people find accents charming."

Nuri stopped pacing and smiled wryly. "Don't push me, Jon. I've already read Mailer's *Tough Guys Don't Dance*."

Saarto laughed. "You're almost as arrogant as I am. Now you'll have to learn to be as tough."

The dancer said quickly, "You still work out yourself, I assume?"

Saarto nodded and pushed out his chin slightly.

Nuri stiffened and made a show of tensing his stomach. "Good. Get it out of your system, okay? Test me if you like, with your fist. *Now*."

Saarto shook his head. "Forget it."

Nuri stepped closer, smiled thinly, and suddenly planted his own fist squarely in the bodyguard's stomach. Saarto winced but held his ground. He stared at Nuri, but made no move to retaliate.

Nuri lowered his voice and asked, "Do we understand each other better now?"

18

WITH THE EIGHT-HOUR time difference, it was three in the
morning in Moscow. KGB Colonel Bruna Kloski's comfortable, three-room apartment at 27 Varzhinskoya Street was in an
excellent part of the city and boasted much sought-after Czech
furniture and a modern Japanese spinet piano. The bed she
slept in was an antique, reputedly once owned by Grand Duke
Vladimir, uncle of Czar Nicholas. There were two modern
Swedish telephones on the nightstand, one for Kloski's
personal use, the other a direct, secured line for KGB matters.

Replacing the KGB phone on its hook, she stared at it
irritably. There had been two calls in succession that had
disrupted her sleep, but they'd both been important. The first
brought strange news from Lubyanka Prison; the second was
from the KGB Special Cyphers Office. The message that had
come in from the United States still rankled her. Kloski lit one
of her English Players and deeply inhaled, cursing the apparent
failure of the contract killer in Los Angeles.

She considered for several minutes, then thumbed through
the address book she kept beside the bed. Finding the number

of her KGB driver, she dialed quickly and waited for the ring. On the opposite wall over the chest of drawers, a mahogany-encased Fabergé clock, its pendulum stilled for years, looked uselessly down on the scene. Her conversation with the driver was terse and brief; he would pick her up in less than twenty minutes.

Kloski dressed swiftly and stepped into the kitchen alcove to rinse her mouth with a solution of baking soda and wintergreen. Going to the front of the apartment, she pulled aside the plum-colored brocade curtains and stared out at the darkened city. She would wait by the window, alert for the driver's signal on the quiet street below.

Outside, the Moscow night had warmed a few degrees and the five inches of snow that had fallen earlier in the day had turned to gray slush. Kloski knew the next sustained snowfall would be the third storm of the season; the law of averages had taught Moscovites that it would remain for the duration of the winter.

Kloski thought for a moment about the American general being held prisoner in Lubyanka. While waiting for her driver to arrive, there would be time to once more look over the *zapiska* on one Austin Shaeffer, United States Army. She retrieved the file from her leather briecase and went back to the window. Turning on the floor lamp, she once more scanned the American's documents.

After several minutes Kloski heard a short horn blast on the street below. She winced at the driver's impudence and forgetfulness. Had he been a civilian sounding a horn in this part of the city, a fine would be in order. She put General Shaeffer's *zapiska* back in her brief, turned out the lamp, and left the apartment by a narrow-tiled stairway to the ground floor.

A brisk, damp wind whipped through her legs as she hurried to the staff car. She cursed her negligence in not wearing heavy cotton, olive drab panty hose. Holding open the door to the brown Volga sedan was her driver from the KGB Guards division. The man had obviously dressed hastily, for his tunic was partially unbuttoned and one of the blue KGB emblems on his lapel was food-stained. Considering the odd hour and her need to hurry, she decided to reprimand him later. She crawled in the back of the car and snapped, "To Lubyanka."

The driver accelerated quickly. The car—with its telltale

government license plate MOC—looked like an ordinary Volga, but it had a souped-up engine and special ballast over the rear wheels. Kloski knew it could overtake any vehicle in Moscow. The driver sped down the priority traffic lane of Kutuzovsky Prospect toward KGB Headquarters and the adjacent Lubyanka facility.

Dzerzhinsky Square was ominously quiet when they arrived. As usual the identification process—despite her rank—was time-consuming and tried Kloski's patience. When finally admitted to basement level A, she was greeted at the end of the corridor by yet another guard, this time a young officer she recognized.

The KGB lieutenant was dressed in a light blue lab coat and wore a a holstered pistol at his waist. He sluggishly rose from his desk, stiffened, and saluted. "Good evening, Comrade Colonel Kloski."

"It is *morning*," she said gruffly. "You received my authorization to see the American prisoner?"

"Yes, Comrade Colonel. And you arrived just in time. General Shaeffer is being transferred at dawn."

She looked at the jailer sharply, extending an open hand for the key. "So I understand. Can you tell me who requested this move?"

"*Ordered*, Comrade Colonel," the lieutenant stuttered through his Georgian accent. He handed her a ringed cell key. "Army High Command. The Minister of Defense, Marshal Poskrebyshev. And the orders were countersigned by Chairman Baranov himself. The American is to be transferred to the custody of Colonel General Kirichek at Strategic Directions West."

Bruna Kloski was pleased at her luck in finding a talkative, friendly officer on duty. She tapped the jailer's key under her chin, contemplating for a moment. "Viktor Kirichek is a marshal in the Warsaw Treaty Organization. What would the commander of the combined East German and Polish Group forces want with the American prisoner?"

The young lieutenant shrugged. "I know only that General Shaeffer is to be dispatched temporarily to one of our military stockades in East Germany."

"Which one? Where?"

The guard leafed through some papers on his desk. "The orders don't say."

Kloski committed what information she did have to memory. Her staff would pursue the matter later. "Thank you, Comrade Lieutenant." She followed him down the tile-lined corridor.

When they arrived at Shaeffer's cell, she peered through the wire-mesh window. Under the glow of the blue night light, Kloski saw a figure asleep on the bed. She flicked on the room's brilliant overhead fluorescent, opened the door and went inside. Watchful, but following her instructions, the smock-clad jailer remained outside the entry.

Austin Shaeffer rolled over on his coat, blinking his puffy eyelids at the harsh light. "What the hell now?" he grunted groggily.

Kloski gave him an affable smile and glanced around the chamber. Hardly a prison, she reflected. This Western provocateur had been provided accommodations more like a university dormitory room than a jail cell, although the chamber had no windows. The furnishings were spartan but comfortable, in fact *luxurious* by Lubyanka, Lefertovo, and Butyrka prison standards. Shaeffer had a desk and it was piled high with books—Soviet-approved texts, of course. On a wooden stool nearby she saw that Shaeffer had been working on a partially complete model of an outdated, 1960s era MIG fighter. The corner of the room was equipped with a modern commode instead of the Turkish toilet found in the old sub-basement horror cells. Kloski swore softly at whoever was responsible for Shaeffer's unneccesary comfort.

The general sat up in his bed, rubbed his chest through a wrinkled T-shirt, and stared perplexedly at her. "They've taken my watch away but I can sure as hell tell when I've had less than two hours sleep. Now I'm honored by a woman officer yet?"

She looked at him seriously. Shaeffer was a chunky, florid-faced individual with a whiskey nose, square jaw, and small brown eyes. His forehead and puffy, spinnaker cheeks were mottled with freckles. He looked younger, much younger, than Soviet officers of equal rank.

Kloski cleared the airplane model off the only stool and sat down. She reminded herself not to rant or intimidate; not now. This was the time to fold her hands in her lap and politely listen. She knew all too well how prisoners loved to talk if given the right opportunity. Solitude did strange things to a man's priorities. Calmly, she asked, "You know who I am?"

Shaeffer nodded. "Unfortunately, yes."

Kloski shifted on her seat. The stool was small and her buttocks hung uncomfortably over the edge. "You believe the widespread myth that I am a monster?"

"I know only that you head the Fifth Directorate. That, in itself, is enough." Shaeffer reached to the bedside table, retrieving a flat box of *papirosa*—the thin, pungent Russian cigarette that was half cardboard tube, half tobacco.

Bruna Kloski knew that most foreigners would as soon smoke dried camel dung to the strong *papirosas*. She withdrew her own box of English Players and tossed it to him on the bed. "Your captors don't permit your American legation friends to furnish you with decent cigarettes?"

General Shaeffer scowled. "I'm permitted nothing from the outside but personal correspondence—two letters a week." He lit one of the cigarettes, staring through the smoke. Pulling the bedclothes around his waist, his eyes went to a pair of prison khakis on the end of the bed. "You want me to get dressed?"

"No. That won't be necessary. I won't keep you long." Kloski lit her own Player, continuing to observe Shaeffer.

He looked back at her, his eyelids appearing tired and wrinkled in the face of a young man. Smugly, he asked, "Why is it everyone who comes to visit me wears a uniform? Are there no civilians, no plainsclothes diplomats in your country?"

Bruna risked a smile. "Authority is important to Soviets. Like Germans, when three Russians are gathered together, the one with the uniform deals the cards."

"Even if it is a woman, of course?"

She nodded, letting the triumph show. "Is it true, General Shaeffer, that you personally know the American President?"

Shaeffer looked away, shrugging off the question. His eyes followed a cockroach as it snatched a crumb from beside the desk and scuttled across the floor.

Kloski asked, "Your food is satisfactory?"

"Not exactly caribou, heathcock, or Crimean caviar, but I've grown accustomed to the fare. The roaches seem to thrive on it."

"General Shaeffer, it is the KGB's belief that you were interested in our signals and surveillance regiment—the SPETS-NAZ Brigade. It is no secret that this regiment represents the eyes and ears of our army land forces. There is also the matter of photographs you took of a pipeline construction project."

"Unwittingly. The charges are a fabrication. All bullshit," the American said firmly. "The pipes are stacked in the damned background. I stated before and I'll say it again. I was returning to Moscow as a private tourist."

"A flimsy story, General. In Russia, we say *b'elymi nit kami*—that it is sewn with white thread."

Shaeffer frowned and shook his head. "Wrong. I wasn't spying on your almighty Soviet Army."

Kloski gathered herself and rose to her feet. Imperiously, she retorted, "The Red Army is indeed powerful, General, but you would do well to remember that the Committee of State Security is even more invincible. The KGB has an administrative staff of over a hundred thousand, and four times that number of *armed* men and women, yes? And should we need them, a half-million informers at our fingertips."

Shaeffer's face hardened. "As always, I'm impressed with your fondness for numerical emphasis. But what does all this have to do with the *initiative* of the average foot soldier?"

Irritated, Kloski snapped back, "Tell me, how do they differ from your average American recruit?"

Shaeffer took a drag from his cigarette before responding. Smugly, he said to her, "In World War Two your soldiers were known for blind obedience, even throwing themselves before tanks. Americans, by contrast, can be led, but never pushed blindly."

"In fact, General Shaeffer, a softness that you and other U.S. military leaders may regret."

"Colonel Kloski, we've covered all the pleasantries and unpleasantries. What the hell do you want with me in the middle of the night? A blood test? Urine sample? My diary? It's on the drawer of that desk. Read it yourself."

She let out a sharp sigh. "No. I need your cooperation. A State internal matter that is important to me but of little consequence to your welfare. Do you know *where* you are being sent early in the morning, and for what reason?"

"No, I don't."

"Who sent for you?"

Shaeffer shook his head.

"General, it would be wise for you to speak the truth. When

Soviet Army Intelligence is finished bleeding you dry, I suspect you'll be returned forthwith here to Lubyanka, again under KGB supervision." She gestured around the room. "I can ensure that your amenities are not arbitrarily withdrawn. While I have little influence at Army Command circles, I do get my way around here."

Shaeffer sniffed. "I believe you and the point's been taken. But I speak the truth. I don't know what the hell's going on."

"Perhaps so, perhaps not. And perhaps it does not matter. We will travel not far behind. Observing, General. I shall make a point of meeting with you again."

Kloski moved toward the door, kicking the airplane model out of her way.

He looked back at her hatefully.

She paused in the doorway, permitting her eyes to curl in a half smile. "You should trust me, General Shaeffer; you have nothing to lose and your life to gain. Possibly even your expedited freedom." Noting the prisoner's perplexed look, Kloski smiled to herself. Despite Shaeffer's try at arrogance, she saw that his small dark eyes in their shadowy sockets were remote and frightened. She had one last important question for him. "General, are you familiar with the American concussion bomb being tested in the California desert? Could you verify the guidance plans for this weapon if they were placed before you?"

Shaeffer had a startled expression, quickly masked.

Good, Kloski thought. She'd say no more tonight; the germ of an idea had been planted. That was enough.

Closing the door to the cell, she turned the key and considered for a moment. She frowned. This U.S. Army general seemed to know less than she'd expected about the upcoming personnel trade. Unless she were lying. Shaeffer would have to be watched closely. Though events were accelerating at a startling rate, his usefulness was far from over. Kloski would wait until Khamsin Ahmed forwarded the stolen weapon plans before having the American general killed.

The assassin had spent most of Thursday shopping for a substitute toupee. Not having time for a fitting and the usual two-week delay in fashioning a custom hairpiece, Khamsin had been forced to make do with a wig he'd found in one of the beauty shops on Hollywood Boulevard. Though the dancer and actress had eluded him by leaving the beach house temporarily, he wasn't worried. Khamsin knew their exact schedule at the nation's capital. Accordingly, he'd booked a flight to Washington, D.C., and taken a room at the Watergate. As requested by his superiors, he'd left a forwarding telephone contact back in Los Angeles.

He wished he hadn't. Khamsin dreaded the reprimand that would eventually come down the line, most probably from the KGB *rezidentura* in New York. The explosion at the film studio had made the news wires, and now Nuri's and Tina's visit to the White House would make an even bigger story. Moscow would be livid.

Staring out the window of his Watergate room, Khamsin debated where to go alone for dinner. He hated Washington, D.C., finding it a lonely city after federal workers rolled up the carpet for the night and went home to the suburbs.

With bitterness, Khamsin fantasized on the ultimate assignment—the assassination of the American President. Khamsin wondered how much the job might pay and who would pay it. The next time he went to Libya or Lebanon, he would discuss the possibilities with the proper parties.

Right now Khamsin wished he were home in Paris, back in the Latin Quarter. Though he'd only been away a week, it seemed like a month. He thought with pride of his comfortable pied-à-terre. Despite the lackluster outer appearance of the buildings along sloping Rue Mouffetard and the neighborhood's prevailing odors of Near East cooking, acrid wine, and cat urine, he'd seen fit that the interior of his apartment was elegantly furnished. Cost had been no consideration.

Since moving from Marseilles a decade earlier, Khamsin had done financially well from his work in the world's hot spots. In his free time London, Montreal, and Monte Carlo were also favorite cities, but Paris was home, and he had not spared the creature comforts there for himself or his dark-skinned lover.

Khamsin wanted to get this annoying KGB assignment over with once and for all and get back to Danielle Ponty. Provided that she'd not disappeared again in one of her periodic temperamental outbursts. Whatever, a man of his scarred appearance could not come down too hard on a woman.

Beside the bed, the telephone gave off a soft ring. Still

daydreaming of Danielle, Khamsin went up to it in a daze and answered in the language of the desert, as he did at home.

The officious long distance operator in Paris didn't understand Arabic.

Khamsin snapped out of his melancholy, and said, *"Alors? Ici Monsieur Ahmed. Qui est à l'appareil?"* Propping a pillow against the satin-padded headboard, he eased back on the bed. *"Oui, oui."* No, this was Moscow. "Yes, I am ready." Khamsin didn't speak Russian, but the KGB woman Bruna Kloski, like himself, spoke passable English. "This line—can we speak freely, Colonel?" he asked boldly.

Her voice rasped back on the wire. "It's scrambled. A circuitous patch through a Paris exchange. You doubt my circumspection, Comrade Ahmed?"

"I am not your comrade, *mon colonel.* Despite my political sentiments, our relationship is purely of a business nature. You call me personally for good reason, I suspect?"

The voice on the line hardened. "Perhaps I should have known better than to trust a deposed former Algerian policeman who is also the illegitimate son of a Pigalle prostitute. Your mixed blood and mixed loyalties apparently create confusion rather than efficiency. Your Foreign Legion background likewise did nothing for you."

He replied angrily, "My record speaks for itself, Colonel."

"Interesting. Beaten at Dakar, Algiers, Mers-el-Kebir, and Saigon."

Khamsin fought to control his anger. He hated the Moscow bitch for dragging out his family skeletons.

Bruna Kloski continued: "I am sorry for you if the immediate situation cannot be rectified, my friend. You do plan to finish the matter, give it your full attention?"

Sighing with displeasure, Khamsin got a grip on himself. "Of course, Colonel."

"Your numbered bank account in Zurich will not be the only thing to suffer should you fail. You will make this delay up to me, Khamsin. Now the other matter in Los Angeles. Did you make contact with our American publisher friend?"

"A rather crass individual, but he's cooperated and I have the documents."

"Excellent. Was it necessary to twist his arm?"

Khamsin laughed. "No, but his fee was exorbitant."

"Money is of no consequence."

"True. Money speaks much louder than bodily threats, *madame*."

"It is Colonel. *Comrade Colonel*. Do not forget your station."

"*Mon Dieu!* My station, thankfully, is in Paris and not in the Kremlin. But let us not argue. Have you additional instructions, Colonel?"

"Only *questions*. How long is our quarry scheduled to be in Washington, D.C.? Will you take action there or when he returns to New York?"

"He is heavily guarded here in the capital. The Secret Service is assisting the FBI. We must use caution; you'll have to trust my judgment."

"I want the dancer eliminated by the most expeditious means possible before he leaves for Paris!"

Khamsin exhaled slowly. "Why this haste? *Au contraire!* I've been thinking it would be an easier assignment in Paris, where I know the city well. And there is yet another possibility. A month from now when he plans a trip to Austria—*death on the Danube*. Ah, so dramatic, *non*?"

"*Nyet! Nyet!*" Bruna Kloski's voice grew more malefic. She swore in Russian, then said quickly, "Convenience is not a consideration. We require immediate implementation of our plans for good reason. Do you hear me well?"

Khamsin replied with deliberate slowness. "I do. May I ask why the rush?"

"You try my patience, Khamsin. Time is working against you. We may have competition in this matter."

"Competition? *Je ne comprends pas*."

"Others who plan to capture the dancer alive, then secretly return him back to Moscow. You must prevent this!"

"Such talent. To waste him, a pity."

"My superior demands liquidation. You will be successful."

"Of course."

"Let me put it another way." Her voice grated in his ear. "We'll not tolerate additional blunders like those in California. If I have to administer Nuri Baranov's coup de grace myself, I am prepared to do so; but in that inconvenient event, it will be for an individual named Khamsin Ahmed as well."

19

THE PRESIDENT and First Lady proved outstanding hosts. Nuri was impressed. Showered, refreshed, and back in his tuxedo, he sat forward at the elegantly set table and picked up the silverware. He wiped it carefully as was his Russian custom, too late seeing Tina's glare of disapproval. Nuri glanced around the candlelit table. He was still piqued by the President inviting the Soviet Ambassador and his wife, and wondered over the reasoning; he hoped to find out later at the post-dinner meeting in the Oval Office. In the meantime he and Tina would have to endure the discomfort.

Nuri counted the places. *Chortova druzhina*—a devil's dozen, including Tina and himself. Besides the First Couple, the other guests seated for dinner and accompanied by their wives were Soviet Ambassador Vassily Chekor; the U.S. Ambassador to Moscow, Gregory Hewett; French Ambassador Jacques Dumas; Kirsten Ellsworth, publisher of Washington, D.C.'s largest daily newspaper; and, of course, Madame Dulac. At the last moment Harry Kaufmann and his wife had sent regrets from Hollywood.

During the first two courses Soviet Ambassador Chekor seemed determined to hold the President in captivity; their discussion had taken on the tone of an argument. Chekor had studiously ignored the dancer from the onset of the evening, applauding without enthusiasm during the ballet performance.

Nuri watched the boastful Russian diplomat continue to badger his host.

"But Ambassador Chekor," the President interrupted, "you have to admit that pride encourages aristocracy. In wealth, intellect, even in your *communes*."

Chekor smiled facetiously. "A bird is known by its flight, Mr. President. Only wide-eyed children are without pride. There is a difference between vainglory and self-respect."

"I'll buy that, but false pride also separates men." The President turned and looked directly at Nuri. "Like father and son."

Refusing to look in the dancer's direction, Chekor glowered and went back to his dinner plate.

Nuri felt embarrassed. He looked at Tina, and from her expression knew she shared his discomfort. Across from them the newspaper publisher's wife broke the silent impasse. She burbled, "Do you feel any deep-seated fear before you are about to perform, Mr. Baranov?"

Nuri smiled. "I try not to dance for applause, only the perfection of the art. But still, audiences can be demanding— and sometimes frightening. The answer to your question is yes."

The publisher himself, Kirsten Ellsworth, spoke to him for the first time. "It's a shame we won't see the U.S. Dance Company this season here in Washington." He flicked a glance at the French diplomat and his wife, seated nearby. "Paris will be fortunate next week."

The French couple smiled as if a political coup had been announced.

Nuri finished his entrée. An alert waiter immediately removed the beautiful Lenox plate emblazoned with an outer ring of small golden eagles. The others, too, appeared to be finished. A silver cart that might have once belonged to Catherine the Great was wheeled in, piled high with fruits, elegant desserts, cheeses, coffee, and liqueurs. Nuri stared at it in wonderment, then turned back to publisher Ellsworth. "I'm pleased that you enjoyed our performance last year, but your newspaper's music critic was less than flattering in her review. If I recall correctly, in referring to my Bolshoi heritage, she called me the best nineteenth century dancer in the twentieth century."

The table took on a sudden quiet as the publisher thought for a moment. He finally replied, "One reporter's will-of-the-wisp opinion, and of no consequence."

Tina wasn't willing to let it go at that. "Mr. Ellsworth, your newspaper is one of the most influential in the country."

Frowning, Nuri added, "I'm sorry, it's just that I have no patience with critics. Too often they are self-serving, elitist snobs."

The French ambassador's wife beamed. "*Bravo, Nuri.* I must agree. In France we are inundated with critics . . ." she paused as a waiter placed an ornately decorated rum cake before her. "Even there are the food critics! Ah, *très belle!* See this gastronomic artistry from the White House kitchen. Monsieur Baranov, I compare your dance critics to fussy Parisian snobs who always find a hair in their bowl of soup. And why? When they sit down to dine, they examine it too closely, shaking their heads until hair falls in the bowl. *Eh bien,* I say the world has had enough of critics!"

Nuri and Tina both laughed, while the others—except for Ellsworth—smiled politely. The Russian woman at the other end of the table self-consciously patted at her outlandish bouffant.

"*Mon cher*, please." The French Ambassador scowled at his wife, then turned to Nuri. "I'm afraid credit for my mate's cleverness should properly go to the German poet Hebbel."

Eyes sparkling with gentleness, the First Lady smiled and changed the subject. "Tina dear, I'm told we're fortunate to have you with us on so short a notice. Do your career schedules often come into conflict?"

Tina sighed. "Very much so."

The President and the Soviet Ambassador had ceased their verbal fencing; they, too, were looking Nuri's way.

Nuri shrugged. "Too often our relationship is like the song, 'Two Ships that Pass in the Night.'"

"Ships? You mean *yachts*, yes?" The voice of impending doom was Vassily Chekor's. The Soviet diplomat raised his voice. "Money, yes? If all goes well you may soon own a ship of your own. Isn't that what you're after, Nuri Baranov? Yachts, the good life of the *imperialist*?"

A pall descended on the table.

Nuri kept silent as he watched Chekor light a Moska-Volga cigarette with a gold Italian lighter. The Ambassador was a Chukchi-Aleut type with a mahogany face, wide-set nostrils, and thick, wet-combed hair. Through a haze of smoke he smiled at Nuri for the first time, revealing horsey teeth. Nuri shuddered. The cunning Chekor had all the charm and stealth of a Siberian tiger.

Chekor leveled a finger at Nuri. "Dancing should be sacred, not a pretext to attain fame and capitalist money." The diplomat's eyes flashed toward Tina. "Or a rewarding career in film, possibly?"

Tina sat rigidly in her chair.

Nuri felt trapped. Boldly, he ventured, "Come now, *Comrade Ambassador*. Tell us what is really bothering you tonight."

"In diplomatic circles, word travels quickly. I am curious, Nuri Pavlinovich. It has come to my attention that you try to be a writer as well as a dancer. Such a cornucopia of talent! In Moscow you are known as one of the *samizdats*." Chekor thoughtfully examined his fingernails. "Tell me, is it also true that you plan to visit Vienna? At the same time as our Bolshoi Ballet?"

Nuri was stunned but determined not to let it show. He said calmly, "A mere coincidence. But also an ideal opportunity to see old friends on the stage, you must admit. That is all that troubles you?" Nervously fingering his dessert spoon, Nuri wondered how the Soviet possibly knew.

Chekor scowled and stumbled to his feet. His wife looked confused and embarrassed as he folded his napkin with a flourish and pressed it to the table with a clenched fist. He said loudly, "No. There is much more. Article Seventy, yes? Distributing for the purpose of undermining or weakening the Soviet regime. Slanderous fabrications which defame the State and Soviet social system." Chekor's puffy face turned red as the Russian flag.

Nuri was sorely tempted to laugh but decided he was in trouble enough. Feeling Tina's foot pressing down hard on his toe, he tried to find diplomatic words for the crude, angry thoughts welling up inside him. He looked at Chekor, sighed, and said calmly but emphatically, "Perhaps you should read what I have written before you cry foul, Ambassador. You obviously distrust my objectivity. It is possible that both capitalism and communism are unfortunate lies to the people? The capitalist lie is a subtle one, but unfortunately, the communist lie is blatant, more powerful, and more dangerous. You'd do well to believe me when I tell you KGB head Fiodor Talik is evil and must be properly exposed. Had Marina Pleskova lived, she too, was prepared to join me in revealing the true character of this dangerous individual. Talik is even known to sexually harass and intimidate pretty ballerinas at the State Theatre. And there is even worse news about his assistant, Bruna Kloski, who heads the Fifth Directorate. Do you wish for me to go on, *Comrade Ambassador*? This is hardly the place."

An awkward hush fell over the table. Chekor glared daggers at Nuri.

Visibly shaken by the altercation, the President looked hard at both of them. "Gentlemen, please. You'll defeat the purpose of meeting tonight."

There was a definite explosiveness in Chekor's small, Napoleonic eyes as he pulled his wife to her feet. Turning to face the President, he bowed slightly and said in a calm, determined voice, "My compliments, Mr. President, for a splendid dinner and fine wine. A most pleasant evening despite my differences with Mr. Baranov. You and your wife are always enjoyable company, but now, if you'll forgive me, I've changed my mind about carrying messages for the defector." Chekor looked at his watch. "It is late, and with your kind permission, we would like to be excused."

The President looked up, troubled. "I can't convince you to stay for a few minutes longer? What of our meeting plans?"

"My apologies, Mr. President, and good night."

Chekor looked around the table. All eyes were on him, including Nuri's. To reach the exit, the Russian had to pass by the dancer's end of the table. Leaning over Nuri's shoulder, his breath heavy with wine and cigarette smoke, Chekor whispered coarsely, "The gulags have infinite patience, my friend. They will yet see you out, dead and forgotten."

Vassily Chekor drove swiftly to the imposing Soviet embassy compound on the rise overlooking the city. He sent his wife to their private quarters on the second floor then went to his office and summoned the duty communications officer. Above the ambassadorial desk were large photographs of the three most important men in the Soviet Union: Chairman Baranov, Security Minister Talik, and Defense Minister Poskrebyshev. Not one of the pictures was higher than any other, though Vassily Chekor had his own distinct preferences for the highest post in the USSR.

Leaning over the desk, Chekor wrote rapidly, reporting his attendance at the White House and the appearance of the Soviet Chairman's son. Most important, he would tell Fiodor Talik about the file of news clippings and other biographical data his research staff had assembled and sent in the courier pouch to film director Natasha Chernyskaya. The packet of material about actress Tina Conner still perplexed Chekor. Why did the Chernyskaya woman need it?

The Ambassador thought about calling Talik directly to discuss the troublemaking dancer, but finally decided against it. He would have to be careful going through routine Foreign Ministry channels. The KGB general would shield him when the big shakeup came, but in the meantime, Chekor still reported to Foreign Minister Tieslin, one of the Pavlin Baranov's lackeys.

Jon Saarto stood alone just outside the White House entrance, inhaling the crisp winter air and feeling genuinely pleased with himself. Though he hadn't made it to the dining table with the others, the President of the United States had paused in the corridor to give him a firm enough handshake and a wish for good luck.

Considering the strange scenario confronting him, Saarto wondered how long it would take to come up with the productive information he needed. The days ahead would be unpredictable and dangerous, but it was no worse than continuing the masquerade with Brian Beck, trying to protect him from his sundry enemies in Los Angeles. There, Saarto had never known what psychotic with a Saturday night special might lay in wait for the infamous publisher. Nuri's enemies, by comparison, were big league. And they appeared *organized*.

Saarto thought about the celebrity lovers. Tina Conner's Hollywood lifestyle Saarto understood to a reasonable degree, but he suspected Nuri's aesthete, east coast world would be alien to him, full of surprises. No matter—an assignment was an assignment, and Saarto would learn as he went along. For starters, he'd try harder to get along with the dancer. So far it had been like trying to communicate on different wavelengths. Saarto knew little about art and the theatre, and admitted it; nor was he an intellectual by any measure. Even when it came to spy novels, he preferred James Bond to John Le Carre.

Again he checked his watch while waiting for Tina and Nuri to emerge from their private session with the President in the Oval Office. Saarto still pouted, annoyed because he felt he should have been included in that meeting. He was sure the agenda had been security.

Saarto glanced up as Niles Donnell, the FBI agent who had accompanied them from California, hurried up the walkway under the portico. The muscular, glum-faced black man had in tow an attractive young woman Saarto recognized.

Donnell looked troubled. He said quickly, "Bad news. Your meticulous planning, to put it bluntly, Saarto, has turned to shit. I'm afraid our security net back at the Four Seasons Hotel has been penetrated."

Annoyed with Donnell for ignoring her, the woman with the long black hair winked at Saarto and made a pretense of introducing herself. "Mr. Saarto, my name's Diana Vespucci from the CIA. It's my job to help you find another hotel."

20

NURI REFLECTED on the post-dinner meeting with the President, the CIA director, and the U.S. Ambassador to Moscow. All three men had tried to convince him that he should drop out of the U.S. Ballet's European tour, remaining in New York, where his safety could be reasonably ensured. At first Tina had kept her silence, but then she, too, concurred with the others.

Outnumbered, for brief moments Nuri had wavered. In the Soviet Union under similar circumstances. he would not have had options; he'd have been given explicit orders. One did not receive suggestions from his father or other Russian leaders, but *instructions*. Making decisions were a wonderful new experience for him, but they were sometimes painful.

Danger or not, he could not and would not leave the dance tour. When he'd told the President this, a sustained silence fell over the Oval Office. The real look of disappointment, however, came from Tina. The issue was obviously not over between them.

Whatever her plea, he *couldn't listen*. If he didn't go on the tour, how could he get to Vienna and help the others? The KGB

155

colonel would be there with the Bolshoi, but he wasn't afraid. In fact, the opportunity to confront Bruna Kloski away from Moscow was irresistible. Nuri couldn't kill this beast, it wasn't in his makeup. But he had something on the head of the Fifth Directorate, and perhaps some vile form of extortion or blackmail would work. None of this he dared tell Tina, not for now.

From the corner of his eye Nuri saw commotion among the White House protective staff in the corridor. He excused himself from the First Couple, who were preoccupied with Tina discussing her latest film.

Nuri strolled up to Jon Saarto and asked quietly, "Trouble?"

The dour-faced bodyguard pulled him around the corner, out of Tina's earshot and view. Niles Donnell and an unidentified woman followed. Saarto looked at Nuri. "An unfriendly reception committee has slipped past us back at the hotel. And they're not a delegation of your fans."

"Oh, hell." A grenade of anger exploded within Nuri. He looked at the others. They appeared momentarily defeated. Beside Saarto and the black FBI agent was a young woman who neither of them had bothered to introduce. Nuri stared, disarmed by her commanding presence. She returned his curious gaze but remained silent, deferring to Saarto.

Nuri managed a smile and was about to make his own introduction when the bodyguard interjected, "There were three of them—tough looking characters. The bellhop tipped us off."

Niles Donnell added, "And they're not any of our Bureau men. Nor are they CIA. I've checked."

Nuri bit back his bile. "I'm exhausted. Returning to the hotel would be dangerous?"

Saarto smiled thinly. "Here's a new word for your vocabulary. *Dicey.*"

Nuri didn't understand and didn't care; he let it pass. "Did anyone get a good look at them?"

At last the young woman stepped forward, her pleasant perfume preceding her. "I saw the trio jump into a taxi. I tried to follow but they slipped away in heavy traffic."

Donnell belatedly introduced her as a CIA operative. "Nuri, meet Diana Vespucci. A crackerjack with the 'Company's' European operations. Once you get to Paris, you're out of the

FBI's jurisdiction and I say good-bye. She'll be numero uno in charge.''

Dark eyes flashing, Diana Vespucci edged forward and shook Nuri's hand. He was surprised by the firmness of her grip—it was much like those of Russian women. The CIA director had alerted him moments earlier that one of his people would be lending a hand, but he hadn't indicated it would be a female. Nuri sighed. All he needed was one more intrusive bodyguard of *either sex*. "I intend to move like quicksilver, Ms. Vespucci. I hope you can keep up."

Diana replied, "You sound a trifle querulous. You're unhappy with the government's efforts to date?"

She was close and the perfume had begun to intoxicate him. Nuri wondered if it, too, were federal issue. He demurred politely. "No. Just unhappy with Paul McGinnis's tragic, unnecessary death." Nuri glanced over his shoulder, wondering what was keeping Tina and the First Couple.

Diana Vespucci said swiftly, "All of us are saddened. The agent's death, the plot on your life. The CIA is concerned over what happens next. Your father's life may be on the line."

Nuri said patiently, "So the President insists. I must discount this. My father is a strong leader with highly-placed friends. He will survive. Furthermore, when he learns of the Fifth Directorate's reprisal against me, I suspect he'll see to it those responsible are punished."

"Don't count on it," grunted Saarto.

The CIA woman looked at Nuri sharply and added, "You really intend to declare a private war on the Soviet government?"

"Only the head of the KGB." Someone had briefed her, Nuri thought. She sounded like Tina.

Diana straightened the blouse under her tan tweed pantsuit. Her moist, pretty lips smiled at each man in turn. "The Paris office will do what it can."

Nuri studied her. Diana Vespucci wasn't exactly pretty, but there was a visceral appeal about the young woman that compelled him to look long and hard. Lean, smooth, still tanned despite the season, the CIA operative was nearly as tall as himself. Her long black hair was coiffed and pinned back on each side, framing a classic Mediterranean face. Her lashes fluttered over intense brown eyes that were large and warm. *Cow eyes*, Nuri reflected. She wore only a hint of makeup beyond her coral lipstick. "You look nervous, Ms. Vespucci," he finally quipped. His staring had obviously penetrated her facade of calm.

All she said was, "Call me Diana."

Nuri nodded and turned back to Saarto. "We forego the Four Seasons luxury, then?"

Niles Donnell replied, "We're making arrangements to move you into the Madison."

Saarto frowned. "That's still downtown, just up the street. I say no."

"Hold on a minute, hotshot," snapped Donnell.

Nuri looked at both men with impatience. He had a plan of his own. "Gentlemen, Tina and I will discuss the problem and make our own decision. Please do me a favor and wait outside by the limo? And make no arrangements whatever until we join you. Diana, I'd like you to remain a moment."

While the two bodyguards shuffled off in annoyance, Nuri met her look of puzzlement. *Diana Vespucci*, he reflected. The name was a tongue twister, but he liked the musical sound of it. He grinned at her. "I'll be brief. Tina will be here any minute and I don't need her interference—or panic. Diana, we need your help now."

She looked at him sharply. "Counseling or a strong arm? Take your choice. I'm damned good at both."

Nuri smiled. "I've been listening to too many *professionals*. I don't want saturation protection, only to disappear. Some privacy with Tina." He held up his hand. "Hear me out before you reject my plan."

She nodded.

"First, leave the White House ahead of us. Find a taxi and make sure you're not followed." Nuri thought for a moment. "On the way out to National Airport there's a high-rise hotel by the highway."

"The Holiday Inn? That isn't the kind of Four Seasons luxury Tina's expecting."

"Screw what either of us *expect*. Just get out of here fast. Register in your own name, yes? Then go into the cocktail lounge and wait. I'll send Saarto in to pick up the room key. Leave it to Tina and me to get to our room separately and unobserved."

"A pregnant idea, but supposing the hotel's booked?"

"No problem. We'll try the routine again at Howard Johnson's or wherever."

The skin on Diana's face tightened. Raising an eyebrow, she asked, "What about me at the desk? A lady arriving without baggage?"

Nuri winked at her. "Talk fast. You'll be wiser for the experience."

Northeast of Washington, just outside a Baltimore Airport business hangar, an orange-and-blue-striped Falcon jet was being serviced by a pair of aviation mechanics. A white Plymouth sedan with three men in it drove across the apron and halted a short distance away from the business jet. A tall, broad-shouldered individual with a lumpish, square face stepped out of the car and approached the nearest workman. "Your flight crew, Nordstrom. Do they remain on call?"

Instantly recognizing the big man, the ground crewman stepped forward and asked cockily, "So who wants to know? The general himself?"

"We work for McCulloch. That's enough for you. So where's the crew now? I've got a message."

"The pilots are holed up in a motel off the Washington Parkway. They can be here in forty minutes notice."

"Good. Tell them we've encountered a delay. A minor problem securing the cargo. We'll have a better chance in New York."

The aircraft mechanic looked annoyed. "Bullshit. How long do you expect us to remain on standby?"

The tall man reached in his pocket and withdrew an envelope. "Additional *waiting expenses*. A little bonus beyond the basic agreement. Summon the flight crew and take the plane up to Suffolk County Airport on Long Island. All you have to do is maintain a low profile and continue waiting. The three of us will fly up tomorrow night and keep you posted. Questions?"

"The same refueling stops and ultimate destination?"

"You've got it. The landing arrangements behind the curtain are too complicated to change at this point. Tell the pilot his instructions hold. And be prepared for a hasty departure."

Nuri sat uneasily in the back of the blue Mercury sedan, gazing out at the Holiday Inn parking lot. Up front, Niles

Donnell sat alone behind the wheel. Tina, shadowed by Saarto, had gone ahead into the lobby to meet the Vespucci woman, as planned.

All Nuri wanted now was a measure of quiet and privacy for the night. Again he wondered about all the high-profile protection the President had assigned him. Did these Americans really believe they stood a chance against Fiodor Talik's headhunters, playing by their own code of ethics? Nuri would cover his bets and go along with the FBI and CIA while it suited his need, but only for Tina's sake. Saarto, Donnell, and now Diana Vespucci might be of assistance in running interference, but in the end Nuri would have to confront the enemy alone. His icy resolve was strengthened, not weakened, by each new KGB-inspired confrontation.

It was just after 10:45, and from across the parking lot Nuri could see that the Holiday Inn appeared reasonably quiet. Predictably, Tina had agreed to the change of hotels with disappointment, for their room back at the Four Seasons had been sumptuous.

Nuri saw Diana Vespucci step out of the lobby and hurry over to the car. He was still fascinated by her manner—quick-stepped, confident, coolly professional. And as long as Tina wasn't around—undeniably sexy. Sliding in the backseat beside him, she said, "I ran the interference at the desk as you wanted. Tina's upstairs, so far unrecognized." To the FBI man up front, she asked, "Who retrieves the luggage back at the Four Seasons?"

"Already working on it," Donnell replied. "Give my men another half hour."

She smiled sagely at Nuri. "You're going to be a challenging problem, Mr. Baranov. After flying an administrative desk in Paris for two years, it'll be a pleasure to stretch my legs again. And my *brains*."

Nuri grinned. "In Russia we call it 'putting a little mud under one's heels.' Mind if I make a suggestion? That we dispense with formality and use first names?"

"Good, I'd like that, Nuri."

In the dim light she looked sultry and disturbingly flirtatious, but at the same time tough—not unlike a few of the female KGB operatives and militiawomen Nuri had seen in Moscow. He guessed Diana Vespucci made Saarto and Donnell uncomfortable by her assertive, competitive manner.

Gypsy eyes flashing, she spoke again. "Nuri, Niles—I'm bushed and have to run. For the rest of the night you're on your own." She opened the car door, but before stepping out, said to Nuri, "Until New York, then. We'll rendezvous in time for the flight to Paris." Winking, she gently touched his chin. "I suspect you'll have your fill of me in France. *Bon soir, monsieurs*," she said musically.

The car door closed and she was gone. Donnell shifted uncomfortably behind the wheel. "Jesus. So much for the new look of Area Two, the agency's European Control. That's some Sicilian dish—and I don't mean pasta."

"Thank God I'm happily involved," Nuri said dully.

"You should be so lucky. Incidentally, I hear Vespucci's a kung fu expert."

"Fine. I'll dance around her best moves."

Donnell snickered. "I could handle the martial arts, but I'm not sure about that slight moustache. She needs either a shave or a wax pull, for chrissakes."

Ignoring Donnell's gibes, Nuri checked the time. Saarto had asked that he wait a full ten minutes before proceeding into the hotel's service entry. Restless, Nuri's eyes were drawn to a sleek red Ferrari Quatrovalvole that had just pulled into the lobby entrance. A conspicuous gold MD emblem was fixed to the rear license plate. Two bellhops came out to the curb and hustled to unload a set of expensive luggage and golf clubs. The poised driver, in his late thirties, handed over the keys to one of the attendants and went inside the hotel.

Nuri remembered how Jon Saarto had joked with him earlier on the plane from Los Angeles, insisting that communism or not, the dancer had been raised on a silver spoon. Seeing the affluent young physician's wheels nearby, Nuri thought again about life in Moscow, his own indulgent two-room apartment in the best part of the city. His monthly salary in the Soviet world had exceeded four hundred rubles—at the time far more than the earnings of the average Russian doctor, engineer, or scientist. Here in America an MD made four or five times more than a hero artist at the Bolshoi.

Reaching over the front seat, Donnell tapped his arm, ending the reverie. "Stop drooling over the wheels, kid. In Russia you lived in clover all your life, right? Over here the field's just a little more fertile and you see the results more

conspicuously." The FBI agent's brown eyes sparkled. "The
promise of capitalism includes toys like that, pal."

Nuri said, "Always promises? The promise of communism
is the same as capitalism—full employment. *A dream around
the bend*. All too many of your black brothers would
understand that, I suspect. Do you like poems, Mr. Donnell?"

"Not particularly."

"Too bad. Listen anyway to a Russian favorite:

> In the fields the rampant weeds
> Have still not turned to wheat
> But soon my brothers, we will shit
> Through a golden toilet seat."

While Niles Donnell laughed, Nuri watched two crowded
mini-vans pull into the hotel driveway and halt a short distance
away. An organized tour, apparently, and it was about to
unload.

Donnell checked the time. "Let's get you inside before that
mob overruns the parking lot."

Nuri climbed out of the car, his eyes scaning the lettering
that ran along the side of the vans. VIRGINIA BALLET ACADEMY.
Donnell tried to hurry him across the driveway, but Nuri was
curious. From the beginning he'd been inquisitive about any
kind of dance organization in America; too often they were like
alien entities in an inhospitable cosmos.

Nuri watched the passengers—obviously high school and
college students—disembark from the vehicles. Most of them
were young women—beautiful, sweetly muscled. The four or
five young men in the group were full of bravado but coltish; a
couple of them had fluted voices. The driver of the first vehicle
appeared to be the group's leader or instructor. He was an older
man but lean and muscular, and wore a tartan tie and a woolen
jacket with leather elbow patches. Nuri took him for a former
dancer turned choreographer.

Curious over the assemblage, Nuri couldn't resist moving in
closer. "Virginia Ballet?" he asked with genuine interest. "A
private, professional dance school?"

The group's leader looked up with impatience but turned
wide-eyed when he recognized who was confronting them. He
responded haltingly. "A coalition of suburban groups. Operating on a shoestring, of course. I'm both startled and honored,

Mr. Baranov." He looked at Nuri's black companion speculatively, then continued, "You're here at the capital for a performance or a personal visit?"

Nuri shook the man's hand. "Relax, please. I'm not an apparition."

"My name is James Berkowitz. I'm the school's director and official chaperone."

The dancers gathered around Nuri in varying degrees of curiosity. A few were occupied with their luggage, but most of the women immediately recognized him. "Nuri Baranov," they whispered excitedly.

Berkowitz cleared his throat. "This is an unexpected *preview* for all of us."

An irritated Niles Donnell tugged at Nuri's arm. "Damn it, Nuri. No one's supposed to know you're here. Let's go."

He pushed the agent's hand away and scanned the cluster of dancers. "Preview? I don't understand."

"We're leaving on a study tour, Mr. Baranov. Two weeks in Europe. Paris, Moscow, Leningrad, and London. Three days in each city. We will see you perform in Paris, of course."

An eager young ballerina, on the skinny side, spoke up: "And especially we look forward to visiting the Bolshoi."

Nuri thought for a moment about their tour. Raising an eyebrow, he seriously asked, "How soon will you go to Moscow?"

Berkowitz thought for a moment before responding. "In five days."

Nuri nodded. An idea took hold, but he would consider it later when he was alone. He smiled back at the faces gathering around him, wondering who among them were the lead dancers. One of the girls reminded him of Marina Pleskova when she had been younger. Another dancer, a lanky, six-foot-tall male, had the same muscular build as his own but wore glasses and had carrot-red hair. Without eyeglasses he would be a near lookalike.

"Will we like Russia, Nuri?" came a young voice from the rear of the group.

"You will love its people, especially the land itself."

Another student asked, "You love the Soviet Union so much after what communism does to its art?"

Nuri said lightly, "The USSR is often called 'Mother Rus.' Could not a mother love her ugly child?"

The tall male dancer Nuri had noticed before stepped forward. "I'm impressed with your style, Nuri. My name is Mark Washburn. I hope someday to leap with your strength and finesse."

Another voice: "We're all your devoted followers."

Nuri shook his head. "Such surrender overwhelms me. But pilgrims and mendicants belong in the Middle Ages, not in creative America today. You must *follow no one*. Set your own style. As I've learned in your country, do your own thing, yes?"

A scrap of paper and a pen were thrust forward, but Berkowitz caught the hand, restraining it. "Not now, people, please. Nuri, we will be attending the performance of the U.S. Dance Company in Paris. There are but fourteen of us in our group. Would it be an imposition to send our programs backstage for your autograph?"

Nuri laughed. "And why not? But I would be insulted if the Virginia Ballet troupe doesn't come to my dressing room personally to visit. I'll leave word at the stage door." He thought for a moment. There might be more to what Nuri had in mind for them in Paris and Moscow, but he needed time to put it together.

They all applauded him. Eyes surveying the parking lot around him, Nuri reflected for a moment. "Provided, of course, each of you do me an important favor."

They looked at him expectantly.

"You must mention to no one that you saw Nuri Baranov this evening. At least until I am quietly out of the city tomorrow and back in New York. A secret between us, okay?"

The group looked confused, but immediately they all nodded in agreement.

An impatient Niles Donnell finally pried Nuri away and pushed him bodily in the direction of the hotel's service entry.

21

DIANA VESPUCCI'S LIE to Nuri Baranov had rolled out effortlessly. The truth was, she had no intention of retiring early, for an Army general friend was expecting her in his hotel room. Her affair with Frank McCulloch was still one of the best kept secrets in the nation's capital.

From the Holiday Inn Diana took a Diamond Cab back across the river and headed for the Watergate. She made sure she wasn't followed by asking the driver to backtrack around the Lincoln Memorial then change directions on Constitution Avenue. The dancer and actress would be safe for the night; Niles Donnell and Jon Saarto would see to that.

Gazing out the taxi window, she thought of the complications ahead. General McCulloch's Army security types had failed in their plan for the Four Seasons Hotel. She'd already suggested that McCulloch's men hold off and not try again, instead waiting to catch Nuri in New York when Tina wasn't in tow. Better yet, in a couple of days the Russian defector would be outside the country of his own accord; a kidnapping in Paris might be easier than the plan to transport him from the States.

Unfortunately the Army general was as impatient as he was
stubborn and determined to have his way.

Diana considered her dual role, the divided loyalty between
her own employer the CIA and her friend at the Pentagon. She
would have to be wary, extremely careful, for there had been
other agency contenders for the job of protecting Nuri Baranov
in Europe. Diana had made her own request for the assignment
appear as casual as possible. Fortunately for her pal General
McCulloch, CIA Director Lindsay had taken the bait. Besides
her hands-on agency experience in Paris, Diana claimed it was
her understanding and love of ballet that made her a highly
suitable candidate for the job. She was, in fact, a virtual addict
of both dance and opera.

It had never entered her mind that she might someday be
accused of treasonous conduct. She was involved with opposing governmental departments, perhaps, but they were all
working for the same country, saluting the same flag. For
Diana it was merely a matter of internal policy. The important
thing was General Shaeffer's safe return. It was clearly a matter
that the military establishment, and *not* the U.S. President or
the CIA, deserved to win. Diana believed in Frank McCulloch.
If her reasons for obeying him were personal as well as
political, *no big deal*; everyone owed a favor once in their
lifetime.

Dismissing the cab, Diana entered the Watergate's lobby and
hurried to one of the house phones. She took her compact and
freshened up her lipstick while waiting for the operator.
"Room 807, please."

An instant later she heard McCulloch's voice on the line.
She asked in a sultry voice, "General, you didn't nod off while
waiting for me?"

"Not a chance. I was about to ring up the room waiter for
ice. You hungry?"

"No. Just a nightcap, love. Make it the usual, or do you
remember?"

"Dry sack, rocks. Or has your taste changed since our last
interlude at that chateau near Provins?"

"You're a lecher and a dear." Softly, she added, "Give me
fifteen minutes to go to my own room and freshen up. I trust
I'm spending the night?"

McCulloch chortled, "Just try to stay anywhere else while
you're in town. When do you go back to Paris?"

"In two, maybe three days." She hesitated. "Frank, about the dancer . . . I'm concerned."

"You're doing fine," he said sharply. "I need your help, Diana. Don't back down on me now, please. The kid will be safe."

"Still, Frank, I think—"

"Diana, dammit. We're on a hotel phone line for chrissakes."

"I'm sorry. I'll be up in a few minutes." She slowly hung up, hurt that McCulloch's tone had been more brusque than necessary. He might be the United States Army Chief of Staff, but he was still a married man out on a fling, and he'd have to learn to handle her more tenderly. After working abroad for two years, Diana Vespucci had learned a little about continental gentlemen and *class*. Her four-star general friend needed a measure more of it.

Diana turned away from the house phone. She headed for the elevator but stopped in her tracks when she saw a familiar likeness pass by on the opposite side of the lobby. A face that belonged in Paris, not Washington, D.C.! The hairpiece was different, but the gaunt, distinctly mottled face was instantly recognizable. She'd seen it before, not in person, but in the confidential files of underworld figures she kept at her Paris office. Diana was certain that it was Najeeb Ahmed—the terrorist and contract killer known as *Khamsin*.

Nuri was relieved to get out of the ruffled shirt and tux. Predictably, the scenes of their arrival at the White House were on the late evening TV newscast. They were both ready for bed, but Nuri continued to watch the report with interest. Tina was unusually quiet and appeared agitated. When the news ended, Nuri went over to her where she sat snuggled against the pillows on the bed. He held her gently, but she didn't respond.

"Nuri," she whispered through her lips, warm on his cheeks.

He waited for her to continue.

"I want you to cancel the tour. Stay in New York." She spoke rapidly, almost too rapidly for him to fathom. "If the U.S. Dance Company fires you for breach of contract, come out to California and teach or choreograph for the movies. Or

I'll help you set up a dance school somewhere in Connecticut. We can—"

"Tina!"

"No. I won't stop. You listen. When the tour's over you want to meet me in London, then we go to Vienna, right? Where you play out your great escape scene with the Bolshoi." She hesitated, staring at him. "I'm not going with you. And if you care for me, you'll forget the entire damned scene."

Nuri took a deep breath, whistling as he let it out between his teeth. Quietly he said, "You've supported me until now."

Angrily Tina shouted, "You didn't tell me that one of General Talik's key assistants would personally be in Vienna, riding herd on the Soviet dance tour. This Bruna Kloski is reported to be a cold-blooded murderess."

He lowered his eyes slightly. "Who told you this?"

"Gregory Hewett, our ambassador to Moscow. And the CIA chief concurred on the intelligence. In the hallway outside the Oval Office."

"I shouldn't have let you sit in on the meeting," he replied severely. "What did you expect, Tina? You can't drain a swamp without finding hungry reptiles."

Tina slid off the bed and went to the window. She parted the blinds, looked out only briefly, then turned back, once more venting her vexation on him. "I intend to talk you out of this madness."

"You're even pretty when you're angry."

Tina brushed a long lock of hair out of her face. "Will you come to your senses or not?"

Nuri remained silent.

She pointed a trembling finger at him. "You're going to kill yourself. I want no part of it. Why, Nuri? Why?"

"*Bol'noy vopros*—a sore question." His lips tightened as he looked around the hotel room, considering ways to escape her censure. Irritably he added, "I'll answer you fully in my book. You'll just have to be patient."

"What about us?"

He ignored her.

Furious, Tina picked up her travel case and hurled it at him. Nuri dodged to one side, watching it strike the headboard and scatter her makeup.

She shouted, "No, no, no. I'm not interested in meeting you halfway on this one, Nuri. Whatever it takes, I'm going to dissuade you from going. Next year, the year after—you'll admit I was right and see all this in a different perspective. I'll be damned if I'll cooperate and co-sign your death warrant with either this evil Bruna Kloski woman or General Talik!"

He sat on the edge of the bed. "Your scythe has struck a stone, Tina. Let's change the subject. Come here."

She stiffened. "When do we get on with our life together? And when do you stop worrying about everyone in Russia getting their hair fashioned by the same comb?"

He replied seriously, "I have a chance to be a part of Soviet history. If the lead in a remake of *Gone With the Wind* were offered you today, would you turn it down?"

"Yes, if it ruined our relationship. And Scarlett O'Hara is an irrelevant comparison."

"Please, Tina. Sit beside me and calm down." He stared at her, waiting.

"I've made up my mind. When I finish my two picture contract, I need a rest." She spoke cautiously, edging toward him an inch at a time. "Next year. I need a break from Hollywood, a big break. I'm thinking about moving to Vermont or Connecticut." She hesitated, then said with sarcasm, "You think you'll still be around, to come up weekends?"

Nuri digested her words in silence.

Tina prodded, "You're not listening."

"To the contrary. Anything to bring us closer together makes me happy."

Tina was near enough now for him to pull her toward him. He smiled at her. "I say *great*."

At last her eyes softened; once more they sparkled like topaz. "You have a peculiar habit of calling everything *great!*"

He grinned. "My socialist upbringing. In Russia it was the Great October Revolution and the Great Patriotic War against Fascism—the battle you insist on calling World War Two. We also have the Great Bell Tower." Nuri widened his smile, posturing. "And most important, *great* ballet dancers."

"The only time you come off that gold pedestal of yours is to stand back and polish it." She shook her head and said quietly, "Nuri Baranov, you're sailing through life as though you were a pirate ship that never enters a harbor."

He exhaled slowly and lay back on the bed. For the past several minutes Tina's words had been like sharp rapiers, scotching his fantasies. But she was right about one thing: he'd love a New England retreat to get away from the intensity of Manhattan. They could spend more time together, less flying across the continent. And it would be perfect for his writing.

Before Tina could marinate further on her plan to disrupt his tour or turn the night into one of her protracted discussions, Nuri was determined to make love. Gently he untied the ribbons on the neckline of her nightie. She didn't object, even edging a little closer. She surprised him by responding to his advance by tracing her fingers up and down his neck.

They looked at each other for a moment, then kissed with passion.

For reasons he couldn't understand, Nuri felt more aroused than usual. Did the argument have something to do with it? The carnal light was there, but apparently only flickering in Tina's eyes. He needed to *slow down*, throttle back, but it wasn't easy with a fully charged battery. Feverishly he kissed her lips, cheeks, neck, and breasts. Now she, too, was aroused and bending over him, her long glistening hair brushing over the blond fuzz on his stomach. With his swollen, erect penis cradled between her breasts, she let her body undulate back and forth.

Nuri swore softly to himself. No, wait! Suddenly, prematurely, he ejaculated, covering Tina's bosom and neck with globules of sperm. She gave up a light gasp, pulled away, and managed a smile. "Oh, my God!" Her sustained look of astonishment was broken by a sharp rap on the hotel room's door.

"Ignore it," Nuri whispered, pulling her back to him.

Tina let him kiss her one more time, then nervously edged away as the knock came again, this time louder.

"Who is it?" he called in annoyance.

"Jon Saarto," boomed back the familiar voice.

Tina scrambled out of bed and wrapped her body in a large bath towel. Nuri pulled the bedclothes over him and waited irritably while she padded to the entry.

When Tina opened the door, she was greeted by a flask of Dom Pérignon pushed toward her by the bodyguard. Saarto looked embarrassed when he saw her disheveled hair and the towel.

"Sorry," he said in compressed voice. "I figured you two were still watching the news. The dance students staying on the fourth floor chipped together and wanted you to have this." He handed over the chilled champagne, then continued in a more cheerfully determined air, "Shall I send up a waiter with an ice bucket?"

"No," Nuri called out from the bed. "Tell them thanks. And Jon, no more interruptions, agreed?"

Saarto's eyes flicked from Nuri back to Tina, hesitating as they focused on her neck and chest. He rubbed two fingers together, implying an uncomfortable stickiness. "I think you forgot something, boss lady." He smiled sagely.

Tina glanced down and blinked. She pulled the towel up higher. "Conditioner, Mr. Saarto. For your information, I was about to rinse my hair."

The bodyguard nodded and backed out of the room. Locking the door, Tina came back to bed with a sheepish grin. "So much for symbolic equations. Do you still want to play?"

Nuri snickered, "You're not embarrassed?"

"Around that clown? He used to work for a porno publisher, for God's sake." She winked. "Now where were we?"

Nuri swallowed hard, mustering his energy. "I think I'll need another five minutes."

"Braggart. I'd better give ten. In the meantime I'll open the champagne." She headed for a pair of hotel drinking glasses on the dressing table. Grinning, she said, "Let's hope the bubbly will reactivate your pleasure center."

"Fine with me."

"Your problem, sweet, is that you're oversexed. Are all Russians as consistently horny as you?"

"Want help with the cork?"

She smiled coyly. "No. Only with your own. Keep it in the bottle a little longer." Gazing in the dressing table mirror at her smeared bosom, she frowned, disappeared into the bathroom and closed the door.

Nuri lay back and listened to the water running. Tina Conner was driving him crazy, interrupting his orderly plans for the immediate future. He had to regain control. Still, he would be nothing now without her. He was complete, for the first time whole—with himself, with Tina. Was he ready to settle down, possibly raise a family? Give up the performing career and teach dancing in New England to be near her? Nuri thought about what the President and CIA director had told him privately after the White House dinner. Why was he surrounded by alarmists, suspecting the worst?

After he helped his friends at the Bolshoi, he would do better than secretly escape on weekends to the country with Tina. He'd propose to her, escape to New Zealand or the Australian outback, possibly even take up ranching. All this if he could finish a couple of dance seasons and increase his nest egg.

When Tina reentered the room without her towel, touching words came to his mind, but somehow he couldn't utter them. Too often words were superfluous. He crawled out of the bed and went up to her.

Standing together nude, they clinked glasses and drank the Dom Pérignon.

22

THE TENSION BUILT steadily in the Oval Office. Shirt collars rumpled from sweat as they argued among themselves, the three men attending the President had become thin-skinned and irritable. The Chief Executive, growing weary of the debate, turned his eyes toward the clock on the fireplace mantel. Though it was Saturday and his schedule was clear, it was well past lunchtime. The meeting had continued for an hour, longer than he'd intended.

Defense Secretary Fleming looked exasperated as he rose to his feet and said in a sonorous voice, "Sir, an investigation of every intelligence echelon in the military will take time. We're contending with days, not hours." The "sir" was purely for effect. All three men in the office were on an informal, first-name basis with the President.

Donald Lindsay cleared his throat. "Indeed. You have my sympathy." The CIA director was a morose individual with a thick-set body, watery eyes, and fleshy double chin. The extra pounds made him look a decade older than his forty-five years. Lindsay continued to stare at the Defense secretary. "I suggest you face the facts, Mr. Fleming. My people tell me the culprits are operating out of the Pentagon. That's your bailiwick."

The President gave up on his pipe and dropped it in a huge alabaster ashtray. Leaning back in his leather chair, he looked at Lindsay and Fleming gravely. "Gentlemen, I think I've heard enough. Ambassador Hewett here has a plane to catch at Dulles. He's about to deliver my personal greetings, several policy statements, and I suspect a few hospitable words of his own to the Soviet Chairman and foreign minister. Whether, at this juncture, Hewett's going to be able to promote a summit meeting by year-end, is pure conjecture. But I'll be damned if I'll have his efforts torpedoed by unilateral acts from any of my subordinates—military or civil." The President paused, glancing wearily around the room. "As an infamous former occupant of this office put it, do I make myself perfectly clear?"

The Defense secretary and CIA director nodded, without enthusiasm; Fleming seemed unaffected by the President's directness. Lindsay closed and locked his CIA briefcase, buttoned his jacket over his paunch, and rose to his feet. "I'll continue to monitor the situation as best I can, Mr. President. Perhaps now you better appreciate my belief that all international security matters should be under one roof. *My own.*"

Hillary Fleming glowered and mumbled under his breath.

"Your point's been taken," said the President. He paused for effect, then grimly added, "And again, for good reasons, duly ignored. God knows the CIA's tentacles are long enough." Turning to Hewett, he softened his tone. "Have a good trip back to Moscow and a pleasant tour of duty, Ambassador."

"Any word for me to pass on to our imprisoned friend, General Shaeffer?" asked the diplomat cautiously.

Before the President could answer, Fleming interjected, "I suspect, Ambassador Hewett, you'll find a way to avoid the ghoulish truth."

"Which is?" asked the President with irritation.

The Defense chief lowered his head. "I'm sorry, Mr. President, but your determinate policy seems to indicate you're prepared to let one of our important military leaders rot in Lubyanka."

In a passenger lounge at New York's Kennedy Airport, the public-address system announced the last call for SAS Flight

12. Nuri and Tina stood halfway down the boarding tunnel, holding hands, not wanting to part.

Tina looked at Nuri seriously. "Before breakfast I saw you studying that Michelin map of Vienna. I'll try once more. Put the idea away, Nuri. Please. Stop playing Hamlet before it's too late."

He duly laughed. "Hamlet is a drama of weakness. I am not weak."

Tina shook her head and held his arm. "No. I'm talking about another role—like duty and self-denial. A shitty heroic task that in your case is unnecessary, far from preordained. *Give it up*."

"Tina, I love you. But this has nothing to do with our future together. We've discussed this at length before."

She replied quickly, "*Before*, your existence wasn't so fragile. Promise me you'll not even *think* about helping one solitary friend in Russia so much as blow his nose. At least until we're back together. Please Nuri, for me."

He half shrugged, half smiled. "We'll talk when we meet in London. Go now, you'll miss your flight."

Tina kissed him a lingering, sentimental good-bye, only to be interrupted by a sudden tap on her shoulder from FBI agent Niles Donnell, who had approached from the terminal end of the tunnel. He said quickly, "Nuri, I suggest we leave now, by one of the lounge's outside exits. My men spotted three familiar faces out on the main concourse. Some characters that were identified back at the Four Seasons Hotel."

Nuri kissed Tina again then gently steered her toward the plane entry. He took off down the tunnel, following Donnell.

Approaching the flight attendant standing beside the 747's door, Tina hesitated. She glanced one more time back up the ramp. Nuri had disappeared. The attendant was waiting for her to step into the plane so the boarding tunnel could be backed away.

The Scandinavian Airlines jumbo jet was scheduled to depart at six o'clock for Copenhagen with a connecting flight to Stockholm. Despite the off-tourist season, it was crowded with a mélange of businessmen, traveling relatives, and a crowd of cinema buffs and film exhibitors, who, like Tina Conner, were bound for the Tenth Annual Svenska Filmo.

Tina had asked Jon Saarto to go ahead with her carryon bag

and settle into their first-class seats. She felt flustered as she thought again of the connecting flight from Washington, D.C., to New York an hour earlier, and the friction that seemed to have developed between Nuri and the bodyguard. What had begun as a personality conflict had turned into obvious jealousy. She wished now that she could have left Saarto in New York, instead traveling to Sweden with the studio publicist Polly Grant, but Harry Kaufmann would have none of it. Polly had been sent ahead to pave the way and meet her at Stockholm's Arlanda Airport.

Tina was stuck with Jon Saarto. He would even have an adjacent room to hers at the Sheraton Stockholm Hotel. She suspected Nuri would do no better for privacy, for he'd be dogged constantly around New York by Niles Donnell and other FBI agents. The dancer had also said something about a woman CIA operative accompanying him when he left the country, but he hadn't elaborated on the details.

Tina found her seat in the first-class section. Jon Saarto sat waiting, a contented smile on his face. It was the first time she'd seen the tall, Finnish-American so ebullient. She couldn't help but feel her bodyguard had found his element and was reveling in it. "You'll survive the separation," he said smugly. "Put away the sour face."

Feeling a pang of guilty embarrassment, she turned to him. "I wasn't moping over Nuri. For your information, I was thinking about Sasha."

"Who the hell is *Sasha*?"

"My dead dog."

Saarto put away his grin and retreated into silence. Tina studied him, trying to read his mind. The bodyguard's hushed manner, she reasoned, wouldn't last for long. For the next ten hours he would have her as a captive audience and they would get to know one another much better. She fastened her seat belt. Thank God it would be a night flight, she reflected. If necessary, she'd take a Nembutal for uninterrupted sleep. Outgoing, ambitious, good-looking hunk that he appeared to be, there was something about Jon Saarto that bothered her.

In his twelfth-floor hotel room Khamsin stood before the mirror, trimming his sideburns and the hair in his nostrils with a pair of surgical scissors. He'd arrived tired and without reservations in Manhattan, and had to call five hotels before securing a room here at the Summit. At least the lodging was conveniently located.

Placing the scissors back in his toiletry kit, Khamsin retrieved a length of dental floss and worked it through his gums, all the while smiling ear to ear and admiring his perfect teeth. He tried to avoid looking at the inferior substitute toupee. He needed to get back to Paris and be properly fitted for a new hairpiece.

Khamsin thought about finishing the job he had started, the necessity for starting from scratch, planning all over again here in Manhattan. Nuri Baranov's twists and turns, along with his increased protection, were becoming annoying. Never before had Khamsin expended so much effort on an assignment. Until now he had contract killing down to a science. They weren't outsmarting him, they were trying to outnumber him!

However difficult, Khamsin needed to finish the Nuri Baranov matter and catch a flight back to France. He was tired of this fox and hound thing and wanted to get home. He sorely missed the wild mulatto woman who shared his bed and board but was so useless at domestic matters. His place would be a shambles if he didn't get back soon.

Khamsin flicked the dental floss in the waste container, rinsed his teeth with mouthwash, and glanced at his Rolex. He was famished, and determined to enjoy a leisurely dinner before starting to track down the dancer. He'd already obtained the address of the U.S. Dance Company's rehearsal hall from the telephone directory, though young Baranov's apartment telephone was apparently unlisted. No matter, for there were other ways of eliciting this information. All the operational details would come together quickly enough in the morning. Khamsin knew he'd need a driver he could trust and sophisticated weaponry. Fortunately, the KGB *rezidentura* who lived on Long Island had promised both.

Khamsin put on his full-length, brown leather coat, looped the belt, and went back to the mirror to check his appearance. He'd almost forgotten to apply a generous amount of L'Homme cologne behind each ear.

Now he was ready to explore the city. He would have a fine meal, possibly at an Algerian or Moroccan restaurant; a choice California wine would be a change of pace from his French favorites. At seven o'clock, as prearranged, he would telephone the *rezidentura* on Long Island from a pay phone.

Despite his earlier setbacks, Khamsin felt a renewed confidence and growing excitement. As much as he looked forward to satisfying his growling stomach, he was even hungrier to see the new laser gunsight rifle that had been promised him here in New York.

Tina lifted the glass of Pinot Noir from her dinner tray, sipping it slowly as she gazed out the 747's window. She saw turbulent storm clouds over the Atlantic thousands of feet below and a full moon off to the right; above the plane the stars were radiant. The first-class dinner service warmed Tina's spirits, putting her in a lighter mood. Even the bodyguard sitting next to her in the aisle seat seemed less burdensome. Saarto had opened up quite freely during the past hour and Tina was certain she knew more about his past than he knew of hers. Oddly, however, not once since boarding the plane had Nuri Baranov been discussed between them.

Saarto was also proving a measure less bellicose and a degree smarter than she'd first thought. Thus far their conversation had revealed that he'd lived in Ohio and Indiana prior to moving to Los Angeles; that years earlier he'd been a boxer and a prize-winning marathon runner. Twice before the bodyguard had visited Scandinavia; first while a high school student, when he'd spent a summer in Helsinki Finland with a grandmother, and more recently with his porno-publisher employer on a business trip to Denmark and Sweden.

Saarto was also qualified as a single-engine private pilot. Even before the captain's periodic flight-progress announcements, her travel companion had calculated with surprising accuracy the 747's location.

Saarto had seen every one of Tina's motion pictures, not that they were historically significant, but the films had given them a common ground for conversation.

The bodyguard's voice suddenly took on a new tone. "What business does Nuri have with the Overseas Film Distribution Service—a Beck subsidiary? You know of an employee there named Tangerine?"

Tina felt puzzled and let it show. "I've never heard of the company or the lady. Unfortunately Nuri doesn't tell me everything."

"He should. I keep reading about your perfect affair."

She looked at him, mildly annoyed. Saarto was staring at her again, a trifle too satisfied. She checked herself. "Nuri and I are planning more than a symbiotic affair, Jon. Perhaps someday even a marriage. Or is that a bit old hat for you?"

He didn't respond. With the lull in the dialogue, Tina held the wine goblet to her lips and gently closed her eyes. Ignoring Saarto, she thought about Nuri back in New York and prayed he would be safe. She suddenly hated herself for following through with the film festival appearance instead of just cancelling the damned trip. Saarto's newest query bothered her more than she would admit to him. Who was *Tangerine*? An odd name, she reflected.

When Tina reopened her eyes, standing over her in the aisle was a wheezing, pear-shaped young man. He wore horned-rimmed eyeglasses and a rumpled corduroy suit set off by a polka-dot bow tie. An expensive Nikon swung from his neck.

"Ms. Conner?" he brazenly interrupted.

The stranger had either a Brooklyn or Bronx accent; California-raised Tina couldn't decide which. She started to respond, then changed her mind, deciding instead to let the bodyguard beside her earn his keep.

Saarto dutifully glared up at the intruder. "The lady would like a little privacy." He hesitated, studying the ferretlike face before him. "Haven't I seen you somewhere before?"

The photographer deliberately ignored Saarto. He smugly withdrew a business card and handed it across to Tina.

Saarto intercepted and scanned the card himself.

Shifting uneasily behind her fold-down meal tray, Tina felt like a trapped animal. She watched Jon Saarto's impatience turn to anger.

The intrusive photographer spoke again. "I'm sorry to interrupt your meal, but all of us have different showbiz jobs to do. When and where the opportunity presents itself."

Saarto tore the business card in half. "I remember now. And I'm not impressed, Mr. Grundy. Either by *Street* magazine as a gossip rag or the scumbag publisher you work for."

The photographer stiffened, but stuck to his guns. "Come now, Mr. Saarto. I'm told that as late as last week you were employed yourself by the Brian Beck publishing empire."

Tina watched anxiously as the bodyguard's fists tightened on the sides of his food tray. Saarto said heatedly, "So what the hell do you want?"

Tina sighed with impatience. She knew precisely what the

intrusive Grundy was after. Paparrazi photographers had become a miserable way of life for her.

Blinking convulsively behind his glasses, Grundy gushed, "A breaking photo story, of course. My first candid shot of the Stockholm festival, okay? Simple enough, the two of you merely enjoying an in-flight dinner. Really no intrusion at all, is it?" He brought up the motorized camera.

No flash, Tina reflected. Working with fast film, he'd have a half-dozen shots in a matter of seconds.

Saarto looked at the confining fold-down table in front of him then glanced around to try to signal the stewardess. None were nearby. Saarto pointed a threatening finger at Grundy. "Beat it, now."

The photographer continued to adjust the lens on the Nikon.

Saarto used his elbow, driving it into the intruder's fleshy stomach. Tina's hands shot up to her mouth as Grundy cried out and doubled over in pain. Tableware throughout the cabin clattered as the other startled passengers looked up in surprise. A few without lap trays jumped up from their seats. The alarmed flight attendants at the back of the cabin hurried forward.

"Give my regards to Brian Beck, you bastard," Saarto whispered coarsely to Grundy.

Crimson-faced and choking with anger, the photographer backed away, but he managed to get off several shots from a safer distance up the aisle. Flipping Saarto off with his finger and mouthing incoherent imprecations, he staggered back into the tourist section.

23

A BALLET REHEARSAL HALL was the wrong place to be on a Sunday morning, and Nuri was in an off mood. He felt restless and edgy, more in the mind for a fast game of racquetball than practice for his upcoming part in *Firebird*. There were two others with him in the rehearsal room—the company's choreographer, Kurt Meisenheimer, and the accompanist, Marguerite Dulac.

The United States Dance Company, like the New York City Ballet, performed at Lincoln Center. But unlike the latter group, which was a permanent Center resident, U.S. Dance maintained offices, rehearsal studios, and scenery storage space a short distance away in a privately-owned building on Amsterdam Avenue. Nuri found these facilities spacious enough, though not as modern and comfortable as the top-floor, air-conditioned practice room at Lincoln Center's New York Theatre.

Kurt Meisenheimer had called a break to get himself a drink of water. While waiting for the choreographer to return, Nuri went to the one wall without mirrors and opened a window to

181

look outside. The sky over Manhattan was overcast, and the sparse traffic on the one-way street four stories below reminded him that it was Sunday. The evening before, after taking Tina to Kennedy for her flight to Europe, he'd gone out to dinner with Meisenheimer and Monica Roberts, the company's financial manager. The pair had been genial hosts, but Nuri had been reminded that he'd fallen far behind as a result of his leave of absence. "Tina Conner is only one cog in your wheel of fortune," Meisenheimer had snidely reminded him. "It's time to go back to work."

There had been several changes in *Firebird*, including a new partnering for Nuri. Annette Lipton would dance the other lead, and he was pleased. There was also a minor revision in the excerpt from Copland's *Rodeo*. These changes would effect Nuri's opening night performance in Paris, and he desperately needed practice time, alone and with the ensemble. After dinner Nuri had returned to his apartment on Sixty-sixth Street and retired early, getting his rest for what was in fact turning out to be a rigorous Sunday morning.

Nuri came away from the window. Thus far he'd worked with the choreographic genius Meisenheimer and accompanist Dulac for over two and a half hours. Meisenheimer was in his sixties, but his body was nearly as lean and tight as when he first came to the U.S. from Austria as a young dancer. He had a face with high, sharply-planed cheekbones, bushy salt-and-pepper hair, and small brown eyes with large lids that made him look like an impenetrable lizard. His gestures were slightly effeminate, but his voice was powerful and his conversation brilliant.

A fiery, temperamental type, Meisenheimer seldom smiled during rehearsals, but at social events could be extremely jovial, and to the annoyance of Nuri and several other straights in the company, often brazenly free with his hands. Meisenheimer never touched alcohol and had only one self-acknowledged vice: he was a pederast, the type who drooled in church over altar boys. Nuri tolerated the choreographer's eccentricities as an Olympic runner might rely on a one-of-a-kind coach with a boozing problem.

Nuri went back to his pliés, observing himself in the wall mirror. He felt sloppy, his muscle memory corrupted by the short vacation and the one short performance at the White House. He slowly shook his head and said to the approaching choreographer, "Sometimes I wonder why ballet is so damned complex. Isadora Duncan was clad only in a skimpy tunic when she danced barefoot and alone on an empty stage."

Meisenheimer scoffed. "Yes. And your great Russian choreographer Fokine, was influenced by her." He signaled Madame Dulac at the piano and they began again.

Nuri danced.

"More elegance! Lighter on the downstep," Meisenheimer shouted.

Niles Donnell casually poked his head in the rehearsal room doorway, but Meisenheimer, with a flutter of his wrist, shooed the FBI agent away.

The accompanist repeated several bars of a theme, but Nuri hadn't caught the rhythm of the step. Marguerite Dulac's wrinkled face smiled at him and she simplified the music, as she often did, plunking out "Five-foot-two, eyes of blue." Nuri was getting tired. The rehearsal had gone on long enough, and he was having trouble sustaining movements to the retards in the music. Determined, he shuffled back to the barre and picked up the beat there. Madame Dulac, helpful as ever, drifted into "Humoresque." Choreographer Meisenheimer zestfully tapped a pencil on the barre, stressing the timing.

Nuri smiled, keenly aware that this was a technique used for years to drill dancers, purportedly originated by Balanchine's talented accompanist Boelzner. Nuri remembered the pianist's improvised words to "Humoresque": *My favorite pastime after dark is goosing statues in the park, if Sherman's horse can stand it why can't you?*

Finally satisfied that he had the step's timing mastered, Nuri paused to laugh.

The choreographer ran a hand through his thick hair and looked at him speculatively. "I think we've had enough for today. Your solo work is excellent." He paused in thought. "Tomorrow morning we will rehearse en masse. The bond between yourself and the corps de ballet is too fragile, Nuri. You sometimes do not feel the presence of the others. You'll have to work on the collective look."

Nuri retrieved a towel from his tote bag and grinned at Meisenheimer. "Don't you think I've had enough of *collectives*, Maestro? Perhaps the bond you seek should be in the music and the hereditary dance steps."

The choreographer frowned and shook his head. "The

American way is not to look grand and noble, but young, fresh, and exhilarated."

Nuri nodded, too tired to argue. He pulled off his ballet slippers and slipped gray sweats over his tights.

Meisenheimer nervously wrung his hands. "We will work together. And you must help the others with their awkward legs. I'm not about to take to France a troupe of grasshoppers and frogs."

Nuri fumbled with an old pair of Reeboks, then gathered up his things. He said seriously, "Maestro, I'd very much appreciate a favor." He turned to Marguerite Dulac, who was gathering up her sheet music. "I need your help, too, madame."

They looked at him speculatively.

Nuri gestured toward the double doors to the rehearsal hall and lowered his voice. "Outside the FBI agent waits. Niles Donnell and his companions follow me everywhere and I feel like a fugitive." He pointed to the opposite end of the long chamber, to the exit they all knew led to an enclosed rear fire escape. "Instead of a cool-down exercise I need—" Nuri started to say a game of racquetball, but thought better of it. Meisenheimer wouldn't hear of it. *The wrong muscles!*

The dancer quietly continued, "I need a break from these government agents who follow me like bloodhounds."

Meisenheimer frowned. "The protection is for your benefit."

"No. The danger is exaggerated. In this city, you know yourself it is simple enough to disappear in the crowd. I'm sick of it, Maestro. It's like being a goldfish with a cat staring at you from outside the bowl."

Madame Dulac gave him a sharp glance. "How can we help?"

"I don't like sticky scenes," said Meisenheimer uneasily.

To the accompanist Nuri requested, "Play one more selection. The two of you remain here until I'm downstairs by the way of the rear stairway. My friend outside will assume I'm still practicing." Nuri watched the old woman amble back to the piano. She played from memory, a selection from the ballet *Coppelia*. Meisenheimer slumped down in a folding chair and glowered at Nuri. Nervously tapping his foot, he whispered, "Go quickly."

Nuri scooped up his tote bag and dashed for the rear exit.

* * *

On Sundays the KGB Annex building near Moscow's outer Ring Road was relatively quiet. Savoring the solitude but at the same time annoyed that he'd been called in to the office, Fiodor Talik polished the two-centimeter thick glass top of his desk with his sleeve. This finished, he idly examined several efficiency reports while waiting for the telephone to ring.

Talik felt lethargic. Though the stubborn bronchitis still lingered, he was hacking far less often. Feeling a measure better, he'd removed the cumbersome woollen scarf from his neck. Talik glanced at his desk calendar. Four miserable days had elapsed since he'd last savored a cigarette, and he could stand it no longer. Let the smoke send him to his death bed; he was going to enjoy a Prima now.

Talik reached for the sculptured bronze bear with five interlocking, chromium rings in its upraised paws. The cigarette lighter was a souvenir prototype proposed for the 1980 Moscow Olympics by Factory Number 76 in Minsk. The novelty item never went into manufacture—Talik had never inquired as to why—and it was now a one-of-a-kind collector's piece. Once more he pushed the interlocking rings down. The bear's head tilted back, spouting a narrow butane flame; at the same time a hidden music box tinkled the first few bars of the "Internationale." Talik had to activate the mechanism twice before his Prima lit.

He sat back, savoring the delicious smoke. It was almost lunchtime, and once more Talik thought with annoyance about making this special trip to the office on Sunday. Talik could have gone directly from his country dacha to the Hippodrome for the winter harness racing were it not for the timely matter Bruna Kloski needed to discuss with him. He hoped the important communications from America had come in as she expected.

Talik impatiently checked his watch. His private sanctuary had never been so disturbingly quiet. Impatient and restless, he went over to the window. He looked up at the sky as if beholding a miracle: the gray clouds over the Soviet capital had parted, revealing a brilliant sun in a patch of blue. He smiled. If the weather held, it would be an omen of good luck for his wagering at the track on Begovaya Street. It pleased Talik that he personally had been responsible for an increased amount of

the Hippodrome's revenues going to subsidize the Bolshoi
State Theatre.

Behind him the red telephone buzzed. Talik stepped over to
the desk, picked it up, and routinely identified himself. As
expected, it was the woman colonel calling from the Fifth
Directorate. Bruna Kloski's voice sounded tinny, as if she'd
caught a cold or were in an echo chamber.

"Where are you calling from, Comrade Colonel?" he asked.

"The basement medical laboratory, General. The speaker
phone is on while I work."

Talik furrowed his brows. "May I ask what you're doing
there on a Sunday?"

"It is quiet except for the animals, and I can be alone to
experiment. The miniature pneumatic weapon we discussed
earlier is almost ready."

Impatient, Talik said, "We will talk about the device later.
Right now I am interested only in the 'prodigal son.' There has
been nothing in the international news about his demise."

"Comrade General, we are still working on the matter. The
one called Khamsin feels success is imminent."

"He's experienced failure?"

"Yesterday. Minor setbacks, Comrade General."

"I expect results, no matter the cost."

Kloski went on: "Good, for his fees are exorbitant. Perhaps,
before this terrorist succeeds in his efforts, there are factors you
wish to reconsider."

"Proceed, but quickly, Colonel."

"Why not let the Americans feel a measure of success while
they quarrel among themselves? When the dancer arrives in
Paris, these conflicting interests will be so preoccupied warring
with one another it would be a simple matter for our own
people to capture Nuri Pavlinovich alive. And then I pull him
by the tongue, yes?"

"*Capture?*" Talik's indifference hardened into rebuke. "I've
already foreseen these possibilities and I reject them outright.
You'll do likewise."

On the line, Bruna Kloski's voice seemed edgy. "Of course.
Whatever you will, General."

"I do not want Nuri Pavlinovich brought back to Moscow,
either by Red Army intelligence or KGB personnel. You will
understand this! I realize, Comrade, that you delight in
interrogation, but you will not have that opportunity with the

dancer. Nor will you prosecute him. Your assignment stands; he will be *neutralized*. I want to see ice water in those veins of yours, Colonel. The logistics of the matter are not that difficult and the odds are with us; the third, the fourth, the fifth try, what does it matter? You must succeed. And in New York or Paris, not Moscow. If he expires in the West, others can be blamed."

"Of course, Comrade General Talik. There will be no martyrs on Soviet soil."

"I trust you, Colonel Kloski, but I suggest you ride harder on your contract personnel." Talik leaned back in his chair and glanced out the window. "You should get out of that basement laboratory and enjoy the pleasant day, Colonel. Outdoors the sun is shining."

Talik hung up the phone and looked at his watch. He wondered why Bruna Kloski took such personal interest in the medical laboratory. Was it some morbid fascination with new forms of death? The doctors who ran the KGB research facility had twice complained to him that she was going through test animals at an alarming rate. Talik wondered if the dedicated woman colonel ever rested. He put the thought away; it really didn't matter.

Rising from his desk, he strolled to the window and signaled to the chauffeur in the courtyard below to bring the car around. Overhead there came a heavy rumble and the clouds slammed closed again. The Moscow sky was as it had been: a monotonous gray with the promise of snow.

24

NURI LEFT the building by the rear door and doubled back to Amsterdam Avenue. For the first time in days he was alone, and he felt better.

Until he happened to glance down the street. His heart caught in his chest and he wondered now if he'd relaxed too quickly. Niles Donnell was nowhere to be seen, but three musclemen sat inside a United Parcel delivery truck and they were looking his way with more than a cursory interest. *Nyet!* It had to be his overheated imagination. But a package delivery on Sunday?

Quickening his step, Nuri hurried uptown toward his apartment, on the other side of Broadway, just off Central Park. He shivered at the cold. The big electrical sign on the Citicorp building several blocks away put the temperature at twenty-nine degrees. When the sign flashed the time, Nuri quickly calculated. With the six-hour difference, it was dinner time in Stockholm, and he'd promised to call Tina before seven. He'd go home first, try and reach the actress, then afterward head for the YMCA three blocks south and luxuriate in the Jacuzzi.

Tightening the strap on his shoulder tote, Nuri walked rapidly, as was his custom. Pedestrian traffic was minimal, so he was able to keep a reasonably clear view of the street in both directions. Still, he felt uneasy. He pretended to look in a shop window so he could unobtrusively glance back toward the parcel-delivery truck he'd seen parked on the opposite side of Amsterdam Avenue. The vehicle had gone around the block and drawn up a short distance behind him; its cab was empty now, the three men not in sight. Nerves tightening, Nuri resumed walking.

Turning the Lincoln Center corner at Sixty-sixth, he hesitated for several seconds, then threw a swift glance back around the buildings. The men were there on the Amsterdam sidewalk, on foot, quickening their pace in his direction. Nuri's heart began to pound. He cursed himself for avoiding Donnell outside the rehearsal room. Was the trio behind him a part of the FBI surveillance team? If so, they presented no problem. But if so, why hadn't he been informed—and introduced? And why did they need a truck?

On Broadway near the subway entrance, Nuri had to dodge a herd of camera-laden tourists bound for the fountain courtyard at Lincoln Center. He pondered what to do next: he might lose the individuals behind him by dashing underground into the IRT and doing some backtracking, or he could try to outrun them on the street. His high-security apartment was a little more than a block away.

Nuri approached the subway kiosk. Beside him a woman dropped a magazine—one of several she carried under her arm. He retrieved it, but before he could call out, she'd stepped into a cab. He was about to toss the copy of *Paris-Match* aside when he noticed the face staring at him from the black-outlined cover. It was Bolshoi *ballerina assoluta* Marina Pleskova! French journalists, as usual, were quick to respond to an international news event.

As Nuri glanced at the face of innocence on the magazine cover, he was suddenly startled by a brilliant red pip of light that crept across the magazine and began to move along his arm toward his chest.

Nyet! Padazheetye! What's this? Nuri's mind clicked to something he'd seen on television weeks before. Panicking, he dropped the magazine and jumped. He felt the wind of a bullet by his cheek as he rolled into the subway entrance, skidding down several steps in a series of bone-jarring whumps. The mortifying reality of what was happening had come instantly to him. *A laser-equipped gunsight!* Foolproof, fast. Deadly efficient.

Nuri's heart thudded. Traffic on Broadway was light. Before grabbing the magazine he'd seen a metallic blue station wagon creeping by on the other side of the street but thought nothing of it. While diving for the protection of the subway entry there'd been a fleeting glimpse of a burst of flame from the vehicle's rear window. The laser-equipped weapon had to have a silencer not to be heard over the street noise. All he'd heard was the sharp clang of lead ricocheting off the side of the kiosk—a place where his head should have been had he hesitated a fraction of a second longer.

No one paid any attention to him as he now sat, badly shaken, on the subway steps. Benevolent, helping hands for drunks and loiterers were nonexistent in Manhattan. He pulled himself together, rose to his feet, and deliberated. Under cover of several people ascending the steps, he cautiously poked his head far enough out of the subway entry to survey the street. Some fifty yards off the blue station wagon had pulled over to the curb. A tall, wiry man in a felt hat and full-length brown leather coat stepped away from the vehicle and crossed the street, heading swiftly toward the IRT entry where Nuri stood. His companion in the station wagon moved off in traffic.

Nuri's stomach pushed against his throat. Nearby, on the sidewalk, the three individuals who had posed as delivery men were also headed his way, from all appearances oblivious to the other adversary. *Friends or foes?*

Nuri couldn't take a chance. There wasn't time to work it out in his mind, even if he could think straight. Heart racing, he whirled and dropped down into the subway, leaping the steps three at a time. In his tote bag he found a token, fumbled with it in the turnstile, then raced to the far end of the platform.

Nuri was desperate for one of three things: a telephone, a subway patrolman, or an immediate train. He suddenly remembered that it was Sunday; this meant curtailed service. Worse, Sixty-sixth Street was a local, and not an express stop. Only a handful of passengers stood on the downtown platform with him and none waited across the way for a northbound train. *I'm trapped*, he flashed.

He did find a telephone booth and was about to step inside

when he saw the tall man in the leather coat come striding out on the platform. The gaunt-faced individual, who appeared to be in his forties, looked hungry, ratlike, and dangerous.

Nuri stared. The man looked familiar. Beneath the wide-brimmed hat was a uniquely disfigured face. *Los Angeles! The electrician outside the film-studio rehearsal hall!* The man's eyes scanned the area until he saw Nuri in the doorway of the phone booth, then he stepped forward, one hand in the leather overcoat.

Nuri shuddered and took off. Feeling an unfamiliar rush of panic, he pushed through several people and leaped down into the subway's concrete roadbed. His chest heaved as he charged down the dark tunnel, avoiding the six-hundred-volt third rail. Ahead of him, alongside the track, the holding signals dropped off in the distance toward Columbus Circle. Green, green, amber, red. Swallowed up in the grime, dampness, and oily coppery smell, Nuri ran faster.

Several hundred feet into the cut he paused to catch his breath, pressing himself against the unyielding, soot-covered uprights beside the track. He looked around the pillar, back in the direction he'd come. His pursuer had jumped down into the tunnel and was following.

Nuri swore aloud in Russian, then English. "*Sookin sin!* Son of a bitch!" Silhouetted against the lights of the station, the man looked more menacing than before. He stepped forward, the long-muzzled gun now removed from his pocket and extended before him.

Nuri was surprised to find his entire frame trembling. How was it possible for his strong, muscular legs to fail him? No, it was the ground rumbling beneath hs feet. Piercing the dark shaft was the headlight of an oncoming train. It moved too fast to be a local. Nuri saw the man following him leap out of the way, pressing himself against the side of the tunnel.

Doing likewise, Nuri held his breath against the dirty wall. Just inches away three hundred tons of express hurtled past. When the train was gone, the shaft seemed even more silent and ominous than before. Nuri heard footsteps again. Despite the chill in the tunnel, he was sweating profusely. Terrified, he began running again, advancing along the side of the roadbed from pillar to pillar, seeking concealment as best he could. He paused in the glare of a small light marking one of the emergency escape exits. Spotting a ladder, Nuri went up the shaft like a rabbit.

The view of the city through the steel sidewalk grating at first startled him. Buildings soared up at exaggerated angles while inches away feet trampled dust in his eyes and nose. There were plentiful undersides of women's skirts he didn't have time to admire. Shouting frantically to clear the pedestrian traffic, he heaved open the steel grate and scampered out onto the Broadway sidewalk, then paused to catch his breath.

Nuri scanned the street in both directions. Predictably, not a policeman in sight when needed. He had to think quickly. Spotting several empty metal garbage cans by the curb, a plan struck him. The would-be assassin pursuing him would have to pocket his gun to climb up the escape ladder.

Nuri moved quickly. He grabbed one of the refuse containers and cautiously edged up to the open grate. Almost immediately his assailant appeared from below, climbing quickly. His hunter's eyes scanned the sidewalk and street as he reached the top of the steel ladder.

Hesitating only long enough to commit the scarred, Mid-Eastern face to memory, Nuri brought down the first container over his opponent's head and shoulder. He pushed hard on it, then kicked for good measure. The man underneath swore loudly in French as he briefly lost his grip on the ladder and fell backward several rungs.

Nuri ran, dodging pedestrians. He had just one priority now. He needed to get back to his apartment and get on the telephone, make a call to the nation's capital. The emergency 800 number the CIA director himself had provided two nights ago in the President's office.

No! Under the circumstances he wouldn't use his own telephone line. A pay phone booth would be safer.

25

UNLIKE MOST federal offices with their weekend look of abandonment, the CIA was open for business twenty-four hours a day, seven days a week. Diana Vespucci, with six years on the job, understood this well and took her days off when and where she could get them.

The austere quarters she occupied had four desks separated by obscure glass dividers, its purpose to provide work space for field operatives temporarily called back to headquarters at Langley. There were no files, and the phones had only a second-level security clearance, though scrambler lines were available in the Control Conference Room at the end of the hall. Diana was almost finished with a bothersome stack of travel expense forms when a duty secretary hurried into the room.

"A coded trouble call originating in New York," the woman said seriously. "Ted Andreason has the duty but he claims the matter should be referred to you. It's from the dancer—Nuri Baranov."

Diana quickly gathered up the forms before her and

crammed them into her Pierre Cardin briefcase. She rose to her feet. "He's calling from a secured line?"

"No. From a pay phone in upper Manhattan."

"Then I'll take the call in here. I'm alone."

"Very good, Ms. Vespucci. I'll put it through." The woman stepped out of the office and closed the door behind her.

Diana picked up the telephone and with a pencil eraser punched in her own code to activate an automatic taping. She waited for the switchboard hookup. After several clicks she heard Nuri's unsteady voice. "Hello?" he asked hesitantly. "Who is this?"

"Diana."

"Who?"

"Diana Vespucci," she replied with impatience. "You've forgotten already?"

"I remember." Again, an uncertain pause. "I was instructed to call this number if complications developed."

She frowned and sat back down at the desk. "There's a problem up there the FBI can't resolve? Where's Niles Donnell?"

The dancer's sharp intake of breath came clearly over the line. "I left Donnell back at the rehearsal hall. By now he's discovered that I gave him—how do you say it—*the slip*? He must be searching for me on the street or at my apartment. I made a mistake, but let me finish."

Diana looked with displeasure at the broken nail on her index finger, silently cursing General McCulloch for his reck-lessness the night before. "Go ahead, Nuri, I'm listening."

"It looks like I have more than one enemy on by back." His voice was stronger now, less shrunken.

She knit her brows. "I'm afraid I don't understand." The fabrication had rolled out effortlessly.

"A sniper tried to shoot me. Is that clear enough? Near Lincoln Center. He looked like an Arab—a tall, wiry character who jumped out of a blue Toyota station wagon. I'm positive it was the same bastard tracking me in Los Angeles. He followed me into the subway."

"But you're safe now?"

"Yes."

"Can I assume the immediate crisis is over?" she asked dispassionately.

"Look lady, what is this? You sound bored."

"Sorry. I just happen to believe in resourcefulness. From what I understand, Nuri, being a creative type you have plenty of it. After all, you did escape the clutches of the KGB when you defected. You're safe for the moment, or you wouldn't be calling me."

"The hell I am."

"Please control yourself."

"Ms. Vespucci, you should be a Russian, you're so poetic and cold-hearted. Do you want the rest or not?"

She answered him softly, "Proceed. But call me Diana."

"Jesus Christ. Listen, Diana. it's obvious the KGB wants me eradicated. And I'm not expecting the diplomats—contrary to the President's noble expectations—to convince Fiodor Talik to back off on his death sentence. But there's obviously more to worry about, like *who else wants to get their hands on me*? And for what reason?"

"I don't understand, Nuri," she lied.

His voice sharpened even more. "Three men in a delivery truck were also following me, ready to move in at the same time as the gunman in the subway. They didn't take potshots in my direction, but they were big bastards and looked far from friendly."

"Our agents seldom do."

"They were your spooks, then?"

Diana bit her lip, suddenly feeling trapped. "I'm not sure. I'll have to check into it."

"That's too vague!" Nuri screamed back at her. "Listen, Diana. I want no sinister characters following me unless I'm formally introduced first. You can tell the CIA director that's the way it has to be. Do we understand each other? If I have to, I'll go all the way to the President. Your additional protection was his idea in the first place."

She demurred politely, "I'll look into the matter. It's not that I'm sitting here in Washington doing nothing, Nuri. For starters—"

"No bureaucratic double-talk, please. Keep it simple."

Annoyed, Diana finished her sentence. "One, we've a half-dozen people working with the FBI, combing through left-wing extremists and possible contract men capable of being KGB *rezidenturas*. Two, there's a pair of new doormen sharing the duty at your apartment building; the regulars have been temporarily replaced with our men. Are you still listening?"

"Go on."

"Item number three, I've reached an agreement with the U.S. Dance Company management. Your announced charter flight to Paris tomorrow night has been moved up two hours and will depart from Kennedy instead of Newark. The press will be furious over not being notified, but the ballet management will blame it on administrative error."

He came back at her. "Is that it?"

"No. I'm concerned over what you've just told me. If it will make you more comfortable, I'll fly up this afternoon. In the morning I'll assist Niles Donnell to make sure your final rehearsal comes off without incident." Letting out a sigh, she slowly added, "Other than setting up a cot beside your bed tonight and holding your hand, there's damned little else I can do."

There was a short, muffled laugh on the line. "Tina wouldn't buy it," he responded quietly.

"Have it your way, but trust me."

"I'll try, but it goes against the grain of my nature. I need to know you a little better."

"That can be arranged."

She waited through an uncomfortable silence at the other end of the line. Finally he said, "Diana, I'd like you to do me a favor. I've already asked Donnell and been turned down. Do you have any influence with the FBI on my situation?"

Puzzled, she thought for a moment before responding. "Only on certain phases of the operation. Why do you ask?"

"This bodyguard of Tina's—Jon Saarto. He's purportedly a fringe benefit from her employer, First Consolidated Studios. I'd like an expedited background check on him. I suspect the FBI already has this information."

"No way. You're a private citizen with no need—"

The dancer cut her off. "I'm not even a citizen yet, remember? But I am the lead participant in this mess. Please, get me a file on Saarto, Diana. How long will it take?"

"A couple of days—if I'm lucky."

"Look, you cooperate with me, and I'll bend over backward to cooperate with you. Okay? Do it, for both of us." The line from New York went dead in her ear.

Nuri left the drugstore phone booth but didn't go immediately to his apartment. Instead, he took a cab to a sporting-goods

store in Brooklyn that he knew was open on Sunday. Never
before had he entertained the thought of owning a handgun; the
American love affair with personal weapons had always
seemed odd to him. But for the first time he was afraid and
unsure of his safety. Regardless of U.S. government assurances, including those he'd just heard from Diana Vespucci, he
felt alone and helpless in a jungle of predatory animals. Even a
caveman with a club and a pack of sharp stones would be better
off, he reflected.

The cabbie, like many others he'd come across in New
York, was a Russian-Jewish exile, but Nuri, with problems of
his own, was in no mood to pursue a lively conversation in
their native language. Fortunately—as was often the case in
Manhattan—the driver didn't recognize him.

Nuri paid the fare, went quickly into the store, and began
perusing a long glass showcase with row after row of
handguns. Beyond the counter on the wall was an equally
impressive assortment of rifles, shotguns, and legally modified
automatic weapons. Never in his life had Nuri seen such an
arsenal; he stared in wonderment for long minutes.

A hostile-looking salesman who wore an alligator shirt and a
thick gold chain around his neck came up to Nuri and went
through the motions of assistance. The clerk showed him
several weapons and after a few pointed questions put aside the
larger caliber pistols in favor of the lightweight, easily hidden
automatics. He checked the clip on a .22 Bernardelli and
extended it in the palm of his hand. "Hundred ninety-five
bucks," he said smartly.

Nuri picked up the gun gingerly, examining its finely tooled,
blue steel finish. "I'll need a permit for this?" he asked
innocently.

The clerk grimaced. "Of course. How long you been in New
York, for Christ's sake?"

Nuri ignored the barb; he'd been asked the same question
more times than he cared to count since his defection. "I'll
need to carry it with me at all times."

The sardonic expression remained on the clerk's face.
"What you do with it is your business, but you'll need a
concealed weapon permit."

Nuri placed the gun on the counter, suddenly remembering
that permits took time. An investigation, his immigration
documents. It flashed through his mind that in a matter of hours

he'd be traveling to France. There would be aircraft boarding inspections, metal detectors, overseas Customs hassles to contend with.

Behind the counter the salesman glowered, waiting for his decision. A bearded, big-bellied character in camouflage pants and jacket came up beside Nuri and beckoned the clerk. "If he can't make up his mind, I need some help."

Nuri glanced at the customer, noting the silk-screened T-shirt inside the open khaki jacket. On it an upraised, muscular arm was tattooed with the name "Mom" while surrounding it a semicircle of bold white letters proclaimed KILL A COMMIE FOR MOMMY. Frowning, Nuri glanced at the gun display case one more time. His mind raced as he remembered the words of the great Russian dramatist Chekhov: "Don't put a loaded rifle on the stage unless someone intends to fire it."

Nuri shook his head and shuffled out of the store. The gun would have to be purchased later, after returning from the tour. *If he were still alive*. Instead of hunting down a taxi, Nuri jogged all the way to the nearest subway station.

The Moscow sky held a promise of snow flurries to come as the small crowd gathered in the cemetery adjoining Novodevichy Monastery. The pathway around the gravesite was covered with a layer of ankle-deep snow, trampled down and soiled by countless footprints. Dressed in black except for his gray Astrakhan fur hat, the Soviet Chairman stood uncomfortably behind the members of the mourning Pleskova family. Pavlin Baranov was accompanied by a personal aide and bodyguards, as well as two friends—Natasha Chernyskaya, the famous director at Mosfilm, and Alexi Stanovich, a senior editor from *Literaturnaya Gazeta*.

Natasha said quietly to the Soviet leader, "I did not know the ballerina well, but she was looking forward to working with me on a short film on the dance. She gave no indication of undergoing personal stress."

Next to the attractive woman director, editor Alexi Stanovich added with a shrug of indifference, "Self-destructiveness is not always so simple to diagnose."

A black-kerchiefed *babushka* who stood in front of them turned and glowered; she was fully prepared to scold them on a need for silence when she belatedly recognized the Soviet

Chairman. Lowering her head, she turned swiftly back toward the gravesite.

The Orthodox priest's eulogy droned on.

Baranov grew restless. He said quietly to his companions, "We must discuss the matter of the Bolshoi incident in more detail, but later. Perhaps, Natasha, you can bring your editor friend out to the dacha for dinner this evening?"

She and Alexi nodded. Pavlin Baranov pulled up the collar of his woollen overcoat, glanced up at the sky, then once more surveyed the scene before him with mixed melancholy and impatience. He wondered what his runaway son—who had once been Marina Pleskova's constant companion—was doing and thinking at this very moment. He desperately wanted Nuri to be here, to witness this scene. Since a *Pravda* photographer had taken pictures moments before, Baranov made a note in his mind to send Nuri a news clipping of the memorial service and obituary. After all, he, Baranov, had used his influence to have the prima ballerina interred in this Arcadian setting outside the monastery walls. Novodevichy was a privileged place where visitors, atheist and devout alike, could wander among the birch trees to gaze at the graves of notables, from Shostakovich and Prokofiev to Nikita Khrushchev and even to Stalin's wife—who, like Marina Pleskova, had committed suicide.

A meter-high, gray marble plinth stood at the head of the ballerina's grave. Mounted to one side—in the Russian custom—was Marina's photograph in a weatherproof glass-and-metal frame. There was no plaque. Baranov knew the workmen would install it later, and if the gravesite were like others in the immediate area, it would be surmounted by a *memento mori*—in this case, undoubtedly, bronzed ballet shoes.

Pavlin Baranov looked around him, searching the faces of the gathered mourners. The priest had finished his eulogy and the crowd was breaking up. Aside from the immediate family, most of the Bolshoi company was present, as were several student friends of Marina's from the University of Moscow. An aide handed the Soviet Chairman a spray of pink roses. Placing it beside the grave, Baranov shook hands with the survivors, had a few brief words with Bolshoi Artistic Director Pyotr Maryinsky, then turned to leave. His friends from Mosfilm and *Literaturnaya Gazeta* had already departed the scene.

Trudging through the snow toward his chauffeured car, the

Chairman was distracted by agitated voices at the edge of the cemetery. A group of university students who had attended the graveside tribute were being confronted by uniformed KGB personnel supervised by a woman officer. Baranov immediately recognized Bruna Kloski of the Fifth Directorate. Why was this KGB heavyweight interrogator here?

Baranov thought about Fiodor Talik, wondering why Kloski's superior had not shown his face at the memorial service. Peculiar behavior for the KGB general. He, of all people, was one of the Bolshoi's most dedicated patrons! No other Politburo member had expressed such devotion to the theatre's continuing welfare.

Curious, Pavlin Baranov was about to stroll over to the disturbance when one of his bodyguards blocked his path. An aide scowled. "Comrade Chairman, please. It may be unsafe. I will have a report sent to you later, at your pleasure."

Baranov shrugged. The snow began sifting down again as he was escorted back to his long black Zil. He climbed inside with his entourage and pulled the white curtains closed. Immediately the vehicle headed out of the monastery grounds and raced up Pirogovskaya Street toward the Kremlin.

The distance back to the upper West Side seemed endless, and Nuri had plenty of time to think. He double-checked the street in both directions before cautiously approaching his apartment building. Sure enough, at the far corner was parked the same United Parcel truck seen earlier on Amsterdam Avenue. The same three men hovered beside it, but thus far they hadn't looked his way. If he crouched behind parked cars, he could easily make a dash for it, beating them to his apartment entry. So much for an afternoon at the Y or going to a theatre, he reflected. Better to stay locked in his flat until Diana Vespucci or Niles Donnell arrived on the scene.

Nuri scuttled toward the building, arriving safely. He entered with his key. Diana was right; there was a new lobby attendant. Nuri nodded, but the replacement man was stone-faced and gave no indication of recognizing the dancer.

As Nuri rode the elevator to his seventh-floor apartment, he thought again about the CIA woman. There was something disquieting about her behavior that bothered him, and he'd yet to get a handle on it. He wondered, too, what had happened to the FBI agent back at the rehearsal hall. Had Donnell come searching for him?

Arriving at his door, Nuri keyed both deadlocks and pushed it open. Just inside the entry on the polished parquet floor was an envelope that had been pushed over the threshold only recently—a certified letter postmarked three days earlier in Los Angeles. The doorman or building super had apparently signed for it and slipped it inside. Nuri did a double-take as he noted the return address; OVERSEAS FILM DISTRIBUTORS; this followed by a handwritten annotation, *Tangerine*.

"Impossible," he whispered aloud, remembering what had happened in Los Angeles. *Tangerine was dead*. He closed the door, wondering whether the letter had been written before her murder or somehow delayed in the mail.

Heading for the kitchen, Nuri tore open the envelope. He frowned in concentration as he examined a folded note that enclosed several six-inch-long, 35mm black-and-white positive filmstrips. A hastily scribbled message read simply, *For your information—goodies gleaned from the latest air freight out of Moscow*. The note was signed, *Love, Tangerine*. Nuri was still baffled by the timing. The film obviously contained information he'd been waiting for, messages passed on by Marina and Dimitri at the Mosfilm end of the line.

Opening the refrigerator, he blanched at the smell. Something left over from before his vacation had given up the ghost. He grabbed a can of Diet Pepsi, quickly closed the door, and snapped the tab. Taking a long swig, he took the drink with him, padding down the hall to his darkened bedroom.

He pulled open the chromium Levolors, letting daylight flood the room. Blinking, he sat on the bed and took off his shirt and shoes. Once more the wall-sized blowup of Bruegel's *Wedding Party* fought for attention with the vivid zebra stripe of the king-sized bedspread. Nuri's apartment wouldn't have suited many young men his own age, reflecting as it did his peculiarly esthetic tastes and/or confusion. He walked barefoot across the pieced white sheepskin rugs to the front of his dresser and gazed in the mirror. His face looked drawn and tired.

Nuri searched frantically through several drawers for his hand magnifier, then finally gave up. He'd have to take the film into the den that served as his improvised darkroom and use the enlarger. Needing a pleasant distraction from all his troubles, he stopped in the living room and slipped a CD on the stereo unit. It was Midnight Oil, the foot-stomping, powerful rock group from Australia. Nuri turned up the volume, retreated into the den, and took the dust cover off the enlarger.

Nuri really didn't give a hoot for photography one way or the other. What basic equipment he owned, begged, or borrowed was born of pure necessity; it enabled him to get filmstrips in and out of the Soviet Union. Turning off the overhead light, he slid the first film section into the enlarger and carefully focused. He read the message. It was week-old material, sent by Marina Pleskova before her death, informing him that she was working diligently to get his manuscript pages into the right hands. His first chapter had already been printed and distributed by the Moscow underground, she advised.

Nuri studied the handwriting and terse, even-toned message, eyes clouding as he thought of her. No indication at all of any personal stress, nothing that would indicate an impending suicide. Nuri took a sip from his Pepsi, then slowly advanced the filmstrip through the enlarger. He found the frames he'd been waiting for—the last-minute changes in the Bolshoi travel itinerary, along with travel accommodations and technical data for the theatres where the dance company would perform. There was one element missing from the film: the total number of dancers who wanted to defect when the time came. Marina was gone; that left three Nuri knew about, provided they hadn't changed their minds. What if there were more? He needed to make plans.

Nuri backed away from the image on the enlarger's platen. After what had happened in Moscow and Los Angeles, he wondered if he could any longer rely on this material. If the KGB caught Marina, they might also have closed in on Dimitri Kollontai, the assistant editor at Mosfilm. Nuri now felt more certain than ever that Fiodor Talik had been instrumental in Marina Pleskova's death. He wondered if there had been personal motives beyond Talik's reprisal for her underground work.

For Nuri the KGB general's profound interest in the welfare of the State Theatre organization had always been suspect. Was he attracted solely by the company's pretty ballerinas? Marina had once told Nuri how Talik had made improper advances to some of the women in the chorus. Had the KGB head accosted

Marina Pleskova and been violently rebuffed? The ballerina was noted for her quick temper.

There had been other discomfiting incidents. Twice before a Security Ministry official had been caught with sticky fingers in the wrong underpants, and those incidents had been hushed over because of the perpetrator's rank. But none of the boys at the Bolshoi had forgotten the KGB colonel's name: *Bruna Kloski.*

Nuri smiled to himself as he thought of the dance company's inner turmoils, the personality conflicts, his own artistic battles with Pyotr Maryinsky. *Damn you, Pyotr Borisovich, and your classical rigidity and reliance on minor league acrobatics! Very soon you'll see what a former gymnast can do.* And who but Nuri Baranov would dare to disturb the great Soviet bear by running off with a few cubs from its den?

He wondered if the others who wanted to escape were still safe following Marina's death. In some small way could they be relied upon to help in his vendetta with Fiodor Talik? He needed to communicate with these individuals, but mail and the telephone were out of the question. Nuri thought again about his meeting with the Virginia Ballet Academy and their immediate tour of Europe and Russia. *Maybe.*

Nuri wondered how General Talik might eventually meet his demise. The KGB minister was a cautious man, attended constantly by bodyguards, but Talik was greedy and prone to imprudent indulgences. Raiding the ranks of the Bolshoi chorus and entertaining them at private candlelit dinners appeared to be one of his indiscretions. Nuri wondered if there were a drug, or some natural scheme of things that might induce Talik's demise. Death to the general and his assistant Bruna Kloski might be the only way out, but who would see to it? In the Soviet Union orderly redress for what was occurring—not to mention hundreds of other incidents Nuri didn't know about—would be next to impossible. Fiodor Talik with his Richelieu mentality was too powerfully entrenched.

Nuri was resolved to make contact with his friends behind the Iron Curtain. He had to find out if film editor Dimitri Kollontai was safe. He thought of other names at the Bolshoi. Pasha. Olga. Certainly his friend Timur Malovik would risk helping him if he knew the immensity of the threat.

One by one Nuri examined the filmstrips in detail, committing the information to memory as best he could. Occasionally he made notes. Marina had code-numbered each frame so there would be no chance of tampering in the transmittal. When he came to the frame designated END Nuri was surprised to find additional film he hadn't run through the enlarger. He glanced at the strip curiously and slid it into place.

Nuri's heart skipped a beat as he gawked at the half-dozen images before him. He didn't comprehend the drawings, symbols, and monotonous columns of data, but he did understand the words TOP SECRET, WARHEAD GUIDANCE SYSTEM, and U.S. NAVAL WEAPONS CENTER were meaningful enough.

Nuri turned on the room lights, opened the door as if in a trance, and wandered into the living room. His mind spinning, he slumped into the sofa. *What was happening? Who did these photographed documents belong to and how had he come by them?*

If he told Niles Donnell or Diana Vespucci about it, all hell would break loose and he'd probably never get out of town tomorrow. But he couldn't leave the film here or take it along. The damned priorities were shifting again. *Burn it!* He'd played the role of the *Firebird* often enough!

Nuri felt a growing anger that he was somehow being played for a patsy. Tina had given him a bundle of admonitions before leaving for Stockholm. One in particular echoed in his brain: "It won't work, Nuri. You don't stand a chance. The KGB's an unstoppable centrifugal force."

26

VENTURING OUTSIDE Stockholm's Concert Hall, Tina shivered at the cold. Winter nightfall, she'd discovered, came incredibly early in these northern latitudes. It was only four o'clock and already the festival's arc searchlights raked the sky over the city. Despite the weather, the crowd milling around the bronze, nine-figure sculpture called Orpheus was in a festive mood. Colorful, international flags fluttered in the brisk Baltic wind over the auditorium entrance. Stockholm police, aided by a group of film festival ushers in smart blue and yellow uniforms, set up a cordon around the throng of departing celebrities. Tina, accompanied by bodyguard Jon Saarto and studio publicist Polly Grant, had to fight her way through the crowd.

Tina tightened the belt on her white, woollen knit coat and pulled its mink fur collar up against her ears. Unaccustomed as she was to the climate, she felt reasonably happy; for the sake of her job she'd tried her best to put Nuri's troubles temporarily out of her mind. Her latest picture *Short Sentences*, had been greeted enthusiastically enough at the festival—at least so it seemed by aloof Scandinavian measurement. She'd noted that regardless of the Svenska Filmo event, the atmosphere in the concert hall lobby following a screening was different than in New York or Hollywood. Here there was a distinct, somber cadence, and though the scene was intellectually stimulating, it seemed to lack joy and spontaneity. Tina blamed it on the weather.

She'd already been told her picture wasn't a winner, which didn't come as a surprise. Thinking commercial all the way, First Consolidated had entered the film in the Swedish competition purely as an introduction to the European market. Harry Kaufmann was noted for commercial projects—big, flamboyant films rather than the kind with art-house and film festival appeal.

Now that *Short Sentences* was out of the running, Tina had been asked to vote on the finalists. As one of the judges, the party invitations had been too numerous to count and she'd been forced to choose carefully.

As they jostled their way through the crowd, her publicist admonished, "I don't know, Tina. You could be making a mistake. Maybe you should just cancel out tomorrow night, forget it."

Tina looked at her with impatience. Polly Grant was a bespectacled redhead, a thirty-year-old mother of two who lived in Santa Monica and had never been to Europe before. Tina suspected the highly-skilled publicity aide—who reminded her so much of *Auntie Mame*'s Agnes Gooch—was having the time of her life at the film studio's expense.

Before she could respond to Polly, Jon Saarto interposed, 'Make a note that for once I agree with the publicity department. Go ahead, cancel. Cultural representatives, *bullshit*. Natasha may be a hotshot director at Mosfilm, and this Alexi what's-his-face purports to be an important literary editor, but they're still Russians. I don't trust them." Saarto pointed Tina toward the transportation waiting at the curb.

"You're being paranoid," she shot back. They still had a distance to go through the crowd. Fighting off more elbows, Tina ignored the autograph hounds but smiled as best she could for the cameras. Giving up an exasperated sigh, she asked the publicist beside her, "What about Harry Kaufmann? What does he think of the Soviet invitation?"

Polly peeked out of her bundled scarf and shook her head.

"What can he think? Natasha Chernyskaya's an old friend of his."

Tina frowned. She turned to Saarto and said in an even tone, "Look, I may have been dead tired, but in a fit of curiosity I did accept the dinner invitation. And I owe this one to Nuri. *Contacts*, Jon. He needs them. If I can get Nuri and his irate father back to speaking again, just possibly—"

Saarto stopped so fast Tina collided with him. He looked at her, then admonished, "Nuri's not here, but in Paris. This broad from Mosfilm—you really think she's on your side? And that oaf with her? *Literaturnaya* something or other. I say *funny money*, both of them. They have to be KGB."

Tina glared at him. "Jon, move out of my way. Snubbing them would be impolite. Besides, what have I to lose?"

Polly Grant, with a perplexed look, came up between them. "Nothing. It's a free meal. Now keep moving; it's cold out here."

Saarto exhorted, "Look, Tina. I have a suggestion. Polly here has worked hard, she wants to get home to her kids. And you need a break from people. The crowds are getting to you. Forget the dinner engagement, and we all clear out of here tomorrow afternoon. Two days early."

She looked at him and laughed. "God, don't tempt me. The studio would crap."

He wasn't finished. "I'll even make you a deal. Take me off the payroll for two days. I'll foot the bill and take you skiing nearby, either Hammerby and Fiskatorpet."

"Well, well," said Polly cattily.

"Find the car, please, Jon," Tina prompted, ignoring his suggestion.

The four long volvo 969 GLE sedans at the curb all looked alike to Tina, but Saarto pointed out the one with their assigned chauffeur. Purportedly the driver was a Swedish employee of the American embassy, but Tina figured him to be a CIA operative. They climbed inside and the Volvo headed out into the congested traffic.

Tina thought about Saarto's bold invitation. The bodyguard was turning out to be more than an employee; already even Polly had called him a friend in need. But a ski trip, hot buttered rum, all the rest? She needed an alfresco affair with Jon Saarto like she needed a rotten script or an insufferable director. Tina turned to the publicist and whispered, "Would you like to go schussing with our friend in the front seat?"

"No thanks," came the immediate reply. "But if you're thinking about letting the cutting out early, I wouldn't mind." Polly hesitated.

Tina smiled. "Of course. You can start packing tonight. I'll manage tomorrow's schedule alone."

Overhearing this, Saarto turned in his seat. He looked unhappy. "What about you, Tina? Still going to dinner tomorrow night in the Old Town?"

"Yes. And you're joining me at the table. You'll love it—a chance to sharpen up your Russian." Tina thought about the Soviet dinner invitation. Profound curiosity more than anything had prompted her to accept. She'd already done everything else expected of a celebrity in this city. Swedish food was superb, and twice Tina had begged off luncheon smorgasbords in an effort to cut back on the mounting calories. The day before, as a personal guest of the mayor, she'd dined atop the Kaknas Tower, and the view of water-fringed Stockholm had been breathtaking. No wonder the city was called the Venice of the North.

As for Svenska Filmo itself, Tina had struggled to remember the many important and not so important people she'd met. Kaufmann would probably quiz her when she returned. But the glitter and glitz had been suffocating. She smiled and abruptly asked the others in the car, "Did either of you hear if Lisa Ehlmann is coming out of retirement long enough to make an appearance tomorrow? And I'm still waiting for word on the Ingmar Bergman tribute."

"I'm sick of rumors," Polly replied, shaking her head. "Fellini was supposed to fly up from Rome last night, and who's seen him?"

Tina called to Saarto, "And you'd have me leave all this excitement for a mere ski vacation?"

"After a miserable evening with the Reds, you'll beg me to carry you off."

Nuri nestled in the aisle seat of the DC-10, racking his brain over not only the woman who slept peacefully by the aircraft window, but also Tina Conner. He still didn't know whether to discuss the secret weaponry filmstrips with Diana Vespucci or not. The U.S. government's intentions still worried him, and in his panic not to be caught with the incriminating film, he'd burned it the night before. He now wondered if he could be sent to prison for this, or if he'd committed one of those vague American crimes like paper shredding.

Actually, his concern over the mysterious filmstrips had been overshadowed by what Diana had told him this morning, that the CIA was certain now that his father, Pavlin Baranov, was in mortal trouble in Moscow.

So the hounds were after *both* father and son! Apparently Fiodor Talik already considered Nuri a dead man. If such were the case, the dancer had nothing to lose playing the role of the gladiator. Somehow, he would win the ultimate game with the KGB minister; if he could find the right weapon.

Nuri glanced sideways. He still didn't know what to think about Diana Vespucci. At least the vivacious young woman had followed through in New York exactly as promised. Prior to his final rehearsal this morning, Nuri had gone for his usual early Monday A.M. hour with his speech coach, learning little more than the proper pronunciation for the new word, "mellifluous." Diana Vespucci often spoke in a *mellifluous* voice, which intrigued him.

The company rehearsal, last-minute trip preparations, and his accelerated departure for Europe had come off without any problems. The press, however, according to his fellow dancers, had been "neatly fucked over" in the process. Many publicity-eager members of the company had been angered, and a few had vented their rage on Nuri. But soon after the flight took off from Kennedy Airport, Meisenheimer was in the aisle with an apology. He gave a detailed accounting of what had happened to Nuri offstage in New York and what the group might expect in the way of additional security precautions should the dancer's problems escalate. Diana Vespucci, too, had surprised everyone by openly discussing the gravity of the situation. The grumbling ceased, and the rest of the flight had gone without incident. To the last performer, they supported Nuri completely.

The World Airways charter finally began a wide circle preparatory to setting down at Charles de Gaulle Airport. Nuri wondered about what restrictions, if any, Diana Vespucci would place on him in Paris. She'd told him earlier that he needn't worry over her working alone in Paris, that in fact she would be assisted if necessary by manpower from the Deuxieme Bureau. The French, she'd explained,˜ were highly proficient at international intelligence matters.

Diana still slept soundly. Once more he admired her peaceful, attractive face, her full, ripe body. The night before she'd slept on the convertible sofa in his living room, and they'd talked for hours before retiring. And yet he still distrusted her. Why? She'd refused to drink while on duty, but had repeatedly looked at him with wanton, sooty eyes, and the sexual chemistry between them had approached a near melting point. Only a cold shower and the portrait of Tina that dominated his bedside table had set him back on an even keel.

Nuri squirmed in the airline seat. Diana Vespucci, like many young women of Latin extraction he'd met in America, had an interesting kind of vitality. There wasn't a shy hair on her head, and in her windy, effervescent manner, she'd even frankly admitted to being oversexed. Her earthy manner was so radically different from Tina's. Intrigued as he was, Nuri wondered why the Agency had chosen such an effusive woman for their Paris operations. Somehow he had to get the temptress beside him out of his thoughts. Better yet, out of his presence. He needed Tina Conner's company badly.

Nuri was determined to find a telephone the minute the plane was on the ground and call her in Stockholm. Regardless of the hour.

The FASTEN SEAT BELTS sign flashed on and Nuri was tempted to secure Diana's, rather than wake her up. It would require a little manipulation—a hard tug here, a little probing around her body there. Nuri hesitated. Instead he gently touched her shoulder and grinned. "Wake up, guardian angel. *Nous arrivons*!"

27

CAFÉ LUNDSKALLERN was located in Stockholm's Old Town. The cellar restaurant, with its half-timbered, brick facade set off by turn-of-the-century coach lanterns, was on a cobbled, medieval-appearing street that was so narrow Tina's driver had to park the Volvo two blocks away. Lundskallern's owner had devoted the entire first floor to the kitchen as well as a shop featuring Swedish cookware and steel cutlery. A tired oak staircase led down to the popular dining room.

Jon Saarto tugged on Tina's sleeve as they paused just inside the entry. "It's too quiet. I don't like the smell of it."

She smiled back at him. "The only thing I smell is fish. What else is new in Stockholm?"

He stubbornly continued, "I think it's a setup. They'll probably record our conversation. All this will come back to haunt you and Nuri, I'll lay any odds."

"So what have I to hide? We'll make a point then of spicing it up. Judging from the reaction to their two films at Svenska Filmo the Russians could use some excitement in Stockholm."

A plump woman spread her embroidered apron in an old-fashioned curtsy, took their coats, and escorted them down-stairs. The cellar consisted of a large room with lace-covered, candlelit tables, a brick-lined alcove for wines, and an ancient wooden bar to handle the overflow customers. Tina noted that the room was half empty and her hosts had not yet arrived. The woman seated them at a cozy corner table reserved for four.

Saarto grinned at Tina. "Good. I suggest first to arrive, first to depart. We beg off early, right?"

The waiter came to take their order for drinks. Saarto groaned at the tab for imported booze but ordered Cutty Sark on the rocks.

Tina asked for Ramlosa mineral water with a twist of lime. When the drinks arrived, she touched glasses with Saarto.

"Za vashe zdorove," he toasted.

"Your Russian sounds convincing to me."

Saarto sipped his drink and grunted in agreement. "It should be. I learned it from a native—my mother. Do me a favor? Forget for the evening that I speak the language. Amazing what I can pick up playing it mute. Especially during heavy-duty conversations."

"Devious, but intriguing. Have it your way." The body-guard's eyes were consuming her again, and she avoided them. *Damn his persistence.* Tina squirmed slightly, tracing her fingernail over the patterned lace tablecloth. "Jon, I'd like to be frank with you and clear the air."

He beamed. "I'd like nothing better."

Tina hesitated. Leaning forward, she whispered, "I'm getting the uncomfortable impression you'd like to explore my erogenous zones." She waited for his reaction.

He swallowed quickly, then grinned. "We hardly know each other. But on the other hand, I'm no prude. Let's say I'd consider it a part of my job responsibilities."

"Listen to Mr. Wonderful. You don't understand."

"I am wonderful. Try me on for size."

She shook her head. "Sorry. Forgive my bragging, but my wildly athletic dancer friend is already more than I can handle. On top of that, I happen to love Nuri dearly and I'm looking forward to the moral cachet of marriage." She paused to wink. "All this despite your irresistibly charming nature, of course."

Saarto sipped his scotch. "What's wrong with encounter sex? Married love is a woman's romantic notion saddled on a man. I believe in honest relationships—whatever their duration, they should satisfy emotionally, physically, and intellectually."

Tina cocked her head. "*Intellectually*, Mr. Saarto? This coming from a former prize fighter no less?"

He looked at her pensively. "You call me *Mister* one more time and I leave you here alone to face the wolves. As for intellect—it's just one more part of the soul, lady. Socrates said to make love with the soul is the greatest victory."

"He could afford to say that. I understand he was an ugly man." Her eyes shifted to the cellar's entry. "Time for business, I'm afraid. Our somber-faced Soviet hosts have arrived." Tina smiled inwardly, watching with amusement as Alexi Stanovich came waddling toward them like a plump goose.

Natasha Chernyskaya followed close on his heels. Tina found her a striking contrast, the very picture of elegance. The young woman, appearing even more striking and beautiful than when they'd first met, wore a sable fur piece over the shoulder of a hand-painted fashion gown.

Saarto sluggishly rose to his feet. Tina offered her hand to the Soviets, making a sustained effort to be as graceful and courteous as possible. *Into the bear's lair*, she reflected.

The evening proved a heavy one. Tina worked hard to contain her festering dislike of Alexi Stanovich, who did most of the talking during the five-course dinner. The more the Russian tried to ingratiate himself with her, the more she suspected his journalistic endeavours were only a cover for more sinister KGB responsibilities. The bulky Soviet literary editor was of indeterminate age and had one of those indigenous, Asian-stock faces, set off by hair and a goatee the color of dirty dishwater. His wide lips were thick and chalk-colored and he had the quick eyes of a ferret. Stanovich's body started small at the head and got bigger, much bigger, toward the belly and hips. Too often the grinning editor would neglect his napkin and leave food particles on his goatee. Often he would speak with his mouth full. Tina tried to avoid looking at him directly.

The attractive young Russian woman accompanying Stanovich, however, proved a more than pleasant dinner companion. Over their dessert of Swedish ice cream and cake, Tina continued to study Natasha. Prestigious film director aside, she could also pass for a beautiful actress. Petite bodied, slim, with fine bones, she wore only a trace of pink lipstick to highlight her smooth, winter-ivory complexion. Her hair, sparkling in the candlelight, was the color of burnt umber, fashionably coiffed to one side and held in place by an elegant brushed-gold barrette. Natasha's eyes were the color of gunpowder and appeared just as volatile. She commanded as much attention in the small dining room as did Tina.

Unable to suppress her curiosity any longer, Tina asked, "Your burgundy and silver dress—it's stunning. Where did you find it?"

Natasha smiled. "It's one of the hand-painted creations by Moscow fashion designer Aelita."

Tina nodded, impressed. Natasha had taken her time eating, picking at her food like a bird. Her manners, unlike Alexi Stanovich's, were immaculate. She sat perfectly erect, alert, politely nodding, and seldom smiling. Tina wondered about her expressive eyes, what lay behind them and what special cinematic insight they possessed. She speculated over the Russian woman's directorial skills and what filmmaking was really like behind the Iron Curtain.

Looking up from her dessert, Natasha appeared to be reading her mind. "We seem to have taken you by surprise, my American friend? Alexi and I are not quite what you expected?"

Tina blushed. She *had* been pleasantly surprised. Her anticipation had been for an evening of swilling vodka rather than sipping moderately on fine wine. She said to her host, "Natasha, what you've told me about your film career is fascinating." She turned to the editor. "I'm equally impressed with your work at the magazine, Alexi. My escort tonight may be boring you with his silence, but you must forgive him. He's been running his legs off for me—working very hard—since early morning at the festival. I suspect he's half awake."

Alexi prompted, "Balancing work and pleasure, of course. In the Soviet Union it is called *zakoldovanny krug*—the bewitched circle."

Saarto stayed mute as he looked at Tina with impatience.

Tina said suddenly, "I'm curious, Natasha. Why did you really invite me to dinner tonight?"

The Russians looked at each other. Stanovich patted his lips with a napkin. "We are well-motivated."

A bent, bearded Swede with a viola wandered up to their

table and, without being asked, began rendering a folk ballad.
His song alternated between Swedish and English lyrics:

> "*Skara, skara havre*
> *Vemskall havren binda*?"
> Reap, reap the oak sheaves
> But who will reap them after?

Natasha and Tina smiled, but Saarto drew a blank. Alexi
Stanovich grew impatient. He brusquely waved the entertainer
away and looked at Tina seriously. "Natasha here met your
dancer friend on two occasions. I was not so fortunate. Though
I once wrote a book on Soviet regional theatre, including the
ballet."

Tina nodded and finished her wine while waiting for him to
elaborate. Once more she had to stifle an untimely urge to
smile, for the portly editor looked more like a poker player
from *How the West Was Won* than the intellectual, worldly
type.

The waiter approached and they all ordered coffee laced with
cognac. Without asking permission, Stanovich lit a long
Kazbek cigarette. Tina winced at the acrid smell.

The editor's eyes narrowed. "Ah, friendship between
different cultures is good, yes? In the Soviet Union Natasha
and I have a special friend, a very important person indeed."

Tina tilted her head.

Natasha placed a restraining hand on her companion's thick
wrist. "Later, Comrade Stanovich. You must learn to be more
subtle."

Jon Saarto shook his head dourly and interjected, "No. I
admire frankness. Please, let's get to the point."

Tina glanced at Saarto then turned back to the film director.
The salmon almondine dinner had been excellent. The wine
and liqueur-spiked coffee were beginning to take hold. She felt
a comfortable glow and was willing to go along with almost
anything—except a political argument.

The Soviet woman's eyes flashed. Abruptly, and with
firmness, she said to Tina, "Your dancer friend is sorely
missed at home, Tina Conner. You must understand the
motivation behind what we have to say."

"Missed?" Tina stiffened slightly. "Nuri has told me
otherwise."

"As have U.S. government intelligence sources," added Saarto astringently. His words seemed to hang in the air like an unpleasant room deodorant.

Glaring back at the bodyguard for several seconds, Stanovich's quavering, fat lips broke into a smile. His stomach shook as he laughed. "Intelligence! What does the *danseur noble* know or care about either CIA or KGB intelligence matters?"

Nervous, hesitant smiles were traded around the table. From her purse Natasha withdrew a folded, slightly tattered program from an old Bolshoi performance. She placed it before Tina. The program was two years old and the color picture on the cover was of Nuri Baranov paired with another dancer. The ballerina he held aloft Tina didn't recognize, but it wasn't the ill-fated Marina Pleskova.

Tina scanned the program and found Nuri's dance partner's name in large type on the second page: Glasha Tenin—one of the secondary principals he'd once mentioned. More times than Tina could remember, Nuri had mourned not being able to bring a collection of photographs and other personal mementos out of the Soviet Union with him. Tina turned the page and saw a likeness of Marina Pleskova.

"Have you seen Miss Pleskova dance?" Tina asked abruptly.

Her own voice betraying agitation, Natasha replied, "We were scheduled to work together professionally. A short documentary film." She paused, slowly shaking her head. "Most people love for the wrong reasons. They love to lose themselves, like Marina. Alexi and I both attended her graveside rite. Let us not talk of sad business tonight." Reaching across the table, she turned the program over and pointed to a curtain call photograph of Nuri bowing to a Moscow audience. "The program has historical significance for Nuri Baranov, a nostalgia piece. It is yours to keep, Tina. A delicious discovery, yes?"

Tina examined the picture of Nuri closely. She'd never seen so many flowers on stage; they were everywhere, surrounding the dancer, even caught by the camera flash in midair. She nervously looked up.

Across the table Alexi Stanovich was smiling at her, his reptilian eyes gleaming. Avoiding his stare, Tina continued to fix her mind on the Bolshoi program. The coffee continued to warm her, and she felt a familiar euphoria. Gazing at the Bolshoi cover photograph, she thought about Nuri's strength, his muscular body—lithe and cursive in tights as he made great gravity-defying leaps. And there were the perfect pirouettes. And the pas de deux—she would give anything to be his dance partner, to be held high in his arms on the stage.

For the first time Natasha sat back in her chair. "After seeing this program, you don't think Nuri would be welcomed back in Moscow? Next to our cosmonauts, who else do we have for proper heroes?"

"Unfortunately, you have more military heroes and more damned medals than any nation on earth," Saarto contradicted.

Stanovich nodded in agreement. "And they are well-earned. But still, our world is at peace and our war heroes grow old, yes? I suspect Natasha here misuses the word 'hero.' If you prefer, Nuri Pavlinovich was a notable *individual* in Soviet life."

Saarto edged closer to Tina and said softly, "Look, boss lady, do we sit here all night listening to platitudes? Ask them what they want."

Natasha smiled. "We seek nothing. We only offer you a golden opportunity."

Feeling suddenly uncomfortable, Tina retired into silence and sipped her coffee.

The Russian woman leaned forward, her golden barrette sparkling in the candlelight. "Tina dear, you must listen carefully. We would like you to come to Moscow, to meet Nuri's father, the Soviet Chairman. I am authorized to make any necessary arrangements."

Tina's heart froze.

28

In Paris, Nuri's room at the Hotel Meurice was luxurious by
any measure. He felt a little guilty and annoyed at having to
stay here while the rest of the company was billeted at the less
expensive George V. Again, Diana Vespucci had made the
arrangements, with only the maddening explanation that there
were security implications and that he should be cooperative
and patient.

Nuri straightened his white knit turtleneck and pulled on a
navy-blue jacket. It was time to leave for the theatre and the
long awaited U.S. Dance Company's debut in Paris. Kurt
Meisenheimer was scheduled to meet him downstairs in the
lobby in ten minutes and they would ride to L'Opéra with Diana
Vespucci in her rented Renault.

Nuri looked in the mirror. Brushing the lint off the lapel of
his sport jacket, he thought of Jon Saarto accompanying Tina
night and day in Stockholm. Again he felt an uncomfortable,
irrational flash of jealousy. Nuri wondered how he might
possibly arrange an even swap—Vespucci for Saarto. He
couldn't decide which would be worse—having the belligerent

private detective on his back or continuing to nurse a festering concern over Saarto's continued companionship with Tina.

The telephone on the Louis Quatorze desk rang shrilly. Nuri hurried over to pick it up.

"*C'est vous,* M'sieur Baranov?"

"*Oui.*"

"Let us speak your new language, *Comrade Baranov,*" the voice continued, in English, but with a strong French accent. "I traveled a considerable distance to see you in America. A wasted effort. You left me with some nasty lumps from the New York subway incident, *bon ami*—the garbage can, do you remember? What's done is done. I am in more familiar territory now, and you are the one who is out of his element."

Nuri exhaled sharply and asked, *"Who is this?"*

A short silence, followed by, "A well-wisher, yes? My real name is unimportant, but you may call me Khamsin. Like the desert wind, I come, I go. Always swiftly. I wish to bid you luck on your debut tonight at L'Opéra. Ah, these glamorous first nights at the theatre!" Another pause, followed by, "Give it your all my friend, for it will be your last performance anywhere."

The line went dead. Nuri stared at the phone.

The atmosphere inside the small Swedish restaurant had turned from cool to frigid. From across the dinner table Alexi and Natasha continued to look back at them with benign smiles.

Tina exchanged concerned glances with her bodyguard.

Ignoring Saarto, Natasha spoke intensely to Tina: "I personally would like you to be my guest at Mosfilm Studios." She paused, thought for a moment, then added, "I'm sorry, that is of secondary importance. A father and son reconciliation is what matters, yes? If only for a brief visit—this would, of course, be for you to decide. You should come back to the Soviet Union with us now, or immediately following Nuri's performances in Nice or London. There is time in his schedule before he resumes the season in New York."

Tina felt dizzy. She couldn't believe what she was hearing. *What kind of madness was this?* She put aside her coffee and shook her head. "Please. You needn't go on. The idea is preposterous. Unthinkable."

Stanovich scolded with his finger. "Kindly hear us out." He gestured for Natasha to continue.

The attractive film director sat forward and said calmly, "Nuri would only go back to the Soviet Union if you led the way, Tina Conner. This would be a wonderful experience for you. Perhaps you might even someday marry Nuri Pavlinovich, yes? Russian wedding receptions are very colorful and exciting." Natasha smiled and poured on the charm like thick cream. "Think of it. All Nuri's friends and relatives, a wonderful reconciliation. And much of Soviet officialdom would attend. Forgive and forget, as you like to say in English. The guests, following local custom, would carry a branch of some kind for marriage good luck—willows, acacia, and our national tree, the strong white birch."

Stanovich took over as if on cue. "And the food. Ah! I tremble in anticipation to think of it."

"I'll bet you would," Saarto conceded without smiling.

Ignoring the building tension, Natasha eagerly continued, "In Moscow, of course, it is the tradition for newlyweds to visit the tomb of the unknown soldier. And, considering the family background, at the wedding we could have Ukrainian dancers—clapping hands and singing the old regional song, 'Sinoe Platoh'—'Blue Kerchief.' Has Nuri played this favorite for you on the balalaika?"

"No." Tina hesitated. "I only discovered this past week that he was a pianist."

"Ah! Then there is a possibility you make love to a stranger, yes?" Natasha paused, her face posed now, porcelain pretty. "Most everyone in Moscow knows from our television that Nuri Pavlinovich is not only a splendid dancer, but that he has musical talent as well."

Tina felt a pang of uneasiness and defeat. She watched Alexi slowly shake his head, gathering as best he could additional arguments to support their cause.

The determined editor finally said, "You have been propagandized by the Western press and no doubt think of our country as dark, ignorant, and bestial. Such myths! Nowhere on earth could you feel such warmth as would be your reception by the Soviet peoples. The revolution has been good for our character."

Tina said swiftly, "But not good for Nuri. Nor those anesthetized leaders who made artistic life difficult for him." She felt bolder now, strong and sure of herself.

Natasha replied softly, "A past misunderstanding."

"Rather mildly put," snapped Saarto with a scowl.

Stanovich looked at him through narrow eyelids. "Perhaps you both misunderstand the revolutions's culling-out process, the party's heritage of leadership."

Tina held his glance. "Mr. Stanovich, I'm not a scholar and I make no pretense at understanding political affairs and your belief in dialectical materialism. But I do remember my drama and literature courses in college. And I vividly recall the words of Balzac:

> "In revolutions as in storms at sea, solid
> worth goes to the bottom, while the current
> brings light trash floating to the top."

Alexi Stanovich's waxy face flushed. "Come now, my dear. Let's not resort to transparent devices!"

"Balzac was a malcontent," added Natasha with finality. "Let us talk seriously of your meeting with Soviet Chairman Baranov."

Tina mustered her resolve. "I'm sorry. You don't seem to understand. For me the proposal is out of the question. I suggest you discuss the matter with Nuri."

You do not understand Russian stubbornness," Natasha complained. "He would never meet with us. He is afraid, yes?"

Saarto shrugged and leaned forward. "And why shouldn't he be? And as for tonight, how do we know we're not being confronted by the KGB?"

Stanovich chortled. "Preposterous."

Saarto tried again. "A binary agent, perhaps?"

"No. We are not of the KGB," insisted Stanovich. "Even if we were, Soviet State Security is preoccupied with nuclear physics, guided missile systems, and military microelectronics. Certainly not ballet dancers."

Tina asked in a compressed voice, "Yes, but what about ballet dancers who would be outspoken authors?"

Stanovich's eyes went dull, his expression morose. "I don't understand."

Saarto said quickly, "You're lying."

Tina waited numbly as the Russian stared daggers at Saarto. Natasha had not lost her composure. Calmly, she said, "I stand by my words. We are not KGB and you will be treated well in Moscow, Tina."

Tina could feel her bodyguard's growing contempt. Saarto had only wound up before; now came the pitch, a fastball, inside. "We've heard the fate of Americans in your beloved Moscow. It's well-known that there's a U.S. general, Austin Shaeffer, being held in prison there."

"Ah, yes! The militarist adventurer." Stanovich pointed a finger at Saarto. "We are not discussing army spies tonight, but talented artists, no? But as for this Shaeffer, our countrymen might call him a devious, spying fascist—or worse—but I am not a dinner host without manners."

Saarto bolted to his feet. "Screw your manners and your hospitality. We'll pay our own tab."

Angered now herself, Tina grabbed the outspoken body-guard's sleeve. She said to him, "*Sit down, Jon.* I've seen too many bad performances tonight. I hardly need yours as well." To the Soviets across from her, she added, "I'm sorry. I promise he'll remain silent for the rest of the evening." To Saarto she gave a hard, sidelong glance and whispered, "That is, if you plan to keep your job."

The fragile scene was interrupted by the waiter with the check, which Stanovich silently paid.

Natasha, her voice more strident than before, asked Tina, "Would you consider compromise? We are prepared to make alternate arrangements if you would be willing to accompany us to Helsinki, Finland." Natasha's eyes studied her carefully. "It is entirely possible the Soviet Chairman will come to meet you there—secretly, of course."

Tina grew increasingly uneasy; the wile of the evening was becoming increasingly apparent. *Why were they so persistent?* Abruptly, she said, "No. I'm sorry. May we be excused?"

Natasha sat erect. Sharply, she said, "Stop being the sweet, wide-eyed pussycat, my dear. You are in a most enviable position to help your paramour."

"I disagree, and I'm not interested." Tina pushed back her chair. "Thank you again."

Saarto curtly bowed his head as they both stepped away from the table.

From the corner of her eye Tina glimpsed Saarto palming off a small card to Natasha. *What's going on?* Startled as she was, Tina pretended not to have seen the incident.

"Do svidaniya," Stanovich snarled, without getting up.

Natasha added, quietly, *"So tsyetami upokoy khristos."*

Saarto gently pushed Tina up the stairs to the exit. At the top of the landing she turned back to him. "What did she say, Jon?"

"The Orthodox prayer for the dead," he said grimly. "Give rest, O Christ, to the soul of your servant."

As the hostess brought their coats, Tina said to Saarto, "That calling card you passed to Natasha. Do you want to tell me about it now or later?"

He gave her a resigned look. "The Russian lady was playing knees under the table." He smiled thickly. "I didn't want her to feel rejected, so I gave her my room number at the hotel."

"God, no wonder feminists hate men. You're more than an enigma; you're the most two-faced, sexist individual I've ever met."

"Not really," he sniffed. "When a woman's horny, I merely try to oblige the whim. I also know how to keep sex and politics separated. My own iron curtain of determination."

Tina ignored Saarto and headed for the exit.

She felt genuinely refreshed to get out of the restaurant. The air was cold and damp with the smell of the sea as they strolled along the Old Town's narrow street. Around the corner they found the Volvo sedan parked where their driver had left it, but two other men were in the front seat, individuals Tina didn't recognize. She felt Saarto tense as he pulled away from her arm, wary.

The door on the driver's side opened. "Miss Conner? And Mr. Saarto?" The man's English had a pleasant Scandinavian accent. He thrust forward his identification and Tina scanned it briefly. Something about a U.S. Trade Legation representative. Saarto examined the card more closely and seemed satisfied. He whispered to her, "CIA cover. I told you we shouldn't have dined with the Russians."

The driver hastily explained. "If you doubt our authority to replace your driver, I suggest you call the embassy for clarification."

"That won't be necessary," said Tina, anxious to get back to her hotel room. "But be forewarned. I'm tired and hardly in the mood for interrogations tonight."

The driver opened the Volvo's rear door for them. "Our only instructions are to see you safely back to your hotel."

"Fine," Saarto grunted. "Then let's move out."

As they drove down Kungsgatan, Tina felt a strange uneasiness. Possibly it was the quietude of the individual up front on the passenger side—an overgrown, brutal man with rough-cut gestures who had yet to open his mouth. His bored expression seemed almost contrived. And why did it take two of them to replace the first driver?

The Volvo sedan didn't turn toward the hotel on Tegelbacken, as she expected. Instead the driver accelerated, made two turns, and took an expressway that led north out of the city. The signs flashed by so quickly Tina didn't catch the name of the route. Was it a highway, or a *vagen, gatan,* or a *berg*? Swedish street terms left her confused.

Saarto leaned forward. "The hotel—you've missed the turn."

The only response from the front seat was the blue barrel of a .32-caliber Czech automatic that was suddenly leveled in his direction. The man on the passenger side who firmly held the weapon faced them with a sardonic smile.

"*Very carefully* Mr. Saarto," he ordered, "you will reach inside your jacket and retrieve your gun. You'll kindly note that my own automatic is aimed at Tina. I will not hesitate to pull the trigger if you make the slightest wrong move. Slowly, very slowly, slide your weapon across the top of the seat, handle first."

Tina was positive the man's pronounced accent was Slavic, not Swedish, like the driver's. She watched helplessly as Saarto complied with the request. Tina's head spun in disbelief; her stomach felt like it was filled with double-edged razor blades instead of a fancy Swedish meal.

The man up front pocketed Saarto's gun.

Looking out the window, Tina made a mental note of the route marker on the expressway shoulder; their vehicle appeared to be northbound on European Highway 3.

The driver said in the rearview mirror, "We regret this inconvenience, but it's not entirely of our making. Had you cooperated and emerged from Lundskallern with your dinner hosts, all this would be unnecessary. Now you must suffer the discomfort. You will regret your belligerence."

Tina looked at Saarto, her heart racing.

He swore, "Bastards!" The bodyguard's eyes, too, spat venom at the men up front, without effect. The gun barrel leveled over the seat back continued to stare back at them with single-minded indifference.

Tina shrugged and whispered irritably to Saarto, "So much for passed notes and a midnight rendezvous with mysterious women."

In the cobbled street outside the cellar restaurant, Alexi Stanovich looked both ways to make sure he and Natasha were alone. He motioned her into the protection of a shop doorway and whispered, "We must now separate, Natasha. You will go quickly back to the Americans' hotel. Use whatever chicanery necessary, but you must retrieve their luggage."

"Alexi, I'm concerned. How long do we dare detain them?"

He spread both hands and sighed. "It is to be determined by higher authorities. But we are fortunate, Comrade Chernyskaya. Fate is with us. Earlier, you heard the radio transmission from the planted microphone in their car, yes? We couldn't be more fortunate, comrade. Tomorrow morning you will send off a cable to your friend Harry Kaufmann at First Consolidated Studios. Sign Tina's name, of course. Be sure to place a copy of this message in her publicist's message box at the Sheraton. And you will use your creative talents to compose a delicately worded wire for Nuri Pavlinovich in Paris. He is staying at the Hotel Meurice."

Natasha nodded, but looked at him with furrowed brows. "In each message I say that Tina will be indisposed for two or three days?"

"*Nyet, nyet.* Do not use the word indisposed. Americans are less formal."

Natasha thought for a moment. "How does this sound, comrade? 'I am taking a needed holiday. Going skiing for several days, safely escorted by Johann Saarto. I will try and call you when I am situated.'"

Alexi smiled. "Excellent, my dear. Excellent."

29

FOR FIVE YEARS their ritual had continued; the first Monday night of each month the five of them would get together to enjoy a bachelor meal and spend the rest of the evening gambling in a basement room at the KGB's Dynamo Sports Club.

Originally, before Fiodor Talik had been promoted to the Politburo post of Minister of Security, the group had taken turns entertaining in their individual Moscow homes. But with Talik's increased responsibilities, secrecy requirements necessitated that they confine their comaraderie and freewheeling conversation to a secure facility that could be properly monitored by his protective staff. The basement room at the Dynamo—just below the basketball court and adjacent to the swimming pool—met their needs perfectly. If any of them consumed too much liquor, there was the steam room just down the hall, with professional masseurs to work out the kinks in their tired bodies. And there was the twenty-four-hour-a-day cafeteria to cater to their appetites.

Though the hour was late, General Talik was in an unusually

jovial, loquacious mood. With him in this exclusive Dynamo lounge were three friends, all of them reporters, from Radio Moscow, Tass, and the Novosti Press Agency. Alexi Stanovich, the fat editor from *Literaturnaya Gazeta*, was out of town at a Swedish film festival and not in attendance, but Talik really didn't miss him. Of the lot of them, Alexi was the one he was least able to confide in. The ill-at-ease feeling had grown to near distrust over the years.

Seated in comfortable, overstuffed chairs before a large, rear-screen Mitsubishi TV, Talik and the others thumbed through thick, spiral notebooks. On each page was a photograph of a horse with a number on its saddle, and beneath this, two columns of pertinent data that included the animal's age and other physical characteristics, as well as racing history, riders, and winnings to date. The sophisticated system had once been designed for Las Vegas casinos.

Fiodor Talik enjoyed this private chamber; its use was limited to KGB officers with the rank of colonel and above. Talik himself had donated the large-screen TV and gambling game to the Dynamo Sports Club with the stipulation it be used for entertainment only, and no wagering for rubles. From the start no one heeded the prohibition, just as the rule against wagering on card games had long been ignored in the KGB facility. The spruce-paneled room was small but comfortable, with several framed, color photographs of Soviet bombers and fighters lining the wall.

Fiodor Talik scanned another page in the racing game's instruction booklet. "The combinations in this collection are endless," he said quietly, glancing at several photographs of jockeys, then comparing their records. "For our next race I'm teaming up rider number thirty-two with a filly named Cinnamon Stick." Talik went to the miniature computer console, typed in the pertinent data, and returned to his comfortable chair. "While the rest of you take your usual time deliberating, I intend to replenish the vodka." He snapped his fingers and the young steward who stood just inside the door came up to him, a note pad and pencil ready for the order.

Talik requested a five-hundred-gram bottle of Pertsovka vodka, several lemon wedges, and a platter of fish delicacies on crushed ice. The steward left the room, passing Talik's KGB bodyguards, who stood attentively just outside the entry.

Talik placed twenty rubles on the table in front of the large-screen TV. His friends had not yet coughed up their wagers; they were still mulling over the racing combinations.

The image on the rear-projected screen was divided into horizontal corridors, permitting up to a half-dozen entries in each race. Since there were only four of them in the room, the game went that much faster; they used only four entry combinations at four gates.

Irritated as usual by the delay, Talik studied the others. Misha Tsvetokov. Viktor Sinyavsky. Vladimir Kassil. He enjoyed socializing with these men because they did not impinge upon his Kremlin leadership responsibilities or his secretive KGB functions in any way. These men usually drank and talked of sports or sex, but tonight the group's conversation had centered on food, this topic brought on by the tough steaks encountered earlier in the dining room at the Union of Journalists' Club. Talik once more considered his associates individually.

Misha was a program producer and writer for Radio Moscow. When sober, he was the best propagandist in all of the USSR. A self-righteous party tyrant, Misha Tsvetokov had small eyes deeply set in his forehead, an aggressive hawk's nose arched over a determined mouth, and the neck of a vulture. He was slender and quick, with all the movements of a predator.

Vladimir Kassil—the chain-smoking, managing editor for the Novosti News Agency—was a short, cherubic figure built close to the ground with dumpy cheeks and chin. He had limpid eyes and sparse blond hair plastered over his scalp with scented pomade. Vladimir was the most talkative member of the group, a perpetual complainer forever pointing out the ills of Soviet life but seldom concocting remedies.

Talik looked at Viktor Sinyavsky—the foreign correspondent for Tass, who spoke fluent French and German, plus enough English to get by. He was a big, robust-complexioned bachelor with short-cropped brown hair and a tiny, unlikely voice, almost delicate. To Talik's annoyance, Viktor often spoke in monosyllables, forcing the others to strain to hear. Reputed to be a ladykiller and a prolific patron of the black market, Sinyavsky had a craving for fashionable French colognes and underwear. All three of Talik's companions were in their mid-forties.

Cigarette wet in his lips, Vladimir ran his knobby fingers

dextrously over the computer keyboard. When he was finished keying up his entry, the others took their turns. Then they all dug in their wallets for rubles to match Talik's wager. Wordlessly, Talik activated the system with the remote control.

The race took the same time it would have taken at a track, plus a good minute of post-time hyperbole from an American announcer.

The arrogant Misha, smiling for a change, won the pot. He looked at Talik, and with the pontifical air of an undertaker, said, "Not so difficult, if you calculate carefully. One of the few imported games I enjoy, General. Much easier than fighting the crowds at the Hippodrome."

Talik said succinctly. "You like it because you win, comrade."

As one they raised glasses and drank the last of the vodka.

Vladimir glanced at Talik apprehensively. "The material I write about young Nuri Baranov—his reception in Paris. The story is of minor consequence. Perhaps it should be buried on the back pages of *Izvestia*. On the other hand, Fiodor Borisovich, if you were to tell us more about this *manuscript* of Nuri's, his apparent madness for writing mistruths, I could—"

Talik waved his hand in protest. "No, no. As I explained during dinner, the information is proprietary. It must be withheld until—"

"This is not a plenary session," Misha boldly interrupted. "Or a news conference. We're not only professionals, but your friends. A journalist needs leads."

"Mind your tongue, Misha." The slight voice of protest was Viktor's. "Our *friend* Fiodor here will have you counting the trees to Siberia."

Talik frowned. "You are like mice, fussing over trifles."

Misha persisted. "I am curious. Can the dancer write? I wasn't aware he had a gift for polemics."

"Nuri Pavlinovich is not another scholar writing historical diatribes on Stalinism," Talik snarled. "Our young defector friend prefers to tease us with his imagination. He writes *fiction*."

Vladimir said, "Ah! But didn't you say that in his initial chapters, the book's antagonist is in reality *you*, Comrade General?"

Talik scowled, adding, "But his lead character is a *criminal of the State*. In his confusion the author has reversed the role of the villain. Nuri should be writing about his father. The son's accusations are as sharp a thorn in my side as the meddlesome Chairman."

"Two boots make a pair," interposed Viktor.

Surprised, Talik looked at the tall correspondent from Tass. "That from you—Viktor the moderate?"

Viktor shrugged. Again, the small voice: "My error, The idiom was purely an observation and not an opinion. I have no quarrel with Pavlin Baranov. Why do you still dig a pit for him, Fiodor Borisovich?"

Talik smiled his secret pleasure. Viktor's comments had only partially dampened his euphoria. He thought for a moment, then looked back at the Tass correspondent narrowly. "You still sit on the fence, then?"

Misha made a point of interrupting. "Where is the vodka, comrades?"

Fiodor Talik sluggishly rose to his feet. "It arrives soon enough." The earlier drinks had taken hold, and he felt testy. He stepped to the wall of aircraft pictures, stabbing a finger at a color enlargement of a Bison-C bomber. "Gentlemen, do you know what it takes to get this Myasishchev 4A off the runway? Well over eight thousand kilos of thrust from each turbojet! *Power!* Our friend Viktor Gregorovich here needs to better understand this. *Highly concentrated, properly applied power.*" Steadying himself against the photograph, Talik continued, "History has taught us that moderate men are pushed aside by zealots as a matter of course. It was Lenin who made the Revolution, not Kerensky, Chernov, and other moderates. Absolutism means progress."

The others looked at him askance. Vladimir looked bored as he blew great clouds of smoke toward the ceiling.

Talik spoke louder, his tone a measure didactic. "I'm in the mood to speak my mind tonight, comrades. I trust none of you have long tongues."

The heavy lids over Vladimir's eyes lowered for a moment. He stubbed out his cigarette in an ashtray and said slowly, "Do I detect another anti-*glasnost*, anti-Pavlin Baranov lecture, Comrade General?"

"Glasnost!" Talik inhaled sharply. The room was deadly quiet, the amiability of the evening having vanished into thin air. Talik didn't mind at all, for it was as if he were swimming in adrenaline. Stoutly, he announced, "I detest Germans, but

they have a wonderful term for world welfare. *Weltan-schauung*—the conception of global life in all its aspects!''

Misha pushed out his vulture's neck and raised an eyebrow. ''Meaning?''

Talik sat back down and pounded a fist into the palm of his hand. ''Reality. Life as it is. I say we have had enough of our Chairman-Premier's innovation and experimentation, his pipe dream of détente with the West! The future should be an extrapolation of the past.'' Talik looked at the others seriously.

Misha rose to his feet; he, too, stood a bit unsteadily. He brusquely announced, ''Comrade General, it is late and I must leave. Lyuba will be waiting up for me.''

Talik sneered, ''You are not tired, but piqued, comrade. You still live with the woman from behind the cheese counter, no? Until you do better, you should remain here with your friends. Sit down, dear Misha, and hear me out.''

There was a knock on the door and the steward brought in a tray with a bottle of vodka, red caviar, smoked salmon, and thinly-sliced rye bread. Talik signed the check, opened the bottle, and quickly poured. The waiter departed.

Shrugging with annoyance, Misha lifted his glass. ''If I cannot leave, I drink seriously.''

They all laughed and raised their glasses.

Misha turned to Talik. ''Well? Proceed then, Fiodor Borisovich. What do you have to say?'' He gave a mock salute. ''We wait impatiently.''

Talik frowned. Always, Misha was like a dog nipping at his heels. Determined to have his way, Talik said with vigor, ''Only a fool believes that periodic wars are not *inevitable*. As long as it is human nature for men to quarrel, it is logical for nations to make war. Radiation sickness may be bad, but history is rife with crueler ways to die.''

Vladimir shrugged. ''True. Perhaps we have learned to tolerate death. Consider the world's man-made calamities.''

Talik nodded. ''*Nine million* Ukrainians and Russians died in the 1930s' famine. *Six million* Jews were annihilated by poison gas or bullets, thanks to the Nazis. More recently, almost *two million* Cambodians massacred in one man's vicious genocide.''

Viktor stared at Talik with a puzzled look. ''And you would advocate another man-made holocaust?''

''You have caviar on your chin, dear Viktor.'' Talik smiled

and helped himself to a service of salmon. He swallowed quickly and continued, "Nuclear war is a problem, but it can be solved in the laboratory of time."

Viktor said stiffly, "On one statement I concur with our former premier, Khrushchev—that after a nuclear holocaust, the living will envy the dead."

Talik shook his head. "The living will shape a new world on the bones of the old, my friend. I have had much time to consider this. Gentlemen, you don't mind that we set aside the wagering? It isn't often I can explore my thoughts with erudite journalists."

Misha looked at him. "Thoughts or *plans*? Do you use us as litmus paper to test your future policies?"

Before responding, Talik poured himself another pepper vodka. This time he sipped it sparingly. "Let me tell you about the United States, yes? Its military concentrates on sophisticated, high-profit offensive weapons. Complicated equipment that is unreliable. And unlike the Soviet Union, the U.S. has no civil defense whatsoever. Americans believe that machines and technology are important, not people; their civil-defense planning mentality does not go beyond molehill survivability. U.S. leaders do not even encourage or show their citizens how to dig."

Vladimir lit another Prima cigarette. His plump cheeks were flushed from drink. "What are you getting at, Fiodor? It is as if you are possessed tonight. I, for one, would prefer to get back to the horses."

"In all good time. Hear me out. I say let them retaliate by bombing Moscow! More Soviets will survive than Americans in San Francisco, Los Angeles, and San Diego combined! Our subway system is the largest and deepest in the world. Ah! You think our opponenets don't worry over this inequity? Consider the KGB's apprehension of the American general, this Austin Shaeffer—caught red-handed photographing Moscow's civil-defense facilities."

The Tass correspondent frowned. "But above ground our cities would cease to exist."

"With some of the inferior construction, it would be good riddance. We would start again, and do it right. More important, our center for economic gravity has shifted eastward, the most critical facilities hidden underground. Great distances separate these new growth areas from Western borders. Time, distance, and the weather have always been to Russia's advantage.''

Misha again started to rise to his feet, but Talik waved him back into his chair, telling him, "My dear friend from Radio Moscow, do you fear statistics? We have only ten cities with populations over a million—an aggregate total of twenty-five million people. This is less than ten percent of our country's total. By contrast, forty-five percent of the U.S. population lives in thirty-five cities of more than a million population.''

Viktor rustled in his chair. "Today's lust, tomorrow's locomotion, dear General? You concern me. I trust it is the pepper vodka.''

Talik sensed the chill in the room. Were they mocking him? His words, obviously, had stolen the well-being of the group, but it didn't matter; these men needed to be awakened from their stupor. "You should be taking notes for later developments, comrades, and not making jokes. I have carefully researched these matters. The Pavlin Baranov–dominated Politburo has its head in the sand. After nuclear confrontation, recovery time for the capitalist system, their GNP, would be a minimum of twenty years. In the USSR, with rigid State implementation of civil defense—protecting people and industrial production—recovery would be a matter of three or four years.''

"How many of our population would we lose?" Viktor's voice was even more subdued than before.

"Not more than fifty million. We lost twelve percent of our peoples in the Great Patriotic War against Fascism, emerging far stronger politically and militarily afterward.'' Talik hesitated. He finished off the rest of his vodka before continuing. "Today, allowing for population growth, we could absorb the loss of a third of our people and be no worse off than at the end of World War Two. The Americans can't seem to comprehend this.''

Misha's face was a pale mask. "Even if you are right, it is madness. Let's now change the subject and speak of more meaningful things—like Lenin's 'radiant future of mankind.' ''

The Radio Moscow producer ignited both Talik's pride and temper. The pompous Misha Tsvetokov was no fool, but he was an incurable romantic! "Misha, I have news for you. The *future* of the world will be in Siberia and Alaska. Both would experience only minimal nuclear fallout.'' Talik hesitated,

studying them individually. There was no mistaking the doubt
in their faces.

Viktor, who had spent considerable time in New York as a
Tass correspondent, looked back at him gravely. "If you want
to win a war with the Americans, Comrade General, you have
to start thinking like them."

"Never! Not if I can help it. They are a peculiar breed of dog
that can't be disciplined. Puppies, seeking the world's love but
never earning its respect. Laying waste to the American cities
is the only way to rid the world of imperialism and the disease
of conspicuous consumption."

Vladimir wiped the sweat from his fat neck. "We've all had
too much to drink," he groaned. But of your 'master plan,'
Fiodor Borisovich. I am curious. What of the other great
powers?"

"Japan is militarily helpless. And I would not attack
Germany, France, and England." Talik paused, regretting he
had used the pronoun *I* instead of *we*. He continued, slower,
more carefully weighing his words. "These countries will
become impotent, disorganized without the free-spending
Americans at their side. Enlightened socialism will prevail."

Misha said quickly, "And what of China?"

"Resumption of the Moscow-Peking axis will be facilitated
by a staged attack on one of China's cities—it will appear to
have been made by the Americans. Wake up, Misha. Are you
listening?"

"You have touched a raw nerve, Comrade General." Misha
slowly shook his head. "I cannot speak for the others, but my
shattered psyche needs time to recollect itself. You speak of
nuclear weapons as if they were mere toys, some new parlor
game, instead of instruments of cosmic destruction."

Viktor promptly added, "I agree with Misha. It is madness.
How can you destroy the United States without a terrible,
unrecoverable reprisal?"

Talik replied in an even voice, "We will lose Moscow,
Leningrad, Kiev, Odessa, Vladivostok, and perhaps a dozen
lesser metropolitan areas, yes. And much of our military
arsenal. But the Soviet Union is the largest land mass on this
planet, and millions of our foot soldiers will go to earth—
spread over the vast steppes and terrain that afford no ready
target for incoming missiles."

Viktor's face looked dangerously taut, but Talik went on.

"Mother Rus lost twenty million citizens in the last war, my dear Viktor. The world is overpopulated. We can lose even more of our population today. Like the lemmings—at the peak of population growth these rodents make spectacular mass migrations to the sea in an act of self-destruction. A *brilliant* solution."

Vladimir had been about to sink his teeth into an open-faced sandwich of pink salmon and caviar. He grimaced instead and put the delicacy aside.

Talik smiled and blandly continued. "Nature's culling-out process. The strong survive to continue the line. In ten, fifteen years, radioactivity will be a negligible factor. What is a score of years in the life of our planet?"

For the first time Talik felt uncomfortable. Though the vodka had made him blurry-eyed, it hadn't obscured the sharp looks of incredulity and displeasure on his friends' faces. *Cretins. They didn't understand.* Misha and Viktor looked as if they were preparing to commit him for treatment. Talik knew now that he'd spoken too freely. The bond between the others— fragile from the beginning—was shattered.

It appeared to be Viktor's turn to goad him. "Comrade General, what of this 'nuclear winter' our scientists predict will follow any missile Armageddon?"

Why were they fighting him? Had they forgotten completely the power he wielded? Carried away on the intoxication of his plans and the pepper vodka, he admonished, "The cold will numb the pain. The Soviet Union can survive on its own for a thousand years. It is a very rich land. We may not eat meat, but we will survive. If Pavlin Baranov is permitted to bring back détente, the world will never change, and that would mean a tragedy for our children and their children."

"Comrade General—" Viktor began.

Talik looked with contempt at the journalist. "Remember Berlin and Dresden after the war? And their appearance ten years later? Ruins are fertilizer, the compost for new civilizations—the stronger, wiser people of the future. *Ultimate socialism*, Viktor."

Misha mooched a cigarette from Vladimir, lit it, and stared at Talik through a cloud of blue smoke. "I'm sorry, Fiodor. We've been friends for too long for me not to speak with frankness. I don't agree with your cynical deceptions."

Beside Misha, Vladimir's double chin quavered as he

shrugged and looked at Talik with downcast eyes. He added, "Nor can I applaud these whims of yours, Comrade General."

Talik replied in a venomous hiss, *"Whims? Possibly they are plans*, no? I do not need your mealy-mouthed support, my dear Vladimir. Tend to your mindless editorials. There are many in the Presidium who will rally to my cause."

Eyes rolling back and forth between Vladimir and Talik, Misha said thickly, "The vodka affects the metabolism of my brain, but still, I detect your craving for more power, Comrade General. As your friend, I'm not a dedicated fan of Chairman Baranov; but neither do I advocate deposing him by force. Nor have I ever endorsed a nuclear showdown with the West."

Staring numbly at Talik, Viktor sputtered, "You would have Soviet Russia exchange a cuckoo for a hawk?"

Talik wasn't amused. His blind friends were more than an annoyance; they'd become a menace. And Misha, the usually stalwart party man, appeared to be the most stunned son of a bitch of them all.

Viktor and Vladimir muttered something, but Talik shook them off. They *know* what I'm planning, Talik reflected. *All three of them*. They knew the difference between drunken hypothesizing and resolute determination. Did they also sense *impending action*? Had he said too much? Talik cursed to himself. Focusing as best he could through the pepper vodka, he tried to squeeze out the meaning of this sudden rebellion. His friends had supported his driven nature before; why had he failed to ignite them now? Talik felt light-headed. His talkativeness had been inexcusable. Might these journalists commit their thoughts to words? Somehow, he would have to deflate their tires.

While Talik cogitated, the others silently gathered themselves and headed for the door. It was a moment of contrived pleasantry; each man bid him a pleasant enough good night, but there was a look of despair and coldness in their eyes. Vladimir hesitated a little longer in the doorway than the others, then he, too, was gone.

The bodyguards entered the room, attentive and expectant. One of them was Talik's personal aide, A KGB sergeant. "Shall I summon the car, sir?"

Talik ignored him, continuing to speculate on what resources he should use to keep the men who had just departed muzzled.

At least until mid-week, four days hence. By then the Politburo showdown—bloody or otherwise—would be concluded.

Abruptly, he turned back to the aide. "Yes, Comrade Sergeant. Bring my car around. But first have your men immediately arrest and detain the three journalists who just left this room. Have them turned over to Colonel Kloski with instructions that they are to remain completely incommunicado until further notice. No interrogations, and see to their comfort. But absolutely no visitors or phone calls."

"Yes, Comrade General." He saluted and hurriedly left the room.

Talik noticed that Vladimir had left behind half a package of cigarettes. Talik lit one of the Primas, savored the smoke, and tried to put the Soviet journalists out of his mind. The press was a problem in Russia just as it was in America. Talik thought about Brian Beck's vast publishing empire. The KGB's relationship with Beck was on perilous footing, for all the greedy publisher wanted was more and more money. Still, Talik couldn't have Beck eliminated just yet. The greedy American turncoat with his ready-made news network might yet prove a useful propaganda tool in the West.

While waiting for the sergeant to return, Talik was glad for a few moments' solitude. With the others conveniently out of the way, he knew his euphoria would soon return. The only distaste he felt now was the thought of going home to his ugly wife. Talik tried to keep his mind on the gargantuan mission he'd assigned himself, but again his sexual appetite was aroused.

Once more he began savoring thoughts of pretty ballerinas. Exciting thoughts, like more than one attending him at the same time. He considered two Bolshoi women in particular, and wondered what form of chicanery he might use to enjoy their company tonight. Talik even conjured a picture of Marina Pleskova in bed, but the memory of the sordid hanging scene interfered.

Talik tried to put the sordid fantasy away, but Marina's voice continued to summon him from out of the darkness. She was screaming, accusing him of lust, the debauchery of artists, and the perversion of innocence.

Talik stifled her cry by roaring back, "Beauty and power are the perfect complement, deserving of each other!"

At last he had peace, for the vodka did its work. He slept so soundly at first and didn't hear his aide reenter the room and summon him.

The sergeant had to raise his voice to a shout. "Comrade General! I've followed instructions. Your friends are in custody and your car waits outside."

30

AT L'OPÉRA it was time for the curtain to go up. Nuri stood in the wings, forcing himself to put the ominous phone call out of his mind. It was his first visit to the reputed City of Light, and threats aside, he was determined to make the most of it. Tonight was important, and he felt exhilarated. New York with its pizzazz and business hype had been vigorous and exciting, but the French capital was another world entirely. To Nuri, Paris was a rich, historical tapestry that had been stitched together by the world's master artists; he'd need time to savor its textures. Unfortunately there wasn't enough of it on his schedule.

From the first rehearsal earlier in the day he'd been impressed by the magnificence of L'Opéra. He'd discovered that the theatre was one of the few places in the world where elephants still tramped across the stage in performances of *Aida*. Nuri felt pleased that tonight this venerable, grand stage, as well as the audience out front, would belong completely to the U.S. Dance Company, and during the next few minutes,

239

specifically to Nuri Baranov and prima ballerina Annette
Lipton as they performed Fokine's version of *Firebird*.

His costume was based on native Russian dress—a fur-
edged hat, bejeweled tunic, and specially designed high leather
boots. The stylized setting of the castle in the trees, executed
on stage in soft, earthy pastels, was ready and waiting, as was
his dance partner, Annette Lipton.

Inhaling several times, Nuri primed himself for the great
physical effort of his next few minutes before the footlights. He
waited impatiently for the full swing of the melody, then
dashed out from the wings.

Ballerina Lipton's golden feathers shimmered. She was in
perfect harmony with his every move. The music's exciting
tempo increased. There was an air about this stage, this famous
building, which Nuri liked; the entire company seemed caught
up in its magic. It was something scintillating beyond his own
presence, though Nuri knew, instinctively, that he was considered the sun of the troupe, the others a scattering of
interesting planets.

Now he was alone as Stravinsky's music soared; it was again
time to conquer space, the moment for dazzling *tours en l'air*
fireworks. The *Artifice*!

Out front, even the galleries sat hushed in anticipation.

Nuri had never felt such swelling energy and intensity of
purpose. Propelling himself forward, leaping ever higher, he
danced as he'd never danced before. He held the French
audience completely spellbound.

The snow goose, batting its wings and neck tucked against
the cold, had the moon all to itself as it flew over the lonely
Swedish cabin. The log and stonework structure was the only
light for miles around the isolated countryside. Flying only a
hundred feet higher, the bird might have seen across the
forested hills to the southwest and the carpet of lights that was
Stockholm. The snow goose avoided the thick column of
smoke rising from the cabin, banked over the adjacent beach,
and headed down the Baltic coastline.

The vacation retreat was a rustic, two-bedroom affair with a
combination living room and kitchen. Tina had been locked in
one of the small bedrooms with a portable kerosene heater to
ward off the cold. She knew only that Jon Saarto's wrists were
taped and he'd been kept in the main room to be closely

watched. Since the bedroom's tiny window was barred, they'd left her unbound, though still the walls closed in on her. Nursing her claustrophobia, Tina once more checked her watch. After being locked in for over an hour, she was considering shouting and pounding on the wall.

She curled up on the bed instead and tried to sleep, but the noise in the outer room continued to distract her—loud voices conversing in Russian and a television station tuned to a Swedish station. Tina wanted desperately to be in the main room, seated beside her bodyguard. But if Saarto were still in there, why was he so conspicuously silent? She suddenly thought about his ski trip invitation, how foolish she'd been to decline.

One of her captors entered the bedroom without knocking. It was Sven—the driver who had deceived them with his phony credentials. Tina felt sure that he was a genuine Swede and not one of the Soviets. Sven had changed from a business suit into an Icelandic fisherman's sweater. Without speaking to her, he dropped an armful of books on the bed and started to back out of the room.

Frustrated, Tina called to him, "Mr. Silent? Such talkative hosts. I'm getting a very poor impression of Soviet hospitality."

He looked at her with annoyance. "My friends are Russian, I'm not."

"Of course. But still the dedicated communist, I take it."

He nodded.

She laughed and scanned through the book titles. "That explains the tired literature."

He said sharply, "I've been instructed to make your stay as pleasant as possible. You'll be permitted only enlightening entertainment."

Tina held up a copy of Tolstoy's *Resurrection* and looked at it askance. "Like this ponderous collection? I'm already well-informed on the Soviet Union. Nuri's given me ample tutoring. If you really wish to be charitable, please bring me some magazines."

Sven hovered uneasily in the doorway, his pale blue eyes glittering with zeal. "You Americans are so demanding, always in a rush. The Soviets move quickly, too, but in a more purposeful way. I suggest, Miss Conner, that you examine the volume with the blue cover. Gogol's *Dead Souls*."

Tina briefly picked up the book but on second thought tossed it back on the bed. "Release us now and I'll not only read it word for word, but see to it all my friends in Hollywood receive a copy." She smiled tartly.

Sven retrieved the text she'd flung aside and thumbed quickly through several pages. He looked up with a wry smile. "Nuri Baranov was negligent in not reading to you Gogol's famous passage about the three-horse sled, the troika. You must listen to this."

The prose came back to Tina. Nuri *had* discussed the work with her, but uninterested at the time, she'd fallen asleep. Grabbing the book out of Sven's hands, she said, "Forget it. Nuri's provided me with enough homework. I'll read it myself. Later, okay?"

Annoyed, Sven ran a hand through his receding blond hair, grumbled in Swedish, and slowly left the room.

Tina heard the key turn in the lock. Sighing with fatigue and annoyance, she perched on the edge of the bed and flipped open the Gogol work. She remembered that the Russian author was Ukrainian-born, like Nuri. Feeling more genuinely bored than curious, she quietly read aloud the passage that seemed to move the Soviets so strongly, her first love Nuri included.

> "And you, Russia of mine—are you also
> speeding like a troika which nought
> can overtake? Is not the road smoking
> beneath your wheels, and the bridges
> thundering as you cross them, and
> everything being left to the rear, and
> the spectators, struck with the portent,
> halting to wonder whether you be not a
> thunderbolt launched from heaven?"

Nettled, Tina paused. *Heady stuff.* She reflected a moment, then skipped to the end of the passage.

> "Whither then, are you speeding,
> O Russia of mine? Whither? Answer me!
> But no answer comes—only the weird
> sound of your collar bells. Rent with a
> thousand shreds, the air roars past you,

for you are overtaking the whole world,
and shall one day force all nations, all
empires, to stand aside, to give you way!''

Yuk and double yuk. So much for *Dead Souls*, she mused.
Curious, but under the immediate circumstances, hardly
inspiring. It was a rotten time for heavy thinking. Tina lay back
on the bed, staring at the ceiling. She tried, not too successfully, to put the mad, disparate elements of what had happened
into place. Nuri was in grave danger, more so than she or Jon
Saarto appeared to be.

Tina felt like a pawn. The question now was what could she
personally do to end or at least diminish the threat. Should she
try to be ambivalent with these people, fight them, or
cooperate?

Khamsin Ahmed sat attentively in one of L'Opéra's second-
balcony seats, less than two hundred feet away from his quarry
on stage. Beside him, in a low-cut gown that emphasized her
ample bosom, his lover Danielle Ponty gazed down at Nuri
Baranov with bored detachment.

Khamsin had been fortunate in picking up the last-minute
tickets to the U.S. Dance Company performance, though in
Paris anything was possible if one had the funds and contacts.
Khamsin had never lacked for either. The sight of his victim-
to-be dancing on stage hardly moved him aesthetically, for
Khamsin had never been a ballet fan. His thoughts now were
only on his setbacks of the past week.

Were he not a prudent, meticulous individual, impatience
might easily have driven him to make a spectacular play,
assassinating the Russian defector right here at L'Opéra. *While
he was on stage!* What a shock wave that would send around
the world, though Khamsin's own chances for escape would be
doubtful. On entering the theatre he'd noted a large number of
uniformed police and plainclothesmen, several he recognized
from the Deuxieme Bureau. Also to be considered was the
short-range performance limitation of the pistol he carried in
his shoulder holster.

He really wasn't worried. There would be ample time. He
would strike later tonight or tomorrow, when the dancer least
expected it. *En fin!* Nuri was doomed.

Khamsin shifted uncomfortably in his seat. He felt a slight

headache coming on. Or was it a voice calling to him in
Russian? *A woman's voice*. It was Bruna Kloski. Again, she
was reprimanding him.

Khamsin started to sweat. *Damn the KGB!* Though Kloski
and General Talik were angry that Nuri was still alive,
Khamsin had not come back to Paris empty-handed. Far from
it, he'd obtained some valuable documents and had frightened
publisher Brian Beck into more productivity. Why was this
Kloski woman treating him like a Pavlovian dog?

Beside him, Danielle had sensed his restlessness. She
reached out for his hand, rubbing the moist palm. He looked at
her expressive brown eyes and smiled, regretting now that he'd
made her suffer through the ballet. He was lucky; tonight she
was in one of her subservient moods. Danielle could be a bitch
with her volatile range of emotions. He wished they were home
in bed right now, making love.

Khamsin felt Danielle's hand tighten. The broken record in
his mind that was Bruna Kloski's reprimand faded away,
replaced by the music from the orchestra pit. The Stravinsky
theme grew louder, much louder. Khamsin felt anger as his
eyes tightened on the dancer leaping across the stage. Nuri
Baranov tossed aside his fur cap, letting his blond hair fly with
abandonment. He soared ever higher. The rest of the audience
sat awed by the performance, but not Khamsin. After his
frustrating, unproductive pursuit, his only reaction was contempt.

The Swedish cabin had warmed considerably, and Tina
turned down the portable heater. The bedroom door opened
again. This time it was her other captor—the one who had
identified himself as Gregor Rablin—who stood framed in the
entry. With a wave of his Czech automatic he gestured for her
to come out into the main room. Tina slipped off the bed and
hesitantly stepped forward.

Jon Saarto was there, slumped on the sofa, his wrists still
bound. The television in the corner had been turned off and
Rablin's partner Sven was in the kitchen whistling to himself as
he made coffee. Tina heard boots stomping off snow on the
front porch, and an instant later the cabin door creaked open.
Alexi Stanovich and Natasha Chernyskaya entered the room.
They carried luggage, and Tina was surprised to immediately
recognize it as her own and Saarto's.

Tossing back the fur-lined hood of her parka, the attractive film director looked at Tina speculatively. "We meet again," she whispered. Once more there was the soft, infectious smile.

This time Tina didn't smile back.

Stanovich pushed the baggage to one side and took off his heavy woollen coat and gloves. "Everyone is comfortable, I trust? The Swedes have a way of furnishing their country homes with all the amenities." He turned to Gregor. "Colonel Rablin, I do not expect you to put away that handgun—at least immediately—but I'm sure our guests would feel less intimidated if you would retire to that far corner to continue your vigil."

"If you insist, Comrade Stanovich," grunted Rablin as he sauntered to the end of the room. "But we can't be too cautious." Rablin spoke English with a thick, throaty accent.

Colonel, Tina reflected; he fit the role. Gregor Rablin, whose smile at her was more conspiratorial than friendly, was a big bear of a man, strong shouldered, with a six-foot-two frame held militarily erect. Rablin's battleship-gray hair was bushy but neatly cropped at the ears; his cunning eyes were deep-seated, worldly wise, the skin around them crinkled and tanned. Tina wondered if he had recently seen duty in southern Russia. Rablin was obviously the most formidable of their captors. Turning her gaze away from him, Tina looked at her luggage, wondering how the Soviets had obtained it.

Natasha again smiled amiably and explained: "We were quite thorough. Your studio has been notified, your hotel bill paid. And tomorrow morning a cable will be sent to Nuri."

"I don't understand." Tina choked out the words.

Alexi Stanovich's smile revealed tobacco-stained teeth Tina hadn't noticed in the dim light at the restaurant. He said to her, "Your private secretary as well is under the impression you went skiing." Turning to Saarto, Stanovich added, "With the bodyguard here chaperoning, of course."

Tina frantically shook her head. "But why, why?" Despite her anti-perspirant, tiny beads of sweat were forming in her armpits. She was amazed that it was possbile to perspire and shiver at the same time. Studying the hostile, alien faces around her, Tina felt increasingly apprehensive and unsure of herself.

Natasha looked at her, then over to the hearth. "You are cold? We must add more wood to the fire."

Sven came out of the kitchen and tossed two more pine logs on the fire. Dripping with pitch, they caught hold immediately.

Tina said numbly, "I'm thin-blooded, accustomed to warm climates."

Natasha's charcoal eyes sparkled with mischief. She said, "Ah, the sunshine of Hollywood. If nature has made you a parrot, it is difficult to play the role of the penguin." She pointed to the luggage in the doorway. "When you leave here you should dress more warmly. You have thermals, sweaters? Where you are going it will be even more cold."

Tina stiffened, for Natasha's words seemed to hang on her like Siberian icicles.

The film director strolled over to the bar separating the kitchen from the living room and poured several cups of coffee from the pot Sven had placed out for her. She glanced back at Tina. "Sit down, please. You will have coffee?"

Tina nodded.

Natasha glanced at Saarto, noting his bound wrists. "Can you manage the cup, Mr. Saarto?"

"I'll pass," he snapped.

Tina wearily seated herself in a tole-decorated wooden rocker. Feeling an increasing contempt for the Russian woman, Tina folded her hands and stared at the ceiling. "What did I do to deserve this?" she asked dully, for Jon Saarto's benefit.

The bodyguard shrugged, and without asking for permission, struggled to his feet. He stepped closer to the stone fireplace. Gregor Rablin didn't interfere, but his gun hand followed Saarto's every move. Grumbling to himself, the bodyguard stared in silence at the crackling blaze.

Natasha circled the room with a serving tray, offering coffee in huge ceramic mugs fired with orange roosters.

Tina took hers with milk but no sugar. In her fear and paranoia, she suddenly wondered if Natasha might be playing a shell game with the five cups on the tray, one or two of them spiked with God knew what sedative. Tina decided it didn't matter; she was miserable anyway. If they wanted to put her to sleep, fine. If Natasha were foolish enough to drug her to elicit talking, the Russians would be in for a big disappointment. There wasn't a damned thing of interest she could tell them. Tina feared only one thing: physical restraint. Since childhood she'd been unable to endure close confinement. She dreaded the thought of being bound and gagged and would give a stellar performance, if necessary, to avoid it.

So far the four of them had kept their distance, relying on Colonel Rablin's Czech automatic. Sven was armed as well. Tina still wasn't sure about Natasha and her oafish friend Alexi. She made up her mind to remain as calm as possible and try not to give the impression that she was a frightened animal, which was very much the truth.

Alexi Stanovich slumped into the place on the sofa that Jon Saarto had vacated. Folding his arms before him, he gave Tina an exasperated stare. "Do you still foolishly believe we are of the KGB?"

Tina swallowed her coffee, glad for the warmth but grimacing at the bitterness. Sven had made a batch of espresso. She sipped one more time, placed the cup aside, and looked back at Stanovich. "What do you expect after all this? I'd be insane to think otherwise." She rocked back and forth in her chair, trying to hide her nervousness.

Stanovich continued, "The only insanity would be your continued stubbornness not to assist your intimate companion Nuri. He is in considerable trouble."

Tina stopped rocking. "No thanks to you."

Natasha put aside her serving tray, sat down next to Stanovich, and glanced at Tina. "The gentleman in the corner of the room is Army Colonel Gregor Rablin, from Moscow. Our Swedish friend Sven over there works for the colonel's SPETSNAZ group as a local undercover agent—what we call a sleeper."

Saarto interjected, "Now that we've seen his dirty laundry, he's no longer a sleeper."

"All the more reason you have for trusting us," admonished Stanovich, with a shrug. "We reveal our cards, you show yours."

Saarto bounced back: "Bullshit! Where's our assigned driver?"

Sven spoke up from the kitchen. "Safe enough, in the loft bedroom. Unfortunately bound, drugged, and still asleep, but he'll be released unharmed after you have cooperated with us."

Tina felt anger. She said sharply, "I should cooperate with Soviets? KGB assassins have made attempts on Nuri's life!"

Natasha sympathetically nodded. "So we have been told. A regrettable internal matter between warring Soviet bureaucracies that must be rectified at all costs. Only young Baranov's father has the power to resolve this."

Tina anxiously leaned forward. "And what makes you think the Chairman himself is not responsible? During Nuri's final five months in Moscow father and son did not even speak."

The Soviet editor smiled. "We assume nothing; we know. As I explained, my dear, Natasha and I are friends of the Soviet Chairman. In my position as a literary editor, I am prudent. I do not necessarily write about everything I see with my own eyes, yes? But I remain alert. There are convulsions in the Kremlin over *glasnost* and Pavlin Baranov's interest in resuming détente with the West."

Natasha added, "We expect an impending Politburo power struggle. Possibly a violent one."

Stanovich shrugged, revealing again a thick, pasty smile. "Tina Conner, you are being difficult. We would like to be your friends, as well as Nuri's and his father's. You must think rationally."

Tina tried to swallow back her rage. She began rocking again, faster. Alexi was trying to soothe her with his soft, warm voice, spreading it on like balm, and she didn't like it. Tina shifted her stare to the pretty woman director who was nearer her own age and involved in a similar career. Bitterly, she asked, "And you, Natasha. Do you concur with everything your confrere has said?"

"To the letter, as you would say in America. Tina, we cannot possibly help Nuri if we're unable to reach him." She pointed to the man in the corner, the one known as Colonel Rablin, who still menaced them with his gun. "This gentleman is not from the KGB, but is an intelligence specialist from the Soviet Army's diversionary force, SPETSNAZ. He is from the elite Moscow Military District Regiment."

"You tell her all this so freely?" Calmer now, Saarto raised an eyebrow.

Rablin said quickly, "I suspect we have no choice if we are to have your cooperation in this matter. None of us favors force."

Stanovich struggled to his feet and swaggered across the room to the fireplace. He warmed his hands briefly then turned to Saarto and extended both arms expansively. "Pick up with us and we can be generous. You fight us, and we fight you."

Saarto groaned, "You've got some balls, Stanovich. You, too, Colonel, with that gun in my face. Cooperation? With my wrists bound as your goddamned prisoner—no way."

Tina quietly added, "My friend has a point."

Rablin said to her, "The constraints on your bodyguard are only temporary. Until our situation is more secure and both of you can be trusted completely."

"Bullshit," grumbled Saarto.

Tina had a jarring thought. She suddenly wondered if these people, the Soviet Premier himself, knew about Nuri's book and the initial chapters secreted into Moscow. Would the KGB have kept this vexing matter to itself? Tina needed to backtrack, do some rethinking. *Ask more questions and bid for time.*

Stanovich's coarse voice jerked her back to the reality of the moment. "In another forty-five minutes it will be time for our rendezvous. You must make up your mind, my dear. One way or another, we'll get Nuri Pavlinovich back in Moscow to confront his father. Perhaps there, in full view of the Soviet peoples, he will be safe from the KGB, the long arm with the knife. Who knows? There is even the possibility he would strengthen his father's position against certain aggrandizing KGB leaders."

Saarto looked at the Russian steadily. "You're referring to General Fiodor Talik?"

Natasha smiled. "His reputation evidently precedes him in the Western press."

Tina stopped rocking and sat forward in her chair. "You're blackmailing Nuri and using me."

Natasha smiled again. "No. We are saving Nuri's life and preserving your romantic affair. We are also securing the position of the Soviet Chairman. There are rumors that Nuri Baranov has some diabolical plans for several members of the Bolshoi Ballet's touring company. Are you a part of this?"

The Russian woman's words drowned Tina like acid rain. She lowered her head. "No, I'm not."

"Then you would do well to listen. They plan another defection, I am sure. You must stop Nuri from doing anything foolish and extremely dangerous. If not for himself, for many others. And their families."

Tina exhaled sharply. *How did they find out about Nuri's plans for Vienna?* Tina felt surrounded and outnumbered. "I demand to talk with someone from the American legation in Stockholm."

Natasha nodded. "Of course. Within a few days. But I doubt if your government has any real interest in your domestic matters. We offer you a *choice*, Tina. You come to Moscow in good faith, willingly, as my guest, visiting both Mosfilm Studios and your future father-in-law, the Soviet Chairman. At the same time you request that Nuri join you."

"Future father-in-law? Ridiculous. Nuri hasn't even asked me to marry him!"

"He will."

Tina shook her head. "Go on with your mad suggestion."

"Ah, the intricate details. These, properly, will be a family matter for the three of you to work out in Moscow. Nuri Baranov has won enough applause and victories for himself. Perhaps it is time he won a victory for the Soviet peoples and his father."

Tina exhaled and shook her head. "Now what's the grim alternative?"

Stanovich folded his hands over his paunch and said wearily, "Unfortunately, we would be forced—to coin an unpleasant expression—'to feed you to the wolves.' These two men would continue to hold you here. Our arrangements for this secret sanctuary have been well thought out, I assure you. Your captivity will be temporary, but out of necessity uncomfortable. Nuri would be informed that you are being held hostage, only to be released when he stepped off the plane at Moscow's Sheremetyevo Airport."

Tina's spirits sagged. "There will be international repercussions," she said, without enthusiasm.

Colonel Rablin smiled thinly. "Not at all. We have carefully considered this aspect. The motivation for your abduction given to the Western press—a monetary one on the part of purported terrorists—will be quite different from that secretly explained to your husband. Nuri would surely consider your safety and welfare to be a large matter compared to his making a three-hour flight to Moscow."

"A one-way trip," said Saarto flatly. "Despite the whitewash, you're all scumbags."

Natasha frowned. She went up to the fireplace beside Saarto

and ran her hands over his curly brown hair. "You're an attractive, extremely photogenic man, Mr. Saarto. Possibly, during your visit to Moscow, I'll cast you in a silent part in one of my films, yes? But first you must end your annoying belligerence." She turned back to Stanovich and said firmly, "Force will be unnecessary. Tina is a professional *actress* and she will be cooperative."

31

NURI CONCLUDED his performance with a double *tour en l'air* to the knee, then bowed his head to accept the applause. The audience immediately came to its feet, roaring with approval. Annette Lipton returned and took her own bows, and she, too, received a sustained ovation. But when the entire corps took the stage, the shouting from the balcony was unmistakable. "Nuri! Nuri, *on veut*, Nuri!"

There was no telling how long the ovation might have continued had Nuri not called it an evening with one bow deeper than the others. Slowly, he backed away into the wings.

Kurt Meisenheimer waited for him with a locked-in-place smile and a towel. Nuri apologized to the choreographer. "Those last steps," he gasped, "I'm sorry, Maestro. I felt grotesque."

Meisenheimer took hold of his shoulder. "No, no. You can bend the legs to be classically beautiful, or you can shape them for a charged effect, as you did. You looked magnificent!"

As they hurried toward the dressing room, Nuri saw agent Diana Vespucci grinning at him and applauding with the

others. Her eyes danced seductively. Nodding to her, he felt
sudden amusement in her following him everywhere. The sexy
woman hardly looked like a CIA operative, or even a typical
U.S. government employee. As usual, her body commanded
attention, and even the blasé French stage hands gawked. Her
dress, even her posture, were too unsettlingly erotic. Nuri
smiled to himself as once more she followed at his heels like a
dedicated fox terrier.

Nuri stepped inside the private dressing room and found it
mobbed. Several Parisians, many he didn't know, gathered
around him, curious; each could have been a minor character
from a Truffaut film. A short, tuxedo-clad individual with
bushy white sideburns extended his hand. "Come stay in Paris,
Nuri Baranov! Your modern Moscow is made for work, early
to rise, early to bed, no? And New York may be dynamic, but
here, ah!"

Nuri laughed. He knew the well-wisher was one of L'Opéra's
directors. Nuri shook his head, replying, "I understand,
monsieur, Paris is made for humanity, for the heart."

A nervous, hesitant laughter crept around the room. Nuri's
accompanist, Madame Dulac, elbowing the autograph seekers
away, drew up beside him. "*Eh bien*, Nuri. To be happy in
Paris, you must love it with your mind; hearts can be too easily
broken. Ah well, no matter. You will learn to avoid cheap
sentimentality." She waved a hand in the air toward the throng.
"Out! *Sortez-vous, s'il vous plait*. Monsieur Baranov needs
privacy, *oui*?"

The well-wishers backed slowly through the door. Several
hesitated. A gray-haired, diamond-necklaced dowager—Nuri
had met her before the ballet and knew her to be the mayor's
wife—tugged on his arm. She spoke haltingly in English.
"Nuri, you must join us for coffee, a late drink, perhaps? We
must discuss your brilliant execution tonight of Stravinsky and
Shosta—"

Nuri grinned and shook his head. "Some other time, please.
As for Shostakovich and Stravinsky, performing these works
tends to agitate me. I'm sorry madame, coffee affects me the
same way."

A reporter waved a pencil to get his attention. "Monsieur
Baranov does not like the *Artifice*?"

Nuri shrugged. "The audience loves it. What else matters?
"Perhaps, in one respect only, I'm like the infamous Joseph

Stalin. I dislike cacophony. Whether the choreography is Fokine's or Bejart's, *Firebird* is a gaudy ballet."

Kurt Meisenheimer stepped forward. "Nonsense. The dissonance was electrifying." Like many choreographers, he was fascinated with the music of Stravinksy.

Nuri turned to the others, who were still being urged to the door by Madame Dulac. "*Bon soir*, good friends. *Merci* and thank you," he called after them. Nuri saw three familiar faces in the doorway shouting to him, and he instantly placed them. The young dance students he'd met a few nights earlier at the Washington, D.C. hotel.

Striding toward the entry, he escorted the dozen or so beaming faces past the others, into the dressing room. The group was excited, everyone speaking at once in the vapid psychobabble of American suburbia. Nuri closed his ears to the clamor, proceeding to autograph ballet programs as rapidly as possible. From the corner of his eye he saw Diana Vespucci hovering on one side of the room, her eyes scanning each of the guests briefly with a look of expertise. Beside her stood two alert gendarmes.

When the excitement had finally settled and all their praise for his performance was expended, chaperone James Berkowitz introduced his charges one at a time.

Nuri eagerly shook their hands. "And where do you all go from here?"

"Moscow first, then Leningrad." It was a soft girl's voice. "We're very excited about it."

The young ballerina was perfect for *Giselle*, Nuri thought.

The tall, red-haired youth with glasses edged forward. Nuri recognized the student from before—his near lookalike.

"Remember me? I'm Mark. Nuri, is there a message you wish us to take to your friends at the Bolshoi?"

Deliberating, Nuri leaned back against the dressing table. He slowly shook his head. "If my book were finished, I'd let each of you smuggle in a chapter." Putting away his sardonic smile, he said seriously, "Yes. If you should meet my dancer friend Timur Malovik, ask him for a message. Bring it out of Moscow with you. Tell Timur I am puzzled, sorely concerned why he did not watch closer over Marina Pleskova. They shared an apartment." Nuri thought for a moment. "Also, I have a message for Pyotr Maryinsky, the Bolshoi's artistic director."

Beside Nuri, Kurt Meisenheimer shrugged with impatience and spread his arms. The dressing room had become uncomfortably warm, and now it was suddenly quiet.

Nuri reached for a jar of cold cream and began removing his face makeup as he continued. "Tell the Russian maestro to go to work on the Bolshoi repertoire. If he works diligently at modernizing the school, I shall someday send my children back to Moscow for ballet lessons."

They all laughed.

Nuri's expression turned serious as he quietly added, "And give the company my condolences over Marina. Her death was as much a surprise to me as to any of them." Nuri lowered his head and sighed. "I'll never understand it."

Meisenheimer interjected, "None of us do." He looked nervously around the room. "Shall we change the subject? This isn't the time to dwell on bad news."

Nuri looked up. "Agreed. We're in Paris, not in the dark, sodden world of Moscow." He lifted the cold cream jar and forced a smile. "To *La Ville Lumiere*! Have you all been to see the sights?"

As one, they nodded.

"Sacre Coeur, the Eiffel Tower, Notre Dame today." This from a young female voice. James Berkowitz added, "Tomorrow the Louvre and the catacombs."

Nuri smiled. "Ah! I went with my dancer companions this morning to the Louvre." He thought for a moment. "But this *catacombs*, you say? Interesting. I know nothing of it."

Marguerite Dulac came up to him. "Graves beneath the city," she whispered with a frown.

Berkowitz apologized: "Being short on time in Paris, we took a vote on what to do. Some of the more bizarre sights won out."

"Gruesome," advised Madame Dulac, wrinkling her nose in distaste. You would be as well off in the *égouts anciens*!

The sewers of Paris," translated Meisenheimer.

Nuri laughed. "Nonsense. Imagination is good." He looked around the dressing room, making sure there were no unfamiliar faces with big ears. "If you'll schedule your tour after my rehearsal in the morning, I'd like to go along. If I can do so *quietly*. You're still able to keep a secret for me?"

Meisenheimer touched his arm. "You forget. After rehearsal the entire company will visit the Pompidou Center."

Nuri winked at the choreographer. "You taught me that no ballet step is holy, Maestro. Nor are any of the company's free-time itineraries. The modern art can wait."

Around Nuri, the girls from the Virginia Ballet giggled in anticipation. The young men cheered. Nuri wiped off his face with a damp towel and smiled. "Until tomorrow, then? I've made up my mind."

Diana Vespucci smiled and shook her head. *The dancer sounded like a damned Egyptian pharaoh.* Diana had listened to the dressing room dialogue with concerned interest, allowing the visitation of the young Americans to run its course. Several times she'd frowned in Nuri's directon, anxious to clear them out, and each time her efforts had drawn a cutting look of censure. Obviously, Nuri was in his glory and enjoying every minute of it.

She glanced at her watch, then back to the handsome performer who seemed to radiate so much virility. Little did the Russian defector realize the infectious nature of his smile. Something awkward and unpermissible was tugging at the back of her mind. Were Nuri's vitality and sexual vibrations rattling her?

Diana knew her own weaknesses too well, and one of them was an unabashed willingness to gamble on one-night stands. She admitted to enjoying variety, no strings attached; like pressure valves, quickie affairs were a wonderful release from boredom. She wondered now what Nuri Baranov thought of her, beyond his posed iron curtain of indifference.

Her conscience suddenly rebuked her. *Stop scheming, Diana, it won't work. Nuri is happily involved. You have a job to do. Your assignment can't be influenced by trivial things like personal emotion. Redirect yourself to the task at hand, operative Vespucci.*

With an audible sigh she forced herself to take her eyes off Nuri before he caught her staring. So much for fantasies with hunky blond dancers. She would file the silliness away immediately, before she made a- dangerous, embarrassing mistake.

Diana had listened carefully to Nuri's abrupt change of plans for the next day, and the new itinerary pleased her. Very much so. The catacombs under Place Denfert-Rochereau would be far less crowded than Pompidou Center. And far more convenient for General McCulloch's three Army friends.

Slipping unobserved out of the dressing room, Diana headed for the pay telephone booth she'd seen earlier by the theatre's stage door.

Tina stood in the snow-covered pathway outside the farm cabin, her spirits at a low ebb. Now that the awaited hour for their clandestine departure had arrived, she was surprised to discover Natasha Chernyskaya had no intention of accompanying them on their boat journey across the Baltic. Jon Saarto had already been led off through the snow toward the nearby shoreline by Sven, Alexi Stanovich, and a young Russian naval seaman who seemed to have appeared from nowhere. Colonel Rablin remained beside Tina, waiting patiently for her to say good-bye to Natasha. One of his hands clutched her suitcase, the other was buried in his jacket pocket. Since Saarto had been escorted off, Rablin had put his gun away, though Tina suspected he still held it in readiness.

"Come, we must keep up with the others," he prodded.

"You'll be safe," Natasha said with finality. She started for her car, then paused, turning back and smiling at Tina in reassurance. "Button your coat before you freeze."

Tina shivered. Tightening her fur collar, she looked at the film director with reservation. "If what you've proposed is so upright and free of guile, why can't I fly with you from Stockholm to Moscow?"

Natasha stared back at her. Despite the three-quarter moon, it was too dark for Tina to accurately read the Russian woman's eyes. Natasha replied, "Secrecy, my dear. Your face is too well-known in the West and publicity must be avoided until *after* your meeting with the Soviet Chairman." She added coolly, "For Nuri's sake, especially, we must have absolute security. Certainly the KGB must not know of your itinerary. You must trust Colonel Rablin and Alexi."

Tina felt abandoned. "When will we meet again?"

"In Moscow. Do not worry yourself."

"You're being vague, Natasha."

"Alexi will bring you to Mosfilm Studios. I'll watch over you carefully from that time on. It is good enough?"

Tina nodded without enthusiasm.

"Vsevo dobrovo," Natasha added, pumping her hand.

"Peace and friendship." Smiling, the film director turned and stepped off through the snow. Several seconds later she backed a white Saab sedan out of the driveway.

Tina waited, feeling dismayed uncertainty as she watched the vehicle disappear beyond the wooded rise.

Colonel Rablin glanced at his watch and gestured toward the pathway the others had taken. Overhead, the moon had disappeared behind a cloud. The snow was only eight or nine inches deep but Tina had trouble finding the footsteps of those who had gone before her.

Her mind flashed back to an appearance in one of her parent's amateurish home movies; as a small girl she'd skipped around the patio of Grauman's Chinese Theatre, carefully placing her feet where the famous had left their permanent impressions. Sixteen years later Tina had placed her own celebrity footprints as big as life in the wet cement. And finally, down Hollywood Boulevard a short distance, there was her own star blinking back at her from the sidewalk!

The moon came back out and she saw the footprints in the snow more clearly. The trail from the farm cabin to the beach descended gradually for several hundred feet, then leveled off before dipping between two rocky crags to meet the shoreline. The little bay, set between a steep wall of granite on one side and a natural rock jetty on the other, was well-hidden. Small swells broke gently over a gravelly, agate-strewn beach that sparkled in the moonlight.

Tina looked up in amazement at the seventy-foot-long, camo-painted air-cushion vehicle nosed up on the beach. She and Colonel Rablin came up beside the others. Saarto stood close beside her as the Russian seaman steadied the boarding ladder that extended over the sea skimmer's flexible apron. Alexi Stanovich was already up on the deck, conversing with the crewmen.

Though the prospect of a midnight boat ride had no appeal to Tina, the brisk sea air was refreshing. She felt far better than she did confined to the stuffy farm cabin. She looked at Saarto, glad his wrist bindings had been removed. "They're finally convinced you won't fly the coop?"

He frowned back at her. "How could I? I'm being paid to protect you, remember?" He pointed to the air-cushion craft before him. "Ever been on one of these hot-air machines before?"

She shook her head. "Have you?"

"Four yeas ago in Finland." He quickly explained, "It's used there and in the Soviet Balkans for passenger service. Called a *Skate* and carries a couple dozen people. I suspect this baby is a military version." Saarto looked up to the deck. At Stanovich's urging, he proceeded up the boarding ladder.

Colonel Rablin called after him, "You are correct, Mr. Saarto. This is a 'Gus' class surface skimmer, assigned to the Soviet Navy. At fifty-five knots cruising speed, we should be in Tallinn in just under four hours."

It was Tina's turn at the ladder. Saarto waited at the top, extending his hand. When she was safely on deck, Colonel Rablin and the Russian seaman on the beach came on board. The Swede named Sven headed back up the beach toward his cabin.

Rablin immediately escorted Tina into the narrow center cabin, urging her to take a seat and try to be comfortable.

Saarto would like to have stayed out on deck, but the speed of the craft would prevent this. The thought of being cooped up for over four hours in one of these deafeningly loud tin cans repelled him. He glanced to seaward, then back to Stanovich, who was watching one of the seamen bring in the boarding ladder. Saarto boldly asked, "Supposing we have Swedish Navy visitors?"

Stanovich looked back at him, empty-faced. From the Russian's expression, it was clear he had the same concern. Saarto heard Stanovich repeat the same question, this time in Russian, to the young naval officer standing in the cabin hatchway.

The officer, apparently the surface skimmer's commander, replied quickly to Stanovich, "Only an outside chance, comrade. Our forces have set up a major undersea diversion thirty miles down the coast near Spillersboda. The Swedes are more interested in submarine penetrations than a remote blip on the radar that nine times out of ten turns out to be one of their own fishing boats. Or at worst, a straying Finnish trawler."

Saarto fought back an urge to comment that the air-suspension vehicle's tremendous speed would be picked up on local radar scopes, but he wasn't about to let on that he understood Russian. Not yet, anyway.

Minutes later, when he was seated beside Tina in one of the aircraftlike, orange flotation-cushion seats, he understood more fully about the coastal radar situation. Their skimmer moved excruciatingly slow, under twelve knots.

Colonel Rablin explained, "We take no chances until we are out of Swedish waters."

Some twenty minues later, as they passed through the neck of the Alands Hav, the hull beneath them quivered and the skimmer accelerated, taking off across the peaks of the waves like a hydroplane.

Rablin said to them, "We're fortunate. The wind is moderate. The weather prediction for our Baltic crossing and entry into the Gulf of Finland is for reasonably calm seas."

Saarto looked at him in the dim red light of the cabin. He wondered what "reasonably calm" meant. Through the vessel's side ports they could see the stars were out in full, with only a few spotty clouds in the sky. The moon was higher now, and slightly behind them. He turned to Tina. "You prone to seasickness?" It was an awkward try at igniting conversation, in any event foolish because any attempt at dialogue was difficult under the loud din of the engines.

"No," she replied. "If I get ill, it's over worse concerns than the sea."

Colonel Rablin smiled and shouted from across the cabin, "You'll not experience mal de mer on a suspension craft. The journey will be smooth as glass."

Alexi Stanovich ignored them and shuffled up front to join the vessel's commander in the small wheelhouse.

Gazing at Rablin, Saarto again raised his voice to be heard over the roar of the aircraftlike engines. "Why this, Colonel? What happened to those super-fast Soviet hydrofoils we've heard so much about?"

Rablin smiled and moved two seats closer so he wouldn't have to shout. "It was necessary to use a Soviet Navy vessel. The smaller patrol craft—the Slepens, Stenkas, and the Pchela hydrofoils—are all operated by the KGB frontier guards."

Saarto was impressed. Their captors had covered all the angles.

The colonel's eyes remained on him. Rablin smiled thinly and explained, "We are under special assignment; most secret orders from the Navy Chief of Operations, who in turn receives instructions from High Command and the Ministry of Defense."

Tina looked up. "And the KGB. How does it fit into this?"

"Not at all. And that's why you are so fortunate."

Saarto leaned forward. "A proprietary question, Colonel. What's the difference between your SPETSNAZ Brigade and the so-called diversionary forces of the KGB?"

"From your standpoint or mine?"

Saarto frowned. "Why the qualification?"

Rablin paused to light an American cigarette; he took his time, savoring the filtered smoke. Finally, he responded. "From the standpoint of Soviet security, an important difference; but this is classified information, my nosy American friend." He hesitated, smiling again. "Suffice it to say, we belong to the Central Army Sports Club, while our KGB counterparts are members of the Dynamo Sports Club. That is all you will be permitted to know. You must simply trust me."

Saarto glanced at Tina, watched her shrug and look the other way in boredom. She appeared to have shut down for the rest of the night. Tina looked tired, but with the noise from the three 780-horsepower gas turbines, he doubted if either of them would get much sleep during the crossing to Soviet Estonia. He watched Colonel Rablin turn on the small reading lamp on the arm of his seat and bury himself in a Leningrad newspaper.

Saarto didn't mind Tina's retreat into silence at all; it would allow him time to think, come up with a plan. He'd already made up his mind to give the impression of tacit cooperation, but at the very first chance was determined to get through to friendly Western authorities—preferably American and the CIA. Back home they needed to know where they were, what the hell was going on.

Saarto flashed on his former assignment with Brian Beck, recalling that muckraker's ability to sensationalize and spread the news. If action in the way of spectacular headlines were required, Beck might be the man to get the ball rolling. No, Saarto mused, things weren't that fucking bad, not yet. Still, he had to break ground somewhere. Tina, in her panic over Nuri, could become too damned malleable; God knows what the Reds might talk her into doing.

Saarto sat in silence for a good half hour, trying his best to pull the abstractions into sound, workable realities. There had to be a way out of this mess and he was determined to find it.

Colonel Rablin finally tired of the newspaper and turned out his reading lamp. Saarto got up from his own seat and strolled across the vibrating deck to the window on the port side. He suddenly wondered if the term port and starboard applied to a speeding air cushion. Christ, was he on a *boat or a plane*? Because of the dim, red glow of the skimmer's interior, Saarto could see the moonlit sea outside perfectly. He continued to stare at the horizon for several minutes.

Saarto felt a warm hand on his shoulder as Tina came up to him. She, too, appeared restless. Together they watched sea spume splash over the bow of the craft and temporarily obscure the glass of the port. Saarto looked at her beside him and measured out a smile. "I've done a rotten job for you so far, boss lady."

Tina looked at Saarto in the strange crimson light. "*Boeuf merde*, or if you prefer, bullshit. Pardon the cheap vulgarity, but where would I be without you? Alone with these vultures?" Feeling his arm move hesitantly against her, Tina tightened.

She edged away slowly, an inch at a time, trying to make her retreat seem less of a spurn. Some inner summons told her to return to her seat immediately, avoid an embarrassing scene, try for some sleep. But she was restive. Ignoring her conscience, she continued to stare out the window beside the bodyguard. The steady roar of the skimmer's engines was like a dirge for her, the sound becoming increasingly foreboding the farther they moved away from the friendly Swedish shoreline. A *Russian sound*, she reflected. *A warning*?

Tina gazed out over the Baltic, acutely aware of the gravity of her predicament. Right now she'd give anything to be beside Nuri to confront the Soviets as a unit. Together. *Getting to Nuri*, that was the plan she'd rationalized in her mind, and she'd do it whether Jon Saarto helped her or not. She exhaled slowly. At present she *didn't* have Nuri beside her. There was only Jon Saarto. Her heart skipped a beat as the bodyguard's arm brushed against her again, warm and comforting. *Damn him!* This time she edged back quickly, without embarrassment.

Tina didn't need Jon Saarto's closeness, but she did need his strength. She'd be glad when the short voyage was over and they had docked at Tallinn.

Saarto pointed through the glass. Before Tina's eyes, far off to the north, the horizon opened up into a string of sparkling lights.

"Helsinki," Saarto said in her ear. "My grandmother lives there. A shame we're passing it by. She'd have rolled out the red carpet for the two of us."

Tina looked up at him, twisting her lips. "Where we're going I suspect I'll see enough *red* carpet."

The sea swells gradually changed direction and the skimmer yawed, wallowing momentarily in the troughs. Tina braced herself and grabbed Saarto's arm. The Soviet pilot adjusted the throttle, eased the rudder slightly, and the craft steadied as it picked up speed.

Tina quickly let go of Saarto's arm. Backing away from the glass port, she went back to her seat and retreated into silence. Saarto, his face blank, slumped into the seat beside her.

Alexi Stanovich came out of the pilot house and found a seat at the front of the cabin that faced Tina and Saarto. He said nothing, continuing to stare at them with the satisfied look of a zoology professor admiring a pair of prize specimens he'd just collected.

Unable to sleep, both Saarto and Stanovich continued off and on to glare disfavorably at each other, but Tina, despite the overpowering clamor of the skimmer's engines, lowered her head and dozed off.

32

NURI STARED uselessly at the carved traceries on the hotel room ceiling. Despite his body's fatigue, he couldn't sleep. Though the one calling himself Khamsin had yet to show his face or telephone again, Nuri still couldn't believe what had happened a few hours earlier when he'd retired to his hotel room. He'd immediately placed a call to Stockholm, reasonably sure he would rouse Tina. Though they weren't scheduled to talk again until tomorrow night just before dinner, Nuri had felt a fit of impatience and loneliness. He'd also wanted to tell her of the resoundingly successful reception Paris had given the U.S. Dance Company. Hardly was he prepared for the shocking news from the Sheraton-Stockholm's reception desk—the word that Tina Conner, her personal secretary, and bodyguard Saarto had all cancelled their remaining reservations and checked out a few hours earlier. It didn't fit.

Nuri's irritation mounted. Where had Tina gone? Why had she changed hotels without leaving a forwarding address or sending him a wire? True, there had been the good luck message and flowers she'd sent to his dressing room at

L'Opéra, but these had obviously been arranged for earlier. His mind wandered, conjuring up possible explanations that ranged from somber to downright silly. It was entirely possible she was en route to Paris to surprise him, or had even gone ahead to set up a warm welcome in Nice, the next stop on the tour. Tina was like that; she would go a long way for a silly surprise. There was also the remote chance that Harry Kaufmann might arbitrarily have called her back to Hollywood.

Nuri stretched, turned on the bedlamp, and looked at his watch. It was almost four in the morning. He had to put the uneasiness away. This wasn't the first time he'd momentarily lost track of Tina because of conflicting schedules, and it probably wouldn't be the last. If he didn't see her pretty face today in the flesh or receive a phone call or telegram before dinner as scheduled, he'd contact the Hollywood studio. In the meantime, sleep was a priority or he'd be useless for the second, and last, performance the next night at L'Opéra.

He turned off the light. In the room he could just make out the carved flowers in the plaster filigree that bordered the ceiling. He wasn't sure, but he guessed they were morning glories. Monotonously he began counting them as if they were sheep. He finally lost count, drifting off into a frightful dream where the sheep had become horses.

The nightmare was familiar. Nuri saw legions of Oprichniks—the dreaded secret police who fulfilled Czar Ivan's bloody dictates; the barbarous men who dressed in black, rode black horses, and swarmed through the country with dog's heads and brooms hanging from their saddles. The dog's head symbolized their task to worry the Czar's enemies, the broom to sweep treason from the land. Again they were chasing Nuri, but this time it was through the streets of Moscow! The dancer was forced to run for his life, and when he looked back, he saw that these hounds were not the ancient Oprichniks, but the men of the KGB. And there was a woman among them!

The sea skimmer arrived at the Soviet naval facility docks in Tallinn an hour and a half before daylight. Colonel Rablin and Alexi Stanovich escorted Tina and Saarto ashore and into the back of a waiting Ziv sedan. "You are fortunate," Rablin explained to her. "By landing a military base, we have avoided both the Soviet Customs office and the KGB frontier guards."

Tina was too tired to be relieved or even care. She heard Jon

Saarto mumble another of his periodic objections to Rablin, but she couldn't make out the words and didn't ask the bodyguard to repeat. They were driven to a small brick navy officer's barracks near the dock, where she and Saarto were permitted to clean up in separate quarters. The building appeared to be heavily guarded. Her room had a narrow, tightly-made bed in it, and Tina wanted to crash immediately, but she'd been told sleep would have to come later. Alexi Stanovich brought in her luggage and told her to hurry. She was to be permitted a hot bath, change of clothes, and breakfast.

The ornate tub with its exposed brass fittings reminded her of the one her grandmother once used. Beside it, hanging on the spotlessly clean, light blue tile wall, was an old wooden-handled brush that looked like the one she used at home to bathe Sasha. Tina ignored it, musing that her back didn't need scrubbing as much as it needed a good massage. Substituting her own bar of Dove soap for the distasteful-smelling orange one the attendant had provided, she settled back in the water and tried to unwind.

After forty-five minutes the attendant—a large, hearty woman in a khaki dress—knocked on the bathroom door. In fractured English she told Tina it was time to leave.

Tina felt better after stepping out of the bath and briskly drying off with a thin, army-issue towel. Dressing informally, as Colonel Rablin had instructed, she put on a cotton blouse, heavy sweater, and woolen slacks. Minutes later, checking her watch and following instructions to the minute, she met Jon Saarto and the others down the hallway in a sparsely furnished lounge. Saarto was already seated beside Alexi Stanovich and had been served a cup of hot milk and what appeared to be a cheese Danish. *Hot milk*, Tina reflected. She hadn't been offered that since she was a child with the chicken pox. The food however, intrigued her.

"*Vatrushki*," explained Stanovich, pointing to the pastry. "Sit with us please. We eat a small breakfast, for now there is more hasty travel." He clapped his hands and the matronly woman who had prepared Tina's bath came out of a side room with another tray. "Perhaps you prefer *bulki* instead—the sweet buns?" asked Stanovich. He helped himself to both.

Tina sat down on a tired brown leather sofa, nodded appreciatively to the woman with the tray, and selected one of the *vatrushki*. The woman attendant, who now wore an incongruous white ruffled apron over her khaki uniform, padded off, again without any sign of recognizing Tina as a celebrity actress. Nor had the navy men on the sea skimmer.

It suddenly flashed through Tina's mind that she was a nonentity in the Soviet Union, for her movies had never been shown here, either in theaters or on television. The Soviet public knew absolutely nothing about Tina Conner! She wondered if the Russians knew anything at all about what had happened with Nuri's career in the West.

Sipping the hot milk, Tina felt an odd, new kind of exhilaration. The thought of temporary obscurity strangely excited her. Picking up a napkin from the large serving plate, she noted the Cyrillic letters adorning its outer rim.

Saarto lifted his cup in a mock toast to her as he read the inscription aloud: "Long live communism—the Radiant Future of Mankind!"

She returned his wry grin.

Alexi Stanovich didn't smile. He looked at Saarto askance. "You read Russian very well."

Tina's pulse beat faster. *Damn Jon. Why had he tipped his hand?*

The bodyguard didn't bat an eyelash. Apparently aware of his error, Saarto took a deep breath, smiled, and said calmly, "How I wish. No, Mr. Stanovich. It's just that I've seen that plate before. One of your Soviet athletes presented several during a TV news interview. The Sarajevo Winter Olympics."

Stanovich held his glance for a long moment, then changed the subject. "Colonel Rablin is preoccupied, making contact with Moscow. We expect to leave as soon as he rejoins us."

Seized with curiosity, Tina looked sharply at the plump literary editor. "Alexi, I've a question. In the United States we don't always hear the truth about Soviet national moods, what the people on the street across your land really think."

Stanovich nodded seriously. "The mood of the population in a given city might be assessed. National temperament of our varied peoples—it is *impossible*."

"Moscow, then," she persisted. "Regarding Nuri's defection. I know the official line, but what was the public's reaction?"

Stanovich frowned and thought for a moment.

While waiting for his response, Tina bit into her *vatrushka*. She found it tastily lined with sour cream.

Across from her Saarto put down his coffee and said abruptly, "It's too damned early in the morning to talk politics." He shot a cross look at Tina. "Save your breath, boss lady. Just eat and drink your milk."

Disregarding him, Stanovich said to Tina, "Contrary to what you may believe, not all Russians are interested in ballet or care about dancers. I enjoy literature, and sports, but rarely go to the theatre."

Tina pressed her point. "Still, you're an alert journalist."

His voice betraying agitation, Stanovich said, "Nuri Baranov was sorely missed. It is as if he had disappeared forever, into a *black hole*. But we Russians are an ancient race and understand such things as rapid change, sudden deprivation. The world is full of disappointments."

"I understand," Tina replied. "In the theatre we say the show must go on."

Stanovich nodded in agreement. "During the German final offensive against Moscow in 1941, Lepeshinskaya calmly danced *Swan Lake* at the Bolshoi."

Colonel Rablin strode into the room, interrupting their conversation. "I'm sorry," he stated, "we're unable to fly in to Moscow. Sheremetyevo, Domodedovo, Bykovo, and Vnukovo airports are all too intensely watched by the KGB. It would be impossible to slip past them."

Stanovich was on his feet. "Have you an alternative plan, Comrade Colonel?"

Gregor Rablin said evenly, "Yes. We leave immediately by automobile for Leningrad. From there we take one of the fast express trains to Moscow."

"But the railroad station on our arrival?"

"Our army contacts will find a way to stop the train temporarily just outside the city, where we'll have a vehicle waiting."

Tina's spirits ebbed. More long hours on the road! She and Saarto were both about to speak at once, but Colonel Rablin gestured toward the door.

"We leave now. You can talk en route," he said sharply. "The car is outside, and Comrade Stanovich, you will drive."

The cobblestoned streets of the Estonian city were deserted except for a few streetcars beginning predawn runs. In minutes they were outside Tallinn, eastbound on the two-lane highway to Leningrad. The limousine was an older model Zil but had been reupholstered and smelled of new leather. Stanovich drove with authority and Tina found herself involuntarily bracing and holding on to Jon Saarto's arm. Colonel Rablin, alert as usual, sat up front on the passenger side. The car raced along the empty night road among snow-covered copses, pine groves, and an occasional stand of fir. There was a transceiver radio in the vehicle, and Rablin, monitoring the transmissions, kept it at full volume.

Tina stared out at the darkened countryside, taking in whatever she could see of collective farms, logged-over forests, sleeping villages. Occasionally a freight truck would roar by, blinking its headlights. She brooded, again wondering where Nuri was at his moment. Tina wasn't afraid for herself, but she was terrified over what might be happening in Paris.

After several kilometers, hearing a succession of high-pitched tones on the radio, Colonel Rablin sat forward in his seat. There was a moment's silence and the sound repeated itself. "We're being alerted." Rablin warned Stanovich. "Pull off the highway as quickly as you can. Find a secluded area and douse the lights."

Stanovich nodded, slowing the car and scanning the edge of the road. Finding a wooded-over area, he edged the Zil gently off the pavement between some currant hedges and overhanging trees and killed the engine.

Tina exchanged concerned looks with Saarto. *God, what now?* she wondered. The army colonel checked his watch and settled back as if expecting a lengthy wait. *For what?*

Rablin turned to face Tina. To her surprise, he calmly began relating the pleasures of Leningrad. He told her that there would conceivably be time while waiting for the train to show her a few of the sights. Tina was unimpressed; the only things she wanted to see were a hotel room and a bed.

They all looked up as the sound of a helicopter approached.

"KGB frontier guards. A regular patrol of this route," Rablin explained. "They travel in our same direction, toward the east, and will not return." Sullen-faced, he turned to Stanovich, who sat poised in readiness behind the wheel. "Give them a five-minute lead before turning on your lights and proceeding." Gazing out the window, the colonel added, "You won't need your lights for long. Daybreak is upon us."

Saarto sniffed, "The mighty Soviet Army hides in the woods from the KGB?"

Rablin turned and looked at him with contempt. "Obligatory only when the army finds itself with such *sought after*, talented company," he said sharply, jerking his head toward Tina.

The beat of the helicopter rotors overhead drowned out any further attempt at conversation. A brilliant light methodically probed the pavement in front of the aircraft. The pilot swooped low along the road, but they were under cover of the trees and remained undiscovered. Tina looked out the window. The sky was just beginning to lighten in the east as the frontier guards' helicopter soared past them, moving rapidly on up the highway.

33

BACK IN LOS ANGELES it was one of those hazy winter mornings. When L. Brian Beck was in residence at his Bel Air estate, he spent most of his time in his antique-furnished, combination den and office where the temperature was kept at exactly seventy-seven degrees. The publisher liked the number seven, considered it lucky. Regardless of the temperature outside, his guards and staff assistants never opened the tall French doors overlooking the spacious patio and statuary-filled gardens. Even the room's humidity was controlled by sophisticated equipment that required little monitoring.

Sitting behind a carved walnut desk on a thronelike chair that looked as if it might have come from the Escorial Palace, Beck shouted impatiently into the telephone. Before him was his usual skimpy breakfast—an almond croissant, a small glass of orange juice, and an assortment of vitamin bottles.

A valet struggled to attach a prosthetic right foot to the stump that was Beck's ankle, but the agitated publisher squirmed so much the aide was having difficulty. Across the paper-cluttered desk sat two restive editors who had been called in from Beck's Century City headquarters; both women fussed with the contents of heavy portfolios while waiting for Beck to get off the wire.

He spoke sharply into the receiver. "Don't trifle with me, operator. I'm a busy man. Either put through your caller from Sweden or try later. I'm hanging up." Beck heard a series of clicks, then an excited, familiar voice. "L.B.? This is Phil Grundy. I'm in Stockholm."

"I'm aware of that, you cunning paparazzi. I still pay the bills around here, remember? Get to the fucking point."

"I'm sending a half-dozen rolls of film back to New York tonight. Hand carried by a foxy stewardess friend. Good candid stuff, couple of bizarre couplings you're going to like. Especially that French bitch Yvette Caret. Sorry boss, that broad couldn't act her way out of a Keystone cops comedy if she were part of the chase. But that's not why I've called you personally."

Beck swallowed a couple of vitamin capsules, washing them down with orange juice. Polishing away some fingerprint smudges on the marble base of his pen holder with the cuff of his shirt, he said impatiently, "Well, I'm waiting, Grundy. Explain."

The valet finished lacing up Beck's plastic foot and left the room unthanked.

On the line the photographer's voice continued in measured tones. "I'm not sure, but I may be on to something big. Juicy tidbit for the supermarket tabloid now, maybe some stronger stuff later for the slick. Tina Conner's just up and disappeared."

Beck leaned forward in his seat. "What the hell you talking about, disappeared?"

"That's what I said. Checked out of the hotel, no forwarding address—so help me, that's the official word." Grundy hesitated. "You know me, I start probing right away. Hold onto your ears, boss. The Sheraton's cashier claimed the hotel tab was paid by a woman other than Tina's publicist; what's more, there was some kind of rumor that the superstar just bailed out on the festival and took off on a ski trip."

Beck exhaled impatiently and shifted in his chair. Ignoring the women editors, he scratched his crotch. "So what? And speak louder. It's a rotten connection."

Grundy raised his voice. "Get off my case, L.B. There's

plenty of 'so what.' Tina evidently dismissed this Polly Grant and went off alone with your former bodyguard, Jon Saarto. Nuri probably doesn't know shit about it. And wait until you see the cozy dinner shot I picked up on the plane on the way over. I've got a hot lead here, Brian, and I'd like to follow it up. I owe this Saarto a little surprise.''

"Owe him?"

"Call it a personal grudge."

Beck smiled and said flatly, "That makes two of us." Beck thought for a moment. Grundy's probing sounded better to him all the time. *Street* could use a big-name headline, some incriminating photos. The trendy stuff—fad diets, arthritis cures, increased sex life, secrets of longevity—had become a drag for Beck. Next week he'd tentatively scheduled an exposé dealing with the sexual persuasion of a leading male rock singer. A bombshell on Tina Conner and Nuri Baranov— insinuating a sleazy love triangle would easily upstage that. It was the kind of material the tabloid might milk for months. There was also Beck's plan to incriminate Nuri Baranov on other matters. *The planted filmstrips*. And this exciting new exposé would play neatly into Beck's plans. It was perfect, almost too good to be true.

"Good work, Grundy. It appears I may have Tina Conner finally eating out of my hand, not to mention First Consolidated Studios and Harry Kaufmann kissing my ass. Keep digging and work fast. You need some extra help over there, hire it. Whatever layouts you come up with, I need a mug shot of Nuri's reaction. You listening?"

"Yeah. I follow. But what about Moscow? We have any contacts there for background info on the dancer?"

Beck hesitated. He couldn't help smiling to himself. "As soon as you're off the wire I'll work on it. But your job's to find Tina and my old pal Saarto, then get your ass over to Paris. If necessary, follow that ballet tour, keep after the pretty blond kid in Milan and London. If you can't make Saturday's deadline by air carrier, send your best shots on the laser or satellite.''

The rented Renault darted in and out of traffic on Boulevard Raspail. Nuri was glad that Diane Vespucci knew the French capital so well. He'd quickly discovered she had all the requisite skill, nerve, and ruthlessness of the typical Parisian driver. Morning rehearsal had gone well for him, but half the day was over and still he'd received no word from Tina. Now he could only hope she'd call during their previously arranged hour later in the day, just before dinner. In the meantime, watched over by the woman CIA operative, he'd venture out on the city with his new friends from the Virginia Ballet Academy.

Nuri and Diana arrived at the area above the catacombs ten minutes early. Parking the car, they set off for the pavilionlike entry. Diana raised her voice to be heard over the din of the frantic traffic circle. "Look at this!" she shouted. "With its seven outward radiating avenues, Place Denfert-Rochereau has become the busy Etoile of the Left Bank!"

Nuri ran across the street, trying to avoid the kamikaze traffic. Glancing at his watch, he noted that it was just after two. His ballet student friends had chosen to take the Metro to meet him here at the eighteenth century pavilion that was the catacomb entrance.

Nuri and Diana were approached by two grumbling Frenchmen from the Inspection Generale of Quarries, each of them carrying a heavy-duty flashlight. They promptly insisted that the underground chambers were not ordinarily open on weekdays and that they were being inconvenienced; indeed, someone had pulled strings with their superiors to arrange the special group tour.

Nuri smiled at them as they all waited. The dance students finally arrived, their manager James Berkowitz leading them across the plaza from the Metro station. After an extended round of greetings, they entered the pavilion as a group.

Nuri had to laugh at his suddenly not-so-brave bodyguard Diana, who seemed cheerfully transparent about the security arrangements.

"Sorry, Nuri. I have a lightweight stomach. If it's okay with you, I'll stand watch at the top of the stairs."

The tour guides assured her that although visitors normally were taken some five hundred yards through the labyrinth of galleries to exit at 36 Rue Rémy-Dumoncel, construction work was in progress and today they would explore only the nearby section. Under the circumstances, Nuri and the others would exit from the same entrance they went in. The entire maze, one of the guides explained, was reputed to contain the remains of nearly three million people, and the thousands of skeletons they did see should more than sate their curiosity.

Diana seemed satisfied. She remained at the pavilion entry while Nuri—albeit apprehensively—descended a spiral staircase with the others. The air was damp and smelled musty, and he was surprised to find bright electric lights illuminating the steps. In the limestone-walled underground passages below, he saw what appeared to be hastily erected strings of electrical wire and more lights. "I expected that we would burn torches to find our way, as in ancient times," he said to the guides who went before them. "You have all the modern conveniences."

One of the Frenchmen shrugged with indifference. "*Non.* Only temporarily, while the contractors labor to maintain the site. But who knows how long this will take? Now the workers are gone, on strike. I prefer it when we go back to flashlights and torches." He pointed to the electrical wire. "The amenities are unsightly, *oui?*"

"But comforting," said James Berkowitz.

"*Aux morts*—to the dead," Nuri said boldly. The tour was every bit the macabre experience he'd expected, and more. What they discovered beneath the Paris streets was a vast honeycomb of ancient, worked-out limestone quarries; crammed inside these wormholes were stack after stack of human skeletons.

Nuri swallowed hard as he stumbled on. Dust-and-fungus-covered sanctuaries piled high with bones set at intervals along the tunnel—too many ghoulish chambers and crypts to count. The temporary lights of low wattage, placed with stinginess, enhanced the eerie tableau.

Nuri paused when one of the ballerinas called out to him from the rear of the group. He remembered her name, *Karen.* Working his way back along the line of drained young faces, he came up to her. She held up a Polaroid flash camera.

Too gleefully for the mood of the place, she asked him, "Nuri, may I take your picture? There, before the skeletons."

Nuri shrugged, arched his eyebrows and peered into a large niche where anonymous bones were heaped in a grotesque altar. Reluctantly he ventured inside, leaned gingerly against the pile and waited while she took the picture. Under the circumstances, he didn't feel like smiling.

Seconds later, together, they examined the print. In the *tour de mort* surroundings Nuri might have passed for a prosperous undertaker or the grim reaper. They couldn't help laughing. He took Karen's picture in return, and she made a distinct point of smiling.

"During the Nazi occupation, the Free French went underground here," Nuri explained, trying to be helpful. "These chambers were purportedly the headquarters for the French Resistance."

The girl frowned and came up to him. "It's gross. An ugly charnel house. Let's catch up with the others, please."

Suddenly the lights went out.

Nuri felt for Karen's hand and held it tightly. She started to tremble. It was pitch black, but from somewhere up ahead they saw the brief flicker of a flashlight. Nuri heard a loud scuffling sound, followed by cursing and shouting in French. The glimmer from up ahead went out. Total darkness surrounded them everywhere; an inky opaqueness more intense than Nuri had ever experienced before. In the distance he heard what sounded like violent blows, more commotion, then footsteps pounding in the tunnel. Then the frightened wail of a teenage girl. Other voices, those of the young Americans. They were talking rapidly, crying, calling out.

Nuri's heart thudded. The fear he felt was unfamiliar, and it gripped him like a rigid, unrelenting vise. It suddenly occurred to him that he'd made a tragic mistake, endangering the others. Where was Diana Vespucci when he needed her? And his promised French police protection?

His enemies *knew he was here. Forewarned.* They would never give up, that was how KGB reprisal worked. Viselike— closing in slowly at first, then tighter and tighter.

The girl beside him squeezed his hand. "Nuri, we just can't stay here in the dark," she moaned. "Where are the others?"

"Hold onto the back of my jacket. I need both hands free to work your camera." Immediately he set off the electronic flash and found his bearings. "When I move, you do likewise."

They staggered forward, making their way down the tunnel with repeated flashes of the camera strobe. They found the rest of the group. Berkowitz had his arms clasped around two tearful girls.

"What happened?" Nuri asked, setting off another flash toward the wall, away from their eyes. In the sudden harsh light a row of skulls eerily glared back at him. Nuri grimaced, this time welcoming the returning darkness.

"We don't know." The voice belonged to Berkowitz. "The guides—up ahead. When the lights went out, I think we were ambushed."

Nuri edged forward, setting off two more flashes toward the far end of the tunnel. He saw two familiar figures a short distance apart on the ground. The French guides! Nuri stumbled on, clicking the camera shutter until he drew up beside them. He wondered how long the camera's battery would hold out.

One of the guides appeared to be unconscious, sprawled on the tunnel floor, while the second man groggily sat up and rubbed his head. He pointed into the dark tunnel, away from the route they'd come. "*Ils est parti dans cette direction! Appelez la police!*" Nuri noted that both of their flashlights were missing. *Yes, police*, he reflected. They needed help. Nuri was determined to remain calm; he had to find out if the immediate danger was over or merely beginning.

The conscious guide started to swear, again speaking urgently in French. "*Depechez-vous! Arretez ces hommes.*" The Frenchman gestured rapidly with his hands. Nuri knew he had to get to the street, signal Diana Vespucci, obtain help. The ballet students would be safe for the moment. They were innocent bystanders—he alone was the target.

The only way he could make it was to run back through the blackness, setting off the camera at intervals, only when necessary for orientation. His enemies were here somewhere in this underground maze; they had flashlights and would be waiting for him. But he couldn't just sit here and cower—he had to keep moving! Nuri could feel the cold sweat beginning to form on his forehead.

In the darkness he could hear the labored breathing of the second Frenchman on the ground beside him. He was coming around. The first tour guide appeared to have calmed down, and with difficulty he said in English, "You—the one with the flash camera, *oui*? Make it work again, monsieur."

Nuri obliged him. The group blinked; all of their eyes, Nuri's included, were getting an uncomfortable workout.

The guide crawled on his hands and knees along the far wall of the catacomb. "Again the light," he cried.

Berkowitz kept burning paper matches, but they only dimly lit the chamber walls and kept going out in the draught. Nuri set off another flash, at the same time seeing what the guide was after. A short distance away on a low platform was a skull-and-crossbone display, apparently set up by some humorist to avoid tour monotony. Several thick sanctuary candles, caked with dirt and dripping with wax, rose behind it.

Berkowitz scrambled after the guide and offered his match-book. When a couple of the candles stayed lit, everyone let out a sigh of relief, including the second Frenchman, who moaned, held his head, and struggled to sit up.

Nuri glanced at Berkowitz. "Everyone all right? You'd better count heads."

One of the boys, glancing nervously around him, cried out with alarm, "Mark's gone! He was right here beside me before the lights went out!"

Nuri thought quickly. *Mark*—the tall, red-haired, muscular dancer, who in the darkness, without his glasses, might easily have passed for himself! Nuri cursed under his breath as he re-created in his mind what had happened. The voice on the phone—*Khamsin?* Or someone else? Like the men pursuing him in Manhattan?

Nuri said quickly to the others, "All of you must wait here until I can bring help. You can't search for Mark without more lights."

Nuri retraced his steps back down the tunnel, repeatedly setting off the flash camera as he staggered through the darkness. At last he reached the spiral staircase.

Pausing at the top to catch his breath, he found the electrical switch for the lights below had been switched off. He turned the power back on. Nuri emerged from the catacomb's pavilion entrance and blinked hard at the daylight.

He was stunned to find Diana Vespucci missing. He shouted her name, his heart beating erratically. Nothing but the swirl of traffic.

Nuri swore loudly, first in Russian, then in English. Pedestrians on the nearby sidewalk ignored him. He looked around the traffic circle. Spotting two gendarmes, Nuri ran over to them, pleading loudly in Franglais and gesturing as best he could that a tour group was in trouble in the catacombs below.

Tina grew increasingly uncomfortable. Sitting quietly in the back of the big Zil, she wished she could be visiting Russia under different circumstances. Leningrad turned out to be one of the most beautiful cities she'd ever seen. Even with the overcast, diffused winter sky, it had a romantic, almost poetical mood.

Colonel Rablin's authortative voice, however, thick with propaganda and droning on like a dutiful American Express tour conductor, had become increasingly wearisome and irritating. Beside her, Jon Saarto, too, appeared sleepy-eyed and annoyed. They had been threading through the city for a little over an hour, Rablin and Stanovich explaining that it was necessary to consume time until their train was ready for boarding. Not once had the two Soviets permitted Tina to get out of the limousine to stretch their feet and see the city's purported delights at close hand.

Rablin spoke to them again. "There, on the left bank of the Neva, is the Winter Palace, built in the eighteenth century." He turned, smiling sagely at Tina and ignoring Saarto. "Everywhere, you must admit, Leningrad is a great symphony in stone."

Tina looked at him seriously. "Colonel, I'll admit the golden statues, the architecture, the fountains, and pastel-hued squares are stunning. But as long as we're here, I'd like to go inside the Hermitage to explore, to meet some of the people. Nuri told me Leningrad is a city of musicians—might we visit just one? At least a quick look inside the Kirov Ballet Theatre?"

Rablin glared at her, then studied his watch. "Unfortunately, it is not possible. We will go now to the Moskovsky Station. Our express train will soon depart." His tone became more apologetic as he added, "We must take extreme care. The KGB has its *stukachi* everywhere."

Beside her, Tina could feel Saarto's zest for contention again stir. "Colonel," he said slowly, "your team's been damned informative and you can keep me up all day and night for all I care. But the lady here needs sleep. For her sake, I suggest you find us hotel rooms for a few hours and arrange a later train to Moscow."

Tina had given up on any thought of immediate sleep. Only half listening to Saarto's argument, she was preoccupied gazing out the window at the passing cityscape. She was fascinated that most of Leningrad's taxi drivers appeared to be women.

After a prolonged silence Alexi Stanovich sullenly looked

back at her bodyguard in the rearview mirror. "We're all tired, Mr. Saarto, but the answer is no. Tonight you'll both have comfortable accommodations at Moscow's Cosmos Hotel."

Colonel Rablin added, "The Moscow express will take four and a half hours and you'll have a private compartment. You can rest then as well."

Saarto said unenthusiastically, "Privacy. I'll bet. Don't forget to lock us in."

Rablin didn't respond, pointing instead to the brilliant gold spire of the Peter and Paul Fortress.

Before he could begin another of his prolonged spiels, Tina said calmly, "Yes, Colonel. I know. You needn't explain." She smiled without feeling. "One more gilded trinket of a possessed despot."

"*Dispossessed*," Stanovich snidely interjected.

34

NURI FELT mournful and murderous at the same time. Standing beside the Place Denfert-Rochereau traffic circle, his thoughts spun as crazily as the nearby traffic. Under the circumstances of Diana Vespucci's abandonment, he wasn't sure what to do next. The French police had brought the tour group up from the catacombs. His new friends were shaken but safe, except for Mark Washburn, who was still missing. The gendarmes had called for additional help then gone back below to resume their search.

If Nuri were to get away and find Diana Vespucci, now was the time. A vacant taxicab approached. He hailed it, jumped inside, and told the driver to take him back to the Hotel Meurice on the Rue de Rivoli. Traffic was heavy and the trip to the Right Bank seemed to take forever.

Damn Diana Vespucci! The mysterious bitch from the CIA had fucked him over. Nuri wondered if a part of him had wanted something different after all, like a little erotic sport; had they made love back at his New York apartment, he just might have penetrated Diana's defenses as well and sensed the scam. Why had the CIA operative suddenly abandoned him?

Nuri paid the cab fare and hurried into the hotel lobby. He hesitated by the desk, considering his next move. Again he silently cursed the U.S. government. Nothing made sense anymore.

Under the circumstances he might call Kurt Meisenheimer or the dance company's road manager to ask their help. Nuri remembered it wouldn't be possible; the entire company was out touring the city, probably en route to Pompidou Center. Nuri decided to call Diana's room, which was next to his own; she might have returned to the hotel for some inexplicable reason. From the beginning the alluring woman had been annoyingly unpredictable. Nuri felt anger. White House endorsement or not, the CIA's value to him had become a matter for conjecture.

He found a lobby phone and asked for Diana's room.

No answer. Irritably he replaced the receiver and headed for the reception desk. There was a number at the American embassy he could call, but he would try it from his room. The clerk behind the counter handed him his key and, along with it, RCA and Marconi telegrams. Nuri glanced at them speculatively, but waited until he was in the elevator alone before ripping open the envelopes.

The first was dated Stockholm and was from Tina. He read it with amazement. According to the wire, she'd tried, unsuccessfully, to reach him several times by phone. When? *He'd received no messages.* Leaving the Svenska Filmo early by two days to go skiing in the Dalarna Mountains? Nuri raced through the remainder of the message. The sentences were stiffly formal, economizing on words. Odd, he reflected. Not once had Tina skimped on telegrams. He read the cable again, then shook his head in disbelief. It wasn't what Tina said that bothered him so much, but the peculiar tone—and the information that had been left out. Like some indication of where she would be staying or when she might next try to call him.

Feeling an increased uneasiness, he unfolded the second cable. *From Moscow!* Nuri's heart did a flip. This couldn't be real, he thought; he had to be dreaming. How did his father know he was staying at the Meurice? The message was short and to the point:

IMPERATIVE THAT YOU TELEPHONE ME
IMMEDIATELY STOP VITAL MATTER OF
MUTUAL INTEREST STOP REGARDS
PAVLIN BARANOV. 7CCCP5 65412

Nuri noted the important personal dialing codes, recognizing them to be his father's Kremlin office and the country dacha. The elevator doors opened and Nuri tucked the messages away in his pocket, hurrying down the hallway to his luxurious suite. Diana had told him his two-night stay at the exclusive hotel was being paid not by the CIA, but by a group of wealthy Parisian ballet benefactors.

He paused in the hallway before Diana Vespucci's room. Minutes before, he'd let her phone ring for what seemed forever; he didn't expect a response now, but still he knocked. Hesitating in the corridor, Nuri thought again about his father's cablegram, the surprising, untimely request to telephone Moscow. After what he'd just been through in the catacombs, he was tired and admittedly afraid; he needed a hot shower and a few minutes alone to ponder. It was almost three here; at the Kremlin it would be two hours later; still plenty of time to get through before his Chairman-father left for home at six.

Giving up on Diana's room, Nuri stepped quickly to the next doorway, unlocking the suite that had once served as headquarters for the German general who was Hitler's personal commander of Paris. With its Louis XVI furniture, bibelots, and Aubusson carpet, the accommodations were too grandiose for Nuri's Ukrainian upbringing. When Nuri had first arrived, the bellman had spent a full ten minutes cultivating the dancer's taste for the suite, in particular telling him all about General Dietrich von Choltitz.

Nuri entered and closed the door behind him. Leaning against the wall, he exhaled sharply. The catacomb incident, Diana's disappearance, Tina's strange telegram, the sudden appeal from his father—it was too much, more than his brain could handle. He was a dancer, not a detective.

Blinking, he saw there was something else. His brown flight bag had been removed from the baggage rack near the closet and tossed on the bed. Clothing was flung everywhere. He went to the luggage and saw that the lining was slashed.

"*Bastards!*" He needed to think clearly, take a shower—not

hot, but cold! No, there wasn't time. *At least rinse his face in the basin.*

Nuri hurried into the bathroom. The door was open, the overhead light left on. He stared. A pair of woman's panties were tossed beside the sink. Halting in the doorway, his spine stiffened. The room reeked of cologne. Before him the elegant, brocaded curtain that framed the tub enclosure was partially torn from its rod.

A woman's arm hung limply over the edge of the bathtub.

Nuri's heart froze, for he immediately recognized the pearl ring and perfect, plum-colored fingernails. His first impulse was to call out "Diana," but his breath caught in his throat.

He inhaled deeply, straightened, and stepped into the room. Flinging back the shower curtain, he stared down into the tub in disbelief. Diana was half nude, wearing only the blouse she had on when he'd last seen her at the catacomb entry. But now she wore an additional accessory—one of his own neckties. Thickly knotted in the middle, it had been drawn tightly around her neck, pinching her skin into washboardlike folds. Her blue face and glazed-over, lifeless eyes stared up at him accusingly. Nuri could feel the prickles of sweat forming on the back of his neck.

His mind flashed. *The motive?* Raped, then murdered, or murdered and raped as a convenient afterthought? A wave of nausea pulsed through him. He stood riveted in horror, unable to turn and move his feet away. He wanted desperately to run, but he couldn't even walk.

At last the numbness dissipated. But as he started to back slowly toward the door, he caught the sound of a body shifting, a slight noise behind him. From the corner of one eye he saw a slight blur, an object poised and ready to fall. Nuri whirled.

From his hiding place behind the bathroom door the assailant lunged forward with a second necktie stretched taut between clenched fists.

Nuri barely avoided the garrote by hurling himself the other way, twisting toward the commode. The force of his rush propelled the assailant forward where he struck the tub, nearly falling on top of Diana Vespucci's body.

Racking himself upright, Nuri kicked up and out with his powerful legs, causing his opponent's body to slam against the wall. It was the wiry-built individual with the sharp-boned, pockmarked face—the same man in the leather coat who had pursued him back in the States! *Khamsin.*

Nuri vaulted over the toilet toward the door, but he couldn't escape. His nimble assailant grabbed one ankle, pulling him backward. Nuri held onto the door casing, his mind reeling with panic as he tried to decide what to do next.

Panting and mumbling to himself in a mixture of Arabic and French, his captor twisted hard on the ankle and pulled. For his size Khamsin seemed to have the strength of an ox; his yellow eyes blazed as his free hand groped inside his pocket.

No more neckties, Nuri flashed. *This time it would be a gun!* Summoning what strength he had left, Nuri rolled over and kicked his adversary in the stomach. The assassin let out an agonizing hiss and folded like a beach chair. In a simultaneous movement Nuri brought up a knee to the chin, propelling Khamsin's body backward. The assassin's head landed with a sickening thud against the porcelain rim of the toilet.

Determined, Nuri struck again, this time with his fist, an uppercut to the right eye. The blow wasn't necessary. His would-be killer was already out cold.

The bathroom was caught up in an eerie silence, the only sound Nuri's hard breathing as he stood poised in the doorway. Glancing at Diana's body, he figured he was being strangled himself—on the frightening alternatives. For the first time he turned back the clock, wondering miserably if he should have remained in the Soviet Union. The price of his freedom was becoming costlier by the moment.

Nuri stumbled back into the bedroom, throwing off his sweater and unbuttoning his oxford cloth shirt, now soaked with sweat. From the closet he took out another shirt and quickly pulled it on. He grabbed his jacket, a razor and toothbrush from the scattered belongings on the bed. There wasn't time to pack.

He wondered if his enemy who lay inert on the bathroom floor was working alone. If so, Nuri had to get out of the hotel before his opponent came around. He started for the entry, but hesitated, glancing back at the phone by the nightstand. *Wait*, he'd forgotten his father's telegram.

Nuri paced the floor briefly, then made up his mind. As instructed, he would put the call through to Moscow. But first he would have to bind his adversary in the other room.

Nuri went back into the bathroom. He tried to avoid the

repellent scene in the tub, concentrating as best he could on the limp form in the leather coat slumped against the commode. The man would win no prizes for appearance; the scarred streetfighter's face reminded Nuri of a rotten coconut. *Was he still alive?*

Inching closer to the still form, Nuri felt for a heartbeat. No problem, the victim's pulse remained steady. Nuri poked inside the leather coat, finding an East German .22 automatic and a suede wallet with identification. The man's name was Najeeb Ahmed, not Khamsin. Nuri was confused. Then he found several personal cards bearing the engraved imprint *Khamsin*, followed only by a telephone number. Satisfied, he kept one of the cards and tossed the wallet aside. He briefly weighed the gun in his hand. He decided to keep it.

Nuri rolled the assassin on one side and retrieved the necktie he'd dropped earlier. Khamsin wore an expensive Swiss watch and reeked of cologne. Nuri held his breath as he carefully bound the unconscious man's wrists and ankles. He took his time with the knots, making doubly sure. Satisfied at last, he left the bathroom and closed the door.

It took only moments to get the long distance operator on the line. Nuri gave her the priority access code numbers Pavlin Baranov had supplied on his cablegram. The French operator insisted that she would have to call Nuri back when the circuit was completed.

He glanced again at his watch and scowled, remembering that it took time in Moscow for the intelligence cogs to fully mesh gears—the KGB's intricate process of determining which calls were worth monitoring and by *whom*. An international conversation conducted from the office of the Soviet Chairman would undoubtedly be given priority attention, perhaps directed to the attention of KGB Minister Talik himself. Nuri blanched. What could be so important that his father would take such an accepted risk? Whatever, Nuri would weigh his own words carefully.

Fresh air, that was what he needed. While waiting for the operator to call back, he had to get away from this place that reeked of violence. He strolled to the tall window, opened the shutters, and strolled outside. The sounds of traffic on the Rue de Rivoli carried up to the Meurice balcony where Nuri pondered his next move. *How much should he tell Pavlin Alexandrovich of these violent events, if anything?*

Before Nuri, to the left, was the Louvre, with its cold stone wings framing leaf-strewn gardens. To the right a bumper-to-bumper necklace of cars circled around the Place de la Concorde, for the late afternoon traffic rush had begun. In the distance the Eiffel Tower soared through the traffic smog into the early winter grayness. Though Nuri really wanted to think about his personal balance sheet, the striking Paris landscape weighed stronger in his mind.

He reflected again on Dietrich von Choltitz, who had stood on this same balcony forty years earlier. The German general had been faced with the decision of whether or not to follow Adolf Hitler's mad orders to destroy Paris, raze it to the ground rather than allow the city to fall into the hands of the advancing Allies. Nuri, too, knew what it was like to be outnumbered—a pursued man on more than one front.

The wait for the telephone to ring was intolerable. Nuri thought again about Diana Vespucci, how she had strangely deserted him only to come to this room to be killed. *Why?* And he'd arrived in time to be next! Had she been the one who had rifled through his belongings or had it been Khamsin?

The Soviet Secret Police had a resolute, one-track mind and would never give up. If one of their hunters failed, Bruna Kloski and her ilk would merely send out another. And another. Contract killers, for the right price, were a glut on the marketplace.

The telephone rang shrilly inside the room. Nerves tightening, he turned and reluctantly stepped toward it.

There were four occupants in the light green Peugeot sedan as it headed swiftly down Boulevard Raspail. For the twenty-year-old American dance student guarded in the vehicle's rear seat, the glamour and excitement of discovering Paris had abruptly gone sour. The three men who had abducted Mark Washburn had suddenly discovered that they had the wrong individual, and they were upset.

Mark was afraid and let it show. After examining his passport, his captors had argued and cursed each other, trying to fix the blame for the blunder that had occurred in the catacomb tunnel. They'd wanted *Nuri Baranov*, not him.

As the car slowed and turned into a quiet side street, the driver glanced back, gesturing with his head. The silent, grim-faced individual beside Mark suddenly opened the door, at the same time pushing hard.

Mark rolled into the street, thumping on the cobblestones like a rag doll discarded by a petulant child. His head finally came to a stop against the curb. The Peugeot accelerated and disappeared around the corner.

For Mark the impressions of the incident were blurry, coming and going with irregularity. In his daze he had no feeling of time, only blurred, hard to distinguish faces. The words he heard were all in French, and he translated with difficulty.

"Is he alive?"

"Yes. There's a steady pulse. His head struck the curb."

"An accident?"

"No, no. He was pushed from the car. I saw it."

"See here, in his pocket. An American passport."

The conversation drifted out of Mark's mind. His temples throbbed and he felt sick. The fractured, fuzzy visions would come and go. Curious faces. Breath heavy with alcohol. He saw a staggering, well-meaning *clochard* pushed back by a gendarme. Now ambulance attendants, followed by an oscillating siren.

When Mark Washburn woke up again, he focused vaguely on a wall plaque: AMERICAN HOSPITAL IN PARIS.

35

THE SNOW, accompanied by a blustering, bone-chilling wind, had fallen steadily in Moscow for most of the afternoon. With the weather outside turning grim and raw, the city and its people once more turned inward. The shift in temperament of his Kremlin office staff had not gone unnoticed by Chairman Pavlin Baranov. The Soviet leader had thought several times today about his fortunate son Nuri in Paris, able to drink espresso at a sidewalk café along the Champs Elysées without risking frostbite. Finally Baranov had made up his mind. For far more important reasons than discussing the weather, he'd placed the long-distance call to Nuri.

Baranov sat forward at his desk, scribbling on a note pad as he spoke sharply into the phone. The conversation had continued for nearly ten minutes and still his words had made no impression whatever on his son. Nuri had been miffed at the abbreviated nature of his first call—a request that the dancer go forthwith to the Soviet embassy in Paris where a secured line to Moscow was available. An hour later, when the circuit had been completed, Baranov had placed most of his cards on the table. Nuri, too, had come up with some surprises.

The crude KGB attempts on his son's life were a shock Baranov hadn't been prepared for. The conspiratorial Fiodor Talik would require far closer observation, beginning immediately. Of course, Baranov didn't tell Nuri of his plan, the U.S. Army Intelligence teams, and on the Soviet side, the borrowed SPETSNAZ Brigade people—all assigned to apprehend the dancer. Nor had he mentioned the impending trade of General Austin Shaeffer. Baranov now debated in his mind whether it was time to tell Nuri that he had Tina in safekeeping. He said into the receiver, "Yes, I'm still on the wire! I was thinking. It's a matter of culture, my son. You will never be happy in the West. You'll have one foot in the grave."

Nuri's voice came swiftly back, "You waste my time speaking in circles. Be more specific."

"You're young. Time is passing for imperialism, Nuri. Can't you see this? The West staggers from boom to bust, bust to boom, until it becomes weary and shaky. Soon capitalism will lose its footing at the edge of the grave and socialism will triumph by default. Return, Nuri, while you can."

"You look for the wind in the field, Father. But it is gone and will not return."

"You are an artist. It is your destiny to serve the State, your own culture."

There was a moment's silence, then again, his son's abrasive voice came over the line: "Return for what? Protective internal exile? Hypnosis? Psychotropic drugs? Do you take me for a fool? I'm aware of Russian artists. Like Maxim Gorky, who was practically a prisoner in his last years at a villa in Soviet Russia. There are many, Father, who insist that Gorky was murdered at the instigation of State Security."

Pavlin Baranov exhaled swiftly and sat back in his chair. "Stalin's security forces, not mine."

"With Fiodor Talik, there is no difference. You do not control the KGB."

"You are being impertinent."

"And you have no insight whatever on the meaning of freedom. Do you think I'm not aware of your own Kremlin power struggles?"

"Nuri, listen carefully. You'll reconsider when you understand my position."

"Your position, it appears to me, is to save your own neck. I cannot help. I'm sorry. I only suggest you retire while there's still time."

Baranov grimaced with displeasure and gripped the phone tighter; his son's insouciant manner was one thing, but rude advice was another. "You misunderstand. Whatever my motivation before, my position now is to protect *your* life. And I can't do it outside Soviet Russia's borders." He paused for a moment. "And there is the matter of Tina, saving her embarrassment, yes?" Baranov had let the cat out of the bag; there was no going back now.

There was a stunned silence on the Paris line. Finally Nuri said to him, "I don't understand what you're talking about. Let's not bring my friends into these matters."

Baranov straightened his shoulders and spoke with incisive clarity, "She *is involved*, my son. Tina is on her way to Moscow at this very moment." He listened for the faltering voice he knew would come over the wire.

"You've never lied to me before; why do you grossly fabricate now? Tina is in Sweden—at a film festival." Nuri hesitated. "She is safe."

"If you doubt me, call Stockholm. Try to contact her."

A stunned silence. "The skiing. You know something of this? *Where is Tina?*"

"She is unharmed, in proper Soviet company, en route now from Leningrad to Moscow. Tina Conner has already sent word to me. She is cooperative where you are not. And she is anxious for you to join her here."

"A lie. Tina knows better. I want to talk to her."

Baranov said quickly, "That can be easily arranged, of course. She will be our guest tomorrow at Mosfilm Studios. And in the evening I intend to personally escort her to the Bolshoi Theatre. She will meet the friends you left behind and she will have a press conference. Nuri, you will *listen* to me. It is in your interest to catch tomorrow's Aeroflot flight from Paris to Sheremetyevo Airport. My aides will meet the plane and escort you safely past the KGB. We must appear together, as a family, in the Bolshoi dignitary box. And then—"

"Never! What you suggest is impossible."

"Nothing is impossible. I guarantee you safe conduct."

"Are you in a position to guarantee me anything?"

"Trust me."

"Absolutely not. This is insane, and I'll contact the American authorities. Do you think I was foolish enough to come here to the Soviet legation alone? An aide from the U.S. embassy waits in the next room."

Baranov took his time about responding. He'd need to tell Nuri more to convince him. "To openly discuss our affairs with the Americans would be a mistake, Nuri Pavlinovich. Your actress friend Tina may well be on Soviet soil, but our officials could still deny it. She could simply be held incommunicado at an undisclosed location. The moment you join her in Moscow, however, we will show good faith by releasing an American general in our hands. You've surely read in the news of this spy?"

"You threaten me, Father?"

Baranov confidently continued, "Under the immediacy of these circumstances, the Americans would drag their heels to help you, yes? Even later, if they were forced to do so from international publicity or public outcry, it would be a facade of protest. You haven't forgotten the Korean airliner incident several years back? Any puny appeal from the U.S. government would be ignored. Capitalism, by nature, is impatient and reckless, Nuri. Time is on the Soviet side, and you must realize that. Still, I personally cannot afford this publicity, Nuri, and neither can you. You will return and we will negotiate *privately*. This is more than a matter of national prestige. It is above all else a family matter. You, Tina, and me."

"It's a State affair of the highest order and you know it."

Pavlin Baranov smiled to himself. He'd made his point. Bidding Nuri a soft, underplayed good-bye, he confidently replaced the receiver on its hook. His son would see the light quickly enough.

Baranov lit a cigarette. Instead of thinking about Nuri, he contemplated the portrait of Lenin on the far wall. Not once had he come across a smiling likeness of the Soviet political genius. The somber pose, Baranov reflected, had become an exemplar for all Kremlin officialdom. The only current Politburo member known to smile in photographs was, strangely enough, General Fiodor Talik.

Baranov reflected on what Nuri had told him about the KGB minister. The KGB had its *zapiskas*, but Baranov had a few as well, certainly the important ones, like Politburo members and key military leaders. He reached into his capacious desk drawer and brought out again the three-centimeter thick file that was marked at the top FIODOR TALIK. Again he opened it. He frowned, thinking about the KGB attempts on Nuri's life. Obviously they were instigated by the Fifth Directorate. Nuri had never been known to exaggerate; his claims had to be true. Despite the precautions, Baranov's call to Nuri in Paris may have been monitored by Talik's people, but it didn't matter; not now.

Baranov's mind flashed back to ballerina Marina Pleskova's grisly death—the purported suicide. KGB Minister Talik had once called Nuri a seditious scum, and at the time Baranov, in acute embarrassment, had not dared to disagree. Had his own arrogance and vanity, along with his son's estrangement, caused him to misread KGB portents? Fiodor Talik might be the most brilliant man since Andropov to run the secret police system, but the general's power was getting out of hand—an individualized plague on the Soviet system.

Hands slightly trembling, Baranov continued to look through Talik's *zapiska*. Friends in the army and the party organization had been right after all; his own position had indeed become precarious. A showdown was brewing, and Baranov could only hope his sudden awareness of this horrific threat that was Fiodor Talik had not come too late.

In Paris, at the Soviet embassy, Nuri sat staring at the telephone receiver in his hand. Beads of perspiration covered his forehead and he felt as if he were about to be sick. *They had Tina.* Trying to regain control of himself, he put the telephone down and stepped slowly to the door of the First Secretary's office.

A dour-faced Lithuanian escorted him down the hallway, along with the American official who had accompanied Nuri into the compound. Ignoring both the Soviet and American aides, Nuri took off like a frightened animal. They shouted after him.

He stumbled on the front steps of the embassy building, picked himself up and fled down the street, crossing diagonally at the corner. A taxi squealed to a stop, almost striking him. Nuri swiftly climbed inside. After a short time the nausea eased and his terror once more turned to outrage.

Tina! Nuri was confused over whom to fight—how could he appease his father and attack Fiodor Talik at the same time?

Waiting for instructions, the taxi driver stared at Nuri.
"Hotel Meurice, *s'il vous plait.*"

The cab headed out in traffic. Nuri thought of the odd
priorities taking place in the Kremlin. Though he had little
cause for agreement with his father, he was sure of one thing.
Ideology aside, the combined Soviet Chairman and Premier
revered life. Fiodor Talik had proven himself a cold-blooded
murderer, a crucible for destruction.

Nuri gazed out the taxi's back window. It didn't look like he
was being followed, but he was far from sophisticated in these
situations. Los Angeles, Washington, New York, now Paris.
He wasn't safe anywhere. Like a homing pigeon, he was
headed back to the hotel, but why? There was a killer bound in
his bathroom, a body in the tub. There wasn't time to pick up
his belongings; not time for anything but escape.

The realization stabbed at him: Moscow! Nuri couldn't wage
his battle in the United States, or France, for that matter.
Tracing Tina's disappearance in Stockholm would only be a
waste of time. His father had never lied before; Tina would be
in the Soviet capital tomorrow night. Nuri would have to bite
the bullet, returning to familiar but dangerous territory.
Familiar ways. Familiar faces. Back to Mother Rus. But he
couldn't do it as Nuri Baranov, as his father expected. It would
be impossible, if not ludicrous. His hands would be tied, if not
his entire being incarcerated the moment he stepped off the
plane in Soviet territory.

Nuri made up his mind. He'd go undercover, set up a
masquerade. His first priority after perfecting his disguise
would be finding Tina in Moscow, then getting her out of the
country. Or at least to the American embassy. It would be a
dangerous stunt, but he couldn't think about that aspect; he had
to put it completely out of his mind. For his efforts, the chances
were excellent he'd wind up a black and blue zombie in a
surrealist scene at Lubyanka. But all that mattered now was
finding Tina.

When the cab arrived at the Meurice, Nuri didn't move. He
asked the cab driver to move on, let him out a block away near
a pay telephone booth. Nuri intended to call the Prefecture of
Police, anonymously tipping them off to the grisly scene
upstairs in the bathroom of his hotel suite. He'd feel a degree
safer with Khamsin behind bars. Nuri would also use the phone
to contact James Berkowitz of the Virginia Ballet Academy.

* * *

The professor's office was a book-and-document-littered alcove at one end of the zoology laboratory. Bruna Kloski found both rooms warm enough, despite the small blizzard outside that rattled the double-paned, caulked windows. The KGB colonel had come to Moscow State University to enrich her knowledge of the infamous puffer or blowfish—whose intestines, ovaries, and liver were purported to possess the world's most deadly poison. Kloski was impressed beyond her wildest expectation at what she'd discovered. The oversize, beautifully illustrated book Professor Cherbakov held out before her was fascinating—particularly the numerous color plates of the Japanese *tiger fugu*.

Kloski glanced up at the wiry-haired professor whose acumen she had no reason to doubt. Sergei Cherbakov was a member of the Academy of Science.

She glanced at the clock on the wall behind Cherbakov.

He continued his explanation. "In the Orient the *fugu* is prized for food; it is an expensive delicacy, for the removal of the poisonous flesh requires expertise." Cherbakov pointed to the book. "Note the fused, hard beak, yes? The fish can nip as well."

Kloski stared at the iridescent blue-and-green eyes of the spiny, inflated fish in the photograph. The creature looked far from appetizing.

"It's an insidious form of death," the professor told her. "Oddly, victims are able to think clearly while their bodies rapidly become numb. It is worse than a stroke; they cannot speak or move, and in a matter of minutes, cannot breathe. Death is very quick."

She watched as he put the book away, opened his desk, and retrieved what looked like a small bottle of aspirin. Cherbakov removed one of the pills. Carefully, with a pocket knife, he cut off a few granules—less than a tenth of the tablet. "So little, you need a magnifying glass to examine it, Comrade Colonel. But the amount of aspirin you see before you is the same quantity of tetrodotoxin, the poison found in one blowfish. It is enough to kill thirty persons."

Bruna Kloski had heard enough. She gathered herself to leave. "I am impressed, if not duly frightened, Professor. I will stay away from Japanese menus that are suspect."

"Our Soviet system, fortunately, deprives us of such

gastronomic gambles. I suspect to the Japanese eating *fugu* is more of a delight to the eye than the stomach. It is unfortunate that there is no Japanese restaurant in Moscow with *fugu* on the menu."

"I'm not interested in Japanese cooking, Comrade Professor." She shook Cherbakov's hand and left the laboratory, which had already started to fill with students.

The corridor outside was crowded, and Kloski took her time making her way to the elevator. While she ogled the pretty young boys, she thought about what Cherbakov had told her at the outset of their meeting—that the poison found in *fugu* was twenty-five times more powerful than even curare.

Kloski was suddenly confronted by her driver. Breathlessly, he explained, "Comrade Colonel, while I waited in the car, a message on the radio . . . You are wanted immediately at the KGB Communications Center. A most important Kremlin telephone intercept."

36

Nuri stepped out of the pay phone station, relieved that his near lookalike had been found. Mark Washburn was safe, recovering in the American Hospital in Paris. According to Berkowitz, the young dance student was being watched for a possible concussion and unfortunately couldn't be released to travel on to Moscow and Leningrad with the rest of the group.

Nuri started walking, uncertain of where to go next. Dodging around a group of elderly Americans taking pictues of each other before a tour bus, he headed slowly up the Rue de Rivoli sidewalk. He shoved his hands in his jacket pocket but immediately removed them, feeling contaminated by the cold steel of the gun he found there. He'd almost forgotten it.

Again he paused to get his bearings. Glancing across the Rue de Rivoli toward the Tuileries, he idly watched a nun lead a line of schoolchildren around Le Notre's circular pond. The group was disciplined, hiking along in lockstep. Nuri couldn't help thinking about guided, group travel like the Virginia Ballet Academy's tour. Such blocked-in itineraries were economical, but they had their scheduling drawbacks, as Mark

Washburn was about to discover; out of necessity the injured youth would have to be left behind.

Nuri had a scheme in mind, and it would involve Washburn—if he would cooperate. It was a wild gamble, but it was better than doing nothing. Nuri couldn't just stay here in Paris feeling impotent while Tina was thrust into the Moscow maelstrom.

Doubling back a block to make sure he wasn't being followed, Nuri hastened across the Rue de Rivoli and dropped down into the Metro. He purchased a *carnet* at the Louvre station, boarded the rubber-tired train and rode all the way to the end of the line at Pont de Neuilly. No one recognized him, though a pretty brunette with a student backpack batted her long eyelashes three times in his direction before disembarking at Porte Maillot. After the ugly scene he'd just left at the hotel, compounded by the news of Tina, pretty Parisian coquettes were the least of his concerns.

Sprinting out of the Metro at the Neuilly station, Nuri paused to get his directions straight, then headed up Rue du Château. He had several blocks to hike to the hospital and he walked swiftly, scuffing through the brown, curled leaves on the sidewalk. Thinking of Tina behind the Iron Curtain, he kicked at the dry blades as if they were Russians sent to hinder him. A stiff breeze suddenly snatched the leaves from his path, sending them dancing along the street.

It was no longer a matter of simply trusting the Americans, he reflected. He could no longer be sure who among them was on his side. On the other hand, he wasn't about to trust his father—or any other Soviet. When it came down to it, he didn't dare trust anyone, only his own intuition. Nuri mused over the words "heroics" and "loyalty." He wondered if he were like Hyacinthus, damned to die because two nations—like two Greek gods—were rivals for his love.

There was a serpent in Moscow, and it was far-reaching and convoluted; it could only be stopped by severing the head, not battling the writhing coils. Somehow, Fiodor Talik had to be contained. Nuri personally knew most of the members of the Politburo, well enough to address them by their patronymic. If he were in Moscow, he could warn them, possibly convince them to help his father. Nuri was also familiar with the maze of the Kremlin itself. Still, he panicked at the prospects of attacking Talik with his own two hands. There had to be an alternative.

The American Hospital, with its four-story white facade and wrought-iron fence, was a block away from the River Seine. Taking a firm grip on his emotions, Nuri strode inside the building. When he inquired at the lobby desk about Mark Washburn, the officious receptionist directed him to a second-floor wing and a private room at the end of the corridor.

Nuri ignored the elevator and took the steps two at a time.

The freckle-faced dance student looked up as Nuri entered the contemporary room. The wall-to-wall windows were framed on each side with brilliant orange drapes, and a monstrous bouquet of yellow gladiolas dominated the table next to Mark Washburn's bed. It was the first hospital Nuri had been in since leaving the Soviet Union, and he was amazed by its fashionable decor and nonantiseptic, cheerful appearance.

Washburn smiled at him. He, too, seemed pleased with the luxury of his surroundings. He quipped, "First class all the way, right? I not only get your autograph, but a personal visit as well. *Fantastic!*" He extended an unsteady hand.

Nuri shook it, replying, "Under the circumstances, could I do otherwise? You're only here because of me."

The youth gave him a puzzled look. Washburn's face, beneath the red hair and freckles, looked milky white. To Nuri he looked older than he did earlier.

"Berkowitz didn't explain to you?" Nuri asked seriously.

"He's over at the Prefecture of Police and promised to drop by after to talk. I'm still a little woolly-headed, but yeah, I'm curious. What's going on?"

"Look, Mark, I can't stay long. The fact is, I have to get out of here before Berkowitz returns with gendarmes in tow to ask you more questions." Nuri paused. He went over to the door leading to the hallway and closed it. "How's your head?"

"Sore as hell. I don't drift off anymore—I'm okay. They want to keep me under observation for two or three days. The tour is firm and the others can't wait. Looks like I sit here until they return. If I'm real lucky, I'll get to fly up to London, rejoin the tour there."

Nuri looked at him with concern. "Your parents. Do they know?"

Mark sighed. "My mother's on her way over."

"Good. About that bad show in the catacombs—I was rotten

company and never should have joined you. Your assailants were after me."

"I figured that. Why? And who were they?"

"Mark, there isn't time to explain. You'll have to trust me and keep what I'm about to ask you now to yourself. At least until I tell you otherwise. No one must know. Not Berkowitz, not even your mother. Agreed?"

"Sure. But why all the far-out secrecy?" He tried to sit up, but Nuri gently pushed him back by the shoulder.

"Easy, easy," said Nuri evenly. "The Soviet KGB wants me dead. My Chairman-Premier-father wants me back in Moscow alive. God knows what the CIA wants. I'm in a no-man's land, caught in between. Your mistaken abduction was all part of it." Nuri smiled to take the sting out of his words. "I thought I could fight them, but now—as I believe you put it in America—they have me over a barrel. Diana, the woman agent you saw earlier—she's been killed. And it appears my actress friend has been forcibly taken into Russia."

Mark whistled through his teeth. "Awesome," he said, reaching for his glasses on the side table. Slipping them on, he continued to stare at Nuri in disbelief. "Jesus Christ, and I thought all the excitement was over." He slowly shook his head. "I mean, is all this for real?"

Nuri strolled over to the window and gazed out at the dormer windows and copper roofs of the buildings across from the hospital. The sky was gray with the promise of rain, and a brisk wind continued to hustle the leaves along the street. He turned back to Mark, answering him solemnly. "Yes, it's all real. I can't even go back to my damned hotel room. There's a woman's body in my bathtub."

Mark Washburn's reply was immediate. "Radical. So why are you worried? They'll figure out you're innocent soon enough."

"You hope. Even so, that's not the problem. I don't have time for an investigaton. I can't even stay for tonight's performance at L'Opéra." He paused, studying the expression on the bedridden youth's face. "Those eyeglasses. You're wearing them in your passport photo?"

Mark nodded, intrigued.

"Any chance you brought an extra pair along on the trip?"

"You sure ask strange questions, but yeah, I always keep a

spare around. An old prescription, but they work in a pinch. Why?''

Silence vibrated between them. Nuri clutched the chrome foot of the bed for support. "I'd like to borrow your glasses, American passport, tour-group travel documents, and most important, your Soviet visa papers," he said firmly.

Mark looked back at him, aghast. "Holy shit. Should I let my imagination run riot, or will you elucidate?"

Nuri ran a hand through his hair. Patiently he explained his plan. "I've been on the stage long enough to know how to apply red hair rinse. I'm also great at makeup. With your eyeglasses and a little padding in my cheeks—"

"*Wow.* You're really suggesting—"

"I have to get into Moscow. But *not as Nuri Baranov.* I need your help."

Mark laughed surreptitiously. "You'd really go back in the bear's den and tempt fate?"

"There's no choice if I'm to beat them at their own game."

"*Shit.*" Mark looked at him meekly. Lips trembling, he intoned, "But my passport, without it I'm up the creek. No, Nuri. I just can't."

"I'll make the loan worthwhile. And, of course, I'll pay your Moscow tour cost."

"No. I don't need the money. It's dangerous. Not for me, but for you. You're a dancer, not Batman."

Nuri laughed. "As of now, I'm both. And you can play Robin."

The dance student was friendly enough, and for a long moment Nuri almost forgot his reason for being in the hospital room. "Stop worrying, my friend. You've never heard the words, 'Artists must never be afraid to spit in the dishes they are fed from'?"

Mark didn't smile; he only continued to shake his head in confusion and numbly stare at Nuri.

Leaning toward the bed, Nuri lowered his voice to a confidential whisper. "This I promise you. If I'm successful, I'll do everything—the choreographing myself, if necessary— to get you a guest appearance role. In the chorus, or even a *demi-charactuer* part at a New York performance of the U.S. Dance Company." He stood back, waiting for Mark's eyes to widen. "Berkowitz tells me you have exceptional talent. I have influence." Nuri waited expectantly.

Mark pushed the electric control, raising the back of the bed. He said in a quiet, almost inaudible voice, "Me, on the stage of Lincoln Center? A guest appearance? You're bullshitting me."

"Do you dance well or not?"

Mark's face reddened. He swallowed hard. "Sure. I mean, yes. But the others—"

"The choreographer Kurt Meisenheimer will cooperate, I promise you. Especially when he learns how close he comes to losing me back to the Bolshoi." Nuri hesitated. It suddenly occurred to him that returning to the former's prestigious ranks—his father's assurances notwithstanding—was pure far-out, wishful thinking. "Forgive my dreaming, Mark. More accurately, I should have said, 'losing me to the gulags.'"

"You've actually come up with a plan that will work?" Mark's eyebrows batted nervously.

Nuri felt better; he knew now that in the end Mark Washburn would cooperate. "Give me three days at the most. While I'm gone I'll give you my own identification for safekeeping. Should anything happen to me, you'll have a valuable souvenir, yes? You, my friend, might even become Nuri Baranov!"

Thanks to expertly-welded steel and modern rolling stock, the straight-as-an-arrow track from Leningrad to Moscow provided the smoothest train ride Tina had ever experienced. She'd slept on and off, but now she stared out the window, sipping the hot lemon tea the nattily-attired conductress had brought her.

"Bored or worried?" Jon Saarto inquired.

Tina turned from the window. "A little of both. We've been in the Soviet Union for over eight hours and I've exchanged less than a dozen words with any of the inhabitants. And that dialogue was confined to the woman who drew my bath this morning and our train conductress. I feel like a leper."

Saarto smiled benignly.

The space they shared was one of eight convertible, "soft class" compartments that made up the coach. The door was locked from the outside and guarded in the aisle by a Soviet Army sergeant—one of Colonel Rablin's aides who had mysteriously appeared at Leningrad's Moskovsky Station.

Once more Tina examined the bright green kerchief Rablin

1ad insisted she wear in public. The colonel and Alexi Stanovich hadn't taken any chances with her being recognized as an American while boarding the train. Even a *babushka*'s dumpy overcoat had been provided her. Smiling to herself, Tina folded the kerchief and tucked it in her purse. She thought again of the station in Leningrad, her initial surprise at the makeup of the train's passengers. Instead of the primitives she'd seen in movies about Russia, they were urbanized, neatly-dressed types, definitely on the young side; probably well-paid workers or upper-class bureaucrats. She saw no children. Then she remembered that it was midday and school was in session. It was also early winter, which explained the lack of usual tourists on an express train.

Putting the scene together in her own crazy-quilt way, Tina suddenly felt ostracized and abandoned. The two of them were probably the only Americans on the train. Saarto looked at her, sensing her distress, but offered only an I-told-you-so smile.

They had been under way for almost an hour, with no further communication with Colonel Rablin or Alexi Stanovich, who occupied the next compartment. Tina glanced at the bodyguard who sat opposite her on the blue mohair seatbench. Attached to the window, a small table with a lamp separated them. The bodyguard looked restless. Again he seemed to be categorizing her. When she saw the familiar dancing light in his eyes, she looked away. Some aberration of Jon Saarto's ego had convinced him he could easily get her to bed and that she would respond with unrestrained lust. The truth was, she tolerated the bodyguard with mild boredom.

"Can we speak freely?" she asked, attempting to distract him. "The compartment—could they have bugged it?"

Saarto shrugged. "I no longer give a damn. Tina, about all this cooperation—"

She lowered her head. "No lectures, please."

"Rablin and Stanovich have no reason to listen. Smart money says they're both catching a catnap. Before that big rendezvous outside Moscow."

Tina thought about the hours ahead. "Would you mind spending a little time on my Russian vocabulary? I'll need a purse full of phrases."

He replied quickly, "Russian isn't a language that lends itself to simplified pidgin form. Forget the tourist booklets and take my word for it. Unlike German, Spanish, or French, there's no such thing as speaking a *little* Russian. You know the language or you don't." He grinned at her. "Surprised Nuri didn't tell you that."

"Nuri didn't tell me a lot of things." She tried to conceal her disappointment. She considered for a moment, then continued, her words coming haltingly through leaden lips. "Jon, I read your mind back in the station at Leningrad. You weren't thinking of this trip, but of trains headed in the opposite direction—*north* to Finland. I'm sorry to drag you into this."

"Granny can wait for another day—if I live long enough." He smiled and shook his head. "Interesting country, Finland, Tina. It's not easy to live in the shadow of Soviet paranoia. I remember vividly her telling me about Russia. After the war with Finland, as a part of the reparation, the Soviets demanded that the Finnish coat of arms be reversed. This so the sword-brandishing lion faced west, instead of east."

Tina started to laugh but reconsidered. She thought for a moment. "Supposing, Jon, we get in over our head—"

"We're already in over our heads. And there's ice forming on the surface."

"Hear me out, please. Supposing we have to run for it. You know Finland, and the winter hasn't set in so strongly we'd be buried in snow. If necessary, could we escape overland—cross some deserted area of the Finnish border?"

Saarto pushed himself back in his seat and sent her a look of incredulity. "Tina, we're going in the opposite direction from the Finnish frontier, deeper into the gut of Russia. As for the border area, the trees have been clean cut and Soviet patrols don't pause to ask questions. They shoot without warning anyone who steps across the spare expanse of snow known as the 'carpet of death.'"

Tina lowered her head.

Turquoise eyes gleaming, he grinned at her. "Next time you want to date a celebrity, I suggest you try a different profession. And stay away from the foreigners. Do like Marilyn Monroe, going for DiMaggio. Check out a baseball player."

"Don't be an ass."

"Sorry. Just trying to be helpful."

There was a long, silent interval. Trying to avoid Saarto's distressing stare, Tina gazed pensively out the window at the Soviet landscape. The train was passing through a thick birch forest with no tree over thirty feet high; an area like the others that had been pointed out to her earlier. The trees had been cut during times of strife to provide fuel. Tina thought about the siege of Leningrad; at the time this rail line had been taken over by the Germans in their determination to cleave that hero city away from the rest of Russia.

The train hurtled out of the trees and into farmland. A blowsy, flaxen-haired girl on a tractor looked up and waved. Tina waved back. The farm girl was attractive. Tina wondered if the gesture had been an empty one, a daily ritual for the train, or had the greeting been meant for Tina? Allowing her mind to flash back to Hollywood, Tina stared across the compartment at Saarto. "Marilyn Monroe was an unhappy actress. Were you serious?"

"Just thinking about noncontroversial professions for your future man of the house."

She said bitterly, "For your information, there are more ballet tickets sold annually in New York than *baseball*." Tina couldn't decide which was more depressing, pursuing a dialogue with Jon Saarto or gazing out the window at the dull winter landscape. She changed the subject. "Look out there. The Asiatic, dismal gray Nuri spoke of. He was right. It makes shivers skitter up and down my back. It may be a stereotype visage, but I can literally feel history out there."

"Sure. The violent kind."

There was an awkward silence. Tina continued, "Medieval death, pestilence, barbaric invasions. The scars of World War Two."

"The 'Great Patriotic War,' please," Saarto corrected. "The Soviets are a bit fussy about that." His transparent eyes were on her again, a degree more intense and inquiring.

She smiled back but this time remained silent. Tina suddenly felt uncomfortable, as if a dangerous fantasy, some hidden instability in her, was being aroused by Jon Saarto. It was like he was trying to be the handsome movie–Indian chief's son, galloping by on a horse, snatching her off a covered wagon to carry her away to some mysterious place. Had the bodyguard become a fantasy borne of too many films since her first interest in acting? Tina shook her head; the daydreaming was nonsense and she had to put it away. Trying to doze off again would help. God knows, she was tired enough.

Before she could curl up and settle back in the seat, Saarto was beside her, not near enough to touch bodies, but still, on *her side* of the compartment. *Damn his persistence.* Tina couldn't return his gaze; all she had the energy to do was sit there, head bowed, resigned to listen.

He said awkwardly, "Come off it, Tina. *Look at me* when I speak to you. What good are words when eyes have their own chemistry? Behind that glacierlike facade of yours there's a woman crying to be let out."

She raised her head, looking at him with alert annoyance. "Jon, before you rave on, you're reading me wrong. Very wrong." He reached for her wrist and held it like a concerned male nurse. She dreaded what would come next.

"My God, your pulse!" he said smartly. "Your heart's fluttering like a hummingbird's."

She withdrew her hand, smiling with caution. "Don't be so boorish."

He edged closer and kissed her softly and quickly behind the ear.

Tina started to raise her hand as if batting a fly, but caught herself, instead gently easing several inches away from him and frowning. The gentle rebuke, however, was too obscure for the egotistical Saarto. His arm came sweeping grandly around her, but she caught it firmly in midair and pushed it away.

Tina was beyond surprise now. She said to him sharply, "You'd have me be a liar? I could never live a life of deceit."

Saarto grinned. "You were living one twenty minutes ago. While you were asleep, you tossed and turned. A nightmare?"

Her antipathy flashed. "I don't remember."

"You whispered the name Jon. I was flattered."

"I was probably afraid." Her voice broke. "Damn it, I'm happy, Jon. Very happy with Nuri. Don't try to spoil it." Turning away, she rested her head against the train window, trying to put the cloying bodyguard out of her mind. The thought dawned on her that she wasn't criticizing him as much as she was gazing inside herself.

Propping his feet on the seat opposite, Saarto yawned. Indifferently, he said, "Another *film scene*? You deny yourself, Tina." He chuckled. "All for cheap sentimentality?"

She exploded, "You're a conceited bore!"

"Ah! At last a spark of fury." He hunched his shoulders, pretending to dodge a potential blow.

"And you're not as humorous or beguiling as you'd have women believe."

He shrugged. "Eroticism embraces all of human nature. Who am I to refute facts? Even here in Russia. Socialism triumphant cannot deny it, boss lady. Eroticism is the essential energy of life, its very object."

"*Mr. Saarto*. I'm far from impressed, and I have news for you. Get it through your thick head that for some people, it's impossible to cheat on an orgasm. A simple enough rule and I live by it. *Comprendez-vous?* Sex works or it doesn't. If not, it reflects something missing in one of the partners."

"Continue. What's your stuffy point?"

"In my case, a matter of love. You're barking up the wrong tree."

Saarto glumly got up and resumed his place on the seat opposite her. He said seriously, "Fine. Now I have news for you." His voice had a soothing quality, surprisingly without rancor. "It'll never work beyond the first year. Nuri's as Russian as cabbage soup and black bread. Waving a U.S. flag isn't good enough, Tina. He'll never change. Let me tell you the . . ." He paused awkwardly, searching for the right phrase.

Their eyes locked. Tina said firmly, "Don't elaborate. I understand symbolic equations perfectly. You're pushing too hard, Jon."

"Just like Willy Loman—out selling the territory."

She smiled. "You've got that right. I've already taken note of the *smile and the shoeshine*." She searched Saarto's face, looking for selfishness or insincerity. She found neither. "I'm sorry. We're both tired and irritable. Think what you like, but I'm getting some rest while I can."

His only response was to smile and gently toss a pillow in her face.

37

NURI SAID GOOD-BYE to the young American and hurried down the hospital corridor. With Mark Washburn's eyeglasses, passport, and Soviet travel documents tucked in his pocket, all Nuri needed now was the makeup kit he'd left in the dressing room back at L'Opéra. He pushed open the door to the hospital and stepped toward the street. It had started to rain, a mild, breeze-driven drizzle. Traffic appeared light.

Nuri slammed to a halt, his muscles tightening. Directly across from him was a light brown Citroen with three men inside, and they were all looking his way. Nuri's eyes narrowed. Vaguely at first, then with sudden vividness, he recalled the faces—*the same trio who had pursued him on Amsterdam Avenue in New York City*! It was obvious from their intense stares that they hadn't brought an olive branch to Paris.

This time he felt no panic, only determination to lose the headhunters quickly. But one of the men was already opening the door to the car. Nuri did an abrupt about-face and darted back inside the hospital lobby. He raced through the first-floor corridor, scanning the directional signs. Cornering a startled orderly, he snapped, *"Parlez-vous anglais?"*

The hospital employee nodded.

Impatient, Nuri grabbed the man's white jacket and shook it. "The emergency room entrance—where is it? Or any exit, other than the main lobby!"

The orderly's Pomeranianlike eyes popped in their sockets; all he could do was point.

Nuri took off down the hall. Less than a minute later he was outside the building, breathless, heart thudding, his body pressed against the side of a blue and white ambulance. Outflanking Nuri, one of his pursuers waited at the end of the driveway entrance less than a hundred feet away. He stood there uncertainly, like a hound that had temporarily lost the scent. The man was heavily built and wore a belted raincoat and gray tweed cap.

Nuri heard voices chattering in French. The ambulance attendants appeared to be delivering a patient inside the building. Pressing low to the ground, Nuri edged around the vehicle. He tried the rear door. It yielded and he swiftly climbed inside, nestling down below the curtained windows.

Nuri lay still, catching his breath. The tired linoleum bed of the ambulance smelled of carbolic. So far he hadn't been seen and he was safe, but only for a matter of moments. The meat wagon's attendants would return with their gurney, open the rear door, and make a noisy fuss when they spotted him. And there was no way to beg or bribe them without drawing the attention of the watchdog in the driveway.

Nuri scanned the inside of the ambulance, not sure of just what he was looking for. A lab coat—some disguise? Nothing usable. The vehicle was a modified van with cabinets along one side and no barrier separating the back from the driver's bucket seat. *The keys!* In their rush the attendants had left them in the ignition. Possibly they'd been left routinely; who in their right mind would want to steal a high-profile ambulance?

Nuri felt the gun he still had in his pocket, praying he wouldn't have to use it to get away. Right now he was desperate enough to shoot anybody. The angry wave of protectiveness for Tina was building again, stronger even than his own need for self-preservation.

He scrambled into the driver's seat and turned the key, glad when the engine caught immediately. The man at the end of the driveway turned, but before he could blink in Nuri's direction, the vehicle was in gear, accelerating, tires squealing and fighting for traction as it raced to the street. Nuri cranked the steering wheel, veering to one side. His pursuer leaped out of the way, falling into a pile of dead leaves at the feet of a stunned hospital gardener.

The ambulance bolted forward, skidded sideways out of the driveway, and sped up the center of the street. Squinting into the rearview mirror, Nuri watched his tormentors. The other two had come running around the building, joining the first, who was still struggling to his feet, wiping his face and spitting out dirt and leaves. They'd pursue him with vengeance now. One of the men raised both arms, aiming a gun at the ambulance's rear tires.

Nuri jammed his foot on the accelerator, swerving right, then left, almost losing control. The bullets missed the tires, ricocheting off the rear bumper. Nuri quickly debated whether to brave the unfamiliar tangle of Paris traffic or get rid of the wheels immediately and find a taxi, or better yet burrow into the Metro. Whatever, he needed to get to the L'Opéra dressing room, go to work on the conspicuous blond hair and change his identity.

Before turning the corner, Nuri glanced in the mirror again. He had a comfortable lead, for his adversaries would have to run back half a block to pick up their parked Citroen. Nuri swerved into busy Boulevard Victor Hugo, and immediately wished he hadn't. The thoroughfare was clogged.

Nuri was keyed up now, ready for anything. The ambulance was another first; he'd never ridden in one before, let alone sat behind the wheel. *Why not make it the ultimate experience?* Flipping the switch on the emergency klaxon, he swung out into the opposing traffic and accelerated.

The Moscow-bound express hurtled through another town without stopping. The train was fast, and they'd already covered two thirds of their journey. Saarto checked his watch. According to his calculations, in less than a half hour they would arrive at the blockade point Colonel Rablin had told them about earlier. Saarto would have to make his move quickly, though first there was the business of concocting a half-ass believable story for Tina.

He looked across the compartment, once more drinking in the captivating actress. Shiny brown hair draped over her shoulders and lashes fluttering as if in a dream, Tina slept fitfully, curled up like a Raggedy Ann doll in the corner of the seat.

Saarto once more checked the time. Wiping the condensation off the window, he saw that the train was approaching Novo Zavidovski. There was snow on the ground now and the threat of more to come. Countless Orwellian concrete cells that were workers' apartments suddenly rose everywhere out of the plain. Then factory buildings.

He thought with increasing trepidation what might lie ahead for Tina Conner in Moscow. It would be worse for Nuri, if love proved blind and he swallowed the bait. The Russian dancer had set a damned avalanche in motion; now others were caught up in it. Only one fact comforted Saarto and let some light through the discordant alternatives. Tina was not exactly being tossed into the crevasse of Soviet classless bureaucracy. According to their hosts—Natasha, Alexi, and Colonel Rablin—she'd at least be given VIP treatment and come under the personal protection of the number-one man in the Soviet Union; a reasonable enough arrangement considering Tina might someday become Pavlin Baranov's daughter-in-law.

Saarto rubbed his chin. Tina was famous enough in the West, but not in the Soviet Union. Here the masses, the countless party echelons, even the press, could care little about her welfare. He reflected on a story his grandmother had read to him a dozen years back: something by Willa Cather—a tale where Russian wolves pursued a sleigh across the snow until finally a bridal couple was thrown off to appease them.

Saarto smiled and slowly shook his head. He stared at the dirty dishes on the small table by the window. Colonel Rablin had insisted he and Tina remain in the compartment and had sent the food in. Cabbage soup, white bread and butter, a salad with thinly-sliced, cold sturgeon. And Saarto's first taste of Russian beer.

When the meal had been served, Saarto hadn't let the opportunity for a little horse-trading to slip by. Whatever happened to them in the hours ahead, he knew Russian pocket money might save the day. Accordingly, Saarto had opened his suitcase and shown the train's reporter an alligator shirt, an electric razor, and the most sought-after prize of all, his nearly-new pair of Levi jeans. Saarto had suggested that if the young Russian were interested, he beg or borrow among trusted railway employees to come up with the going price in rubles. Saarto knew that both he and the porter would be breaking Soviet laws, but there was nothing to lose. He was already a goddamned prisoner.

There was a knock on the compartment door, followed immediately by the lock clicking open. The guard outside again admitted the porter to pick up the lunch dishes. This time the young waiter's face appeared even more covetous than before. Tina sleepily opened her eyes to survey Saarto and the porter, but said nothing.

The Russian closed the door to the outside corridor and smiled, revealing uneven teeth that reminded Saarto of canted gravestones.

"Ob eshchat zolotyye gory," the porter said thickly, pulling a wad of bills from his pocket and hurriedly counting them out.

Saarto translated in his mind. The man was grumbling about "promised mountains of gold."

There were a hundred rubles on the table, and after a brief hassle, Saarto gave his jeans, the Izod shirt, and a pigskin belt, but not the electric razor. The porter seemed satisfied as he gathered up the treasure along with the tray of dishes.

Saarto faked a quick stumble and accidental nudge against the porter, and the contents of the tray scattered. While Tina helped the Russian retrieve the mess off the floor, Saarto turned aside, quickly removing the identification cards from the wallet he'd just lifted. He quickly pocketed the documents and tapped the preoccupied porter on the shoulder. "You dropped this."

The Russian looked puzzled as he accepted the wallet, but gathered up the spilled items without comment. He started to leave.

Catching him by the arm, Saarto asked, "The army colonel and fat civilian—they're in the next compartment now?"

The porter hesitated, then replied, "No. In the dining car."

"How long have they been there?"

Wide awake now, Tina sat up in her seat.

The railroad employee was growing uncomfortable. He glanced at the blue jeans over his arm, then back at Saarto. "I don't know, comrade. They are being served now. If you need them, perhaps they'll return in twenty minutes, a half hour. Depending on the service."

Saarto gestured toward the door. "That'll be all. Thanks, pal."

"For an American, you speak very good Russian, no?" He smiled and stepped out in the corridor.

The guard at the door sized up the porter's little haul and scowled, but didn't interfere. Saarto wondered if the army sergeant had been bribed. He looked the guard over quickly, noting the peaked cap, regulation greatcoat with shiny brass buttons, and the service automatic in a waist holster. The door closed in Saarto's face, and again the train compartment was secured from the outside.

Immediately Tina was on to Saarto like sticky wallpaper. "Jon, look at me. Why do you need Soviet money? I thought we were official guests, of sorts. A freebie."

Saarto smiled at her, but didn't respond. He took out his own wallet, withdrew all his American identification, replacing it with the porter's. He handed his own documents to Tina. "Keep this in your purse for safekeeping. I'll need it later."

Saarto examined the small waste receptacle under the window table. It was half filled, containing paper wrappers, cellophane, and a couple of empty cigarette boxes. He added a Russian magazine and the paper placemats he'd pulled off the lunch tray. "Matches?" he asked Tina.

She stared at him suspiciously. "Yes, probably. But first an explanation." She dug in her purse.

Saarto waited for her eyes to meet his. He said bluntly, with a measure of mistruth, "Listen for once, and don't argue back. There isn't much time. I'm going to get out of here, wing it on my own into the nearest town and get help."

Her face turned ashen. "You're not serious?"

He didn't respond.

"No. It would be a mistake," she said emphatically. "I don't need help. Not yet. Wait until I talk to the Chairman or can reach Nuri in Paris."

"All you'll get from Pavlin Baranov is ultra-left-wing dogma. *Pokazukha*—the Soviet's showmanship of illusion."

"Don't mess with my mind, Jon," she sneered. "I have to try."

"Try what? Parlor socialism won't work." Saarto sat forward, gently placing a hand over her lips. "Kindly shut up and listen? I have a plan. You need an *insurance policy*, boss lady, we both need one. You don't stand a chance with the Russians unless someone back home—with plenty of clout— knows you're here."

She pushed his hand away. "Jon, forget it."

"Forget it my ass," he said firmly. "Think it over. The only people in Sweden or the USA who give a damn about you believe the two of us are off skiing, for chrissakes. Nuri may not buy it, but under the circumstances, who knows how he'll react. When your American friends *who can help* find out the truth, it may be too late."

Tina focused on him with alert annoyance.

Saarto continued, "I have to get through to U.S. authorities. Moscow, wherever. If they won't help, I'll notify Kaufmann at the film studio." Hesitating, he tightened his voice. "If worse comes to worst, I've got a former employer in the publishing business, remember? Brian Beck can at least raise a little hell in the press. Believe me, if there's a U.S. government conspiracy involved here, someone has to blow the lid off."

Tina shook her head in wonderment. "Hard to believe you'd ask that loathsome publisher for anything."

Saarto grinned. "In a tornado you run, don't walk, to the closest cellar."

"You're a cynical bastard, you know that, don't you?"

"Thanks. But keep listening. Our friends in the dining car will panic when they discover I'm gone, but they're not about to take it out on you. I doubt, under the circumstances, that Rablin will even sound an alarm on the train for fear of alerting the KGB to what's happening. Probably won't even send out a dragnet for me, at least not right away. You and Nuri are the ones needed in Moscow. Do you follow so far?"

She looked at him with something akin to horror. "Jon, you're mad. You wouldn't stand a chance out there. I won't let you go."

Saarto smiled, rose in one movement, and backed toward the door. "You have an alternative plan?" Folding his arms over his chest, he glared at her and said irritably, "Don't be so pigheaded. I'm not deserting you Tina, just restructuring the protection the best way I know. For the time being you're safe enough; what I need is lead time before that proposed big debut of yours tomorrow night. Hard telling what'll happen when you confront Pavlin Baranov and face his ultimatums."

Her eyes chilled. "You're convinced it'll be unpleasant, come down to ugliness?"

"Yes," he said automatically. "Now hand over the matches. And trust me. Rablin claims he's booked us into the Cosmos Hotel. One way or another, I'll contact you there."

Her bewildered eyes flitted between the wastebasket and Saarto. Finally she withdrew the Beverly Hills Hotel matchbook from her purse and tossed it to him.

38

NURI ABANDONED the ambulance on a side street off Rue de Caumartin and walked the remaining two blocks to Place de L'Opéra. The light rain had stopped, but the cobbles were still wet as he crossed the street, threading his way through stalled traffic. Nuri had a great deal of inventiveness going on in his mind as he approached the theatre, and it had nothing to do with ballet.

Though he immediately recognized Nuri, the backstage watchman gave him an inquiring, almost hostile appraisal. The short, gnat of a man appeared to be in his seventies and spoke only a little English; he kept pointing to his pocket watch while asking about an unscheduled rehearsal. With difficulty, Nuri finally made his point: "I need my makeup kit in the dressing room, monsieur. I will only be there a short time."

The old man nodded and went back to his station by the door.

Nuri thought quickly, trying to figure a way to slip past the old man—unseen—on the way out of the theatre. He wasn't about to spoil his planned disguise by letting anyone in on the secret—*friend or foe*.

Studying the area by the stage door, Nuri came up with a
simple enough plan: He'd set up a noisy diversion and make a
dash for the exit when the watchman went to investigate. A
flower vase from his dressing room, hurled toward the opposite
end of the stage, should do the trick.

Nuri hurried through L'Opéra's darkened, ominously quiet
corridors to his dressing room. He fumbled with the key the
guard had reluctantly loaned him and pushed open the door.
The smell of flowers in the closed-off quarters overwhelmed
him. Nuri left the door open for air and turned on both the
overheads and the string of lights over the dressing-table
mirror. The framed photo of Tina Conner he'd brought along
on the tour smiled at him from its place beside the makeup kit.

Nuri took off his jacket and shirt. He propped the borrowed
passport against the mirror, folded it open to the likeness of
Mark Washburn, and studied the color photo carefully. It was
taken with flat lighting. Good—all the better for hiding sharp
facial features.

The floral odor was more bearable now, and he closed and
locked the door. Nuri chose a temporary red hair rinse and
went to work at the sink. He finally managed to get his hair
tinted reasonably close to the color of Mark Washburn's. The
dance student wore his hair shorter, but that wouldn't be a
problem; passport ID photos were often months out of date.
Finishing with the blow dryer, Nuri studied himself in the
mirror. *Good enough.*

It was time now for the face. Sorting through the makeup
kit, he ignored the fine sable brushes and theatrical putty; this
time he was after youth, not age. He found the flesh-toned
vanishing stick he needed and went to work on the shadows
under his ears and lower lip, determined to make his face more
round, childlike, and less elongated. He took his time. To
complete the illusion, he used plastic padding to puff out his
cheeks. Nuri removed it for the time being, for the mouth
inserts were too uncomfortable to wear for more than a few
hours at a time. He'd rely on them later, when the masquerade
started to get chary.

Disguise would be only part of the picture; from stage
experience he knew that *presence* and *attitude* were equally
important. He would have to concentrate on changing his
posture and gait—try to slump a bit, feign an air of teenage

indifference and boredom. Forget his usual alert, quick manner. *If he managed to remember.*

Nuri put his shirt and jacket back on and checked himself before the full-length mirror. He would need a few more items: a heavy overcoat and scarf for the Moscow deep freeze, and a suitcase with enough in it not to arouse suspicion when he encountered Soviet Customs at Sheremetyevo Airport. After leaving L'Opéra, his next stop would be an inexpensive department store, or better yet, a used clothing shop.

Around him the great French theatre was depressingly quiet, the slightest noise amplified. Nuri stiffened when he heard a slight scuffling noise. Was it his imagination? He cocked an ear and heard it again, behind him! Startled, he turned in time to see a fat mouse scurry across the dressing table and hide behind Tina's portrait. He ignored the creature.

He was ready now, except for the horned-rimmed glasses. Nuri put them on, studying his image in the mirror, comparing it to Mark Washburn's passport photo. The resemblance was startling; it might not fool any fellow members in the Virginia Ballet Academy, but it would satisfy Soviet airport personnel.

Jon Saarto glanced at Tina, then down at the matchbook she'd handed him.

The actress managed a smile. "Always wanted to watch a firebug at work. Is it true that arson investigators often look for wet-stained trousers at the scene of a deliberately set blaze?"

Saarto refused to laugh. "An old wive's tale."

"Please get on with it."

Saarto hesitated before striking the match. "In the remote chance we don't link up again and I bite the wrong end of a KGB bullet—it's been nice."

Her face brightened. "Likewise. I feel like we've both been cast in a Dashiell Hammett film. And as for this scene, let's do it in one take." Sighing, she came up beside Saarto and playfully tapped his shoulder. "Move over. If the entire compartment goes up like a tinderbox, I intend to be closer to the door."

He grinned at her. Tina's touching him and the nearness of her body was like being bitten by a woman without a rabies shot—the cure would be painful. He had to get out of here quickly, before they touched again, even accidentally, before he said clunky, embarrassing words he'd live to regret. Saarto checked his watch once more and looked out the window. The train slowed slightly and rumbled across a girdered bridge, then the snow-mantled forest closed in again as the express gathered speed. Saarto smiled to himself. Tina was right; a fire to distract the guard would be a time-worn scenario, but he was certain it would work. He struck the first match.

It took three tries to get a decent blaze going. Tina watched him, a conspiratorial look in her eyes. He crossed his fingers, praying she'd remember to do exactly as he'd instructed.

The paper in the wastebasket took hold, an untidy little inferno. As prearranged, Tina screamed while Saarto pounded on the door to the passageway. He looked sidelong at her, grinning. She was even a better actress off the screen than on it.

The duty man unlocked the door and threw it open. He stared in momentary amazement at the conflagration by the window. A plastic ashtray Saarto had flung into the fire now billowed thick, ugly smoke. Tina began coughing—for real.

"Vodu!" the guard shouted. He grabbed a towel from the compartment's small vanity, wet it, and began beating the flames.

Saarto shouted in Russian, insisting that water wasn't good enough; they had to find a fire extinguisher.

"Tahm, nah st'yen-yeh!" The frantic sergeant pointed toward the end of the car but he didn't look up, continuing to flail at the wastebasket with the towel.

Smoke surged out of the compartment as Saarto edged through the doorway. He saw the nearby fire extinguisher and ignored it. *Now, his chance!* He bolted along the corridor toward the rear of the train. At the end of the coach he glanced back long enough to see Tina retrieve the extinguisher and hurry with it back to the compartment. Muttering a quick prayer for her safety in the minutes ahead, Saarto leaped through the vestibule and into the next car. More private compartments. He thought about the scene he'd just left; when the fire and smoke were put down, Tina was to convince the guard that Saarto had rushed toward the *front of the train*—ostensibly to seek out Colonel Rablin and Alexi Stanovich in the dining car. In truth, Saarto would flee in the opposite direction—toward the last coach. He had a plan.

A stout-shouldered conductress tried to stop him in the passageway of the next car, but Saarto brushed her aside, growling in Russian that he was on KGB business and in a hurry. Whether the surly woman believed him or not, she stood back, dumbfounded. Saarto boldly plowed on, rushing into the vestibule of the next car. And the next.

When he entered a coach filled end to end with Soviet soldiers, he passed through slowly, making an effort to appear nonchalant.

At last he found the train's last car. It, too, appeared to be a compartmented affair like the one he and Tina occupied. The corridor, for the moment, was empty.

Quickly he examined the vestibule area between the cars. He would have to move fast before company joined him. Beneath the steel footplates, the couplings and buffers rattled as the train accelerated slightly. Saarto withdrew the knife he'd lifted from the luncheon tray and set to work, swifting cutting through the black rubber pleats of the pass-through. First the top, then both sides. Immediately the vestibule filled with wind-driven snow. In the distance, above the wind, Saarto could hear the klaxon of the electric locomotive as the train approached a grade crossing. He hoped they weren't approaching a town of any size.

Saarto pushed the severed divider back and kneeled to examine the coupling between the cars. He noted that the rail equipment was German, not Russian; according to the stamped plate on the frame of the coach, it was made in Hamburg. Having spent a summer working in a freight yard, Saarto knew exactly what to do next. Before disconnecting the air hose and breaking the coupling, he needed to turn off the air-pressure valve. He lay on his face, groping for the small handle beneath the forward coach. The wind plucked at his fingers like an icy scalpel as he twisted.

At last he had it. The rest came easily. Saarto didn't bother with the electrical line; it parted in a shower of sparks as the cars separated. Leaping to the slowing, abandoned coach, Saarto watched with satisfaction as the rest of the train gradually, then more quickly, pulled away. *Good-bye Colonel Rablin and Alexi Stanovich. Take care, Tina, until we rendezvous later.*

When the main train was a good mile distant, Saarto crawled out on the side of the car, waiting until it had slowed to around twenty miles an hour. He hoped the passengers inside were still oblivious to what had occurred, that they'd merely assume there was a minor delay along the track. Russians were accustomed to inconveniences.

Saarto calculated quickly; there was a slight downgrade, and it would be another half mile before the carriage came to a complete halt. Around him was farmland bordered by scrub brush—ideal terrain for finding cover. He needed to move now.

Saarto dropped off the side of the coach, rolled down the embankment and came to a thudding stop, his face buried in drifted snow. The tumble had knocked the wind out of him. Sucking in lungfuls of air, he watched the lone railroad car roll on. When it was far enough away, Saarto climbed to his feet, batted away the snow, and scanned the immediate area.

The surrounding terrain reminded him of upstate New York. The light snowfall had stopped but low gray clouds continued to scud across the horizon; the sky was darker than before, and Saarto figured dusk wasn't far off. He saw a farmhouse in the distance, and over the hill behind it, several columns of black smoke spiraling into the sky. *A village?*

Saarto lurched forward, his soles plunging down into what appeared to be an inch of fresh powder over an icy crust. He saw a road up ahead and took a shortcut across a shallow valley to reach it.

Saarto passed two farms and what appeared to be an abandoned brick yard. A truck roared by, followed by a crowded Volga sedan with a broken chain rattling on a rear tire. He waved, but the drivers took no notice of him.

The village seemed to rise out of nowhere, with few people out on the streets. Saarto shook his head in disappointment. There was still no sign of an expressway to Moscow, and he was sure such a thoroughfare existed. He idly wondered, if and when he did find the main highway, if the Soviets had anything that resembled a Howard Johnson's or even a roadside toilet and pay phone.

Spotting two schoolgirls, Saarto stopped them for directions. They were friendly and cooperative. A short time later he was stomping his feet on the worn wooden porch of what the Soviet children told him was the local post office—the only place where he could make a long distance telephone call. The building's interior was dim and melancholy; the bespectacled clerk who received Saarto was a bloated individual whose somnolent, unsmiling face nearly filled the small barred window. Again, Saarto used his best Russian, this time asking for a telephone.

The fat man's wary look and the gruff, dismissing manner of his response made Saarto feel alien. The postman claimed the long distance line to Moscow had been giving the village trouble, but Saarto was free to try it if he had the rubles to cover a deposit. Studying him, the Russian acknowledged Saarto's language proficiency, then asked if he was Finnish or Swedish.

Saarto shook his head. Abruptly, in a determined, fatuous manner, the postman announced that he'd known all along that Saarto was an *American*. It was obvious by the walk, the way he'd approached through the snow. Saarto stared at him and asked again about the long distance wire. The Russian shrugged, took his money, and pointed to the phone at the opposite end of the room.

Saarto went over to it and read the instructions posted on the wall. He thought for a moment, once more considering his options. What he really needed to do was make contact with the proper U.S. authorities in person—not by telephone. But they were in Moscow. *Proper authorities!* What a crock of shit that turn of words had become.

Whatever, he had to cover his ass—or rather, Tina Conner's. Saarto wanted to call Hollywood and the film studio, but it would be closed at this hour; worse, Harry Kaufmann's unlisted home telephone number was back in his wallet with Tina, on the train. Saarto ran through several personal numbers back in the States that he'd committed to memory; most of them wouldn't be good for an overseas collect call. As repugnant as the remedy appeared, the double-dealing Brian Beck in Los Angeles might be of help to him. Desperate times called for desperate measures. As for this end of it, the worst the Russkies could do would be to cut the connection.

Saarto knew that direct-dial long distance to the West had been suspended since the disappearance of détente. Operator-assisted calls—depending on the time, circumstances, and mood of Moscow telephone personnel—took time to put through.

It was Tuesday, normal working hours for the Soviets, and Saarto was lucky; he only had to wait ten minutes for a circuit to Los Angeles. He waited through several rings at Brian Beck's Bel Air home. It would be four in the morning in

California. Saarto drummed the wall with his fingers. *Damn
Beck!* Why wasn't he picking up the private line beside his
bed?

The Chateau de Plaisir was located upstairs in the 8000
block of garish Sunset Boulevard. Paula Suebray's patrons
were a diverse lot, but one special room at the rear of the
building was reserved for her wealthier, kinky-minded clients
from Beverly Hills, Hancock Park, and as far south as Newport
Beach. She called the exclusive room *le donjon*—the dungeon
or keep. In the trade, Paula's flagellation scene was known as
Reddi-Wip.

Brian Beck was among those who patronized the imagina-
tively-furnished facility on a regular basis, alternating between
several buxom dominatrix types who catered to his sundry
fetishes and fantasies. Once a month he would spend the entire
night at the Chateau. Following his sadomasochistic debase-
ment, he would take his favorite mistress of pleasure to
breakfast at the nearby Hyatt or Barney's Beanery.

Beck preferred to have his torment rationed out in doses,
each mini-orgy followed by a short, recuperative nap. Tonight's "hostess," Sybil, was a new girl, just in from New
Orleans. She'd just departed, leaving Beck alone on the narrow
cot where he'd collapsed nude, red-faced, and exhausted.

For the moment Beck was even too tired to enjoy a cigarette.
Reaching over the side of the bed, he pushed aside his
prosthetic foot, fumbling in the Gucci loafer where he'd stuffed
his wallet and other belongings. He found his Rolex and
examined it in the dim red glow of the chamber. Four-fifteen in
the morning! He'd been here six hours. *Christ, he needed
sleep*. The room, with its fake limestone walls, torture rack,
and assortment of sex toys, took on an uncomfortable chill.
Beck pulled the antiseptic-smelling sheet up over him and
buried his head in the pillow.

Nodding off quickly, he began to dream. A crazy dream, and
it was better than anything he'd just experienced here in the
Chateau de Plaisir's *donjon*. Tina Conner's face floated in and
out of focus. God, what was she doing to him? The image
faded; somehow, he couldn't sustain the ecstasy. Beck was half
awake and shivering again.

Suddenly there was a crashing sound in the building, very
close by. He heard shouts, female shrieks, following by cursing

in the corridor. The door to the chamber shattered. Four men stood over Beck, two of them holding weapons. One of the intruders turned on the unflattering overhead fluorescent.

Beck blinked and sat up slowly. He stared into not one, but two gun barrels, less than a foot from his nose. He looked around the room. The grim-faced, resolute quartet confronting him might have been produced by a cookie cutter. All four men had neatly-trimmed moustaches, preppie haircuts, narrow-striped ties, and conservative gray suits.

"Mr. Beck, we're FBI agents and we have a warrant for your arrest. The charge is violating U.S. espionage laws. You have the right to remain silent. Anything you say can be used against you in court. You have the right to talk with a lawyer and have him with you while questioned."

Beck pulled the sheet closer around his milk-white body, staring at them reproachfully. Sweat had already begun to form at the back of his neck and armpits. He watched the men separate slightly. The tall one by the door stepped forward. A sharp-eyed, burly blond in his late thirties, he patted his Smith & Wesson .38 thoughtfully and gave Beck a measured smile.

He said slowly, "On the other hand, Mr. Beck, you can save your neck by following my instructions to the letter." His words, too, sounded memorized, yet this time they had a ring of authority. "A choice. Immediate arrest, or the opportunity to attend a little swap meet. I'll explain the details en route to Washington, D.C., but suffice it to say you'll be leaving the country for good. My friends here are willing to give you three hours to arrange your financial affairs, choose what personal effects you need, then be escorted to a waiting private jet at the airport. You'll have to decide now, Mr. Beck."

39

GENERAL FIODOR TALIK'S country dacha near Pushkino was situated in a glen, hidden by clusters of birch and gorse and surrounded by a high electrified fence. The structure was half timber, half brick, with intricately carved Mongol eaves and two stone fireplaces, one at each end of the building. Beneath the massive, exposed beam ceiling of the living room, the KGB leader sat in front of the hearth, warmed equally by the blaze and the imported bottle of cognac he shared with the woman colonel he held in secret disdain. Despite the vulgar aftertaste Talik felt following Bruna Kloski's official visits, the colonel had proven to be his staunchest ally. Alone this woman was worth a dozen or more other loyal officers he trusted, for none of them had her tenacity and ruthlessness.

There was one serious flaw in their relationship, Talik thought. Colonel Kloski knew a great deal—*too much*. And this was dangerous in the Soviet Union. Talik idly wondered if this mannish female intended to some day betray him. What personal goals did she have of her own in the scheme of things?

He would eventually be required to eliminate this Kloski,

along with other potentially dangerous aides. *Turn on them before they turned on him.* He had to protect his flank. But all this would come later; for now he desperately needed her efficiency and connivance. Even more important, he needed Bruna Kloski's bloody hands.

Talik sipped from his Rémy Martin and stared at the miniature Solka cassette player she had placed on the table before him.

Kloski's yellow eyes flashed as she asked thickly, "Do you wish to hear it again, Comrade General?"

"Yes. From the beginning." Indeed, some of the dialogue Talik had just heard exchanged between the Soviet Chairman and his dancer son in Paris had bordered on disbelief.

Kloski pushed the reverse button and the tape began rewinding.

While Talik waited, he sipped his cognac and stared into the fireplace. Among the charred, smoldering pine logs, he saw an apparition—an unpleasant one. *Too much of the fine Rémy Martin?* Talik went over to stoke the fire, then returned to the sofa.

The flames burst higher, but the annoying vision didn't go away, instead becoming more vivid, in sharper focus. Talik saw several men in a meeting. In the foreground was his adversary, a younger Pavlin Baranov; the time was twenty years earlier. Talik recognized the scene: another exclusive dacha, this one near Usovo—the country place of the First Secretary of the Communist Party. Talik was there with Baranov. Even at that time they had been disparate figures, though their ultimate vision for Soviet collectivism had been more closley attuned in those difficult times. They were both junior officials in the Ministry of State Security then, working in turn for General Ivan Serov, then Yuri Andropov.

The vision in the flames became more detailed. Talik rubbed his eyes, trying to make the spectre go away, but it persisted. He saw a replay of the socializing that night at the dacha—the Germans would have called such a session "a night of long knives." Pavlin Baranov—the heretic even then—had referred to the meeting as "a hatchet session." Talik had gloated, with good reason to be ecstatic; the sabotage concocted that night had enabled the Politburo to oust revisionist Nikita Khrushchev the very next day. For once and for all Khrushchev's tirades and harebrained ideas had been put out to pasture.

Though Pavlin Baranov himself had wisely not supported

Khrushchev too vocally that night, he'd later passed on some innermost thoughts to Talik. Despite the undisputed problems with the Khrushchev leadership, Baranov had been convinced, and still was today, that the thorny, deposed Premier was a true visionary merely imprisoned by Russia's past. Talik held only contempt for this rationale. Bolder now as Soviet Chairman, Pavlin Baranov still insisted that it was Khrushchev—the self-made, dumpy man from peasant origins—who brought the Soviet Union into the twentieth century.

All lies! Revisionist propaganda, reflected Talik. Khrushchev made too many blunders to itemize, but the big ones still hurt Russian prestige. Never again must the Soviet Union back down as it did in Cuba. The young American President who was so vocal on immunizing the world against the spread of socialist ideas had outfoxed Nikita by nerve alone. And this was the same John Kennedy who fumbled the Bay of Pigs affair and numbly accepted the Berlin wall! As far as Talik was concerned, Khrushchev's Cuban missile fiasco was another Munich.

Talik swallowed hard, trying to put away the memories of those difficult years. But how could he when, regrettably, they were being replayed, precipitated by the half-a-loaf mentality of the incumbent Chairman-Premier? Ever since that night two decades back at the dacha, Talik's relationship with Baranov had been on downhill slide. The current Soviet Chairman was an abomination and had to go. Talik once more felt satisfaction as he stared into the fireplace. The flames shot higher, finally consuming the phantasm. The younger image of Pavlin Baranov disappeared, and along with it, Talik's persistent memories. He looked away from the hearth, determined to think about the present and future. Once more his great design, the thought of sabotaging his old enemy, intoxicated him. Just a few hours longer.

Talik would now listen to the tape again and commit the incriminating dialogue to memory.

Kloski was ready with the cassette. Talik eyed her appraisingly as she sipped her drink. "Before we run through it again, Comrade Colonel, you are positive that your man Khamsin did not complete his task?"

Kloski avoided his eyes, staring into her brandy glass with annoyance. "An unfortunate setback. Our friend blundered and has been captured by the Paris police, Comrade General. It is confirmed."

"There is also the matter of the weaponry plans he was hand-carrying for us."

She thought for a moment, eyes narrowing. "Khamsin will be expecting our assistance, that we will bring him out, perhaps to safety in Moscow."

"Did Danielle Ponty thoroughly check the apartment for the secret documents?"

Kloski nodded. "I suspect Khamsin hid them elsewhere in the city. He was a fool not to take care of this matter before going after the dancer."

Talik thought for a moment, then reached for a cigarette. "Aside from the espionage material, do you need him here to do your will, Colonel?" He gave her a speculative look.

"Certainly not."

"Then Khamsin has ceased to be of value to us. Have him liquidated before he talks too freely."

There was an uncomfortable silence. The Wellington chime in Talik's grandfather clock sounded in the hallway. It was seven o'clock.

He looked at her. "Those crowded eyebrows of yours. Do I detect more bad news, Comrade Colonel?"

She cleared her throat. "Since speaking with his father on the long distance connection, Nuri has disappeared."

Talik winced. His disdain for both the Soviet Chairman and his son once more suffocated him, mushrooming up like an unwelcome tumor in the throat. *Contain yourself, General. Don't lose control in front of this Kloski woman.* Talik stiffened, determined to maintain a facade of calmness as resolute and rigid as the Kremlin wall itself. Considering his options, he said quickly, "You'll see to it that General Shaeffer is not given over to the Americans."

Kloski nodded gravely. "Of course. I'll personally attend to the matter. I have already made arrangements to fly to East Berlin, the first thing in the morning."

"And the Nuri Baranov situation?" Talik studied her.

"He will not escape. The frontier guards have been alerted, and I've assigned additional KGB personnel in Moscow—the largest dragnet the city has ever seen, if necessary. We will apprehend him before he can reach the Chairman." She paused and added maliciously, "His actress friend and her traitorous escorts will be found as well."

Talik pursed his lips. "Move with extreme care. I do not

wish to risk a premature confrontation with the Soviet Army.
You're certain the dancer will attempt to return to Moscow?"

Kloski put down her empty glass and smiled at him with
reassurance. "After hearing this taped telephone conversation,
I can't conceive of another possible reaction from the dancer."

Talik nodded. Sipping his·cognac reflectively, he looked
back at the fireplace, once more mesmerized by the flames.
Quietly, he said, "Whatever manpower you have to assign,
Comrade Colonel—I suggest that the task force be doubled.
We take no chances." He waved his hand with impatience.
"Now play the tape again."

Nuri had spent the rest of the afternoon making arrangements for the next day's flight to Moscow. Already it was
approaching six. Following the neon arrows and other pedestrians along Boulevard Montmartre, he passed several grease-
blown eateries humming with flies and smelling of *pommes
frites*. He was hungry, but first wanted to find a cheap,
inconspicuous room for the night. He rejected two hotels
where the entry stairwells smelled of urine; in another doorway
a derelict's snarling dog frightened him off.

Nuri finally found a place that looked reasonably tidy,
though unpretentious. Climbing to the second-level office, he
rang the bell. A door opened behind the counter. The concierge
was an older woman with a deeply-planed, ugly face with
stretched skin the color of parchment. She reeked of talcum
powder. She greeted Nuri in an impatient, contemptuous
manner, examining his passport with a reading glass and
quickly pocketing his money.

Nuri found his own way to a huge, sparsely-furnished room
with stained wallpaper and a grimy skylight. By size alone the
pad would have been sumptuous in the time of Gauguin and
Van Gogh. Tossing his newly-purchased suitcase on the bed,
he washed and changed into a clean shirt. For the moment the
shabby hotel would be his island of security; his masquerade
was a suspended existence, but at least he was safe.

Despite the day's unsettling events, Nuri was eager for a
decent meal. He left the hotel, leaving the key at the desk.

Shuffling back down the boulevard, Nuri found a small café
that struck his fancy. It was hardly noticeable from the street,
tucked behind a window solid with red gingham curtains. Nuri
took a table near the rear and ordered a thick steak *à la
béarnaise*. He consumed half of it, all of the large escarole and

cucumber salad, and the best part of a bottle of Chateau-Margaux.

It was late when he walked back to his hotel, and he felt light-stepped, a degree more confident. He had to keep reminding himself that he was no longer Nuri Baranov but rather Mark Washburn; he needed to act the part of the young American tourist.

The street was already filled with night people, a good number boisterous, a few drunk. Two prostitutes beckoned to him from their roost above a shuttered patisserie. Nuri flashed on what one of his childhood tutors had told him of life in the West: *Sex, greed, sex, charity, and sex.* He smiled up at the women and walked on.

His hotel still hadn't been shuttered for the night. Nursing his paranoia, Nuri looked up and down the street in both directions before passing through the entry and trudging up the stairwell. "They" were still out there looking for him. Now the French authorities as well would join the chase. None of this mattered. Only Tina. He'd fallen full into the maw of retribution—or was *revenge* the proper word? Nuri needed the pocket-sized English dictionary he'd left back with his other belongings.

Safely in his room, Nuri locked the door and propped a chair against the knob. He brushed his teeth, then stripped down to his shorts. As tired as he was, he couldn't retire immediately following a large meal, so he did push-ups until he'd worked up a decent sweat. But his mind continued its flash dance and he quickly lost count. Giving up the exercise—"monkey drills" as the Americans liked to call it—he flopped, exhausted, on the sagging, too-soft bed.

The hotel walls were thin as cardboard. From the next room he heard a radio playing—Edith Piaf singing *"Les Mots d'Amour."* Nuri hugged one pillow against his chest, tossed the other over his head. He slept soundly for an hour or so, then woke; from then on he was only able to drift off intermittently. Across the way a disco club throbbed satanically into the wee hours; he could hear pounding heels, drums, shouts, and shrill laughter.

Frustrated, Nuri was tempted to rise, wander across the street, and observe the action over a glass of calvados or scotch whiskey. No. He didn't need company. Not tonight. His mind was already too crowded.

* * *

After the pyrotechnics in the train compartment and Jon Saarto's escape, the enraged Colonel Rablin and Alexi Stanovich weren't about to take any unnecessary chances with Tina. They'd taken her back to their own compartment and seated her between them. She felt only a dull numbness up to the two Russians' alternating wrath and silence.

The emergency stop to rendezvous with Rablin's special army detail came off without incident, and they escorted her, undetected, into the heart of Moscow in a Chaika limousine with its curtains drawn. The colonel had been convivial and gregarious in Leningrad, but now, angered over Saarto's escape, he'd become withdrawn and distant. Tina had tried, unsuccessfully, to explain the bodyguard's rebelliousness, that Saarto in fact meant no harm to any of them, that his only intent was to notify the American authorities. Tina had explained that regardless of his actions, she still intended to cooperate with Rablin. Since neither he nor Alexi Stanovich seemed pleased, she, too, had retreated into silence.

Tina was surprised when the Soviets hadn't taken her to the Cosmos Hotel as promised. Instead, Rablin drove her directly to Natasha Chernyskaya's.

The film director's third floor walk-up apartment was suitably grand by Moscow standards for a State artist of stature. It was located by the Literature Museum, just a stone's throw from Gorky Park. There were four spacious rooms, one of which had picture windows with a view of the Moscow River. The flat, to Tina, seemed to be the antithesis of communal society—were it not for the oppressive lobby on the ground floor with its tired Caucasian carpet and prominently placed pedestal with a white alabaster bust of Lenin.

Natasha's furnishings were cozy enough, though the film director's taste was somewhat eclectic—or chaotic. The overstuffed furniture was strikingly modern, probably of northern European import; the walls were crowded with drawings, lithographs, engravings, and one huge watercolor. Tina recognized a Dali sketch, but the other works were signed by unfamiliar Russian names—Rerich, Feofilaktov, Somov, Vallin. The room contained several ceiling-high, glassed-in bookcases with several shelves given over to Royal Copenhagen figurines and Yussupov china. Newspapers, magazines, and film scripts were scattered everywhere, even stacked on the counters in the reasonably modern kitchen.

Despite Natasha Chernyskaya's hospitality, Tina knew she was still a prisoner. Gazing outside, she could see one of Colonel Rablin's men watching the building's entry from across the street.

Tina turned away from the window and watched Natasha set the table. In the background the stereo played a barely recognizable Russian version of the Beatles' "Here Comes the Sun."

Tina quipped, "Colonel Rablin is a lying son of a bitch. He promised to put me up at the Cosmos, with no more guards."

Natasha's eyebrows shot up in an offended stiffness. She tried to smile. "My dear, one shouldn't question the morality and family lineage of the man who holds out his hand to pull you out of quicksand." She finished folding a napkin and looked at Tina seriously. "The change in accommodations, the man down on the street—it is all for your protection. The KGB may be wise to the colonel and Alexi. We have to be cautious. Come, you must be famished after your journey from Tallinn."

Tina sat at the table, listening to her hostess' apology for the simple menu. Natasha said, "The colonel's last minute change of plans caught me off guard, and there wasn't time to queue at the food stores."

Tina's hunger precluded any disappointment in what Natasha considered routine Russian fare. The breaded veal, boiled potatoes with parsley, and glazed carrots were delicious. Tina ate with gusto, feeling a twinge of guilt at accepting more hospitality from the enemy camp.

After dinner they lingered at the table over cappuccino. Tina examined the intricately-formed coffee spoon Natasha had placed before her. The end of the handle was a silver onion dome overlaid with an Orthodox cross of gold.

Natasha said quietly, "When you come to Russia you must not look at facades, for they will disappoint you. Study the small details. Learn to look closely and you'll learn much about our humanity."

"Nuri told me much. It was like seeing your land through the eyes of an artist."

Tina smiled again, and with forced bonhomie tried to penetrate into Natasha Chernyskaya's past. She was anxious to know how the pretty Russian woman became a renowned film director.

The line of inquiry didn't take hold. Natasha said something about being born in the Crimea, the daughter of circus performers, then having been raised in Poland by her grandfather, a high-ranking Soviet officer in the Warsaw Pact forces. She then moodily, if not deliberately, changed the subject, talking instead of the Italian influence on cinema. Natasha told Tina she was particularly interested in Luchino Visconti, that the 1942 classic *Ossessione* was one of her favorites.

Tina was tired and let it show.

Natasha gave up her own room, insisting on sleeping on the pillow-covered day bed in the living room.

Tina would have given an arm or leg to use the telephone to try and get through to Nuri in Paris. She started to plead her case, but Natasha turned her down.

"It would be too dangerous; the lines might be tapped. Tomorrow, perhaps, at the film studio we'll find a way to get a message through. I suspect, however, Nuri will not be at his hotel, but en route to Moscow."

Tina winced and went into the other room. Confused and tired, she crawled into bed. One moment she felt as if she were embarking on an exciting new adventure, the next it was as though she'd been gagged, bound with chains, and tossed into a dank, deep pit from which she would never again see the light of day.

A half hour after Tina Conner had retired, Natasha was startled by the ring of the telephone on the table beside her. She put aside the film script she was studying and answered, trying to keep her voice low.

"*Alyo.*" She frowned, tightening her grip on the receiver. "*Ktoh-eh-toh?*"

Listening with agonized concentration to what was being said at the opposite end of the line, she finally responded, "*Oh-nah zo'yes, oh nah nee-koo-dah n'yeh eed yoht.*"

Natasha glanced warily toward the bedroom door, sighed sharply, and switched to English, whispering, "You should not have called here, Mr. Saarto. And it is a mistake for us to speak in English. Call me tomorrow, at the studio, the previously-designated telephone."

Irritably she replaced the receiver.

40

WEDNESDAY MORNING brought high cirrus clouds and smooth air to the busy flight corridor between Moscow and East Berlin. The Aeroflot Yak-42 slowly descended, then made a wide circle preparatory to landing at Schonefeld Airport. Fastening her seat belt, KGB Colonel Kloski's hands grew clammy. She'd conquered every fear imaginable except flying.

Kloski traveled light this trip. Overnight luggage with a change of clothing wouldn't be necessary, for she planned to be at the Twentieth Guards army installation for less than an hour, then catch a return flight to Moscow. Even her briefcase was lightweight, emptied of its usual voluminous paperwork. Today it contained only a green folder with her priority KGB orders and a small medical pouch she called her "truth kit." This time, in addition to the syringe and bottle of talk serum—her own mixture of sodium Pentothal with a pinch of racemic methedrine—she'd included an ampule of prussic acid. There were also a pair of rubber gloves and a large wad of cotton. Kloski had used prussic acid before and found it a convenient, nearly foolproof liquidation device; its inhaled vapor perfectly simulated the effects of coronary heart disease.

The exciting new *fugu* poison she'd been experimenting with wouldn't be appropriate for the task at hand. Kloski would save that diabolical surprise for tonight, the grand finale she'd planned for the Soviet Chairman himself.

Kloski hoped her intelligence was correct and that the scheduled release of the American general had not been moved up several hours. *No, this would be unlikely*. Soviet timetables were more often delayed or postponed, seldom accelerated. She wondered what travel arrangements Colonel General Kirichek at Army Strategic Directions West had planned for the captive. Would the American be set free at Checkpoint Charlie, or something more dramatic, like the infamous U-2 pilot's return at the Glienicker Bridge? Whatever, it was all *madness*.

Kloski knew Kirichek not only had Marshal status, but he was a Hero of the Soviet Union, influential in both Politburo hierarchy and the party. Kirichek was purportedly one of the "untouchables," and as such, immune to KGB or GRU reprimand. Still, the Warsaw Pact commander and his aides wouldn't dare interfere with her request for one final interrogation of General Shaeffer; it was the Fifth Directorate's mandate to probe and make official inquiries. According to her authorization—signed by Fiodor Talik himself—that was all she would officially do. A few pertinent, final questions. What Kloski *actually* intended to accomplish was a different matter.

Glancing out the plane's window, Kloski marvelled at the growth of East Berlin since she'd been here eleven years ago. She saw the highway leading northwest—one of Hitler's famous autobahns—that led to her eventual destination between Berlin and Eberswalde.

She thought again about the situation in the Kremlin and Chairman Baranov's decision to let the American general go free. *Irresponsible, completely unthinkable*. On the contrary, a proper spectacle, a tough-minded example should have been made of this Austin Shaeffer. In his tomb, Lenin would shudder! Does the Chairman think the Americans, getting their military spy back, would not feel obligated to resume détente and merely look the other way in face of Nuri's return to Russia? The senior Baranov was dreaming again.

Kloski let out a sharp sigh; she needed to slow down, control her excitement. She started counting bodies again. Chairman

Baranov's alliance with the army was strong, but Talik in his role as KGB minister commanded the Dzerzhinsky Division, a combat force of 18,000 men. The Chairman had better than two thirds of the Soviet military machine in his pocket, and up until the incident of his son's surprising defection, he'd been popular in the party organization and the entire Soviet Congress. All this despite his mixed Ukrainian-Latvian origin. The energetic Baranov was a dozen years younger than Fiodor Talik, and some members of the Politburo called Baranov the "boy wizard." Kloski wondered if anyone in the KGB upper echelons might clandestinely support the Chairman. If the KGB had its *stukachi* everywhere, couldn't Baranov have his own infiltrator-informers?

Kloski reaffirmed in her mind what she had to do now. She needed to strengthen her own position as well as Talik's. General Shaeffer's release would be an embarrassment to the USSR and had to be avoided at all costs. And when finished here in East Germany, she would intensify her efforts to find Nuri, have him liquidated. Last of all, there would be the matter of the American actress. If she didn't leave the Soviet Union soon of her own accord, perhaps she, too, would meet with an unfortunate "accident."

Kloski felt the landing gear thud into place as the jet lined up with the Schonefeld runway. Her body involuntarily tightened. *Forget the plane, think of the critical hours ahead*, she repeated to herself. Think of tonight at the Bolshoi State Theatre, when all restraint would be tossed to the wind. She was committed—Fiodor Talik's will would be carried out. The situation at the Kremlin was beyond defusing. Chairman Baranov and his son were doomed, and in the process, KGB Colonel Bruna Kloski wouldn't feel the slightest sting of remorse. If the dancer-turned-blasphemous author were allowed to live, he would precipitate trouble in the Soviet population, particularly among artists and intellectuals. There would be scandals with continuing international repercussions. Nuri's seditious acts against the State had only accelerated the ultimate resolution of power. Externally, Pavlin Baranov had become too "acceptable" among Soviet Russia's enemies. The monster that was communist fulfillment required another image, a return to the rigors of Stalinism. Consolidation of power and carrying out the will of the party was a ruthless, never-ending task.

Kloski smiled to herself. Fiodor Talik was determined to take over the Soviet helm, and she would help him. But he was too old. The KGB general wouldn't live forever, and there would be younger, more energetic hard-liners waiting in the wings. And she would be one of them.

Jon Saarto slowly opened his eyes. He was thirsty, his mouth feeling like residue from last year's cotton crop. Blinking at the daylight streaking through the barn's weatherbeaten walls, he stretched and pushed the hay that partially covered him away. He smarted at its fetid smell.

Trying to play it low-key and remaining unconspicuous would have been impossible had Saarto gone directly into Moscow the night before and tried to register at a hotel without travel documents. After the encounter with the Soviet postal clerk Saarto had doubts over successfully winging it as a local, even with the pilfered train porter's identification. Appearance was now his first priority; he needed to find some Russian clothing.

Saarto had managed to ward off the cold by snuggling up next to a docile cow and pulling hay over himself. At first he'd slept uneasily, not because of a hooting barn owl, but for fear the bovine beside him might roll over and crush him, or worse yet, suddenly rise and drop a damned cow pie in his face. The fatigue finally won out, and he'd dozed off, only to oversleep.

It was well past daybreak, and Saarto had to move. He needed to get into the city, buy some inconspicuous clothing, and find a public bath. He didn't mind looking like a country peasant, but he didn't want to smell like one. Rising to his feet, it took a moment longer to get his bearings. Chickens scurried around him, scavenging in the hay and dirt. Saarto hesitated. The sagging barn door was half open, and he'd left it closed the night before. With measaured steps he inspected the barn's interior, halfway expecting to find a lurking figure nearby. He saw no one, but from outside he heard voices.

Saarto's nerves tightened as he moved stealthily to the half-open door. Pressing himself against the jamb, he risked a peek across the farmyard. A small log and brick house was situated less than a hundred yards away, in the doorway a shawled, stout woman with a child tugging on her arm. Confronting her was a lanky teenager in coveralls and fur-trimmed cap. The young man was arguing vociferously with the woman, all the while pointing toward the barn—in Saarto's direction.

"Pa-shlee-tee pa-troo-lee!" the woman shouted.

Saarto stiffened. He'd been discovered, but apparently there wasn't a telephone in the house. The farm youth appeared ready to follow the woman's urging and go for help. He disappeared around the side of the structure. When Saarto heard an engine turn over, he remembered an old truck had been parked in the driveway the night before.

Saarto cursed himself for not leaving before daybreak as he'd planned. Flinging caution aside, he slipped through the barn door and bolted in the opposite direction from the house, heading out across the field. Saarto plunged through ankle-deep snow for several minutes until he was out of breath, then paused to rest.

He looked back, satisfied that no one followed. Gazing across the plain, he could see buildings on the distant horizon. The fringe of Moscow? He'd read somewhere that the transition from the steppe of a century ago to urban Moscow was strikingly immediate; one moment there would be rustic cabins, fertile fields, forests. The next, there were the thirteen-story apartments that marked the boundaries of a tightly-zoned city.

Already Saarto imagined the smell of diesel fumes. *No, it wasn't his imagination.* At the far end of the field was a small intersection on the Leningrad-Moscow Highway. He saw a road sign as big and blue as any on the Pennsylvania Turnpike, indicating in both Cyrilllic and English the route leading to the ring road that surrounded the Soviet capital. Saarto waited for a break in the truck traffic, then sprinted across the road. A short distance away was a kilometer post that read 28/741, and beyond it, a small diesel fuel station.

Saarto spotted a long, tarpaulin-covered rig that was being serviced. It looked like there was room in the back to mooch a ride. He approached the vehicle guardedly.

In Washington, D.C., the mood in the Oval Office grew ominous. Sweating under the volley of questions that had been hurled at him, CIA Director Donald Lindsay edged back in his seat. "We tried our best, sir. Nuri Baranov's disappeared in Paris."

The telephone on the Chief Executive's desk buzzed softly.

The President picked up the intercom and snapped, "Absolutely no interruptions."

Outside it was raining in the capital, a rotten Saturday to begin with. For the President the morning couldn't have been worse had Russian shock troops landed on Pennsylvania Avenue. From the onset of the meeting he'd been livid with anger. The four powerful men summoned to his office seemed to cower under his onslaught. Before him sat the National Security Advisor, the Secretary of State, the CIA director, and head of the FBI. The latter two men had taken the brunt of his wrath.

The President didn't want to hear the details of what had happened in Paris, and had to force himself to listen. If he didn't, the media would. After six years in office he'd come to hate everything about politics, especially its vulnerability to the press. The news people would be at his throat soon enough on this Nuri Baranov mess. *Reporters were like rapacious hawks.*

Rising from his desk, the President went over to stand by the fireplace, where his aides had kindled some oak logs. His aging schnauzer looked up from its spot on the hearth, expecting either a handout or a pat on the head. The President ignored the dog, continuing to glare at the others who sat in a semicircle around his desk.

FBI Director Lance Byington, a hulk of a man with a square streetfighter's face, looked strangely small and diminutive. He was first to turn and brave eye contact. "I'm sorry, Mr. President. I should have been more watchful over Army Intelligence. However, I'll remind you this clumsy milieu acted only with White House interests and the nation's welfare in mind. Certainly not out of personal motivation."

The Chief Executive glowered. "Poppycock. I give policy orders, I expect them to be implemented. Neither U.S. nor White House interests were carried out. As for Nuri Baranov, he was asked to cooperate with us and apparently declined. In a democratic society that's his prerogative."

The cowed FBI chief leaned slightly forward in his wing-back chair. He was about to speak again, but across from him CIA head Lindsay said swiftly, "Gentlemen, our mistakes and the tragic loss of one of my agents are water over the dam. Unfortunately, Nuri's still swimming in the dangerous current. And I have reason to believe he's up to something." Lindsay hesitated, then continued in an uneven voice, "And I submit it's a damned sight more earthshaking than dragging a few of his fellow dancers out of Russia. Or publishing an underground book."

The President glared with impatience. "You've cleared him of any espionage or the possibility of being a KGB sleeper. What else?"

"A man, like a harassed animal, can take so much threat and be hunted just so long. A trapped quarry eventually turns vicious hunter himself."

"And the implications?" asked the Secretary of State. Gerald Brenner's lean, bronzed face looked a little haggard, his eyes redlined.

Scowling, Lindsay replied, "I say the dancer's more gutsy than we figure. He'll go all the way—for nothing less than Fiodor Talik's throat."

The FBI chief coughed. "Convenient for us, but he wouldn't stand a chance. Even if he did have the mind of an assassin. Which I doubt."

Stepping quickly back to his desk, the President eased his lanky body into the chair and looked at each man in turn. He said somberly, "Try telling that to John Wilkes Booth or Lee Harvey Oswald at their bizarre moments of glory. And God knows, they had less reason to be justly motivated than Nuri Baranov."

"Hear, hear; I say more power to him," announced the bearded, owl-faced National Security Advisor. William Mydlowski had a habit of waiting until everyone else had spoken, adding his two cents last.

The others looked at Mydlowski with grumpy indifference. The President took his time lighting his pipe. Everyone waited, enduring the uncomfortable, ominous silence.

Secretary of State Brenner broke the lull by coughing again. He said slowly, "As for this threat of Talik's, when petty people are caught up in a great internal power struggle or a war, anything can, and usually does happen. Urgency takes on a new dimension."

The President pointed his pipe at Brenner. "Kindly stop turning phrases and get to the point."

"Ambassador Hewett's intelligence sources in Moscow suggest we don't give Fiodor Talik the slightest excuse for a confrontation. The general might use it."

The President puffed on his briar, but he wasn't enjoying the smoke at all. Irritably, he said, "An alarming hypothesis. So much for ex-post-facto observations from our Kremlinologists. As usual, the latest diplomatic word from Moscow tends to be foggy." He paused, turning to Donald Lindsay. "While the CIA's failures are patently clear."

Lindsay flushed and raised his hands in protest. He let them fall back of their own weight. Quietly, he retorted, "Mr. President, I suspect Talik is all hot air. He talks a big future war he can't possibly win. The KGB general dreams of getting in a few good licks, then running for the hills. No one takes him seriously. Certainly I don't, nor does the Pentagon."

NSA head Mydlowski added, "Whatever the Soviets try, we'll survive, gentlemen. Wasn't it one of President Reagan's brilliant Civil Defense advisors who made the remark 'Ants eventually build another anthill'?"

The President didn't react. He sat silently, eyes seething and still riveted on the CIA director.

FBI chief Byington shifted his big frame. He quickly interjected, "I never was a believer in détente. Maybe the right wing's full-court press against the Russians is the only way after all."

The President looked at Byington. "I suggest you stick to law enforcement and let the rest of us worry over geopolitics. Which brings me to those stolen weaponry plans. Has the disloyal publisher done any more talking?"

"Brian Beck needs a little longer to make up his mind. The Bureau intends to give him all the rope he needs to hang himself and anyone else involved."

The Secretary of State leaned forward and changed the subject "There's more bad news: Soviet Ambassador Chekor has been recalled."

Donald Lindsay shrugged. "Not by Baranov. I suspect Chekor's gone back of his own volition to meet with Talik. They're two peas in a pod. Mr. President, what do we do about General Shaeffer at Lubyanka?"

The President shook his head. "I suspect he's already on his way home. As for these other long shots of yours, Lindsay— will they in fact work, or is counting on the CIA like betting on a spavined racehorse?"

The Agency head wasn't about to be put down. "I've already apologized for the Diana Vespucci fiasco, Mr. President. A regrettable loophole. That incident aside, I have complete confidence in the rest of it."

The Chief Executive tiredly rose to his feet. "Gentlemen, suffice it to say I no longer need to have any of you go probing with rectal thermometers to tell me the Soviet bear is running a mean temperature." He paused. William Mydlowski and Gerald Brenner were gazing out the window toward the south lawn, and he wanted their undivided attention. "I suggest all of you listen carefully."

When every eye in the Oval Office was turned his way, the President continued, "The U.S. Dance Company's official explanation to the press will be that Nuri requested to go join his actress friend in Stockholm. From what we now know, it appears the media will have its hands full picking up on a trail that doesn't exist." He hesitated, turning to the CIA director. "Lindsay, have your people intensify their search for Nuri— before the French police trip him up in their dragnet. In the meantime, we buy a few hours, continuing to pretend we know absolutely nothing. The next step is up to the Soviet Chairman."

The FBI chief cleared his throat. "Pardon, sir. What about Defense Secretary Fleming and General McCulloch, their role in all this?"

The President reached in his side drawer, withdrew a couple of Milk Bone biscuits, and flung one of them across the room. It missed his suddenly alert dog by the hearth and wound up in the fire. The schnauzer whimpered, but managed to pick off the second biscuit in midair.

The President turned back to Byington and said incisively, "General McCulloch will never see another star if I have my way. As for the Defense secretary, pass the word: I expect either Fleming's resignation or his head on my desk on Monday morning.

A red stripe on the left arm of a Soviet Army major's tunic signified Deputy Duty Officer. In the case of Misha Ogirkov it also meant unpleasant responsibilities, like seeing to the ugly affairs of a military stockade and in a matter of minutes having to entertain infamous KGB officials from Moscow—a gross-mannered, impetuous woman colonel, at that. Ogirkov had never met Bruna Kloski, but her reputation preceded her. His aide had informed him that the head of the Fifth Directorate had arrived early and was in the next building waiting for him.

Ogirkov did not expect the reputed Beast of Lubyanka so soon. Either Kloski's plane had come in ahead of schedule or his driver had a heavy foot while bringing her up from the East Berlin airport. It didn't matter, for Colonel General Kirichek had ordered Ogirkov to take his time, remaining in the American's cell as long as necessary; he was to finish debriefing General Shaeffer and not allow any unwelcome bureaucrats from Moscow to interfere. Any proposed final interrogation by the KGB could wait. Though he was out-ranked, Major Ogirkov was determined not to be bowled over by this Colonel Kloski; she could cool her heels back at his duty office.

Two faceless satellites in khaki hovered on separate sides of the room as Ogirkov continued his confrontation of Austin Shaeffer. The American general, having just finished a lunch of lentil soup, black bread, and an apple, appeared unusually cheerful.

"To continue. It will be over soon, General Shaeffer. Despite your lack of cooperation, you can expect to be released within the day—late this evening at the latest. Depending on what happens in Moscow, possibly even in a matter of hours. You are fortunate, extraordinarily fortunate. But also, shall we say 'extraordinarily naive'?" Ogirkov watched the stockily-built American's smile disappear.

Shaeffer's face reddened. Clenching his jaw, he said with effort, "I'm tired of conversation, Major. Especially the kind that leads nowhere."

Ogirkov shrugged. "As are my superiors. Playing nurse-maid is beneath the dignity of the Twentieth Guards, men who have a reputation for being the best of troops in the Western sector."

Shaeffer stood by the barred window looking out on an empty parade ground. "Bullshit."

It was Ogirkov's turn to bristle. "I must now bring up an unpleasant subject, General. The KGB is interested in one last visit with you. A few final questions when I am finished here."

"You've made my day."

"I would suggest you answer any queries she might ask you precisely as you did at Lubyanka. Do not add information or deviate in the slightest. Not at his point in the game, General."

Shaeffer came away from the window and pulled out the crumpled packet of English Players Bruna Kloski had given him earlier. "You did say *she*?" He straightened the last cigarette and lit it.

"The head of the Fifth Directorate. A woman." Ogirkov watched the American spit out his smoke.

Shaeffer slowly nodded. "Colonel Kloski. Unfortunately I've already met the Amazon. I suspect she wears camo jocks for underwear."

Ogirkov didn't understand the idiom and really didn't care. "We'll try to keep her visit reasonably short, but I can promise nothing until I examine her orders." He smiled at Shaeffer and reached inside his tunic, withdrawing a photograph that he kept cupped in his hand. "It was all so futile, General. Colonel Kloski would be most eager to know what army intelligence has discovered about you. But it does not suit our interests to chop straight from the shoulder and assist the KGB at this time. Let me say, however, that your intelligence attempt was a waste of time."

"I was an off-duty tourist. Read my fucking file and *you* won't be wasting time."

Ogirkov smiled. "We know exactly what you were after, General Shaeffer. Two things. Construction evidence of our new civil defense shelters, yes? And equally important, information on the underground petrol supply network—according to your own CIA, the system that enables us to refuel front-line vehicles at the German border and beyond." Ogirkov paused, watching Shaeffer's eyes waver slightly. "All outdated intelligence, my foolish friend!" Ogirkov handed over the palmed photograph.

Shaeffer saw that it was of a helicopter. He examined the photo without comment.

"You wasted your time, General Shaeffer. Next week that picture will appear in the British aviation guide *Jane's Military Aircraft*. The helicopter carries over forty tons of petrol. Our V-12 cargo helicopter, General Shaeffer. Simple mathematics should tell you what this means to our support capability for a rapidly advancing front. Who needs antiquated, vulnerable pipelines? And as for our civil defense shelters, the Soviet Union has nothing to hide. Regrettably, your visit to Moscow was a misadventure. You're welcome to the helicopter photograph, of course."

Shaeffer looked at him hatefully. Ogirkov headed for the door, jerking his head toward the two guards who preceded him out of the room. He turned to Shaeffer and added in a cynical footnote, "Ah, the pleasures of West Berlin. Perhaps tonight you will enjoy dinner at one of those *weinstubes* off the decadent Kurfürstendamm, yes?"

Shaeffer smirked, "Thanks for nothing, *comrade*."

Closing the door to the cell, Ogirkov dismissed his two assistants and stepped briskly down the barracks hallway. At the outer doorway he was surprised to be greeted—in less than a friendly manner—by the KGB woman. Bruna Kloski had apparently grown tired of waiting in the Duty Office across the courtyard. Ogirkov straightened his shoulders and saluted. She was tall, with several centimeters on him, and Ogirkov had never considered himself short by any means.

She looked at him with unwinking snake's eyes. "You will tell your Colonel General Kirichek that I have no time to be kept waiting, Comrade Major." She hovered over him, too close.

Ogirkov edged back slightly, trying to avoid her abusive stare and stale breath. Never before had he seen such a combined look of cruel joy and determination in a woman's face. He finally said to Kloski, "I regret the delay, Comrade Colonel."

She nodded toward the inside hallway and extended her hand. "The key, if you will," she said with impatience. "I'll not be keeping your prisoner long."

Forcing a smile he didn't feel, Ogirkov replied, "I will be pleased to accompany you. Follow me." He started to turn.

"No." Her fleshy, liver-spotted hand grabbed his wrist. "It is unnecessary. I'll find my own way. I wish to question the prisoner alone, in privacy. That is our KGB prerogative."

Ogirkov thought rapidly; his orders didn't prevent this. *Poor Austin Shaeffer*. Reluctantly he handed over the key. "Cell fourteen, Comrade Colonel."

He watched her swagger down the hallway, a briefcase clutched tightly in one hand, the jailer's key ring swinging in the other. Ogirkov shook his head. On top of her other disagreeable features, the woman colonel walked as if she needed a good sprinkling of talcum powder between her legs. Ogirkov bit back a smile and turned to the duty man beside the door. "When she is finished, you will check the prisoner, make sure the door is properly secured, and report back to me."

Major Ogirkov proceeded across the courtyard. Once inside the duty office he made himself comfortable behind his desk and once more perused General Austin Shaeffer's *zapiska*. There was nothing he'd missed; it would be a pleasure to be rid of the querulous American. Ogirkov picked up the telegram that had authorized Bruna Kloski's visit to the stockade. An aide had left the additional documents she'd brought with her on his desk, and now he read those as well. Her orders had been signed by the Minister of State Security himself. Ogirkov wondered why the KGB colonel had flown all the way from Moscow on such short notice. There had to be something peculiar going on at the Kremlin.

Ogirkov suddenly had misgivings. Kloski's orders were legitimate, but still—he thought a moment longer, then picked up the field phone on his desk. A communications operator responded and Ogirkov identified himself. He asked to speak directly to the Warsaw Pact military commander, Colonel General Kirichek.

Before the connection could be completed, one of the stockade guards burst inside the office. "Comrade Major! The KGB colonel asks for you! She reports a calamity." The guard paused to catch his wind.

Ogirkov rose to his feet and grabbed his hat. "Speak up! What is the problem?"

"The American general appears to have suffered a mortal heart attack."

41

NURI SAT in a window seat toward the rear of the DC-9, his eyes closed and his thoughts focused on his first moves in Moscow. This second leg of the flight wasn't crowded and he had the row to himself. When the seat belt sign had gone off, he'd taken off his shoes and sat cross-legged on the cushions, sipping at a plastic cup of Dutch beer the stewardess had brought him and listening to music on the stereo earphones. Whitney Houston was singing "Didn't We Almost Have It All." *Appropriate*, he thought, considering his past year in the West.

Nuri considered his hastily improvised change of plans. His only regret was the way he'd disposed of the gun he'd taken from Khamsin. In the rush to change flight tickets, he'd tossed it into an airport rest-room trash container. If it were found and traced, the French police might lock on to his new itinerary.

Rescheduling Mark Washburn's flight ticket to Moscow had been accomplished easily enough the day before, but while in the Air France office, Nury had felt sudden misgivings. Disguise or not, the logistics were *too perfect*. KGB func-

tionaries would undoubtedly be assigned to watch the one daily
flight leaving Paris for Moscow. At the other end, the Soviets
knew Nuri would be coming and they would go over every
passenger manifest with a fine-toothed comb, and particularly
any flight originating in France. Nuri often had strong
precognitions, and each time he trusted them, things went the
right way. This morning when he'd rolled out of bed, the hunch
had been to avoid Charles de Gaulle Airport.

Accordingly, he'd left the Montmartre hotel early, taking a
taxi out to Le Bourget, then caught a plane for Copenhagen
that made a convenient connection with an SAS flight to
Moscow. On the way to the alternate Paris airport, Nuri had
noticed a *vendeuse* holding up a copy of a French newspaper,
on its front page a picture of Khamsin being escorted out of the
Meurice Hotel by two gendarmes. Nuri had bought a paper,
hoping to get the lengthy news story translated later.

The change in flight plan had cost Nuri not only an hour or
two of time, but the last of his traveler's checks for the
additional air fare. He was down to thirty dollars and a few
French francs. He hoped the Customs people in Moscow didn't
ask to see his funds.

The hop from Paris to Copenhagen had gone without
incident, arriving at Kastrup Airport in plenty of time for the
Moscow connection. Nuri had even found time to pick up
some reading material, a package of sugar-free chewing gum,
and a carton of American cigarettes—one more prop to make
him look like a typical tourist. The smokes might also come in
handy for gratuities and petty bribery.

The SAS flight departed on time and was scheduled to arrive
at Moscow's Sheremetyevo Airport at four-fifteen. With plenty
of time to think, Nuri again tried hard to conjugate what had
happened to him over the past nine days. Unfair was too kind a
word to describe it. He had no personal interest in the
internecine, dog-eat-dog politics of the Kremlin, yet he was
being thrust into the fray head first. If it had been remotely
possible, long ago he'd have talked his father into early
retirement or changing professions. Whatever course Nuri now
followed, there was one consolation: he had Mark Washburn's
round-trip ticket in his pocket—a way out of the Soviet Union,
provided he wasn't discovered. All he had to do was
rendezvous with the Virginia Ballet Academy group, clue them

in to what was happening, and leave Moscow on their tour schedule.

But first there was Tina. Without her, nothing else mattered; the Soviets could exile him into the farthest Siberian taiga. Again he wondered what had happened to the bragging bodyguard assigned to protect her. Nuri's father had said nothing whatever about Jon Saarto.

Nuri's mind flashed to Fiodor Talik. For Nuri and Tina to escape would be only half the battle if the general were allowed to live. But how could one man incapacitate the State Minister of Security? First of all, Nuri needed to decide on the *proper place* to do the job. The Kremlin itself? Talik's KGB office on the outskirts of the city? At the Bolshoi Theatre, or perhaps at his country place? Nuri remembered the general's country dacha vividly. He had visited there on several occasions with his father. While a teenager he'd once stayed there on a weekend boar-hunting trip. Nuri weighed the chances. He had a disguise, an excellent cover, but he'd still need help to penetrate the KGB leader's protective perimeter. And most of all he'd need the will to pull the trigger.

Nuri gazed out the window, examining the flat country miles below. He wondered if the plane was still over Poland or if they had passed into Byelorussia. He thought of his father's well-meaning programs, trying to get Soviets to resettle, move to the fertile areas west of Moscow. The benefit programs were better than those offered to homesteaders in Siberia. Nuri knew that the problem was superstition outweighing practicality; the average Soviet felt that too many Germans were buried in this soil and that some day their bodies would rise in anger to reclaim the land.

Nuri smiled and looked away from the window. He'd have more than his fill of Soviet idiosyncrasies soon enough. He'd be better off using the rest of the flight to read the British dance magazine he'd picked up at the Copenhagen airport.

The Soviet Chairman's new driver was a gangly East Georgian with a tight-set mouth and nervous brown eyes. The man wheeled the gleaming Zil limousine into the priority traffic corridor of Kalinin Prospect and accelerated. Police with white batons popped up at every intersection, halting cross traffic and permitting the Soviet leader's vehicle to charge quickly toward the Kremlin.

Though the hour was early, Pavlin Baranov's mind was fully alert. The replacement chauffeur made him uneasy, even though the new man had been recommended by the motor pool and screened by Baranov's personal security force. If his own trusted bodyguard not been sitting up front as well when the limo arrived, Baranov would have driven to the Kremlin himself in his housekeeper's Zhiguli.

Baranov leaned forward in the Zil's gray leather seat and tuned the radio console. Radio Moscow had an agriculture commentary this morning he wanted to hear, but instead he found music. Baranov glanced at his watch, suddenly remembering that he'd left for the Kremlin an hour earlier than usual. He'd listen to the radio report in his office—if he had the time. The day's schedule promised to be hectic. The Foreign Minister had roused him at six, suggesting a luncheon meeting with the American Ambassador, Gregory Hewett. Baranov had refused. *Not yet.* He'd already shown a token of good faith by agreeing to release General Shaeffer. *Why were they in such a panic in Washington?* Did the Americans really believe he couldn't handle the Talik situation with due process? Six votes were all he needed to oust Talik from his position.

Tonight Baranov would have dinner with the American actress; afterward, they would attend the Bolshoi performance. He still hadn't made up his mind about a post-theatre, impromptu news conference. Baranov would decide that after the dinner with Tina Conner. Depending on her cooperation, he might not need it at all. Tomorrow morning he'd call an emergency meeting of the Politburo in the Arsenal Tower and convince them to act quickly on the Talik matter. In a fortnight the Plenary Party Congress would convene to rubber stamp whatever they decided.

General Talik was forever accusing him of softness and negligence. In one respect the KGB leader was right. Baranov should have seen the handwriting on the wall: Fiodor Talik had an evil, pernicious streak and would put to the knife the new humanism that was sweeping Russia. The problem for Baranov was that he still wasn't sure how immediate the danger would be—where and when any rapine plot of Talik's might surface. Whatever, he'd have to be ready.

Baranov patted the small TK automatic inside his suitcoat. It was the first time he'd carried the regulation KGB pocket pistol since becoming combined Chairman and Premier. Carrying the weapon did nothing for his morale, but Colonel Rablin and his Red Army friends had urged it on him—*as a precaution*.

Arriving at the Kremlin, his limousine swept through the wrought-iron gate between the Minister's Building and the Arsenal and headed for its priority parking place. Already the red flag proclaiming his presence was flying from its mast.

Five minutes later Baranov was in his commodious office, surprised to find it disrupted by a pair of workmen. The two men were overseen by a KGB security guard—an officer Baranov recognized and trusted. A stepladder was on the floor by the desk and the heavy mauve draperies had been pulled aside; one of the workmen was putting away his glazier's tools while the other cleaned a new pane of glass in the tall mullioned window that overlooked the Kremlin.

The KGB officer promptly explained what had happened: "I'm sorry for the inconvenience, Comrade Chairman. We did not expect you so early. Last night the cleaning people let a ladder fall against one of the windows and broke the glass. It has been properly replaced, of course." He turned to the workmen, urging them quickly out of the room. "Move, move. Pick up your ladder! The affairs of State cannot wait while you dawdle."

When they had departed, the KGB guard—a cocky young lieutenant—backed out of the office, clicking his boots and bowing slightly to Baranov before closing the door. Baranov took off his eyeglasses, polishing them as he strolled over to the window. He put them back on, examining the replaced windowpane—casually at first, then more carefully, gently tapping the glass, as well as its neighbors, with his fingernail. Then he gently rapped on it with his knuckle.

Baranov stiffened. To confirm his suspicions, he took the letter opener from his desk and gently cut away a small wad of the glazing putty.

The replacement pane—bullet-proof glass of sandwiched acrylic—appeared thick enough, but it had only been *single* glazed. *Deliberately?* The rest of the window was double-thick with a sealed pocket of air between, this to prevent sophisticated laser detection devices from listening to conversations picked up on the minute vibrations of the glass. Baranov felt a tightening in his stomach. Frowning, he backed away from the window and pulled the draperies closed, shutting out both daylight and the chance of eavesdropping. Irate, he placed a

hand on the intercom line, about to call the KGB duty man
back in. He hesitated, reconsidering.

While he mulled over the situation there was a soft knock on
the door. It was his secretary, who also had come in early; she
stepped inside the office, and from the look on her face,
Baranov knew she had bad news.

"Comrade Chairman, I regret to inform you that General
Talik is attending the Bolshoi Theatre this evening as well. And
he asks your permission to share the dignitary box."

Baranov cursed under his breath, then let out a sigh. The
night at the theatre would be a seminal one indeed. He watched
the secretary slip quietly out to prepare coffee. For the first
time in several days the office was caught up in a deadly
stillness. Sitting down at the desk and staring unseeingly at the
portrait of Lenin on the far wall, Baranov pondered.

Up until last week he'd considered Fiodor Talik a throwback
reactionary, a braggart, an annoying gnat in the Soviet
hierarchy—at worst, a tired old Stalinist waving his fist beyond
his time. Baranov knew now that danger had been festering
here for some time. *The seed of an undetected apocalypse?*
The thought lodged in Baranov's chest like bad food that
wouldn't go down. Talik would be like an eel on a hook when
he was confronted. And he would be confronted. *Immediately*.
Tomorrow morning Baranov would see to it that Fiodor Talik
was put in the Politburo's penal seat.

Only some artillery sound effects and a background orches-
tration by Tchaikovsky would have improved the scene. Grim-
faced and milking their misery for what it was worth, the two
wounded Russians huddled together in the foxhole. A third
soldier hovering above them was struck by a grenade fragment.
He fell into the already crowded hole. Grimacing with pain,
the newcomer pulled himself upright, introduced himself, and
withdrew a bloodied loaf of bread and a tin of German sausage
from his tunic. Before they could eat, all three men ducked as a
German tank rumbled over them.

Tina Conner was too far away to pick up the dialogue, and
she wouldn't have understood it anyway. The Mosfilm Studio
back lot was cold, and despite their thermals, she and Natasha
both shivered. Overhead, the dreary gray-flannel sky looked
pregnant with snow.

The foxhole wasn't working. The tracks of the German

panzer kept caving in one side, half burying the soldiers each time it passed over them. The Russian *dublyors*—stunt men— were having a tough time of it, and finally the exasperated director called for a break, shouting for the workmen to dig another hole.

Natasha pulled Tina aside, making room for several gaffers dragging in more cable from the generator truck. "Come, enough of war spectaculars, yes? We will go inside the sound stage for some hot tea."

Tina gladly followed her. "I'm impressed, but tell me, Natasha. Those soldier-actors appear to be so stoic. Are they impervious to pain?"

"They film what is true; it is like docudrama, yes? Ask your American generals about the war. Russian soldiers seldom cry out when wounded."

Tina put the subject away; her thoughts were too tangled on other matters to pursue it.

"Come, there are people you must meet," Natasha urged.

Tina had met more than her fill of Soviet actors, actresses, and production personnel. She'd even exchanged several autographs and promised to send photographs. *If she ever got out of this*. During lunch the studio's artistic committee had set out two long banquet tables at one end of the cafeteria in her honor and there had been endless speeches Natasha had done her best to simultaneously translate. For Tina most of them had a hollow ring. Colonel Rablin and Alexi Stanovich had stood by in the background like proud parents or watchdogs; she couldn't decide which. They were accompanied by two soldiers with automatic rifles and a pair of surly civilians in fur-trimmed topcoats.

Tina and Natasha entered the sound stage, Rablin and his motley group following close behind. It was as big as any Hollywood structure where Tina had worked. They found the refreshment cart and Tina took tea without sugar.

Wherever they went Natasha Chernyskaya seemed to command attention. Here on the heated sound stage she especially stood out. The workmen took sharp notice when the woman director took off her fur-lined coat, revealing a glistening brown pantsuit that clung to her curvilinear body like tanning oil. By comparison, Tina in her wool two-piece outfit felt like a Quaker schoolmarm.

Tina listened politely as Natasha gestured toward a set,

apparently an interior of a Russian farmhouse. "The picture is called *Partisan's Daughter*—like the famous painting. It is one of our more expensive efforts. Not only is its party ideology flawless, but the film is one of the most poignant love stories Mosfilm has yet produced. And I am miserable because I am not directing it."

Tina nodded. The *Partisan's Daughter* company was between scenes; the huge sound stage—one of several on the lot—was noisy, a polyglot of conviviality. Natasha explained that the picture was being directed by one of her rivals, an individual she personally disliked.

"Sergei Filipov, rightfully, should be making army training films, but he has highly-placed friends in the party," she said acidly.

"What is the theme of the film?"

"It's the story of a very old man who rediscovers his alienated family and is penitent for his selfishness after the war. The film's spirituality can be compared with *Wild Strawberries*."

"A propaganda tool?" Tina couldn't resist the barb.

"No. We don't make propaganda pictures at Mosfilm. The story is based on fact."

Sergei Filipov came hurrying up to them. He spoke in heavily accented English. "I am honored, Tina Conner." The smartly attired director was a lean, thickly moustached young man with silver-rimmed, tinted glasses. He had a surprising suntan, as good as Tina's, but an old scar shot down the side of his cheek like lightning, spoiling the effect. He pulled out a crushed box of Canadian cigarettes and continued the conversation in a fractious manner.

Tina responded to his questions as best she could, but it was clear that Filipov was uncomfortable around Natasha. Finally the set behind him was ready and he went back to his folding chair. Grandly, he waved his hands, shouting *"Gotov! Nachnyom!"*

The cameras rolled.

Tina watched in rapt silence, quietly sipping her tea. It was a long take. On the other side of the set Colonel Rablin and Alexi looked her way with indifference. When the scene was completed, Natasha led her by the arm and they began to explore the rest of the sound stage. They walked slowly, taking in the various sets. Again Rablin's two heavies followed at a discreet distance.

Natasha suddenly volunteered, "The problem with proletarian art is that it is too reflective. I would like to be more imaginative, but Russian theatregoers are like Narcissus—they want to be able to look at and admire themselves."

The malaise that had come on in the crowded lunchroom still troubled Tina, but she put up a facade of interest. "Narcissism is an affliction of the talented. Nuri's like that—forever playing roles off stage and loving it. But I understand him."

They continued to stroll, Natasha glancing back over her shoulder to see if they were being followed. She seemed to be leading Tina to a quiet area of the sound stage where they could be alone. Colonel Rablin's men, as if sensing the Russian woman's desire for privacy, didn't follow. Natasha spoke again; in a tone of ironic amusement, she told Tina of the advantages of filming in a socialist state.

Tina wasn't impressed and felt compelled to interrupt. "I appreciate your informative tour, Natasha. But we're only postponing the inevitable and you're putting me through a vicious agony. My mind is on Nuri, not cinema."

"Ah. Maybe you are building a false, make-believe arch, Tina." Her voice was almond-sweet again, as provocative and impetuous as that first night in the Stockholm restaurant. "Do you really believe you can tear out the keystone in Nuri's life and replace it with your own? Without his world crumbling around him?"

"I haven't attempted that. We've started from the ground up. It's one of the traditions of the American melting pot. The ability to rebuild completely."

Natasha looked at her. "You and Nuri would do well to consider the words of the Irish poet George Moore: 'Man travels the world over in search of what he needs and returns home to find it.'"

Though Natasha's words cut like a scythe, Tina admitted to herself that she enjoyed this woman's company. The film director was not only intelligent, but outgoing and genuinely cheerful, unlike the pseudoshyness of the other Soviet women Tina had met at the film studio. But what did she really want? There was something intangible hidden here, beyond the easy, quicksilver flow of Natasha Chernyskaya's talk.

They hesitated beside a darkened set of what looked like the czar's bedchamber. Tina asked sharply, "Why is the KGB so determined to destroy Nuri?"

"I suspect it is *zavarit kashu*—to cook kasha, or grain, yes? It is the Russian phrase to stir up trouble, start a risky affair. The KGB fears the dancer's ideas—the manipulation of our Soviet young people."

"And yet you help Nuri. And me. Why do you hate General Talik, Natasha?"

She replied automatically. "Fiodor Talik only imagines he is a true socialist. It is not so. He lusts for the purple; there is a touch of Tiberius in him. In another way he is like Hitler, and would demand great sacrifices of the Russian people." She hesitated. "But then sacrifice as the agent of change is something you Americans have never understood. Your paranoia over communism blinds you."

Tina was perplexed and annoyed at the same time. She let it show.

Natasha said quickly, "I speak of sacrifice the Russian way. Americans are so comfortable and cautious, always afraid of loss. In the past our generals, to clear a mine field, simply marched a few brigades through it. General Talik would revive this kind of mentality. He is dangerous for our maturing, wiser nation."

"You often speak as if the Soviet Union were a utopia. There are not bad aspects to your life here?"

Natasha shrugged. "Of course." She glanced warily around her. "Soviet life is burdened by a straitjacket of theoretical statistics, quotas, and percentages of acceptability. The bureaucracy is suffocating. But there is compromise in every society."

Tina swiftly added, "You've omitted the possibility of imprisonment. I never hear Soviets mention the gulags. All the Mosfilm razzle-dazzle in the world, including your hospitality, Natasha Chernyskaya, cannot conceal the fact that I am one more Soviet prisoner."

Natasha frowned.

Tina held up her hand. "Wait, please. You need to listen. As for red tape, in America we have bureaucracy, too, but it is much different." Tina shrugged. "We have freedom, and we have large taxes."

"Yes, I know. It is your largest state, on the gulf."

Tina laughed uneasily, but didn't clarify. "I'll tell you about our bureaucracy. In America the government is not designed for high-handed reaching down; it is the citizens who reach up. That's the way freedom must work." Tina felt wired, suddenly ready to take on the entire sound stage from a soap box. Natasha's lengthy ministrations had gone on long enough and it was her time to speak out.

Natasha smiled and adroitly changed the subject. "You look unhappy my dear."

"I'm miserable. None of this conversation fits my organized, comfortable compendium for a future with Nuri. You're all fighting me and I'm outnumbered."

"Things will be better when you plug back into your work."

Tina shook her head. "Such sage insight."

"You could appear in a Russian film, perhaps. Come, we'll go back to my office and explore the possibilities with the artistic committee."

Tina wanted to shout no, but figured it would be better to play the game, see if it took her a step nearer to Nuri. She looked edgewise at the Russian woman as they headed back to rejoin Rablin and Alexi. "Natasha, stop testing me and tell me the truth. As a creative individual, how do you put up with all this?"

"A matter of culture. I work for change from within, no? Or perhaps serving the blind mammoth that is the Soviet State is my destiny."

"How can you ever find your true potential?"

Natasha grinned. "The King Arthur syndrome, my dear. It may be a round table, but when you have talent, everyone knows who's king." She abruptly put away her smile as two somber-faced men appeared from the shadows of the scenery dock. Thrusting forward their identification, one of them said briskly, *"Tovarisch Chernyskaya, mih ha-teem pagavareet s'vame. Nee boytess."*

Natasha looked at them with trepidation, then turned and translated for Tina. "KGB. They insist on questioning me. Privately." Her hands went to her hips and her face turned red as the Soviet flag as she began shouting at the pair.

Tina didn't understand a word, but she could see Natasha was adroit at creating drama.

Suddenly one of the men grabbed the woman director by the arm, the other gesturing for Tina to come along as well. Tina felt a rude shove on her shoulder. Instead of heading back toward the busy film set where photography was in progress, they were directed through a dark passageway in the scene dock.

"They take us to a back exit," Natasha said glumly.

Tina felt a tingling sensation that began at the neck and ran all the way down her spine. Should she shout, try to escape and run back to the others for help? These men showed no weapons, perhaps they didn't need to. The expression on their faces and their identification appeared to have been enough for Natasha; she'd stopped struggling quickly enough.

The last thing Tina wanted to admit was that there was nothing she could do. Wrenching her arm away from her captor, she tried to run, but the big Russian grabbed her again, this time seriously. A fast, convincing hammerlock around the throat ended her struggling. She could barely breathe, let alone fight back.

Just as suddenly the iron grip was released. Tina whirled, squinting into the dim light of the aisle. There was a collision of bodies.

Both of the KGB men took saps to the head and sagged to the floor. Standing over them were two of Colonel Rablin's assistants, who proceeded, unnecessarily, to kick their downed victims in the stomach. Rablin came up from behind and pulled his men off, instructing them to drag the inert forms out of the aisle and into the scenery bins. His assistants quickly obeyed.

Natasha looked horrified. Tina involuntarily grabbed her arm and they trembled together. The comic figure of Alexi Stanovich lurked in the background, silent and watchful. Colonel Rablin glanced about and said angrily, "Under the circumstances, I suggest you leave the film studio immediately. My men will tend to this situation."

Danielle Ponty usually didn't like high places, but she had no choice. The view, however, of the Champs Elysées from Notre Dame's spire was magnificent. It was just after noon, and the sun had come out through a hole in the clouds; all Paris seemed to be shimmering at the great cathedral's feet. *At her feet!*

Danielle removed the plaid overcoat she had made herself and slid the rifle's stock, barrel, breach, and sound suppressor out of their specially sewn individual pockets. Quickly she assembled the components, just as she'd watched Khamsin do time and time again back in the apartment. Last to be added was the telescopic sight she carried in her shoulder bag. It took her just five minutes to put the weapon together but a good half hour for her to get used to the great height.

Danielle brushed the windswept hair out of her smooth brown face and focused again on the Police Judiciaire just to Notre Dame's left. She had read the headlines and done a little probing of her own. Najeeb Khamsin Ahmed was being summoned to that building for a combined interrogation. No less than the Prefect of Police, the Chief of the CRC, and the Director of the Police Judiciaire would all be in attendance. An FBI representative from Washington, D.C., had asked to sit in as an observer, and there were rumors in *Le Monde* that the CIA was also involved. They were expecting a stellar performance from her lover, who was scheduled to arrive in a police van at any time.

Danielle was ready. In a way, it would be a shame to bring their relationship to such a sordid end, but Khamsin had made too many mistakes. Until now the French-Algerian's wealth and connections had provided everything imaginable he wanted. Danielle would give him what he deserved; he had to play by the same rules as anyone else in the game. She, too, was a dedicated professional, and perhaps he would come to realize this in the brief seconds before he passed into the nether world. *How fast was death?*

Khamsin had been a shortsighted fool when it came to matters of love. Did he really believe that a woman of her caliber and promise could go on forever with such an ugly, distorted face? Thank God they were of no further practical use to each other. Nor was her ex-lover any additional value to the KGB. Danielle shuddered to think of Khamsin's wrath if he ever discovered the KGB had literally *placed* her in his apartment—a sleeper in more ways than one! Fortunately he would never find out.

From her perch in the belfry she could see the approach of the police van. It sat at the curb for several moments, waiting for a police escort to come out from the building. Finally two gendarmes opened the rear door and Khamsin stepped into the winter sun.

Danielle exhaled slowly and took a deep breath. Keeping within the spire's shadows, she slowly brought up the rifle, hoping her earlier practice with it would be rewarded. A payoff from the KGB depended on it.

She had only a few seconds. The silencer made the weapon heavy, but she could at least steady the barrel over a gargoyle. Lining up the telescopic sight, she fired twice.

On the street below Khamsin's head exploded in blood.

42

UNCOMFORTABLE VISIONS of what awaited Nuri in Moscow persisted. Twice he'd started to read the dance magazine, but he couldn't concentrate. He finally nodded off, fantasizing not on the current misadventure, but puppy dreams of his bygone childhood in Russia.

When Nuri awoke, nature called and he padded to the aircraft lavatory. Closing the compartment door, he urinated with relief, washed his hands with fragrant lotion soap and briskly rubbed them with a paper towel. Flexing his long fingers, Nuri held them before his eyes. *Could these hands be committed to spilling blood—Fiodor Talik's blood?* There had to be some other way, but what? Long ago Nuri had been taught that in dance the hands were the most eloquent voices of all, that they were responsible for completing a movement or gesture—powerful seals to subtle or grand deeds. *You will do it. Nuri Pavlinovich! It is either you or the general.*

Nuri examined his face. Even with the pasty Mark Washburn makeup, it looked drawn and haggard. Was the entire encounter aging him? He didn't want to think about the terrible truth—that as a model serves a painter, a dancer serves a choreographer and ballet company as absolute reality. That hard reality was that Nuri was nothing but raw material from which the finished work is fashioned. "Grow old along with me, the best is yet to be" was an unlikely phrase for a *premier danseur*. The successful dancer epitomizes physical beauty, proportion, artistic movement. No other talent is so affected by the ravages of time's encroachment.

It was the first time Nuri had thought about these things in months. Exhaling sharply, he left the toilet compartment and headed back to his seat, avoiding the sexy but gabby Danish flight attendants. He couldn't handle anyone else's questions, not now. He had too many of his own.

The seat-belt sign flashed on and one of the attendants reminded them to reset their watches; it was now four o'clock Moscow time. Nuri had already made the two-hour adjustment. Looking out the plane window, he saw that winter twilight had settled over the snow-covered Soviet capital.

Minutes later the DC-9 settled down gently at Sheremetyevo Airport. The aircraft taxied interminably. As Nuri stared uneasily at the familiar terminal building across the field, his every breath became a struggle. He was back in the Soviet Union, again a part of his essence. He was coming home, but it was home for the forgotten.

Arriving at the Bolshoi State Theatre, Bruna Kloski told her two KGB assistants to wait in the downstairs lobby. She headed for the second floor. On the staircase she came upon Artistic Director Pyotr Maryinsky, trailed by a half-dozen instructors from the Ballet Academy. When Maryinsky paused and extended his hand, Kloski shook it without feeling.

Maryinsky said politely, "Ah! Colonel. Do you find everything in order for the visit tonight for our Soviet leader?"

She surveyed him and said spitefully, "Others worry over the welfare of Chairman Baranov. I am concerned only with the arrangements for my own superior, General Talik."

Maryinsky looked surprised. "I did not realize the Minister of Security would also be joining us."

"A last minute decision, Comrade Maryinsky." She bowed slightly and proceeded up the marble staircase.

The Bolshoi people looked at each other and hurried off.

Kloski entered the spacious foyer she knew would be used

that evening for intermission refreshments. For the moment the
hunt for Nuri Baranov would be of secondary importance.
Despite what she and Talik had heard on the monitored
telephone conversation about the American actress arriving in
Moscow, Kloski had serious doubts the dancer would attempt
to return to Russia. Nuri was no fool and would surely think
long and hard about such a dangerous action.

Fiodor Talik's unpleasant surprise for the Soviet Chairman
was all that mattered for the next few hours, and she was
determined that this evening come off precisely as she had
planned it. The logistics and timing must be perfect. Accordingly, Kloski would go over the steps she would follow
during tonight's performance. She'd already noted the program. *Stone Flower* before intermission, excerpts from *Firebird* and *Don Quixote* after.

Kloski watched as two officious women spread a linen cloth
over a fifteen-foot-long table on one side of the foyer. She went
over to it. A curly-haired, statuesque young man approached,
catching Kloski's eye. He stood near her and began laying out
folded napkins and tiny plastic forks. Apparently one of the
waiters, he had a smooth, gently rounded Lithuanian face, firm
shoulders, and perfect round buttocks—the kind of young man
she admired. It was difficult for her to resist the impulse to
touch him.

"The refreshment arrangements, young comrade. Where do
you propose to serve the wine and vodka?"

The waiter noted the rank on her epaulets and quickly
pointed to another table across the room.

Kloski persisted. "And the fish delicacies. Where will you
place them?"

He gestured to the end of the table in front of her, and she
was satisfied. The catering people had agreed to cooperate with
her request; in addition to the caviar, sturgeon, salmon, and
assorted cheeses, they had agreed to stock the buffet with
Japanese sashimi. But Kloski herself had secretly made the
arrangements for one frozen puffer fish. Her plan was to slip a
few of its tainted fillets on the seafood platters *after* intermission, when everyone had returned to their seats. It would be
convenient, neatly contrived evidence, perfect for the pathologists and the history books.

Kloski stole one more glance at the handsome young waiter,
then left the foyer and proceeded to inspect the auditorium

itself. She went into the dignitary box, once more measuring it with her eye. Clucking her tongue with satisfaction, she examined the balcony seats on each side of it. She wanted to be doubly sure her calculations had been correct—the position of the chairs, the velvet curtains, the exits, and most important, the all-important *trajectory*. Nothing must interfere with her own little Bolshoi performance.

Finally satisfied, Bruna Kloski left the theatre.

A representative from Intourist met Nuri as he stepped off the plane. The woman checked his name—Mark Washburn's name—against a computerized list and advised him what hotel the rest of the tour group had been assigned. *The Ukraine.* Smiling dutifully, she gestured for him to follow the signs to Soviet Customs.

Everywhere Nuri looked he could see the bright green cap bands of the KGB border guards—far more than usually congregated at Sheremetyevo. Bullies driven by symbolic power, they scanned each arriving passenger carefully. Nuri was inside the building, but his breath still turned to steam. Something was wrong with the terminal's heating system, for the Customs area was crowded with shivering, irritated people. The Soviet authorities, too, seemed unusually aggressive. Nuri knew he had to remain calm and ignore their taunts, but as a Russian himself, it would be difficult.

Steeling himself, he went through the ritual with the rest of the tourists, establishing the credentials of his innocence. He lathered under the repeating pawing of his travel papers and had to resist the urge to curse at the money-exchange people in no-holds barred, idiomatic Russian. *No! He was an American tourist.* He joined the baggage queue. The multilingual Customs clerk was a lymphatic older woman whose fat hands fingered through his passport with annoying slowness. Nuri felt like a live butterfly, its wings pinned to a mounting board. "Your visa and itinerary forms are in order, Mr. Washburn, but your hard currency declaration surely cannot be correct."

Nuri quickly fabricated, "I lost my money in a Paris accident. The tour's manager will explain my late arrival and he has ample funds for the entire group. His name is James Berkowitz, at the Ukraine Hotel."

She looked at him narrowly, but seemed satisfied with the return ticket out of Moscow.

A paunchy older official abruptly reached over the woman's
shoulder and grabbed the passport. He examined the document
briefly, went back to his desk and picked up the telephone. The
supervisor was obviously a *krepky*—a hard nut to deal with.
Nuri prayed that James Berkowitz, if he was available at the
Ukraine, wouldn't be too shaken up with surprise.

While the Russian waited on the phone and tapped the
passport on his desk in annoyance, the woman Customs clerk
finished examining Nuri's suitcase. She stepped back, disappointed at the meager pickings, but her watery gray eyes
continued to study him. Nuri didn't avoid the woman's
scrutiny; nor did he challenge it. He merely looked on as if he
were bored and tired. In truth he wasn't seeing too well through
Mark Washburn's eyeglasses; the woman was slightly out of
focus.

The supervisor at the desk made no effort to mute his voice
as he interrogated Berkowitz at the other end of the line.
Apparently satisfied, the Russian hung up the receiver and
returned the passport to Nuri. "We welcome all students to the
Soviet Union," he said mechanically. "May your visit be a
pleasant one." He gestured for the next person in line.

Nuri closed his suitcase. His audible heave of relief,
however, was premature. Glancing up the line of Customs
officials, he saw three KGB border guards enter the room.
They were studying faces, not travel documents or baggage.
The Customs people skittered out of the way as they strolled
down the baggage line. Nuri felt horror as he realized that one
of the KGB faces was familiar. The man had once been
assigned to the grounds of his father's country dacha.

Not chancing his makeup on an encounter, Nuri grabbed up
his suitcase and hurried for the exit before the KGB official
strolled closer.

There were fewer KGB men in the outer corridor, and none
in the main terminal lobby. Nuri stepped swiftly to a pay
phone. He had to keep reminding himself to relax, that he was
not the Soviet Chairman's son; he didn't look anything like the
dissident dancer!

Nuri put a two kopek coin in the slot and picked up the
receiver. He waited for the tone and dialed Timur Malovik's
number from memory. He wondered if his fellow dancer had
moved since his roommate Marina's death, or whether someone else was now sharing the apartment. There was no answer.

He suddenly remembered that Timur sometimes taught late-afternoon classes at the Boshoi. Nuri found another two kopeks and dialed again, an even more familiar number, 29-17-51. The operator at the State Theatre answered and Nuri asked for the Academy extension.

He had to argue with two intermediaries, but at last he had Timur Malovik on the line. Nuri said in Russian, "Timur, listen carefully. This is a friend you haven't spoken with in many months."

There was a gasp, followed by an uncomfortable silence at the other end of the line.

Nuri continued, "I can understand your shock. What time do you finish instruction? It is imperative that we meet somewhere immediately."

"I'll be free in two hours, but you can't come here." Timur sounded both afraid and elated, unable to contain his excitement. Nuri hoped the dancer's enthusiasm wouldn't arouse suspicion.

Nuri thought for a moment. "We could meet on the street, near the bus stop at Sverdlov Square."

"No. Too many of our dance people frequent that corner. You would be recognized."

"Perhaps not. You haven't seen my new look."

"Still no." Timur lowered his voice. "Too dangerous. Go out to my apartment; meet me there later. Now I must go."

Nuri hung up, gathered his things together, and headed for the terminal exit. He took a taxi into the city, making minimal conversation with the driver, who had to struggle with English. A zealous party man, he also happened to be down on Americans.

Nuri got out at the Ukraine Hotel. He finally managed to get the stunned James Berkowitz downstairs and out on the street, alone and away from bugged telephones and the ever-present KGB "lobby loungers." Nuri waited until they had walked behind the hotel to the Berezhkovskaya Quay along the river before explaining his masquerade and arrangement with Mark Washburn. Berkowitz listened patiently, but without sympathy. He seemed annoyed at his student back in Paris for cooperating and at Nuri for proposing the shaky arrangement.

"You amaze me, Nuri." Berkowitz slowly shook his head as if he were seeing a mirage. "Whatever you need to do, I promise to cooperate. Provided it doesn't jeopardize the safety of the other students." Shaking his head, Berkowitz looked out across the dark river. "Shit. This was supposed to be a quiet, off-season friendship tour. My wife will never believe me when I get home—if I don't wind up in a Soviet labor camp first."

"Don't worry," Nuri gripped his shoulder. "I appreciate your concern. I promise to be careful."

They parted, Nuri walking in the opposite direction, back toward the central city.

On Kutuzovsky Prospect the huge GLORY TO LENIN sign was peeling badly, and across the way on one of the government buildings a spotlighted red flag hung limply from its masthead. Nuri felt a familiar depression as he crossed the street, mingling with the homeward-bound workers. The mass of humanity looked the same as it did over a year before, the people around him wearing their way of life on their faces.

In Paris Nuri's disguise had worked perfectly. He'd felt comfortable in the masked turbulence of Montmartre, but here he wasn't sure. The people looked at him! Then he remembered. His shoes, slacks, and overcoat were obviously Western, and he wore no hat. All Russians wore hats in this weather. Nuri had forgotten, but it was working to his benefit. He walked faster, more purposefully, in the Moscow tradition. He had to think, and he also needed to get something to eat; he'd need the strength in the hours ahead.

After a ten-minute walk he was on Gorky Street, passing a restaurant with large windows. He peered inside. Despite the tarnished lamps and peeling brocade wallpaper redolent of past elegance, the place was crowded. It was still early. Animated diners were stuffing themselves and watching the passersby. Spotting an empty table in the back, Nuri went inside. He knew that as an "American tourist" he would be given preferential treatment, his place marked with a RESERVED sign to prevent others from sharing it.

Nuri took a seat at a table covered with lace-patterned polyester. He smiled at the surprisingly cheerful, miniskirted waitress, musing that she could do with a couple of inches more on her hem. Her legs were knobby and callused, and he wondered if she moonlighted scrubbing floors.

The restaurant specialized in Georgian food, and Nuri ordered Chicken Tabaka. While he waited for the main dish, he asked for a glass of vodka and some *zakouski* to nibble on. The waitress brought the appetizers and vodka immediately. She quickly poured. Nuri stared at the familiar bottle with the distinctive flying crane bearing a bunch of grapes in its beak. As a tourist would routinely do, he sipped the drink, but couldn't resist chasing it with a cucumber in the Russian tradition. Nuri now felt what it was like to be a foreigner in Moscow, to be stared at in varying degrees of envy, curiosity, even contempt. The sensation mildly amused him.

The main course came quicker than Nuri had expected, and he ate with gusto.

He was almost finished when he noticed that a woman sitting at a nearby table was staring at him. She was accompanied by a pair of young children. Nuri took off his glasses for a better look. The Russian woman was severely pretty and had a polished, streamlined face and brilliant red lipstick, all framed in a blue paisley kerchief. She was slumped recklessly in her chair, pretending to read a copy of *Krokodil*, but her legs were spread purposely apart, the raised skirt revealing perfect inner thighs that merged into secret shadows. She looked up fleetingly from the magazine and again gave Nuri a sultry look.

Feeling cornered, Nuri finished his meal. He was determined not to look her way again, but his gaze was irresistibly drawn back to her. This time she made no pretense of reading. Ignoring the preoccupied children who sat opposite her, she smiled unabashed at Nuri with an expression of sexual cunning.

Not now, you lovely wench, not now. Nuri felt panic, guilt, and curiosity at the same time. He finished off his vodka and asked for the check. The thought of a secret rendezvous with the pretty stranger—stroking her soft, furry mound and moist vulva—would have excited him any other time. But not tonight. He'd almost forgotten how so many Moscow men and women delighted in secret encounters. Tina would never understand this Soviet intensity.

Nuri shook his head. This wasn't the time for delirium or sexual expectation; he had to get out of the restaurant, back to work. Unfortunately he had to pass right by the wanton woman's table to get to the door.

He tried to move purposefully, without looking down at her, but at the entry he hesitated and looked back. Her eyes were still on him, but now she was grumbling in Russian—some-

thing about him being an unfriendly, arrogant American. In his
excitement, he'd again almost forgotten his role.

Nuri stumbled outside the restaurant, dodging the line that
had formed at the door. He smiled, suddenly feeling as tall and
significant as the Statue of Liberty. Again he was caught up in
the inscrutable riptide of Moscow life—a life that in brief, odd
moments in the West he'd sorely missed. The first month in
New York especially, had been lonely and difficult, despite the
new, well-meaning friends he'd made. The escape itself, the
loss of family and Soviet friends, the sharp severance from his
culture, and the sudden melting into an alien civilization he'd
been taught to despise, were all traumatic experiences that took
their toll on his emotions.

He stashed the memorabilia away and headed for the Metro
station at Karl Marx Prospect. After walking a short distance,
he paused to check his watch. There was still plenty of time
before meeting Timur Malovik.

Strolling down the Twenty-fifth of October Street, Nuri
passed the GUM department store's dull facade and approached the edge of Red Square. Above him the neon stars
atop the crenellated monuments glared out on the city, burning
through the early evening mist like watchful ruby eyes. Nuri
felt drawn to the Kremlin as if by some strange force, yet he
knew, instinctively, now was not the moment to penetrate its
nearly two miles of walls. His father worked long hours and
was undoubtedly still in his office within this formidable
fortress. Other important men were here as well, like the bones
of Peter the Great and Ivan the Terrible in their sepulchres.
Nuri sighed with misgiving. He knew that few of the historical
figures in the Kremlin's entombed collection of czars, princes,
and grand dukes had died of natural causes. Murder—by knife,
smothering, poison—seemed a rule of thumb for their precipit-
ous exit from this world.

Strolling toward the subway station, Nuri passed the Tomb
of the Unknown Soldier. Traffic came to a standstill as a trio of
Chaika limousines, their white curtains pulled for privacy, sped
away from the Kremlin, heading east on Karl Marx Prospect at
high speed. As he watched the shiny black Chaikas race off in
the distance, an idea came to him. Russians respected uniforms
and authority; they were also beholden to the long black
automobiles in the priority traffic lanes. Nuri knew that once a
high-ranking official had submitted his cross-city itinerary to

the computerized Kremlin Communications Center, no one would think of interfering with the vehicle. All along the way police held up side traffic with their white batons.

Nuri theorized on what might happen if he were to commandeer a pair of limos, dress a couple of his Bolshoi friends who wished to escape in KGB uniforms, then together with Tina and his father drive north to the Finnish border. The more he thought about the daring idea, the more he rationalized its feasibility. They would routinely halt the limousines at highway checkpoints, but what local authority would dare question the ultimate authority of the Soviet Chairman? A bogus mission for Nuri's entourage and appropriate paperwork would have to be trumped up, but this would be the least of their problems. It would take something daring to get Tina out of Moscow.

The food and vodka had lubricated Nuri's mind, and the scheme took shape quickly. There would be two main obstacles. What to do with Fiodor Talik while the escape took place, and what might happen to Pavlin Baranov when they reached the Finnish border. His father's name would be mud in the Soviet Union for having been a participant—or rather, victim—of such a disgrace. Nuri thought for a moment. *No*, not in his wildest imagining could he talk his father into defecting—never, not in a thousand years, regardless of the circumstances. Pavlin Baranov was Soviet to the core, and loved the USSR and everything it stood for.

Flashing on Fiodor Talik, Nuri immediately had the answer. Why force his father to go along? The KGB minister would accompany them, a gun barrel nudging the general's balls all the way to Helsinki if necessary. The humiliation would be so complete, Talik could never face the Politburo again.

Nuri made up his mind. He would refine the plan and confide in Timur Malovik. Their first priority was weapons.

43

THE LIGHT was waning and Jon Saarto had wasted away the better part of the day without being able to contact Tina Conner. She wasn't at the Cosmos Hotel, as Colonel Rablin had indicated. His other tasks in Moscow had been to purchase some inexpensive Russian clothing and make a leisurely visit to a steam bath, enjoying an invigorating leaf scrub and massage. Afterward Saarto had felt completely restored, ready to scale the Kremlin wall itself if necessary.

The windowless, dimly-lit restaurant had just opened for dinner. Saarto sat at a table near a huge porcelain samovar and ordered a glass of dry light wine. An elderly, crinkle-faced waiter brought back a bottle of Tsinandali.

Saarto sat patiently, sipping the wine. He waited forty-five minutes but Natasha Chernyskaya didn't show, as she'd promised. Glancing at his watch he felt a gnawing apprehension, for he knew she lived very close by. Still, he had only her telephone, no address. Saarto wondered if she were listed in the Moscow directory. *A famous film director?* Unlikely. Saarto paid the waiter, and when he rose to leave, he asked,

"Comrade, are you acquainted with Natasha Chernyskaya the film director?"

The Russian nodded without enthusiasm.

"Her apartment. Which one is it?"

He led Saarto to the doorway, pointed diagonally down the street, and held up a handful of fingers. "The fifth building from the corner."

"Have you seen her today?"

The old man only shook his head and murmured something about Soviet artists and intellectuals being full of shit.

Saarto left the café and pulled up his collar. The city was dark now, and seemed colder. He walked briskly down the street, then suddenly paused. He was no longer about to enter Natasha's apartment building—the tall, brick structure indicated by the waiter—for parked directly in front of it was a white Moskvitch with four men, the two in the front seat in KGB uniforms. They smoked, engaged in dialogue, and occasionally glanced at the buildings, but took no notice of him.

Saarto again checked his watch. Natasha would have to wait. During his unproductive visit earlier, the U.S. embassy had suggested he call back at five-thirty to see if they'd received any word from Washington on his identification. Saarto deliberated over whether to use a pay phone to call them. *No*, he'd backtrack to the embassy compound on Tchaikovsky Street and rattle their cage *in person*.

On his way to the Metro station Saarto passed a theatre billing old Charlie Chaplin films. Hesitating briefly to examine the posters that had been translated into Russian, he remembered that the great revolutionary leader himself was particularly fond of Chaplin. Lenin's wife was known to play the piano in accompaniment to the silent flicks. Saarto smiled at the woman in the ticket window and hurried on.

Seeing a taxi approaching with the small green light burning in a corner of the windshield, Saarto decided against the Metro. He flagged the cab down.

"The American embassy," he snapped in English. Saarto knew that a Russian asking to be taken to that address might just provoke more than a raised eyebrow.

"Yes, sir. You're a tourist or on business, perhaps?" The driver spoke better than passable English.

Saarto noticed on the seat beside him a couple of tattered

pocket books—*Sharkey's Machine* and *The Choirboys*. The
driver spoke to him in the rearview mirror, volunteering that
he'd read both novels twice, that he's purposely kept them in
the cab for possible trades. He stressed that American
diplomats, in particular, were good at providing him with
pocket books. "You have something to trade, perhaps?"

"Sorry," Saarto replied. "I'm traveling lighter than usual
this trip." *An understatement and the truth,* he reflected.

To save time the driver took the Ring Road to the U.S.
embassy. When they arrived, Saarto saw a new shift of Soviet
militiamen on the street—overgrown, brutal men with rough-
cut gestures. They didn't stand at rigid attention but walked
back and forth and talked among themselves. One of them
carried a Drakech automatic machine pistol. The Russians
seemed ready to approach Saarto until he waved the pass he'd
been given earlier.

The U.S. Marine guard recognized Saarto from his visit
three hours earlier and waved him inside, where he was again
ushered into the office of Brent Larkin, the cloying Special
Assistant to the Chargé d'Affaires.

Larkin looked as if he'd just returned from R & R on the
Costa del Sol or the Canary Islands. He was tanned, tall,
bright-eyed, and immaculately dressed, but a trifle slow on the
response. Initially Saarto had asked to see the Ambassador
himself, only to discover Gregory Hewett had been called back
to Washington on an emergency basis. The Chargé d'Affaires
himself would be out of the office until morning. Brent Larkin
claimed to be the only ranking official available to listen to
Saarto's problem. Saarto had to pick up his feet to avoid
tripping on a wrinkled Bokhara rug beside Larkin's desk. The
furnishings in the office looked more Russian than American,
Saarto thought, as he took a seat on a brown leather love seat.

"Mr. Saarto, I'm glad you returned before I left for the day. I
have news."

Brent Larkin's words fell on Saarto as smooth as cream.
"Good. Did Washington, D.C., verify that I am, in fact, who I
purport to be?"

Larkin frowned and sat back down at his desk. He tapped his
wristwatch. "Sorry, we still haven't heard from Washington.
Considering the early hour there, this isn't unusual." He
hesitated, mouth tightening. "The news I'm referring to comes

from Paris; a matter concerning the woman there who would supposedly verify your credentials."

"You still don't believe me? For chrissakes, you thinking I'm a KGB plant? Look, find Tina Conner. She has my wallet and passport."

"You did come to us with only Soviet identification, no entry visa, and only a pocketful of rubles. Americans do not customarily enter the USSR under such circumstances, Mr. Saarto. Should we believe you merely fell out of the sky? But in fairness we're investigating your claims, and, of course, your purported contacts."

Saarto said violently, "In the meantime—"

"Let me finish."

"It's imperative I get through to the White House. If not there, to the head of the CIA or National Security Agency."

"We're working on it, I assure you. Perhaps you're too impatient, Mr. Saarto."

"I dislike fucking red tape."

Larkin shrugged, then smiled for the first time. "We all do. *Nichevo*, my friend. The Moscow equivalent for *manana* and *c'est la vie.*"

Saarto slowly shook his head. It had started to ache. "Save the Bolshevik repartee. And the translation. As I explained before, I speak the language."

"All the more reason you are suspect. Now, do you wish to hear what we've learned or not?" Larkin paused, then continued, measuring his words like a man tiptoeing through a marsh, trying to avoid quicksand. "We did call your Paris contact—this Diana Vespucci. Unfortunately we wound up with the Deuxieme Bureau instead. CIA operative Vespucci is dead and the dancer Nuri Baranov is wanted by the French police for questioning in the matter. He has disappeared."

Saarto's gut did a fast barrel roll—in two directions. *Vespucci! The assassin Khamsin again.* Saarto swallowed hard and said to Larkin, "I'm telling you Tina Conner is in Moscow now. She's being used as bait, and if the dancer isn't here yet, he will be soon enough. We don't have until tomorrow morning to get rolling."

Brent Larkin stared back at him with an enigmatic expression. "Shooting from the hip is for B westerns, Mr. Saarto. Hardly suitable for grand-scale international diplomacy."

"Diplomacy my ass." Saarto's mind raced. If he couldn't

get through to the Washington, D.C. bigwigs or studio head Harry Kaufmann, maybe he could pop a few balloons by playing darts with the press. "Listen, Mr. Larkin. A prisoner usually gets one phone call. And I'm a virtual prisoner in Moscow. Do me a favor and give me one conversation back to the States on one of your secured lines? I'll make it collect. Just one."

The aide thought for a moment. "You'll never make it through to the Oval Office."

"I figured that," Saarto snorted. "No, a line to California. I have another angle in mind."

Larkin waved him off. "I suggest you stop worrying and let us work on it. Go out and find yourself a stiff glass of vodka and relax, Mr. Saarto. If you prefer, there's some good Ukrainian brandy around Moscow. Not only excellent for calming you down, but it's anti-freeze for the Russian winter."

Saarto brushed the sarcasm aside. *The bastard!* "Do I get that secured line or would you rather I go over to the National Hotel, use a pay phone, and broadcast U.S. proprietary matters for all the world to hear?"

Larkin frowned. He pushed several buttons on his telephone, said a few sharp words into the receiver, and handed it to Saarto. "If your credentials hold up, this won't cost you a dime," he said flatly.

Saarto grabbed the phone. The satellite line to Hollywood was established immediately. Saarto knew he could count on L. Brian Beck to raise some hell. The publisher knew the megabuck value of bombshell events turned into exclusive, syndicated news stories. The phone rang several times before it was picked up.

"Beck residence." It was an alien voice, definitely not the publisher's. A new strongarm Saarto hadn't met?

"Let me talk with Brian."

"He's not available. Who's this?"

"Jon Saarto. His former bodyguard. What's it to you?"

"Hold the wire and you'll find out."

Saarto winced in annoyance. A half-awake, distinctly familiar voice came on the line. "Saarto, this is Niles Donnell, FBI. Where you calling from?"

"Moscow."

"Jesus Christ. What the hell do you want with Beck? He's finished, and I'm not at liberty to tell you about it now. Just take my word, it's out of the Bureau's and the CIA's hands. The whole ball of wax. *Understand?* Forget the rest of your mission and get your ass out of Moscow."

The line at the Los Angeles end went dead. The knot tightened in Saarto's stomach as he slowly hung up the phone. The cocksuckers would let Tina swim alone with sharks!

Nuri found the two-foot-high neon M that marked the Metro entrance and joined the rush-hour crowds pushing like cattle toward the escalator. It was a long ride to the bottom—Moscow's subways were the deepest in the world. Nuri, like the others, rode downward in tight-lipped silence.

The clock on the platform changed from 6:04 to 6:05 as he stepped aboard a Red Line car. Enduring the elbows and sweating bodies, he rode the train to the Fruzenskay Station.

He surfaced into the cold night air and hiked the rest of the way to Timur Malovik's apartment on the city side of Lenin Stadium. The traffic on Kharchev Street was muted when Nuri approached the familiar salmon-colored building at number 17. He quickly mounted the steep staircase to the third floor. More times than Nuri could remember he'd climbed these same green tile steps in the company of Marina Pleskova. Again, each landing had its distinct smell: Tonight the second level smelled of baked fish, while the third reeked of an exotic Eastern fare he guessed to be curried lamb.

In the Moscow fashion for shared apartments, there were two buzzers and two nameplates beside Malovik's entry. Nuri noted that the soiled card inscribed Marina Pleskova had already been removed. He pushed Timur Malovik's buzzer and waited. Moments later the door opened. Timur—seeing instantly through the disguise—pulled him quickly inside. After a bear hug of laughter, they looked seriously at each other. In the background Nuri recognized Bach's *Brandenburg Concerto* playing on the stereo; Timur had turned the volume up. *Good.* A precaution—probably unnecessary—against the possibility of bugging.

Raising his voice slightly, Timur spoke first. "Never! Not in a light-year, would I expect to see you again in Moscow. And in costume! It's among your best."

"Unfortunately I keep forgetting the role. I'm supposed to be a young American just out of high school, yes?" Nuri looked around the room. The apartment was as he remembered it. Theatre posters everywhere—the hodgepodge look that might just as easily have belonged to a young dancer in Vienna, London, or San Francisco. The only thing unique about Timur Malovik's place was the huge, glass-covered coffee table with its wire-mesh sides; not everyone kept a small boa constrictor in the living room. *Little?* Nuri glanced at the cagelike coffee table with apprehension; the snake had grown considerably in just over a year's time. "I see Boris Godunov's longer and fatter. He eats well?"

Timur's eyes flashed with mirth. "Often better than me. It's not always easy to find baby chicks, however, to keep him in roughage."

Nuri winced and stepped toward the bedrooms. "Do you mind?" He headed down the hallway of memories, taking in once more the familiar photographs lining its walls. Most of the dusty, framed pictures were committed to memory: poses of Marina Pleskova—her lead in *Raymonda*, the first time she'd danced the *Dying Swan*. There was Timur in *Apollo, Corsaire*. Himself as Prince Siegfried in *Swan Lake*, and as the puppet *Petrouchka*.

Nuri entered the small room that had been Marina's. The furniture was the same, but already Timur had replaced the ballerina's frilly white lace curtains with draperies that looked like dyed burlap. Nuri stood there only briefly, thinking of Marina's death at the Bolshoi. He tried, unsuccessfully, to control the anger slowly building within him, his festering hate of ballet benefactor Fiodor Talik. The questions Nuri wanted to ask Timur about that night at the State Theatre rolled back and forth in his mind, and he didn't know where to begin.

Timur sensed Nuri's agony and pulled on his arm. "Come back in the living room, yes? We'll talk."

They spoke to each other rapidly, Nuri explaining as much as he could in twenty minutes. Timur offered him wine or vodka, but Nuri declined, accepting hot lemon tea instead. He sat at the far end of the room, where he wouldn't have to look at the snake. Nuri could hardly believe the information Timur had for him—a litany of trouble. The film editor Dimitri Kollontai, killed by the KGB at Mosfilm; several of his underground printing friends interrogated at Lubyanka; and most startling of all, *Tina Conner attending the Bolshoi with his father*. Nuri's hands balled and he angrily struck them on the nearby table. "Why is Tina being subjected to this embarrassment?"

Timur shrugged. "There's rumor that elements of the Western press have been invited to the Bolshoi tonight."

Again Nuri thought of the mantle of authority that was the long black limousine. The plan would have to work; he had no choice. He looked anxiously at his fellow dancer. "You're sure, Timur? My father will bring Tina with him to the State Theatre tonight?"

"I'm positive. Pyotr Maryinsky himself told the Academy staff this afternoon. But there is a diabolical turn. The KGB general has suddenly elected to attend the ballet as well. He will join your father in the dignitary box."

Nuri's heart did a fast *fouette*. "I don't understand. Why? A temporary reconciliation of sorts?"

Timur Malovik's eyes turned dark and vacant, as cheerless as an abandoned coal vein. "Certainly not. It's most peculiar that Talik has chosen to attend with the Chairman. A black cat still runs between these two leaders."

Nuri let out a lungful of air. "After all that has happened, do you still wish to flee to the West, Timur?"

"Of course, Nuri." He hesitated, lowering his eyes. "Unless things change for the better here in Moscow. In some ways I love the Bolshoi, yes? But I suspect change is impossible."

"How many others will be with us?"

"Two more that I trust, possibly a third who is indecisive."

"We'll forget the fence straddler."

Timur went on with consternation, "There is also a lighting technician who saw two of Talik's men with a rope, climbing after Marina Pleskova just before she hung herself in *Giselle*. He has been intimidated into silence, and there's rumor he may be sent away—to a theatre in Minsk or Odessa, or some more remote place."

Nuri said quickly, "He's welcome to come with us. I have a plan. We'll have to move boldly and rapidly—tonight. Immediately following the performance, when the dignitary limousines are in front of the theatre. We'll use them."

Timur looked stunned. *"The Chaikas and Zils?"*

Nuri nodded.

"But what about the Chairman and the KGB minister?"

"Leave that to me."

The strains of the *Brandenburg Concerto* had begun to unsettle them both. Timur went over to the stereo, turned down the volume slightly, and looked back to Nuri. "There's more you must know. Talik's assistant, Colonel Bruna Kloski, was at the Bolshoi this afternoon. Checking arrangements for the minister's visit."

"The tigress spraying her territory."

Timur thought for a moment. "Do you think the KGB minister will give up his hunt for you so easily? The tiger is reported to be successful in one stalk out of twenty, yes? Talik and Kloski are persistent people, Nuri Pavlinovich." Timur drew a finger across his throat to make his grim point.

"One week of hell is enough for anyone. I've had enough, Timur. The issue will be drawn and resolved once and for all. How do you feel about General Fiodor Talik?"

"I despise him, of course. If he were here in my apartment, I'd feed him to Boris Godunov. Aside from his political aspirations, the man is vulgar. See for youself tonight; I predict he'll arrange to take one, possibly even two ballerinas back to his dacha—or his Moscow apartment. Wherever he can entertain them unknown to his wife!"

Nuri glanced at his watch. "We'll go to the theatre separately, Timur. You must leave word at the stage door. Find some ruse, but clear me to enter."

"It's not possible to have visitors before a performance. You know that."

"Ah, but it is permitted to make a last-minute costume delivery and check for fittings. *Mark Washburn* will bring in a wardrobe package."

Timur only looked at him with amazement.

Nuri continued, "About that delivered package—we'll need to put it together now. I'll need some tights, supporter, and slippers." He looked down at Timur's feet and shook his head. "Your shoes are too large for me. I'll need your help to beg, borrow, or steal some dance slippers from the Academy lockers."

Timur grew wide-eyed. "Surely *you* have no intention of moving around backstage as a dancer. The maestro would recognize—"

Nuri cut him off. "I have a surprise for Pyotr Maryinsky."

"Nuri Pavlinovich, if I guess correctly what you contemplate, you're walking on the brink of an abyss."

"Better than playing only a pathetic *Petrouchka* for the rest of my life—dancing on the end of a string."

44

"I'M AFRAID," Tina said shamelessly.

Natasha assured her, "Don't get cold feet now, my dear. Dinner with the Chairman is only the overture. We're not even into the first act yet."

Colonel Rablin and his men drove them to a small *ibeza* restaurant on the outskirts of Moscow. The escort, Tina noted, had been increased by two cars and at least a half-dozen armed soldiers. After the KGB confrontation earlier at Mosfilm, the colonel wasn't taking any chances.

The restaurant, constructed of double-walled logs, was set back in a cluster of trees. Rablin waited outside, setting up his own perimeter of men while Natasha escorted Tina into the building. It was warm and the decor was cozy enough, but still Tina felt trepidation. She was only buying time to learn more about the enemy camp, but might the fraternizing backfire? Her heart quickened.

The Soviet Chairman waited for Tina and Natasha in a large private dining room. He kissed them each on both cheeks, then dismissed his official interpreter, insisting that Natasha do the translating—if necessary. Baranov professed to know a little English but had a habit of lapsing in and out of it in a haphazard manner. The three of them sat at a round table covered with pale blue linen and a beautiful centerpiece of white roses.

Tina was surprised by Pavlin Baranov's appearance; he looked ten years younger than she'd envisioned and was nearly as handsome as his son. She watched the Soviet leader's aides—apparently bodyguards—stoke the large, cut-granite fireplace at one end of the room. Pavlin Baranov dismissed the two men and they backed out the door. The Chairman waited until Tina and Natasha were seated, then pulled up his own chair.

The three of them at the table were a friendly triangle of warmth, and for the moment Tina felt strangely separated from the rest of the Soviet Union. Baranov apologized for his inadequate English; he switched to Russian and Natasha translated, almost simultaneously. "You were fascinated by your tour of Mosfilm? What do you think of the Soviet cinema?"

Tina smiled and said tartly, "I saw the exciting fire, but felt no warmth."

For several moments silence hung over them like death itself; Tina's spirits sagged. For an opener, she'd blundered.

A dumpy, pigeon-toed waitress entered with a bottle of vodka and tiny sausage appetizers. She filled three chilled glasses and set them on the table.

Tina looked at the drinks unhappily. A toast would be next, but to what? Oh God, why had she let Natasha cajol her into this affair? Nuri would be unforgiving if Tina's efforts with his father worsened an already delicate situation.

Showing no concern, Natasha said to Baranov, "I'm afraid she is tired from her travels, Comrade Chairman. And we had a busy day at the studio."

Tina smiled nervously, fingering her strand of pearls. She said in a softer tone, "Yes. I'm sorry. The studio's hospitality was exemplary. I hope I can return the gesture to any of your film people who visit Hollywood." She hesitated, considering the Chairman. "Please. There are life-and-death matters—far more important than cinema—that we have to discuss."

Without bothering to consult either Tina or Natasha, Pavlin

Baranov ordered dinner for them. The waitress wrote it down and padded out of the room.

Baranov smiled and sat forward in his seat. The gold cuff links protruding from the sleeves of his expertly tailored gray suit reminded Tina of a pair she'd given to her father on his fiftieth birthday. The Chairman's sapphirelike eyes completely disarmed Tina as he said to her, "I can appreciate your concern. But first I think we should make a toast. A wish for Nuri's safe journey—his swift return to join us in Moscow."

Tina squirmed, making a painful effort to go along with the lightness of the moment. "I'll join your toast gladly for *Nuri's safety*, but I suspect you're in for a disappointment if you believe he'll show up in Moscow."

Natasha translated, apparently unnecessarily, and they raised their glasses. Tina drank only half of her hundred-proof vodka. She stared at the remainder and exhaled swiftly; given a match, she could breathe fire like a dragon. Natasha grinned and patted her wrist. "Take your time with the drink, my dear. The evening is young and you're not a Russian."

"Ah! But there's a chance that someday she might marry one," suggested Baranov with a wink.

Some inner atavistic instinct made Tina raise an eyebrow. She thought for a moment, then said, "May I speak freely?"

Natasha and the Soviet leader both nodded.

Tina said, "I want to talk about Nuri. What will happen to him if he crosses the border and returns to Moscow?"

The Chairman shrugged. "He will be safe if the three of us have our way."

"You're being vague, Mr. Chairman. That's not really good enough."

Natasha interjected, "It is difficult to plan in this hour of political crisis."

Tina felt a familiar panic, a deepened sense of alienation and foreboding. Obviously there would be no illumination of Nuri's status. She thought about Jon Saarto, wondering if the bodyguard made it into Moscow. Would her plan to sweet talk the Soviet Chairman be a waste of time, even hinder Jon Saarto's self-proclaimed mission? No, she had to keep trying, attempt to search out and determine the ultimate threat and intent of the Kremlin conspiracy. She said to Baranov, "Nuri's told me of your enemies. He writes about them in his book. Why are you not afraid?"

"There is no room for personal fear—least of all paranoia—in the crusade for world socialism."

"I'm told that the iron-willed KGB general knows no mercy. Only suppression and terror."

Baranov shook his head. "You sound like the American President and his Ambassador. They, too, overestimate the ambitious nature of our Security minister. Fiodor Talik is an old man whose bark far exceeds his bite. I will see to it that he is taken care of properly, and very soon."

Tina replied, "A wolf without teeth still ogles sheep, Mr. Chairman. And if he's cunning, can always rely on others in the pack to do his dirty work."

The waitress was back with a tray of soup.

The Chairman spoke again, this time with a metallic edge to his voice. "You and Nuri will be safe with Colonel Rablin and his assistants. Unlike the KGB apparatchiks, the army is highly visible, never out of sight; numerical superiority is on our side. But when needed, our military, too, can turn invisible. You must trust us."

"Nuri won't return," Tina said flat out.

Natasha looked at her, hesitating before translating.

The Soviet leader understood. His eyes didn't waver, staring at Tina with frightening concentration.

Tina retreated into silence and picked up her spoon. The herb-flavored fish soup before her—Natasha called it *ukha*—was served in a red and gold enameled wooden bowl. It was delicious.

The awkward silence asserted itself while they finished their entrée. Baranov had instructed the waitress to serve the meal quickly so they wouldn't be late for the theatre, and already the main course and wines were being hurried in.

Suddenly Pavlin Baranov said, "I know Nuri well. If he is not already in Moscow, he will return very quickly. We will all be together soon. I know my son's emotions, his repressed loneliness for the Russian culture."

Tina tilted her head in disbelief. "Do you, Mr. Chairman? Nuri misses his friends in Russia, that is all. If and when he does come back, I suspect—like many other Soviets who have disappeared into the American melting pot—he would do so out of *curiosity*. Food, songs, customs, yes—even your idiomatic language—all this culture is available to him in New

York, Los Angeles, and San Francisco Russian communities. I know. I've been there with him."

Baranov looked at her with innocent surprise. "You sound angry, my dear. This is no time for pyrotechnics. Enjoy your food. The fine Romanian wine complements the grouse, yes?"

Tina could only pick at the elaborate spread. She lowered her voice. "Mr. Chairman, I beg you to face reality."

Baranov seemed to tighten. He put down his fork. "It is you who must face the truth of the alternatives. The first one, yes? You can enjoy your stay in Moscow and reflect this elation when meeting the press at the Bolshoi Theatre. You'll explain that the purpose of your trip is a better understanding between the Soviet and American peoples—one dramatic artist's dedication to reviving the cultural exchange program." Baranov hesitated, studying her. "Equally important, of course, your mission includes *healing the wounds* between father and son."

Tina felt twinges of irritation and fear as she waited for Pavlin Baranov's alternative.

The Chairman sat forward in his seat. He spoke rapidly in Russian: "Or you can attack the Soviet government, claim you were forced to come to Moscow, and disavow my efforts for a reconciliation with Nuri. This option, of course, would unfortunately inspire further retaliation and harassment of Nuri by the KGB, all beyond my control." He smiled and added reassuringly, "I am using you, Tina Conner, to preserve the halfway house I have built in the retreat from Stalinism. *Glasnost* is difficult, nearly impossible in the suspicious climate of the Soviet State." He slowly exhaled and sipped his wine before continuing. "Enough. Perhaps more important than détente and the welfare of all Soviet and American performing artists, your *affaire d'amour* with Nuri is at stake, yes?"

Stunned by Natasha's translation, Tina shook her head in aversion. What had initially been Nuri's personal vendetta against Soviet ballet, in particular the State Theatre in Moscow and one of its directors—the meddlesome, perverse General Talik—had become an international incident. A frightening situation where human lives were negotiable: the Soviet Chairman's, Nuri's, possibly even her own. The press interview would be one more Russian tripwire. Tina had no doubts over Nuri's volatile reaction if he saw her interviewed on television. If he weren't already en route to Moscow, he soon would be! *No, Nuri! Don't swallow the bait. That's what they want.* Damn her lover's stubborn, intense nature; how could one individual take on the entire Soviet world?

Tina had to force herself to eat. Looking back at Baranov, she said shamelessly, "It would be a mistake to use me at one of your press conferences." Her mind raced. "Unless, that is, you're prepared to have me openly question *human rights* in the Soviet Union."

Again her words hung heavily in the air. The Chairman didn't respond, but continued sawing at his baked grouse with a knife. When he did look up, he held her gaze and smiled gently.

Tina felt uneasy. Though it was a dismal get-together, a strange conjunction was taking place between her and the senior Baranov, one she didn't understand. Her sharp words might be spoiling it, but that was a risk she was emotionally compelled to take.

Abruptly he said to her, "The USSR is a young democracy compared to America, but we have made far greater strides in seventy-five years than your country in double that time."

Tina choked back an insulting remark. Instead she waved her hand, admonishing, "Please. Back home we have many cultures. And both progressives and conservatives. But I take no responsibility for those with a 'back of the bus' mentality."

Baranov nodded sagely. "I was thinking further back than that. I understand that as late as 1830 the American Supreme Court decided that Indians were human beings."

Natasha Chernyskaya looked embarrassed, but kept her silence.

Tina felt light-headed. She tried again, increasing the edge to her voice. "We don't persecute religious believers or dissident intellectuals. Nor do we shoot down civilian airliners."

Natasha extended both hands as if to separate them. "Please, please. Our concern is for Nuri, not politics."

Baranov sipped his wine and smiled wryly. "You are serious about Nuri, seriously in love?"

Tina nodded.

"You bring much happiness to my son, I'm sure. Certainly beauty and talent. But perhaps you also fill his heart with alien music that is not good, because he has neither the time nor the disposition to give it permanent form."

Tina saw red; it was as if she were under siege. On the surface Pavlin Baranov appeared to be the perfect pragmatist, an expert at tactical logic; but obviously the thought of losing, or even compromise, hadn't entered his mind. She said quickly, "We are dedicated to one another. Mr. Chairman, I have to ask, do you really believe that Nuri was misdirected, that he merely ran off to the West for personal glory?"

"Yes. Aside from politics, name performers are noted for feeding on their narcissism."

Damn him. Tina pushed herself back from the table and rose to her feet. "Forgive me, Mr. Chairman, but when I get angry I need to walk, dispel the negative energy." She slowly circled the table, to Natasha's chagrin. Baranov looked up in amusement as she continued in a shaky, serious voice, "As for millions of followers, Nuri probably had more world glory when he was here in the Soviet Union. American ballet enthusiasts are much smaller in number, an elitist crowd at best. Now he's fallen into disgrace in Russia, and this bothers him. Nuri fled to the West to improve his art, to *create* in the highly charged environment of New York." Tina paused, stepping out of the way of the waitress who looked at her with curiosity and impatience. Tina looked at the Soviet leader expectantly. "*Freedom*, Chairman Baranov. Moscow had smothered your son. Even when he is with me in the kicked-back environment—I'm sorry—*relaxing atmosphere* of southern California, I can see how restless he is! Nuri needs the vitality of the U.S. Dance Company—and its versatility."

Baranov announced, "And the Soviet people need Nuri's energy and great talent here. Can you imagine what our winters would be like without the colorful theatre season?"

Natasha smiled and calmly interposed, "Dostoevsky wrote that 'Russia is a freak of nature.' The hand of *Russkaya zima*—Russian winter—grips the country in October, choking it by the neck until April. No mid-seasons like you have in America. Here it is more than a physical discomfort. Nuri must have told you this; for us it is a *siege of the mind*."

The small laughter that followed eased the tension slightly.

Tina sat back down at the table. "I'm sorry. All that may be true, but still—"

Baranov interjected, "Winter brings us the excitement of grand opera, folk theatre, and the ballet! Including Nuri's once-in-a-decade kind of dancing. Soviet citizens, by nature, crave the extraordinary. You must understand this. Perhaps, Tina, you know only the bright exterior of Nuri's talent, and not his soul or soft underbelly."

"In a year's time I've come to know both well, Mr. Chairman. Please. I didn't come to Moscow to debate." Again Pavlin Baranov had aroused her antipathies. To her amazement, the dinner meeting with the Soviet leader had worked out precisely as Natasha had predicted—a clumsy sparring for positions. The real battle for her would probably come later, when confronted by General Talik at the Bolshoi.

Tina would refuse to commit herself to Baranov. She needed to stall, find time to think; to come up with a plan. She wanted Jon Saarto around for support, if nothing else. Never in her life had she felt so alienated and alone.

Baranov gently tapped the side of his wineglass to break her reverie. "My innovations for the future can only work if you and Nuri cooperate, set an example."

Tina was disarmed. *"Innovations?"*

"I work for a Russo-American exchange program—a year, two years from now—whenever it can be implemented. A policy where Soviet dancers and other artists of Nuri's caliber will be free to spend specific periods abroad. Proper consideration will be given to marriage with non-Soviet citizens, of course."

Tina stared at him with innocent surprise. Was she dreaming, or was Baranov? She felt sure the tactical dice were loaded in favor of KGB head Fiodor Talik and not the well-meaning Soviet leader across the table.

Natasha glanced at her watch and turned to the Chairman. "We should be leaving now, for we have a half-hour drive to the Bolshoi."

Tina glanced at her half-empty dinner plate, and beyond it to the untouched rum cake dessert. All in all, the dinner had turned dismal. She idly wondered if Russian restaurants gave out doggie bags for later—if her hunger *ever* returned.

45

NURI GRINNED at Timur. "It's been a while since I've ridden in a subway without graffiti."

"Still one of Moscow's treasures."

The train braked at the platform and the doors opened. Nuri hefted the costume bundle over one shoulder and stepped out of the car. Sverdlov Square Station, with its marble and glittering chandeliers, was uncrowded; the rush hour was long over and the theatre crowds had already made their way into the Bolshoi auditorium. Nuri gestured impatiently for Timur Malovik to keep up with him. They stepped on the Metro escalator and rode to the street surface in silence.

Outside there had been a sudden drop in temperature, and the chill penetrated Nuri's bones. He pulled his scarf tighter around his neck, for the cold stabbed relentlessly at his sinuses, cheeks, and throat. He was glad now that he'd dried his head thoroughly before leaving Timur's apartment. The natural blond hair was back again, as he wanted, but prudently tucked beneath a floppy fur cap Timur had loaned him. Nuri also wore a theatrical moustache, Mark Washburn's eyeglasses, and the cheek pads—all items that could be quickly discarded at the critical moment.

Across the square the Bolshoi State Theatre stood out in the Moscow night, floodlights casting an ivory luminescence on its triangular frieze and massive Greek columns. Nuri checked his watch, reasoning that the audience within had been settled for over fifteen minutes. The first ballet would be well under way. Nuri pulled Timur to a halt and pointed to the reserved parking area beside the portico. A half-dozen limousines lined the curb, big Chaikas and Zils. Checking the license plates, Nuri said, "To the left—the first two vehicles, you see? My father's and Fiodor Talik's." Nuri counted the men nearby. "There are four aides and three KGB men in uniform guarding them."

Timur nodded and said quietly, "Do you plan to take your battle into the streets?"

Grinning, Nuri blustered, "My grandfather, who knew both Lenin and Trotsky, was a Bolshevik streetfighter. It runs in the family." Nuri hesitated, then changed the subject. "Timur, the order of the performance, explain it to me again."

"*Stone Flower* is being performed now, before intermission. There will be the *Firebird* and *Don Quixote* excerpts after."

"And the schedule is firm? You will dance the lead in *Firebird*?"

Timur nodded.

Frowning, Nuri thought for a moment. He'd just done one version of *Firebird* in Paris and had his fill of it. "Which choreography? Fokine's or Bejart's?"

Timur grinned. "You're lucky. *Bejart's*. Red leotards, the male phoenix rising from the ashes—the red apotheosis of the people."

"I haven't danced that revolutionary propaganda in three years."

"Perhaps you've forgotten the steps."

Nuri shrugged. "Never. At least the role is suited for a male dancer. Timur, it's time for you to go ahead alone. You're late enough, and Maryinsky will panic. I'll enter the stage door ten or fifteen minutes after you're in the dressing room. Are we together on the wardrobe delivery scheme?"

"Yes. Though I still think for you to dance in my place is madness." Timur paused, looking sideways at Nuri. "May I ask what you plan to say to that packed auditorium at the conclusion of the number? *If you live that long?*"

"I'm still working on it. Go now, or there'll be trouble."

Timur hurried off across Sverdlov Square toward the Bolshoi's lobby entrance.

Nuri wasn't in a hurry. He took his time strolling back to the tall, wrought-iron gate that marked the theatre's stage entry and shipping dock. En route he paused, observing himself in the reflection of a shop window; he didn't see a dancer, but an actor. *A credible one,* he hoped. His mind flashed on the controversial Russian poet Blok, whom Nuri had last read as a teenage student.

> A gleam in the window
> A porch without light
> A harlequin whispers
> Alone in the night.

Jon Saarto may have survived thus far in the Red capital by keeping his wits, but the complicated, tough part was still ahead. He'd watched helplessly as Tina Conner was escorted minutes earlier into the theater by the Soviet Chairman himself. As ever, she looked exquisite, though a bit sullen-faced. Saarto figured the actress had been safe enough winging it on her own; her celebrity status, if nothing else, kept vulnerability to a minimum. He wondered how Tina was taking the brutal reality of Moscow, if she'd finally armored herself and come out of her dreamworld over Nuri Baranov. Or would that be asking too much of any woman in love?

From where he stood across the square, Saarto could easily survey the activity outside the theatre. The Bolshoi edifice, like many buildings in Moscow, didn't look uniquely Russian at all. He vaguely remembered reading somewhere that the ornate, pseudo-Greek, five-tiered auditorium in its original version had been built in the same year as the American Revolution.

Saarto saw an inordinate number of uniformed KGB guards in front of the building; moments before he'd observed more of them pacing back and forth near the stage entry. Saarto knew why they were here and who they were protecting, but these men seemed unusually alert, as if expecting trouble.

Earlier, just before curtain time, when Saarto had ventured up to the box office to inquire about last-minute cancellations or no-shows, he'd heard the strains of the "Internationale" coming from inside the theatre. The ticket attendant had told

him there were no seats whatever, not even standing room; for
tonight's performance was a special one—prepared for visiting
dignitaries from the Byelorussian, Ukrainian, and Moldavian
republics, who were celebrating the sixtieth anniversary of the
Union of Artists.

Saarto was still trying to devise an alternate plan to gain
entry. He knew that once inside, the operation's fine tuning
would have to be improvised as he went along. He thought
quickly. An arrogant bluff was the only answer—*a little
substitution*. If he moved quickly enough with fake identification—one of the green KGB identification cards—he might
con his way past the Bolshoi doorman or ushers. Providing the
other KGB men kept their distance. Ignoring the alert but edgy
Russians in uniform, Saarto concentrated instead on a group of
bantering, smoking civilians who hovered around the dignitary
limos. One of the men—a noisy, paunchy individual in a fur-
trimmed overcoat and hat—appeared to be the junior official in
charge. He also looked KGB. Either out of nervousness, a
suspicious nature, the night's chill, or a combination of all
three, the portly Russian chain-smoked as he paced between
the waiting limousines and the opposite end of the Bolshoi
facade. Apparently something had caught his eye on the street
that led around to the theatre's stage door, for the Russian
disappeared down the dimly lit sidewalk.

Immediately Saarto followed him, keeping to the shadows
and skirting along the street side of several parked cars. After a
short distance the Russian civilian was met by a KGB sergeant
who had apparently stepped away from his companions
guarding the stage door. The two men paused in the darkness.
Saarto edged closer to hear their exchange. A clumsy transac-
tion was taking place, and Saarto could see that the KGB
civilian had purchased a liter of vodka. The meeting was brief,
and the uniformed guard quickly returned to his station several
rubles richer. The civilian turned, concealed the bottle in his
overcoat, and headed in Saarto's direction.

Saarto stepped out from behind a parked Volga and strolled
up the sidewalk. As he approached his quarry, he walked
faster, more purposefully, but waited until he was beside the
Russian before galvanizing himself into action. Timing was
critical, but Saarto had practiced the stunt more than once with
success. Passing the Russian, he suddenly whirled, coming up
on the man from behind. Deftly, using both hands, Saarto

spread his opponent's fur collar apart and pulled sharply downward, using the cumbersome overcoat and sleeves to pin the KGB man's arms to his waist. Before the man could cry out, Saarto spun the Russian's fleshy body, driving a terrible, air-sucking blow into his solar plexus. The KGB man coughed and keeled over, doubling up in pain.

Now Saarto was on top of him, one hand on the mouth, the other searching for a weapon and digging for the precious identification. Finding a Makarov automatic and a fat wallet, he quickly pocketed both. Saarto looked around, considering his plan. The street, thankfully, was still quiet.

Dragging his perspiring victim to the curb and out of sight between two parked cars, Saarto removed the bottle of vodka in the overcoat pocket. He was lucky it hadn't broken in the scuffle. Saarto pulled his captive's head up by the chin. The Soviet gurgled unintelligibly as he stared cross-eyed at the gun Saarto brought to bear on the bridge of his nose.

Saarto said in his best Russian, "Comrade, listen carefully. If you wish to live, you'll do as I say." He waited until the frightened man's breath came easier, then tilted the vodka bottle to his lips. "Now start guzzling. All of it."

The KGB man recoiled, but Saarto menaced him, pushing the gun hard into his temple and forcing the bottle. The Russian would have choked had he not swallowed and kept swallowing.

Saarto wasn't satisfied until three fourths of the bottle had been consumed. "Good, yes?" he asked in a sarcastic whisper. "Now, fatso, you'll remain right here. Just sit and ponder your damned position until the booze takes hold. If you're smart, you'll crawl away, hide somewhere until you're *sober*. Then you'll probably concoct a story, reporting that you were attacked by a hooligan. Consider carefully, *comrade*, what will happen should you be accused of drunkenness on the job—an investigation won't go well in your favor. Especially when your uniformed accomplice back there testifies that he sold you the bottle. Am I correct?" Saarto rose from his haunches and untightened. Still, he held the gun in readiness and kept his face in the shadows so the abashed, confused, and soon-to-be-snockered Soviet couldn't see it.

"You've wasted your time," the doomed man said, his voice already thickening from the hundred-proof alcohol.

"There are only papers—in my wallet—and precious few rubles."

Saarto looked up and down the street. The sidewalk was still empty and traffic was sparse. "Whatever you've got will be enough."

The Russian sneered, his teeth a pale gleam in the darkness. "Your accent—you're not from Moscow . . . but the Baltic area. Possibly . . . even Finland. The militia . . . always hunts hooligans down and . . . I'll remember that voice."

"You just do that, Ivan. *Do svidaniya.*"

Nuri warily eyed the three uniformed KGB guards by the stage door. Tall, broad-shouldered, with faces of gristle, the special-duty men all appeared to have been struck from the same mold. Nuri had timed his arrival to coincide as closely as possible with intermission. He put on Mark Washburn's glasses and slowly approached the alert sentries. The sergeant in charge listened to Nuri's fabrications while his companions probed like ferrets through the wardrobe package. Satisfied, they brusquely waved him on to the next barrier.

Nuri was a bundle of raw nerves as he passed through the all-too-familiar stage door. The chunky woman guarding it sat behind a pulpitlike oak desk, fussing with her coiffure. In her preoccupation, she eyed Nuri as though he were a fly crawling over her dinner plate.

He went up to her, working hard to keep his face muscles taut and the cheek pads of his disguise in place. Smiling was out of the question. The woman was a slight blur because of his eyeglasses, but it didn't matter. Nuri knew her well enough; she was the one the dancers called *charodeika*—the witch. Eyes flickering, she looked at him appraisingly, but accepted his story. Timur Malovik had obviously warned her of an impending delivery. Nuri nodded as the woman unnecessarily explained the way to Timur's dressing room.

Nuri headed on backstage, breathing a sigh of relief. He smiled to himself, and a passing wardrobe mistress thought it was for her. She flirted back, batting her eyes and wiggling her hips as she passed by. Nuri stiffened as Ballet Master Pyotr Maryinsky approached, his face its usual inscrutable mask. He gave Nuri only a cursory glance, without a hint of recognition.

Nuri took the stairs down to Timur's dressing room two at a time, pausing on the landing to allow a score of cheerful ballerinas to pass by. The names and faces that had almost eluded him in the year-long absence from the Bolshoi suddenly came back to him. It was as though he'd never left this great theatre. There was one face missing, of course. *Marina Pleskova's.*

He was about to knock on the door of the dressing room occupied by Timur and several other male dancers, but he hesitated. His heart pounded. What if he were discovered before his plan could be put into action? Nuri felt a strange urge to back off and reconsider. *No!* He'd come this far, and he would have assistance from Timur Malovik. The young Tartar, he remembered, was a master at petty intrigue. Timur had the boldness to pull off anything. Regaining his composure, Nuri knocked.

Malovik was waiting. He opened the door immediately and slipped out into the hallway. Thrusting a pair of dancing shoes into Nuri's hands, he gestured for silence and led the way down a deserted passage beneath the stage. When they were alone in an isolated storage area, Timur said to him, "You can get dressed here."

Nuri took off his hat and coat and opened the package he'd carried for the last forty-five minutes. "The time, Timur—how much of it do we have?" He took off his watch and glanced at it nervously before placing it aside with Mark Washburn's eyeglasses and other effects.

"Enough. Take care with your makeup." Timur withdrew a small hand mirror from a fold in his dancing tights and handed it to Nuri. "Sorry. This is the best I can do. As for the music, beware. There are a dozen or more bars in the middle coda that have been eliminated in the new choreography."

Nuri frowned. "Without consulting Stravinsky or Bejart?"

Shrugging, Timur added, "How can I explain it without practice? You'll have to improvise."

Nuri withdrew the plastic wadding from his cheeks and stripped off his moustache. Quickly pulling on the vermilion leotards, he said dully, "For the past few days improvising has become a way of life. If the audience is as shocked as we expect, the missed beats will be the least of my problems."

Timur turned apologetic. "I'm having trouble rounding up the others, getting an immediate commitment without giving away the plan."

"They have until the final curtain to decide. But *no*

pleading, understand? They come or they stay, but we share no details until departure." Nuri began changing his face makeup, balancing the mirror with one hand and the grease sticks and pencils in the other. He underscored his eyes in the usual manner, made his mouth a degree heavier. His blond hair was a trifle long for the role of the partisan hero-turned-phoenix in *Firebird*, but there wasn't time to properly trim it now. He was relieved enough to have it back to its normal color. It took Nuri another ten minutes to complete the makeup job and finish dressing.

Timur appraised him carefully. "Now the difficult part, getting upstairs and hiding you somewhere in the wings before my cue. I forget—*your cue*. You're still positive you want to go out there before the entire Soviet world with this?" Timur's voice was soggy with regret. "There's no chance of sitting down privately and talking with the KGB minister? A gun at his throat if necessary?"

Gazing in the mirror, Nuri straightened his cap. "Sorry, Timur. I haven't got a gun."

"Words sometimes move mountains."

"Not a chance. General Talik is mantled in evil; he hasn't a shred of social conscience I could appeal to. Now let's go."

They made it to the top of the stairs, but Nuri was forced to turn his face away when several stage hands passed by with a cumbersome prop. Nuri followed Timur by a circuitous route through the scenery bins, around the back of the theatre. They avoided the brilliantly lit area downstage where workmen were putting the final touches to the *Firebird* set.

Suddenly Timur drew to a stop, grabbing Nuri's arm and pushing him back into the shadows. From the opposite end of the stage a tall, uniformed woman strolled their way. *KGB Colonel Bruna Kloski!* Nuri looked quickly around him. A short distance away was a small janitorial closet. Timur read his mind and they both dashed for it.

There was barely room for the two of them, and Timur had to struggle to pull the door shut and secure it. They both held their breath. Seconds later they heard the KGB woman's footsteps outside. The sounds were joined by heavier, sluggish trodding and agitated conversation. *Kloski's assistants?* Now more foot traffic, followed by a scraping noise across the floor. *Again the stage hands*, Nuri guessed. Timur waited for the sounds to cease before sputtering softly with laughter.

Nuri grumbled, "What's so fucking funny? And you're stepping on my feet."

"I'm thinking that this is the closest the two of us have ever been, yes?"

"Forget it, Timur. Don't impose on our friendship. One of these days I'll see you yet turn straight."

Again the twitter close by Nuri's ear. "You'll never reform me, Nuri Baranov. Your dithyrambic passion for womanhood puts me to sleep. For an artist, you deprive yourself of aesthetic pleasure."

"Bullshit. And kindly lower your voice or they'll hear us outside."

"Ah! I've struck a sour chord? Haven't you heard that great artists have the characteristics of both sexes, that genius often demands a bisexual nature?"

Nuri didn't like being a captive audience, and he felt disadvantaged in the darkness; he wanted Timur to be able to see his scowl. Exhaling sharply, he whispered back, "Aside from being contentedly in love with Tina Conner, perhaps this one artist is a connoisseur. Your bird's ass, Timur, does not appeal to me. Nor do other boys. Now how long do we remain in here?"

"Up yours, purist. Be patient." The Tartar retreated into silence, again listening carefully. Outside the closet it was quiet.

Timur opened the door a crack, checked the stage, and eased outside. He motioned firmly for Nuri to stay put. "Don't come out until the end of the overture. We'll change places only split seconds before the entry cue, agreed?"

Nuri nodded without enthusiasm. He wasn't happy with the musty closet.

Timur frowned at him. "Bird's ass! Some compliment." He smiled and twittered triumphantly, "If you're such an *ornithology* expert, you would reconsider *flying* out on that stage. Have you forgotten our old Russian proverb—that a sparrow that has been shot at should be a knowing, wiser bird?"

46

FINALLY SATISFIED with the security backstage, Bruna Kloski hurried to the front of the theatre to join the intermission reception. She checked her watch. Events were proceeding as planned; indeed, the scene was everything her superior Fiodor Talik could have hoped for. Inside her uniform jacket the air pistol with its deadly mini-dart was ready. Kloski knew that outside the Bolshoi building, as a precaution, KGB forces would be taking up positions all over the city. Troop helicopters would soon arrive at Red, Revolutionary, and Konsomol squares, and in another half hour Moscow would be sealed off at the Inner Circle Road, train stations, and airport. Kloski's pulse quickened as the final countdown approached; she was convinced the destiny of the Soviet Union would be decided in the hour ahead.

Climbing the Bolshoi's grand staircase and stepping into the foyer, Kloski surveyed the intermission scene. The glittering chamber was crowded with the most influential and fashionable people in Moscow—all of the USSR, for that matter. Personally, Kloski disliked stylishly attired women; their extravagance went against the grain of her hard-line socialist principles. Tonight, however, with more important concerns on her mind, she wouldn't allow these trendy Soviet women to annoy her.

Kloski saw the Soviet Chairman and the American actress holding court at one side of the refreshment table, while the KGB minister conferred at the opposite end with several dignitaries. As she suspected, both men were making a studious point of avoiding each other.

Under Pavlin Baranov's orders, the members of the press—hovering nearby like watchful, hungry peregrines—would not be premitted to approach Tina Conner until later, after the final curtain.

Kloski helped herself to a slice of seedless rye bread and caviar. She ignored the liquor, instead accepting from the waiter a small glass of lemonade. Tonight absolute sobriety was imperative. The Beluga Malossol was delicious, and she had another generous helping. She wolfed it down, then went back to observing the dignitaries.

Just a few feet away Chairman Baranov patted his perspiring brow and turned to Tina. The Soviet leader raised his glass, crowing, "There is only one way to drink vodka, young lady. Like a hero of the Soviet Union on leave." He winked at Tina. "*Or like* a talented, attractive American movie heroine, yes?" An aide quickly translated.

Kloski watched Tina Conner participate—albeit reluctantly—in the Chairman's toast. All eyes in the crowd were on the actress as she did her best to swallow the lemon vodka in one gulp, suppressing a grimace as it set fire to her throat.

Kloski looked on with concern as the film director Natasha Chernyskaya came up to Tina, whispered at length, then quietly slipped away with an army colonel. Kloski recognized Natasha's companion from earlier when the pair had taken seats in the orchestra. *Colonel Rablin of the SPETSNAZ Intelligence Brigade.* He and the woman director were not even casual friends; the meddlesome Rablin was obviously here tonight to protect the Chernyskaya bitch! Kloski sighed with resignation; for now she'd let Rablin have his way; the woman from Mosfilm would still be questioned, however, but *after* tonight's priorities had been dispensed with.

Kloski scanned the table of delicacies, noting that the Soviet Chairman had sampled only a few items. Baranov, radiating an aura of disquietude, had put his glass down, consuming no more vodka and eating sparingly. Kloski could sense the American woman's tension and increasing discomfort. *Good.* The meddlesome Hollywood slut would suffer far greater turmoil before the night was over. Kloski glanced to the other end of the table. The KGB minister reflected a mood of anticipation, though Talik's face, usually a facade of arrogance, tonight appeared nervous and agitated. Despite his earlier professed confidence in Kloski's agenda, there was a restless nature in his movements and he kept fidgeting with his watch. *A new Strela*, she noted. *Relax, Comrade General, you are in good hands. Trust my judgment.*

The chasm in communication between Tina Conner and Pavlin Baranov seemed to be growing. Tina's face brightened when the warning chime sounded the end of intermission.

The crowd slowly dispersed back into the auditorium, but Kloski stood where she was, waiting patiently for the foyer to clear. Talik came over to her before proceeding with the others into the dignitary box. "I trust, Colonel, you're satisfied with the arrangements?" he asked quietly.

"Perfectly, Comrade General. These will be moments neither of us will forget."

Talik's face narrowed cunningly. Waving a thick finger at her, he whispered, "What happens tonight is unimportant. Marxist science has always been the inevitability of a better tomorrow, not the hastily poured concrete of today."

Kloski wanted to cleverly expand on the idea, suggesting they bury the current Chairman *in concrete*, but she thought better of it. Instead she said simply, "*Lenin zhivyot*, Comrade General."

Talik bore a triumphant expression as he hastened toward the auditorium, two plainclothes bodyguards in tow.

Kloski hurried over to the abandoned refreshment table before it was cleared away. Waiting until the waiters were preoccupied, she reached inside her tunic and withdrew her little diversion for the pathologists—the foil packet containing several intricately cut slices of *fugu*. She glanced in both directions before gingerly opening the wrapping and dropping the leaf-shaped, tainted fillets on the remains of a platter of raw fish. Woe be to the kitchen staff if they partook of the wrong tidbit before a post-assassination investigation could be arranged. *No matter*. In the past far worse sacrifices than a waiter or two had been necessary for the greater welfare of the state.

Saarto checked the clip in the newly-won Makarov automatic to make sure it was full. So far he hadn't needed the weapon, for the infamous green card of the KGB had done wonders opening doors. Saarto crossed his fingers, hoping the vodka had done its work on the porky Russian back in the street.

Without protest, an usher had admitted him into the theatre during intermission. Again by flashing the KGB card, Saarto had just squelched the objections of four people returning to their plush balcony compartment to find him lingering in it. Saarto had entered the multitiered balcony and worked his way as near as possible to the dignitary box without arousing suspicion, but he still wasn't near enough. He'd have to chance slipping in closer, possibly running the gauntlet of other KGB men with legitimate identification. The official seats were virtually surrounded by plainclothes types—mean-faced, alert individuals who spoke with harsh urgency and from appearance alone might moonlight on the Russian weightlifting team. Outside the dignitary box in the corridor were a combination of uniformed KGB guards and militiamen.

Saarto watched Tina take her place between the two Soviet leaders. Edging along the back of the balcony, Saarto pushed the rich red divider draperies aside as he slipped from one private stall to another. The theatre was resplendent in festive light from thousands of cut prisms in the ceiling chandelier and sconces around the balconies. It had been over thirty hours since Saarto had last seen Tina on the Leningrad-Moscow train. Her face blushing with color, she looked rested and alert, undeniably lovelier than ever. From where he stood, however, there was no chance she'd see him. Saarto's head felt cloudy; he drew in a long breath and exhaled slowly, reminding himself not to let Tina's magic distract him.

From their place in the balcony Pavlin Baranov and Fiodor Talik stared stonily at the stage like a pair of caryatids. Tina appeared to be ignoring the KGB minister, for when she did respond to Talik's queries, it was almost with clenched teeth, avoiding his stare and speaking directly to the interpreter who sat in the second seat row.

Feeling vulnerable, Saarto looked around him, suddenly wishing there was a nearby fire escape. Somehow he'd managed all the details neatly enough, including a damned *trap* for himself. Again he inhaled deeply to calm his nerves. *A one-way ticket to hell*, he reflected. He had no one to blame but himself. *Shit.* Saarto's netherworld existence as a bachelor had become half a life anyway; he had absolutely nothing to lose in going for the top prizes on the shelf.

The house lights dimmed. Igor Stravinsky's sonorous notes filled the magnificent auditorium, swelling, filling every corner, stilling the leftover whispers of the audience.

It was then that a tall woman in a KGB uniform sauntered into the balcony area between Saarto and the dignitary box. Even before he caught sight of the glittering, primeval yellow eyes, Saarto knew that this had to be Colonel Kloski of the nefarious Fifth Directorate.

Saarto stepped to the side of the draperies, hiding himself from her possible scrutiny.

Nuri winced. The closet smelled of stage glue and dirty mops. At last he heard the distant tremolo of strings from the orchestra pit. The overture of the *Firebird*. Nuri needed desperately to dance, for his ruminations while waiting in the darkness had given him a slight headache. He felt like a greyhound in a holding box anticipating the race for the rabbit. His heartbeat quickened as he looked forward to interrupting both his father's and Fiodor Talik's cobwebby scenarios; both men were like spiders, one harmless to him, the other poisonous. But both men had spun their snares.

Nuri listened intently to the music. *Now. Time to head for the wings. Minutes were critical. Move!*

Nuri made it to the place on stage his dancer friend had indicated. He could feel Timur's presence on the other side of the canvas tormentor, hear the young Tartar scooping in lungfuls of air as if routinely preparing himself for his stage entry—in this case one that wouldn't materialize. It was all a subterfuge for Pyotr Maryinsky, who would be standing beside Timur with his lighted clipboard.

Nuri's fear returned, burning as bright as the neon stars atop Red Square. He put his mind completely on Bejart's choreography and the panic faded—until he was suddenly tapped on the shoulder.

Nuri froze. *Recognized!*

Shaking her head, a pretty ballerina stared at him. She

whispered, "You are a grave affront to Leninist principles Nuri Pavlinovich. Have you no social responsibility?" When her frown twisted into a cautious but genuine-enough smile, Nuri knew he was safe. She added, "But we love you. Dance, if you must."

He didn't have time to respond. Reflexively, Nuri picked up the entry cue and leaped out on the stage. The fluidity, speed, proper placement of weight, and springiness of step were as close to perfect as he'd ever danced. It wasn't necessary to glance at the audience; he knew, by the terrible silence, that they were stunned with disbelief. It was as if everyone had ceased to breathe at once. Nuri landed downstage center, right on beat in a fifth position, and smiled at the conductor. Yurek Kasatkina's eyes were huge in their sockets.

Nuri didn't dare look up at the dignitary box, *not yet*. He needed to prepare himself for the euphoria he'd feel when he saw Tina. He stole a glance into the wings instead. The Bolshoi artistic director's face had gone white as milk, but beside him, Timur Malovik was all smiles. Nuri had almost forgotten how egotistical, overbearing, and short-fused Pyotr Maryinsky could be. He, too, was the enemy; under the circumstances, might he ring the curtain down?

Nuri softened his attack. His stomach felt as it were doing its own pirouettes. He started to get nervous again, then he felt the modulations of the timbre and his body gave its all, his every sense responding to the mobility of the Stravinsky theme.

At last he had the courage to focus directly on the dignitary box. He saw Tina, and predictably, his spirits soared. Their eyes locked ever so briefly, but it was enough to cause a strange feeling in his chest—exhilarating, but at the same time acutely painful. After the woes they'd been through and were *still going through*, nothing could separate them. Not now. Not his father, not the KGB. The bond was stronger, not weaker.

Nuri risked a glance at his father, who wore a strange, complacent smile. Two seats away, Fiodor Talik's face was florid, stiff and ugly with contempt.

Addressing his fellow dancers, Nuri once more adjusted his mind and body to the *Firebird* role. He was determined that this night would be his—not his father's, the KGB general's, or even Pyotr Maryinsky's.

47

AWED AS SHE WAS by Nuri's performance, Tina trembled with fear. She watched, fascinated, as he did his triple fouettes. At times the dancer seemed to hover over the stage, a humming-bird without wings. As always, his Technicolor eyes had a magnetism of their own, but this time there was more, like the strong, muscular body with its rare combination of masculine bearing and androgynous sensitivity. Tugging the strongest on Tina's emotions, however, was Nuri's unsurpassed power—the irresistible force of his stage presence and character, though now it seemed to be a strong, deeply-imbedded *Russian character* she'd never seen before.

The exhilaration Tina felt was soon replaced by an awful foreboding. Beside her the State Security minister shifted in his seat, livid with anger. Tina nervously turned and looked at him. Scorn flashed in Fiodor Talik's eyes like lightning. Apparently having witnessed enough, he shot to his feet.

Inexplicably, Tina, too, stood up. With shocked restraint, she touched Talik's arm, but her words caught up in her throat. All she could do was sway in dizziness, her legs almost slewing out from under her as she stared at him. Talik seemed ready to shout toward the stage when a glowering Pavlin Baranov caught him by the arm and pulled him back into his seat. Tina needed no urging to sit back down.

The Soviet Chairman said emphatically to Talik, "You forget, Comrade General, that *I am the vlasti*—the incumbent power."

The KGB leader didn't respond. He stared at Tina and the Chairman, his face twisted in contempt. To Tina, Talik may as well have been playing Mephisto on the Bolshoi's stage; the man looked evil and desperate, a maniac pursued by the devil that was his own ambition. She shuddered and involuntarily edged to the far side of her seat.

The atmosphere was charged with electricity. The audience in the nearby balcony was distracted by the disturbance in the dignitary box and looked their way, but downstairs on the main floor all eyes were still transfixed on Nuri Baranov. Except Natasha Chernyskaya's. Tina saw her look up with concern.

On stage Nuri was going into his *tour de reins*—a circuit of fast barrel turns. Tina held her breath. He did them expertly, with height and forceful impact.

Tina's face was hot, her body rubbery. The story of the ballet escaped her, for her thoughts were in total disarray. Tina sat between the two most powerful men in the USSR and she felt oddly superfluous to both of them. Though the rest of the auditorium murmured with excitement and anticipation, the mood in the dignitary box had turned hostile, as if open war had been declared. As far as Tina was concerned now, the entire theatre was filled with enemies prepared to strike at her—*and Nuri Baranov!* And they were completely helpless. Why had Nuri taken the damned bait and returned?

Tina's arms felt heavy and her heartbeat was erratic. Pavlin Baranov seemed oblivious to both her discomfort and the KGB minister's escalating fury. An invisible shield seemed suspended around the Chairman, an unseen barrier as formidable as the Kremlin wall itself. From all appearances there was no room inside the circumference for anything but father and son and a few steely thoughts.

Tina glanced back at the KGB head as he suddenly snapped his fingers to summon one of his bodyguards. Talik whispered in the man's ear and pointed to the uniformed woman who stood in the rear of the adjoining box. The woman's condescending smile awakened something in Tina, revived one of Nuri's earlier warnings. A woman colonel headed the Fifth Directorate and did all of Talik's dirty work. *Wet affairs*, Nuri claimed. Tina had forgotten her name. Why were Russian names such *tongue twisters*?

Talik turned back to Tina, his face less ruffled. He regarded her with a strange, distant smile. "You are right. This is not the time for anger. Let the artist perform." An aide promptly translated.

Tina didn't believe Talik; not one iota. The red sparks in the KGB general's eyes seemed even brighter than before. Tina saw through the grin and felt the malice. Nuri was right; there was something absolute, perverse, and murderous about this individual.

Nuri remembered almost all the choreography and improvised the rest. The concluding scene of *Firebird* was a triumphant meeting of the uniformed partisans and the people of the future. Supported by the rest of the troupe, Nuri danced his finale. In the wings, vain-as-a-peacock Pyotr Maryinsky looked on, his intense eyes continuing to scold Nuri for his audacity; at the same time his lips worked in several directions as if he were unsure whether to frown or smile. Crowding around Maryinsky, several dancers and members of the Bolshoi production staff continued to stare out on the stage with amazement. Some beamed, while others bore cruel, insolent expressions on their faces. All were shocked with disbelief.

Nuri emerged from a circle of ballerinas. His grand pirouettes in the air with their size and sweep left the audience breathless. The end of the ballet was Bejart's statement that the poet, like the revolutionary, was a bird of fire.

Nuri took his bows with the others. The applause and cheering—like nothing he'd ever experienced—sent a shiver of excitement up his spine. Nuri took the reception as gracefully as he could, but it was Tina he'd come for, not the Union of Soviet Artists audience. Looking to the side of the stage he saw Pyotr Maryinsky's face and body were as immobile as a carved sarcophagus. The maestro did not applaud.

While the others took their curtain calls, Nuri went up to Maryinsky.

The Bolshoi artistic director said sourly, "You look good as usual, Nuri Pavlinovich. Yet your style has changed."

Chest heaving, Nuri looked at his old adversary. "The river looks the same, but the water is never the same."

Maryinsky's face twitched. "You are *Narcissus*, dancing on a mirrored stage."

The others crowded around in mounting confusion. From behind Maryinsky, Timur Malovik protested passionately, "Your jealousy doesn't become you, Maestro. There are many, including myself, who are enthralled to dance in the shadow of Nuri Baranov!"

A ballerina came rushing off the stage, pleading, "Nuri! Come back out! Your audience demands you."

Nuri went back with the other dancers. This time they politely stood behind him.

"*Bis, bis,*" the crowded auditorium shouted. More, more. Nuri raised his hands and called back, "*Spasibo*. Thank you."

Saarto stared at the stage in amazement, captivated not by Nuri's spectacular performance, but by the fact the dancer had actually made it to Moscow.

The ovation was tumultuous. *"Spasibo! Spasibo!"* repeated the audience.

Saarto would have to be careful, not let the madness infect him. He turned his gaze away from the stage to the dignitary box and saw that Fiodor Talik was on his feet again. It was obvious that this time his anger wasn't about to be contained— by Pavlin Baranov or anyone else.

Talik raised both arms in an Augustan pose, trying to silence the auditorium, but he went unnoticed as the crowd began clapping in cadence. Nostrils flared and lips quavering, Talik protested in a high-pitched wail, *"Nyet! Nyet!* This will not be permitted!"

In the confusion, the applause drifted off and Nuri, still posturing at center stage, stared up at the KGB minister.

The house lights came up full and the theatre grew strangely quiet. Talik shouted down to Nuri, "How dare you pervert the traditions of this great worker's showplace, Nuri Baranov! You need your head examined!"

Saarto's gaze shifted back and forth between the official box and the stage. Impervious to Talik's sarcasm, the dancer stiffened his shoulders and boldly called back, "Madness? Me? Tell us about your own perversion of psychiatry, General!"

Nuri paused to catch his breath. The audience held theirs. "Would I be diagnosed to have paranoid delusions of reforming society? Will I be accused of 'neurotic moralizing,' or a poor understanding of socialist reality? I'm sure you would like nothing better than destroying my mind and spirit with drugs, make me over into a zombie at one of your 'enlightened' mental institutions."

Talik's face was reddened even more as he gripped the balcony with both hands. Shaking his head, he suddenly shouted, "Moscow has no need of last year's snow. Leave the stage!"

Pavlin Baranov's own anger was mounting as well. He, too, rose to his feet as if ready to tear into the KGB leader. An awkward moment of silence slid by.

Saarto saw a movement in the back of the next balcony section. It was the woman KGB colonel known as Bruna Kloski, and there was a dangerous flicker in her eyes. Saarto could see that she held something in her hand, close to the body. Taking advantage of the auditorium confusion and concealing herself in the draperies, she moved surreptitiously closer to the dignitary box.

Saarto moved quickly, following her as best he could; he watched with alarm as she withdrew a weapon—a silenced pistol? It looked strange, more like an electric screwdriver than an automatic. It had to be a gun, but what kind?

Stepping back into the shadows, Bruna Kloski raised her weapon and aimed it across the balcony. *At Chairman Baranov!* Saarto was so close he could hear her indrawn breath. There wasn't *time to think*. One second Saarto felt the muscles tighten in his calves, the next he was in midair, going for the quarterback sack. He had to smother her aim!

"Pfffft!"

The sound of the air gun's discharge went off close by Saarto's ear as he half tackled, half embraced the KGB woman with an armful of red velvet drapery. The curtains broke free, and Saarto thrashed with Kloski on the floor.

In its deflected trajectory the tiny dart of *fugu* poison had missed the Soviet leader, skimmed dangerously close to Tina, and wound up in Fiodor Talik's lower cheek. With sudden surprise, the KGB minister clutched at his face as if batting a mosquito. The tiny dart was just over a centimeter long, and he quickly pulled it away.

Too late.

Almost immediately Talik appeared puzzled and disoriented. Numbly rolling his head, he started to sit down, but instead slumped all the way to the floor.

Tina's face was a mask of horror as she edged back against Pavlin Baranov for support.

Saarto found Bruna Kloski tougher than he'd figured. She cursed and fought her way out of the draperies. He tried to withdraw his gun, but now the bodyguards were on him like fire ants. They jerked Saarto back, quickly disarming him.

Two women in the nearby balcony screamed hysterically. Tina shouted something, but Saarto couldn't make out the words. Four of the big Russians had him flattened, a heavy shoe pressing Saarto's cheek and head so firmly against the floor his eyes bulged in their sockets. From where he lay Saarto could see the stricken KGB minister's twitching form a short distance away. Fiodor Talik's wordless, paralyzing spasm lasted less than thirty seconds, then he was as still as a stone.

"Shah ee maht!" Saarto mumbled slowly under his breath. *Shah* was Russian for "king" and *maht* meant dead—together a corrupted form of "checkmate." So much for the Soviet KGB leader's sorry play, Saarto flashed. He wondered if there were any other would-be usurpers waiting in the wings. Around Saarto's head there were pounding footfalls, bodyguards pulling Pavlin Baranov and Tina Conner away from the dignitary box, out of the balcony. Vaguely he heard the Chairman instruct his aides, "Don't harm that man. Interrogate him and bring me a report immediately." Saarto heard Tina shout a protest in vain, but her words, too, faded as she was bundled outside with Baranov.

The woman colonel was on her feet, straightening her hair and glaring down at Saarto with cunning yellow eyes. She rasped, "Your name? Who sent you?" First in Russian, then heavily accented English. Her assistants twisted his arm tighter.

Saarto blanched. Fighting off the pain, he said slowly, "Let's just say that like the young actress, I'm an unwilling guest of the Soviet Union."

Bruna Kloski's fury was uncontrolled. She kicked Saarto in the face, drawing blood. Her foot came at him twice again, this time in the stomach. "I'll deal with him later," she snapped. "Take him to Lubyanka."

Oobeet vbayu—killed in action, Kloski thought, gazing down at the still body of Fiodor Talik. An unfortunate accident. Spotting the small poison dart on the floor near the KGB minister's body, she gingerly picked up the tiny messenger of death with a handkerchief and pocketed it.

A bodyguard's attempt to administer CPR to Fiodor Talik proved futile. Kloski tried to find compassion for the dead Soviet official, but there wasn't room for anything but anger and retribution. She also had her own position to worry over. Still, the enemy had invaded the Bolshoi—a deadly scorpion in the tent. He was down there, on the stage. The defector was a creature to be quickly squashed before he could inject his poison.

Kloski looked frantically around her. She grabbed a Kalashnikov automatic rifle from one of her uniformed assistants and pointed it toward the stage, where Nuri, surrounded by flowers and well-wishing fellow dancers, stared helplessly up at the dignitary box. The rest of the Bolshoi company had gathered around him, and Kloski was unable to get a clear shot. As a group they bowed one more time and backed away from the footlights.

The curtain crashed closed, followed by a choking silence.

Kloski whirled, her face covered with perspiration. "I want every exit blocked. No one leaves this theatre, or their seat. Calm the audience by immediately continuing the performance."

Exchanging the Kalashnikov for a service automatic, she raced downstairs and headed backstage.

48

When the curtain had closed, the scene-changing process
backstage proceeded as if nothing had happened out front. Two
members of the theatre's operational staff hurriedly whispered
in Pyotr Maryinsky's ear, but he ignored them, immediately
clapping his hands and spurring his dancers into activity. Sergei
Svoboda—whom Nuri had known before as a *demi character*
dancer—came strutting out of the wings carrying his ten-foot-
high, tapered wooden lance. He looked at Nuri disapprovingly
and took his place on the *Don Quixote* set with several
ballerinas.

Nuri wiped the sweat from his forehead. Timur Malovik
grabbed his elbow, trying to prevent him from returning to
confront Maryinsky, but Nuri was mesmerized by his former
choreographer and determined to hear what he had to say.
Approval was Nuri's Achilles' heel—it meant everything to
dancers and actors alike.

Nuri knew he would only have a few moments. His father
would either send for him or venture backstage himself. Either
way, in a matter of minutes Nuri would be reunited with Tina.

Already he could hear the rumors, the agitated conversation of the other dancers. *The KGB minister had suddenly taken ill. A heart attack? No, there had been a fight in the balcony.* Maryinsky looked frantic as he tried to dispel the speculation and clear the stage. Having seen for himself how Fiodor Talik had collapsed in the dignitary box, Nuri assumed that the KGB minister had been shot with a silenced gun. But by whom?

Under the circumstances, Moscow—the entire Soviet nation, for that matter—would be an armed camp. Nuri knew too well that this would be a foolish time to force anyone's hand and attempt to run off with a couple of official limousines— especially his father's. Nuri would have to wait—a day or two at least—for the dust to settle. *In the meantime . . .*

After Pyotr Maryinsky learned that the rest of the Bolshoi performance was ordered to proceed, he turned his attention to Nuri. "You wish to speak with me?"

"I no longer set your spine tingling, *Maestro*?"

Maryinsky exhaled sharply and glowered at him. "Nuri Pavlinovich, you are not, by any sense of the imagination, the best classical dancer in the world. Even in the West some of your purist reviewers—and I'm sure you've read them—are appalled by your lack of discipline. But you do have a unique, damnable reputation for living up to the moment, surprising audiences and fulfilling their emotional needs. Often with magnificent improvisation." Maryinsky paused, shook his head, and added gravely, "It is difficult welcoming you back to Moscow when you vex our State Theatre. You've also caused much pain here. We cannot forget the Marina Pleskova incident."

Nuri said sharply, "Surely you don't blame me for the demented actions of Fiodor Talik and his hirelings?"

Maryinsky shrugged, lowering his head. "Yes, indirectly. It wouldn't have happened but for your influence on the ballerina." The artistic director paused, studying him. "What has happened to your love for Mother Rus in general, the Bolshoi Theatre in particular?"

Nuri hesitated. "It is fine classic theatre. The best. But I've found a radically different, invigorating lifestyle in America. As for love affairs, I've found one—with Tina Conner."

Maryinsky wasn't impressed. "But there is no *Bolshoi* in the West! And never will be. You forget the theatre is a jealous mistress?"

One of the pretty ballerinas gathered around Nuri chirped, "Perhaps you love only the outward proofs of love! Surely your cultural background prohibits any real—"

"Stop, please." Nuri cut the young woman off by gently touching her lips. "My relationship with Tina prospers. It will grow." Nuri's proximity sense sounded an alarm. Abruptly he turned, spotting a familiar face at the opposite end of the stage. It was Natasha Chernyskaya, anxiously poised in front of the doorway that led to the front of the theatre. She pressed her body against the door until she could manage to prop a chair against its handle.

Natasha was trying to signal him. She waved frantically, indicating for him to run, *escape*!

Nuri stared at her, puzzled. *Why?* With Talik gone and his father calling the orders, he should be reasonably safe now. Who was the film director attempting to slow down and keep from entering the wings? Several puzzled stage hands had gathered around Natasha, each of them as curious as Nuri. She shouted a warning, but her voice was cut off by the crashing sound of the door and chair as they splintered and fell out on the stage.

Nuri's heart jumped when he saw Bruna Kloski push the shattered door aside and come stomping his way. The KGB woman's face looked intent on retribution, a grotesque mask with flashing eyes. She held a pistol in readiness.

Nuri gulped in a lungful of air and moved like quicksilver. Leaving Maryinsky and his entourage of dancers, he dashed for the opposite stage door that led outside. Reaching the wings, he skidded to a stop. *No!* There were guards outside the exit who would easily restrain him. Nuri turned. *The loft ladder!* It was only a few feet away, and he leaped for it.

Adrenaline pumping, he scrambled upward. Leaving the rungs at the first level, he ran a short distance along the narrow catwalk. He found another ladder and began climbing again. Above him, if nothing else, would be the cover of darkness.

Natasha picked herself off the floor where she had fallen when Bruna Kloski battered down the door. She watched with concern as the KGB colonel, without hesitation, began scaling the scenery loft ladder after Nuri. The woman was so intent on getting her hands on the dancer that she'd ignored Natasha. The violence and determination in that face, however, had ripped across the stage. Now, more than ever, Natasha knew it would take a team effort to stop Kloski. Nuri needed help.

She glanced around the stage. The dancer had a small break, for in her lunatic determination and haste, the tall woman colonel—though armed—had come blustering backstage alone. Kloski's corps of bullyboy assistants were obviously still preoccupied with the crisis in the dignitary box.

As for Pavlin Baranov and Tina Conner, Colonel Rablin and his men would see to their safety, if the KGB didn't. With Talik eliminated, the threat against the Soviet Chairman was minimal. *Damned Rablin*. Why couldn't he be where he was really needed?

Natasha stared up at the scenery loft where Nuri and Bruna Kloski had disappeared, not sure of what to do. Was there time to go for help? God knows, she might bring the *wrong* guards backstage, making it worse for Nuri instead of better.

No, she'd have to do what she could herself. There was another ladder on the opposite side of the stage from the one used by Nuri and the KGB woman. Natasha ran to it and struggled up the rungs.

49

NURI HESITATED on the second-level catwalk, debating whether to climb higher. The Bolshoi's stage was huge, one of the largest of its kind—if not the biggest—in the world, but he knew he couldn't play hide-and-seek forever. Time would be against him; when KGB help arrived, the odds would be on Kloski's side. Desperately, Nuri looked around him for a weapon but saw nothing he could put to quick use. Everything was bolted or tied down. *Damnation! What the hell now*? How far was the bitch willing to clamber after him? All five stories?

A response came in the form of a scampering sound on the ladder beneath him. Nuri felt one consolation: it was a long climb, and the KGB woman couldn't shoot while hand-over-handing it up the rungs.

Nuri went higher, against his will. At least his anger was now under control and he could think clearly enough. If Talik were dead, Nuri's major battle had already been won, and yet Bruna Kloski's final skirmish could kill him. She had two advantages—a gun, and if the chase were prolonged, plenty of assistants to converge on the scenery loft and string him up without a trial, just as they'd done with Marina Pleskova. On the other hand, the woman colonel was in unfamiliar territory, while Nuri knew most of this stage like the back of his hand.

He looked down and shook his head. Far below, as if his troubles with the KGB huntress didn't exist, the scene shifting continued. The morbid battlefield scenery for *Firebird* came gliding up into the loft in front of him, while a canvas backdrop of stylized Spanish windmills descended. Nuri paused on a catwalk before the imposing scene of the Polish castle used in the ballet *Bakhcisarajsky Fountain*. Feeling as if he were approaching the castle on a precarious drawbridge that might momentarily collapse, his heart thudded. *Don't look down!*

Nuri had never taken to lofty places; it was probably one more reason he'd steered away from becoming a gymnast. Holding onto a support cable with one hand, he took off his ballet shoes so his feet could better whisper along the loft's narrow walkways. Except for an occasional utility lamp of small wattage, and refracted light beams from below that threw oblique, amber rectangles across a few of the flies, the loft grew more shadowy and ominous the higher he climbed.

As Nuri edged along the eight-inch-wide catwalk, he extinguished two of the utility lights by their pull chains before realizing the clicking sound was giving his location away. She was somewhere near him. He could feel it.

His eyes dilated, adjusting slowly to the darkness. Inches at a time he groped his way along the walkway, determined to get to the other side of the canvas flat, out of the line of fire from Kloski's spot on the ladder leading up from below. Reaching the opposite side of the stage, Nuri stopped, hesitant about passing through a pool of illumination.

Nuri looked down and saw Bruna Kloski, ever so briefly, caught in the same light and peering up toward him. Even from the distance he could see the murderous intent in her eyes, the smirk on her lips.

"You're finally a dead man, Nuri Baranov," she raved, her voice lurid with contempt. "Long overdue for your reward."

Recklessly, Nuri laughed at her. He shouted downward, "I am the *glavni vrag*—the main enemy, yes, Comrade Colonel?" The false bravado did nothing for the increased trembling in his legs. He wiped his sweaty palms on the sides of his red dancing tights, breathing long and hard in an effort to relax his taut muscles and strung nerves. Suddenly he heard a noise from the far end of the flies. There was *someone else* in the loft!

Nuri decided to move. He darted quickly across the dim pool of light, but not fast enough. With a muffled report, flame belched from a silenced gun below him and a bullet grazed his bicep. It went on to clang off a spotlight housing. Nuri felt something, ever so slightly, give in his flesh; the bullet had only scraped by, but it had carried a section of skin away with it. Ignoring the pain, he plunged ahead into the shadows.

Nuri gripped his arm, now sticky with blood; he knew that surviving a minor surface wound would be the least of his problems. He took off his tight dancer's T-shirt and bound it around the injured arm to stop the bleeding. After a few moments the stiletto-sharp pain receded to a numb ache.

He found the ladder and struggled higher into the loft, surrounding himself again with huge backdrops and cycloramas. The scenery loomed everywhere; large luminescent numbers on the back side gleamed in the darkness, echoes of every current opera and ballet in the Bolshoi's current repertory calling out to him. Nuri's shoulder throbbed with each new rung of the ladder; sweat ran into his eyes, stinging and temporarily blinding him.

The darkness in the upper flies was his ally now. While Nuri usually felt a tremolo of fear over high, precarious places, all his fright now was preoccupied by the silenced gun Bruna Kloski carried. Did she have the nerve herself to pursue him all the way to the top? The catwalks there were even narrower, barely wide enough to do a highwire act, let alone serve as a platform from which to aim a weapon.

Nuri's breath came faster. Despite the improvised tourniquet, the blood still dribbled down his upper arm. He needed to rest, not hang onto a ladder as if his life depended on it. Once more, balancing as best he could, he set out horizontally across the loft. Nuri spotted a wider catwalk a few yards away and a half-dozen feet lower, most of it well-hidden in the shadows. He could hide there, if . . . Halfway between was a light bar with enough room to make a transitory landing, swing to gain momentum, then leap to his ultimate perch. *All this if his earlier training in gymnastics came back to him.* He suddenly remembered his wounded arm, how it might botch the maneuver and get him killed.

Below him there came a shuffling noise. Abruptly the KGB

woman's voice shouted up to him. "Come back down, would-be author and enemy of the State!" Her summons bit of sarcasm. "You can go no higher! You might think you are Michelangelo painting the truth on the ceiling, but as I see it, you merely write faslehoods in the sky, Nuri Baranov! Lies that in the prevailing wind of socialism will blow quickly away. Just as you are now about to be blown off your roost by my bullets."

Nuri swore as a small light beam flashed in his direction. He hadn't figured she'd carry a penlight. He ducked a fraction of a second before the gun went off again. Kloski had him pinned down. Terror gripped him, and he knew there was no choice. He'd have to dust off the gymnastics and leap.

Spurring himself into action, he sucked in air, and jumped.

The sudden convulsion in his shoulders when his hands caught the bar wouldn't have fazed him in normal circumstances, but this time a bolt of pain from the wounded arm ricocheted through his entire body. He started to stiffen with agony but quickly caught himself.

No! Don't go rigid. Don't dare stiffen halfway through the swing. Continue, pitch the body, distribute the weight. His arm was on fire, but he followed through. Back, forward, then let go and come up in a tuck! On a foot-wide catwalk? *Never. He wasn't a damned circus performer. You have to try. There's no longer a choice!*

Nuri landed on his feet, pawing the air for balance and quickly dropping to his knees. Exhaling in relief, he remained low, crawling along painfully, pulling himself into the darkness. Kloski was on the opposite side of the flat now and he was safe—momentarily, at least.

Natasha Chernyskaya's eyes, big and frightened, flicked back and forth in their sockets; first up to Nuri, then over to Bruna Kloski, who was at the same level, then downward from her dizzying perch. Exhausted as she was by the climb, she had to go higher, then get farther out over the stage, closer to Nuri. Natasha's arms and legs felt leaden; her mind was hazy but it was trying to tell her something. Finally it flashed with clarity: *You have to get the dancer out of this. Stop the KGB beast once and for all.* But how? Natasha knew all too well that if she wanted to survive herself, Kloski's demise would have to look like an accident.

She knew Nuri was safe for the moment, resting on a catwalk above Kloski, obscured from the KGB woman's view by a canvas drop of painted foliage. But while Natasha tried to decide what to do next, the stage crew below—unaware of what was happening high above them—started to lower the backdrop shielding Nuri! Natasha herself had still not been spotted by Kloski, but she was helpless. She watched with horror as some forty feet away the KGB woman raised her silencer-equipped Strikov and patiently waited for the flat to pass out of her line of fire.

Natasha dropped to her knees and frantically stretched for one of the supporting lines to Kloski's catwalk. Pulling it closer, then shaking it with all her strength, she finally dislodged the KGB woman's footing.

Kloski, unable to keep her balance and barely managing to hold onto her gun, fell to her knees on the narrow gridwork. With shocked surprise, she turned and stared at Natasha. Her eyes widened with delight when she saw that the film director was unarmed. Kloski swore softly and steadied herself, then temporarily ignoring Nuri, she began crawling toward her new opponent.

"It was a difficult climb, am I correct Comrade Chernyskaya? How dare you interfere with me! Your descent will be much easier and quicker, I promise."

The two adjacent catwalks swayed as both women gathered themselves and tenuously rose to their feet. Natasha's heart pounded in panic as she watched Kloski tread even closer, then pause. Smiling and drawing in her breath, the KGB colonel balanced herself as best she could, then raised her gun and drew a bead on Natasha's heart.

50

WATCHING KLOSKI crawl along the catwalk toward Natasha Chernyskaya, Nuri had to think quickly. The film director's face appeared frail and gathered as she tried to put away her fear and accept the inevitable. For Nuri, once more the fury began to rage. Damn this persistent KGB creature and the mean price she placed on human lives!

The pain in his arm forgotten, Nuri pressed quickly to the stage sidewall and a nearby rack of scenery tie-offs. His eyes focused on several coils of rope, following them to their source. He scrambled to release one particular coil. *No!* Forget the rope—not enough time. Simply pull out the wooden stanchion, grab the sandbag, and heave! Below him Kloski was getting to her feet, raising her gun toward Natasha.

Nuri aimed as best he could. He watched the fifty pounds of dead weight sweep across his hastily calculated arc. The burlap sandbag scathed the side of Kloski's face before she could squeeze the Strikov's trigger. More important, the counter-weight's nudge was enough to knock her body off balance. The sandbag's abrasive surface drew blood as well, though the improvised weapon hadn't been aimed accurately enough to pile drive her brain into oblivion, as Nuri had hoped. Nuri saw something else that made him smile: Bruna Kloski was wearing a wig, and it had been dislodged by the sandbag's glancing blow.

Nuri stared down at the KGB colonel, who was now battling furiously to keep her balance. He shook his head as he considered the close-cropped, distinctly male hairstyle the longish blond wig had concealed. The rumors were true! *Kloski was not a woman, but a man.* Nuri's gaze darted to Natasha Chernyskaya; he saw that she, too, bore a look of astonishment.

The wig spiraled down to the stage floor.

Nuri flashed on the past, his brain bombarded with conflicting images of the KGB woman colonel. Staring in wonderment at the scene below, he remembered the jokes he'd heard earlier and dismissed, that the gross-mannered, heinous Bruna Kloski might be a transsexual! Not silly speculation, *but the truth*? A *he*, not a she! *Bruno*, perhaps, instead of Bruna?

The KGB colonel tottered on the narrow perch, arms windmilling for balance as she screamed coarsely, the gun still madly clutched in one hand.

Nuri tightened, but felt no pity for her—*or him.* Nuri was oddly distracted, amazed by what he'd discovered; he was still unable in his mind to reconcile the KGB officer's proper gender.

Natasha Chernyskaya decided for him when she shouted, "He's going to fall!"

Kloski clawed the air, but managed to catch the edge of the swaying walkway with one hand. Swinging tenuously fifty feet over the stage, his fingers turned red, then blue. Desperate for a better purchase, Kloski jammed the gun into his belt and grabbed the edge of the walkway with both hands.

Natasha stealthily edged along the catwalk toward the spot where Kloski held on for life.

"No!" Nuri shouted. "Go back."

The film director ignored him, and with a determined look continued on her hands and knees.

Nuri turned his gaze on Kloski. "So, Comrade Colonel. We now see why the young boys in the Dance Academy so studiously avoid you, yes? Can you hear me, comrade? You secretly march to a *different drum*, no? Transvestite, transsexual, pederast, whatever your curious stripes, it is only fair that you share them with all of Moscow. Shall we lower you down a bit and open the curtain?''

The helpless KGB officer's response was an angry, broken string of obscenities.

Nuri observed with dismay that the lanky Kloski—whatever *his* bona fide first name and patronymic—was proving as strong as a gorilla. Seeing Natasha approach, he'd gone back to clinging with one hand so he could reach for the gun with the other.

The film director had managed to struggle along the shaking catwalk to a point directly above their dangling adversary. Now she began kicking, as hard as she could, at Kloski's remaining handgrip. The KGB colonel's crazed, greedy eyes flashed repeatedly between Natasha and Nuri as if undecided whom to shoot first. His bloodied hand couldn't hold on any longer, and though he tried to bring the Strikov to bear, the narrow walkway he clung to swung crazily and his gun hand waved in useless arcs.

Kloski's bruised and bleeding fingers finally let go, and he swore in anguish.

Nuri watched, horrorbound, as the KGB colonel plummeted to the stage. Kloski's five-story, ghostly scream ended with an ugly sucking sound, for his body had impaled itself on Don Quixote's upthrust lance.

Natasha winced and looked away, but Nuri continued to stare in disbelief. He felt numb all over. After what he'd been through, he needed to see it all, down to the terrible, convulsive finish; if he were below on the stage, he'd be the one to take Kloski's pulse—*to make absolutely, dead sure*.

The ten-foot-high jousting lance was only a wooden stage prop, but it proved unbending and stout enough; the KGB colonel hung there, arms splayed and trembling, skewered as neatly as a kabob. A crimson gore flowed down the arms and upper body of Sergei Svoboda, who had been preparing himself, anticipating the role of Quixote. Despite the rain of blood, in his shocked confusion the muscular dancer had managed for several seconds to hold the lance erect as if he were doing a balancing act at the Moscow Circus. Finally emotional shock and the laws of physics overcame Svoboda. Like a flag mast felled with its standard still flying, Bruna Kloski and the lance crashed to the stage.

Nuri winced and climbed down to the lower catwalk where Natasha held on tightly. She was trembling. The film director looked down at the stage one more time, then back at him. When he steadied her, she studied him appraisingly, as if wanting to confide in him but halfway fearful.

Nuri asked, "You're afraid of me or the height?" Natasha Chernyskaya was one of the most attractive, self-confident women in Moscow, but now she behaved like a nervous bird.

Finally getting a hold of herself, Natasha said softly, "I can't be seen with you, but there are things you should know. Listen carefully, for I'll have to be brief."

Perplexed, Nuri looked into her fluttering eyes. "I don't understand."

"It isn't important that you understand everything. I've been told that no less than the American President has entrusted you, so I must chance doing likewise." She hesitated, studying his reaction. "My cover *zapiska* may indicate I am Russian, but the truth is that I am Polish. A long story that perhaps you will learn more of when you return to the United States. *If we are able to get you out of Russia.*" She looked at him speculatively and lowered her voice. "I am a mole for the CIA, and your friend Jon Saarto was my American contact."

Nuri swallowed hard and said in a determined voice, "All of the Soviet Union knows you for your cinematic art. How is it possible for a talented person to be plunged into the harrowing life of a penetration agent?"

She said reassuringly, "The aesthetic part is the easiest. In fact, enjoyable. It is difficult enough being a lonely man in the enemy camp. A lonely woman is even more difficult. Without my film work, mentally it would be impossible."

Nuri was astonished and let it show.

Natasha glanced nervously around her. From below they could hear the sound of someone climbing up into the loft to join them. She said quickly, "In the balcony an American was taken captive—you know Jon Saarto, of course?"

Nuri erased his smile and nodded.

Again she lowered her voice. "This Saarto is an Agency operative as well, and was sent to infiltrate the Beck Publishing Corporation. He was also to check your bona-fides. Beck thought he was being clever, using the same channel as you to

get espionage material into Moscow. He was a fool. In the end
he used the one called Khamsin Ahmed in Paris as a courier to
carry concussion-bomb microfilms to the Soviet Union. Khamsin never arrived, but it is unimportant. They were fake plans
and documentation, for we were on to Beck two weeks ago."

Nuri slowly shook his head. "I'm familiar with this
Khamsin. He also had another job, to kill me."

Natasha nodded. "About this Jon Saarto. We both must do
what we can to help him. And protect his cover."

"Tina—what does she know about this?"

Natasha stiffened. "Nothing. And it must remain that way.
In Stockholm she caught Saarto passing me a note. He palmed
the incident off as an invitation for a sexual tête-à-tête, and I
trust she accepted it. In reality Jon was making it clear to me
that as far as the White House was concerned, he was not
authorized to travel to Moscow with Tina. The success of our
plan, however, depended on secrecy, last-minute improvisation. Your father knew this, of course. I knew by agreeing to
participate we were taking a chance that might backfire, but
Chairman Baranov had no choice. Now we must do what we
can for Jon Saarto. And if you and Tina wish to escape from
Russia, you must *swear* to protect my cover."

Nuri exhaled, quickly considering the risk of taking Natasha
out of the Soviet Union with him. He looked at her seriously.
"You'll have to come back to the United States with us. Tina
and I will both introduce you to the right people in the
Hollywood film industry."

Natasha grinned and shook her head. "I've already met
many of these people. No. In cinema one must have deep
insight into humanity, understand and experience one's culture
to the utmost. How could I achieve this focus in America?
Here, I know the Russian people, I know what the future
should hold for them. Perhaps there will come a day when I
have nothing more to say; possibly then it will be different."

Nuri prompted, "And *then* would you consider fleeing to the
West?"

She lowered her eyes. "I make artistic statements. I am
already permitted to attend film festivals outside the Soviet
Union. In the meantime I work to improve conditions in the
Soviet republics, and indirectly, in Poland. Never forget that
the motion picture is the 'democrat of the arts.' As for the

future, we will see what will be when I lose my creative energy, yes?" She nervously looked downward toward the stage. "Now I must go. Someone approaches. You must distract them while I slip down the other ladder."

Before Nuri could respond, she disappeared into the darkness.

51

WINCING. NURI tightened the improvised bandage on his arm and hurried to the nearby ladder. He began his descent, to be met on the next landing by Timur Malovik. The younger Tartar stared at Nuri's bloodied shoulder.

Timur said uneasily, "I wasn't sure I'd find you alive. You're wounded badly. We can have a boatswain's chair sent up and let the rigging crew lower you."

"No. I'm all right. Just a messy surface scratch."

"Below, on the stage. She's dead."

"Kloski's not a she. *He's dead.*"

"As is Fiodor Talik out front," Timur added with relief. He lowered his voice. "It's a new scenario, Nuri. You still plan to organize an escape by motor vehicle across five hundred miles of Russia?"

Nuri started for the ladder. "Under the circumstances, obviously not tonight. We'll discuss it tomorrow."

Timur grabbed Nuri's good arm, restraining him. "Wait, please. With Talik and Kloski dead, we need to talk." Hesitating, his face furrowed with consternation. "Do you think your father's interest in reviving the cultural exchange program is sincere?"

Nuri shrugged. "Yes, but he is only one man in the Politburo. After tonight, however, the odds for him achieving his goals appear vastly improved. Why do you ask?"

"I've just talked with the others. They insist that they in fact love the Bolshoi, but merely want the yoke of oppression removed so there is freedom to travel and perform throughout the world—like before. Not all of them are as talented and *daring* as you, Nuri Pavlinovich. Some of us need the financial security blanket a State Theatre can afford our careers."

Nuri let Malovik's point sink in before responding. "*Us*, you said. You, too, are getting cold feet?"

Timur smiled sadly. "You have accomplished much tonight, and opened my eyes. A choice, yes? Perhaps it is a matter of pain—the sharp one of revolution, sudden change, or the dull one of continued oppression. I've been thinking, Nuri. Would I be better off in the West? For homosexuals, Gypsies, Jews, and other minorities, bigotry is the same everywhere."

Nuri dropped a hand on his friend's shoulder. "Whatever you decide, we will be friends."

"And I will still distribute your book here, yes?"

"Save that decision. You may feel differently after reading it. Timur, I'm curious. Did you or your underground friends suspect Colonel Kloski's true sexual identity?"

"I wasn't sure, and didn't want to get close enough to find out."

Nuri let out a sigh. "Unfortunately, we'll never know about Kloski's motivation, what made him tick. What do you think, Timur? Was his masquerade a compulsive need or a frivolous adornment?"

Timur stiffened. "Whatever his secret sexual escapades, I hope they'll be buried with him."

Nuri nodded and dismissed the subject. "They're waiting for us below."

They both started down the ladder. Nuri's shoulder still hurt, but the pain was bearable. As they descended, he said to Timur, "One last favor, and I'm counting on you. There are items I shouldn't have in my possession if by chance I'm searched or interrogated. Back in the area where I dressed— my belongings. You must get there first and retrieve the passport and visa belonging to Mark Washburn. Take it to

James Berkowitz at the Ukraine Hotel. No explanations are necessary; he'll understand. Will you do this?''

"Consider it done."

Stepping back down to the stage, Nuri was greeted by Pyotr Maryinsky, several members of the Bolshoi staff, and a group of dancers from *Don Quixote*. They stared at him with a stricken, horrified expression. Timur Malovik slipped away, unobserved.

Nuri felt his skin grow hot as he glanced at the dead body and the confusion at stage center. He turned to Maryinsky and said emphatically, "Open the curtain, Comrade Artistic Director, and show your audience *real blood*, not red symbolism."

Maryinsky said with exasperation, "Either of them, Talik or Kloski, in their passion would have killed you."

"I wasn't ready to die. There are a dozen ballets I must dance."

"Here or in New York?" Maryinsky asked tartly.

Nuri hesitated, distracted by a commotion at the stage door. His father had entered, accompanied by Tina and a half-dozen bodyguards and KGB personnel. Deferential Bolshoi personnel edged back, making a path for the Chairman's entourage.

Nuri concluded his conversation with Maryinsky, stating simply, "Dancing is the most fragile and temporary of the arts. In ten, fifteen years, the Soviet people will forget me. There will always be others." Swallowing hard and straightening, Nuri turned, intent on greeting his father. But he fell into Tina's arms first. Passionately, they embraced and kissed, while Pavlin Baranov waited.

Nuri then put his good arm around his father, bussing cheeks in the Russian tradition. It had been twenty months since Nuri had last seen Pavlin Baranov in person. The Soviet leader's shoulders appeared slightly buckled from the weight of time, but his blue eyes, the identical color of Nuri's, were as bright and alert as ever.

Words, under the circumstances, were difficult for both of them, but the small talk continued for several minutes. Nuri stood next to Tina, his hand clasping hers tightly. He knew she didn't understand the dialogue, so he explained, "We spoke only of minor things—relatives and my father's health."

There were tears on Tina's cheeks, and Pavlin Baranov handed her his monogrammed handkerchief. The Chairman said slowly, "It is good to get it out of your system, Tina. We Russians call tears 'pearls of suffering.'"

Nuri translated.

Timur appeared with Nuri's street clothing in his arms.

Pavlin Baranov said to his son in a somber voice, "Come. Put on your overcoat and shoes. You can clean up and dress later, for we will go out to my dacha. There we will talk privately of more serious matters."

As they left the theatre and hurried to Pavlin Baranov's waiting limousine, a crowd of people lined both sides of their pathway. The throng was watchful but silent, held back by cordons of militiamen and KGB guards. A dozen young people toward the rear suddenly began shouting in cadence.

"We want Nuri! We want Nuri! We want Nuri!"

Both he and Tina were startled by the perfect, accent-free English. Then Nuri remembered; *The Virginia Ballet Academy*. He waved. The Russian crowd around the Americans watched in shocked expectation, then after brief moments they, too, started shouting and clapping their hands.

52

THE DACHA WAS only partially heated when they arrived, so the Soviet leader's aides hastily turned up the furnace and kindled several logs in the fireplace. A woman physician treated and expertly bandaged Nuri's arm, then departed. Pavlin Baranov brought out a crystal decanter and poured a tawny liqueur into three goblets.

"Fine Armenian brandy, to celebrate." He offered the drinks on a serving tray. "To the 'green snake,' yes?" Baranov smiled and lifted his own glass.

Tina looked at the Chairman, puzzled.

Nuri explained the idiom: "In the West the term is 'pink elephant.'" He ran a finger around the rim of his own glass and looked back at his father with discomfort. "I'll join your toast only when I'm sure our American friend is safe."

"And that you'll free him," Tina added, sliding her brandy snifter back on the tray.

Unruffled, Pavlin Baranov sipped his drink. "We are still determining whether this Jon Saarto is a hero or our enemy. My

428

investigators must be sure. I expect an accounting at any moment."

Nuri said sharply, "Saarto saved your life."

Grave-faced, the Chairman nodded. "That fact will not go unrecognized. Had General Talik and Colonel Kloski succeeded in their ultimate moment of violence, you would have seen a bloody purge unprecedented in modern history. Talik's ambition to reshape the USSR and dictate death with a mere snap of his fingers linked him to policies as hard and cruel as the worst of our czars. Or Stalin."

Tina looked at Nuri, then to the Soviet leader. Intently serious, she queried, "Are you satisfied now that your position is secure?"

Pavlin Baranov calmly replied, "Absolutely. I negotiate from strength. I am nominating one of my friends, a Red Army marshal, for the position of Minister of Security. He is a tough, dedicated Leninist, but less arrogant and far more malleable than Fiodor Talik. I have the Politburo votes, and already, for the announcement, workmen prepare his likeness—a large photograph that will be placed beside mine in Red Square."

Tina listened to Nuri's translation, then asked curiously. "Why are these giant portraits so popular in Moscow?"

Nuri smiled. "Authority is important to Russians. There's a deep anarchy embedded in our character, the need for a leader to venerate."

Pavlin Baranov lit a cigarette and sat on one of the two beige sofas that faced each other by the fireplace. The carved birch coffee table between them was strewn with several Czech and Italian art books, all expensive. The Chairman's gaze alternated between Tina and Nuri as he exhaled a long column of smoke. He said slowly, "The days ahead will be hectic. While the Soviet leadership situation is stabilized, I suggest that the two of you go to a recreational facility at Yalta or Baku to rest." Baranov paused, avoiding their eyes as he struggled for words. "You will need privacy to give proper consideration to Nuri's future in the Soviet Union. *Yours as well*, Miss Conner, if it is your destiny to remain here with him. That choice is yours."

Nuri's spirits took a nose dive. He scowled and threw back his shoulders. "Absolutely no."

"Your lady has not seen the charm of Yalta. Or you might stay at Baku, or the Caucasus."

Nuri flared. "Sanatoria, health resorts, the dying and the dead! Yalta is dull—the whole of Crimea is one vast rest home for emphysema." Nuri's memories of beaches filled with suntanned, distended bellies lying in rows came back to him, the recollection a far cry from the physique-conscious American women he'd admired on the sand at Malibu and Fort Lauderdale. His neck muscles tightened as he sat forward in his seat and said irritably, "Father, you obviously feed on patterned monotony—your so-called scientific socialism. I'm sorry, but there's something in my makeup, possibly from my mother's blood, that makes me thrive on the ferocious energy of the West."

Pavlin Baranov spread both hands and sputtered, "Energy? What energy?"

"Acceptance. Rejection. *On merit.* The artistic vitality and madness of New York City. An artist needs a wall in front of him against which to bang his head. But not one of stone, or an iron curtain." Nuri thought for a moment. "Please. I cannot, will not remain in the Soviet Union. You deceive yourself. This discussion is madness. It's too well-known that I drive a sharp stake in the heart of communism."

Taken aback, the Russian leader struggled to his feet.

Tina pleaded, "If you care for your son, you'll see to it we get aboard the next flight out of Moscow."

This time Baranov didn't need a translation. Understanding her intent, he shot back, "Tina Conner—you don't understand." He paused, then continued in Russian so he could choose his words carefully. "I can use my influence, but Nuri's welfare must be decided by a form of political communion; that is the inevitable way of socialism. Why do you think I beg him to recant his reactionary views?"

Baranov waited for Nuri to translate, then calmly continued, "You ask me to test the limits of the possible, yes? But in our Soviet system it is the limits of the permissible that matter. Our bureaucracy what it is, I alone cannot authorize Nuri to merely pick up and leave again." Baranov sent her a fragile smile then turned his attention back to Nuri.

The dancer gloomily listened as his father unreeled the already familiar evidence against him. Nuri was relieved when the priority telephone in the next room rang shrilly.

The Soviet leader excused himself and stepped away to answer it.

When he was gone, Tina spoke slowly, the anxious voice of a mediator. "Don't battle him, please, Nuri. Just stall for time. In the morning I'll go to the American embassy."

"Dreamer," he scoffed, with more calmness than the moment deserved. Nuri strolled over to the fireplace, having spotted a familiar object over the mantel; it was the balalaika his mother had presented him on his twelfth birthday. Gently lifting the instrument off the wall, he smiled, gave it a brief tuning, and began to play for Tina. He sang:

> "Maiden, maiden, tell me true,
> What can grow without dew
> What can burn for years and years
> What can cry and shed no tears?"

Winking at her, Nuri paused to whisper, "Love." He then went into the refrain, this time singing in Russian.

> *"Toom bah lah, toom bah lah,*
> *Toom bah lah lie kah.*
> *Toom bah lah lie kah,*
> *Toom bah lah lie."*

Nuri's head felt like an attic; there were too many memories that needed dusting off—like the balalaika. *Not now*, he reflected. *Another time*. He put the musical instrument aside and gave Tina a gentle kiss.

His father reentered the room. Glancing at the balalaika on the sofa, Pavlin Baranov said wryly to him, "Nuri Pavlinovich, you are an incurable romantic. Always fantasizing. Perhaps that is your problem. Do you know the meaning of puppy love?"

Not about to be nettled, Nuri gave his father a taut look. "Yes. In the Tretyekovskaya Gallery. There is a painting of a peasant woman allowing herself to be suckled by the nobility's puppies, while her own infant cries beside her in the hay. A sample of Soviet realism in art. By comparison, it is Soviet policy that contemporary masterpieces by Chagall and Kandinsky are preserved but hidden away in storerooms closed to the public."

"Enough, Nuri. Do not provoke me," Baranov snapped. "Do you wish to hear the news on Jon Saarto or not?"

Nuri put away his testiness, becoming suddenly attentive. Tina looked on, exhausted and afraid.

The Chairman brusquely explained, "The Americans responded to our initiative much faster than we envisioned. Perhaps they anticipated us. This Jon Saarto appears to be bona fide, and though he is a CIA agent provocateur, I do owe him my life. He will soon be released, *traded* for the espionage agent L. Brian Beck. The U.S. President has agreed, but only if the exchange can be made forthwith. And *quietly*."

Tina asked, "The publisher has no choice in the matter? As a typical *capitalist*, Beck would have ample resources for his defense."

Pavlin Baranov laughed at this. "In America he's no longer of value; in fact, a dangerous traitor. I'm afraid Mr. Beck's entrepreneur days are finished. When an intelligence organization buys a spy, it owns him totally, irreversibly. If Brian Beck stays in the United States, he will hang or rot for life in prison. Here, he will be given his *freedom*."

Tina exchanged a swift, knowing glance with Nuri, who asked, "Where is Jon Saarto now?"

"Lefortovo Prison. He is safe."

"No!" Nuri shook his head. "If the American is imprisoned, Tina and I will join him, spend the night there as well."

Tina frowned. "Speak for yourself, Nuri."

"Then I'll go there alone."

Baranov scowled. "Don't be foolish. You're my guests here."

"No again. You'll arrange rooms for us—Saarto included—at the Rossiya or Cosmos. Double the guards outside the hotel if you must, but give us privacy and time to think. Away from all this political upheaval and madness."

The Chairman stubbornly shook his head. "Jon Saarto must be kept under custody. We and the Americans both require absolute secrecy."

Nuri was adamant. "Leave that to me. Unless you want us to join Saarto, taking adjacent cells at Lefortovo."

Baranov scowled and poured himself another brandy. "I don't need that kind of hard-hearted reality. To negotiate, you must learn to compromise."

Shrugging, Nuri rose to his feet and replaced the balalaika above the fireplace. He warmed his hands by the hearth before turning back to face the Russian leader. "Since when do

Russians *compromise*? You think I haven't given considerable thought to bargaining? Good enough, Father. If you wish to meet me halfway, listen carefully." Nuri inhaled deeply, girding himself for an uncomfortable concession. "I'll forget the book—no *Kremlin Sword*—until you retire or leave the Presidium and Politburo; this in turn for a complete restoration of a decent cultural exchange program. Specifically, next season you allow the Bolshoi and other theatre companies to resume their visits to the United States. And no harassment of Soviet families left behind in the 'unfortunate event' dissidents should defect to the West."

For twenty seconds Pavlin Baranov merely stared back stone-faced, betraying no emotion. Then he said suddenly, "Agreed." Turning to Tina, he fired off some terms of his own. "And you, my dear, must compromise as well. You have a choice. You can, of course, return to America immediately, or work for three months at Mosfilm Studios."

Startled, Tina pressed both hands against her cheeks.

The Chairman held up his hand before she could protest. "Wait. I haven't finished. Natasha Chernyskaya has agreed to prepare a guest role in Soviet cinema, this to occupy you while Nuri is with the Bolshoi Touring Company. He will go to Vienna, Cairo, Peking, and Tokyo."

Nuri staggered uneasily against the fireplace, his stomach doing pirouettes. "No. A thousand times no." He saw Tina's face sicken with dismay.

Emphatically, the actress said to Pavlin Baranov, "You would force Nuri to dance again for the Bolshoi? He's not a mechanical ghost or a soulless mannequin!"

Nuri sat back down on the sofa and put his arms around her. Tina's cheeks were glistening as his lips brushed against them to whisper in her ear. "It's all right. He'll quickly learn my computer won't accept his software. My father can't win, Tina."

Nuri could feel her rapid pulse and taste her tears. Any shred of tolerance he might have for his father's ideas had vanished now. Nuri would say more to this leader of the Soviet peoples, plenty more, but he had a sinking feeling this wasn't the time or place. His father would never understand that as a creative individual he had mysterious, highly-developed antennae that sensed forces beyond logic and simple understanding. Communism would amputate these invisible wires, substituting more simplified, direct, and controlled forces of its own. Nuri kept thinking of a marionette on strings. *Petrouchka!*

When Nuri's eyes left Tina and flashed angrily back to his father, he was surprised to be greeted by an infectious, almost mischievous grin. The Chairman said smugly, "You will go on the Bolshoi tour—that is, Nuri Pavlinovich, *if we can trust you*. Who knows? There is always the possibility that your ingenious, stubborn nature would again find a way to defect— possibly even at the very first stop. Vienna, yes? I must remind the KGB to be vigilant."

Nuri smiled back with caution.

Baranov's smile broadened. "But then as I grow older I'm inclined to be forgetful." He looked at Tina. "Possibly your charming visit to Moscow will keep me so preoccupied I will neglect to warn the KGB."

Nuri was both gladdened and confused; he needed time to think. Pulling Tina to her feet, he whispered, "Come. It's late." To his father he said, "If it pleases you, we'll continue this discussion tomorrow at your Kremlin office. I trust you'll lend us a limousine and arrange for our hotel? Including accommodations for Jon Saarto, the so-called agent provocateur."

Grave-faced, Baranov nodded. "If you insist. But you will all be heavily guarded. For your protection."

"Of course," Nuri grumbled.

They started for the door. Immediately a dour-faced aide brought their coats.

The Soviet Chairman's voice mellowed. "Whatever you do, wherever you go, there are the chains of servility. In the West it's ruthless competitive exploitation; here it's beaureaucratic manipulation. No one is completely free of the yoke of oppression. It is merely relative."

Nuri shrugged. "As time passes, edges wear down. Even in Moscow."

Tina put on her fur-trimmed hat, smiled, and added, "And according to Gogol, history moves faster in the Soviet Union than anywhere else."

Nuri frowned. "*No Gogol*, Tina. Leave all the intonements to *Izvestia* and *Pravda*." Turning to his father, he tried to smile. "And no more paternal advice tonight, please."

Tina opened the door and shivered. "The weather in

Moscow gets colder by the day. I'm sorry, this California girl has trouble getting used to it."

The Chairman helped with her woollen scarf. "Stalin taught us that winter is Russia's mightiest army."

Two long black Chaikas waited in the driveway. Nuri and Tina bid the Soviet leader good night and hurried over the frozen walkway to the first vehicle and crawled inside. It was warm, for the driver was expecting them and had kept the engine running.

As the two limousines passed out of the inner gate and disappeared down the snow-lined driveway, Natasha Chernys-kaya emerged from her place of concealment in a back bedroom and joined Pavlin Baranov in the dacha's doorway. Despite her heavy sweater, she started to tremble, and the Chairman held her in his arms.

"It is a mistake, Pavlin? There is a stone in my heart that we cannot tell them. They will inevitably learn of us."

Baranov gently kissed her neck and closed the door. "Not now, Natasha. Later, perhaps, when the stage is far less crowded."

EPILOGUE

SAARTO LOOKED as the cell door clanked open. Brent Larkin from the American embassy entered, along with one of the Lefortovo Prison jailers.

The Special Assistant to the Chargé d'Affaires smiled. "You're free to leave, Mr. Saarto. The Soviets have agreed to put you up in a de luxe hotel for the night. Come morning, it's my job to see you off at the airport."

Saarto shrugged. "I take it I've blown my cover."

"And your welcome in the Soviet Union."

"What about Nuri and Tina?"

"Relax. They'll both get out—sooner or later. I still have to buy your ticket. Any special destination? Washington, New York, Los Angeles?"

Saarto thought for a moment. "None of the above. I need a vacation. Make it Helsinki. It's been a while since I've visited Grandma."

The raw, bitter cold night had inundated Moscow. For the first time in a week the snow clouds had dissipated and the stars were out in full splendor—a brilliant canopy that even upstaged the illuminated red stars atop the Kremlin spires. Tina and Nuri found the city a deserted stage—enchanting and mysterious.

It had required a little persuasion, but Nuri had convinced their driver and guards to let them out near the GUM department store so he could show Tina an illuminated deserted Red Square at night. It was finally decided the couple could stroll the short distance to the Rossiya Hotel, but the half-dozen KGB men in the second limousine would follow on foot.

Bundling themselves, Nuri and Tina walked slowly, hand in hand. They found the wide square empty except for a few policemen, street cleaners, and tourists with tripod-mounted cameras. The clock on the Spassky Tower read just after one. Nuri could sense Tina's fatigue, and he pulled her closer. "You said once that when you were married you wanted it to take place in an exotic place?"

She looked at him uncertainly. "How can I select the spot when I've yet to be asked?"

Nuri kissed her, then nuzzled his face in her hair and whispered, "I'm asking you now."

She stared at him, catching her breath. Her radiance made him instantly forget the joyless world surrounding them—the place described by many Soviets as the "Jewel of the East." Nuri waited for Tina's response, blocking out all other thoughts; there was just one word that was important now, and she whispered it in his ear.

"Yes."

Nuri grinned and ecstatically looked around him. To the trio of KGB men waiting several yards away, he whooped, "She accepts! We're going to be married!"

The Russians shrugged and looked at each other.

Nuri pointed toward the illuminated turnip domes of St. Basil's with its fairy-tale, candy-striped cupolas twisting into the sky. "You want to be adventurous, look there. Come spring or summer, we'll fly your parents to Moscow, along with an American minister of your choice, and be married on the steps of St. Basil's. Come, I'll show it to you."

Before Tina could wearily object or even consider the matter, he led her into Red Square. Their official KGB watchdogs followed at a discreet distance.

Approaching the imposing cathedral, Nuri gestured toward

the circular platform near the entrance. "We call it Labro Mesto," he said to her. "The umbilicus of Russia, perhaps the world."

They were distracted by a bundled *babushka* who crept toward the platform, placed three small votive candles on the steps, and lit them. She crossed herself in the Orthodox tradition.

Tina said quietly, "I'm trying to remember the cathedral's history. Didn't Ivan the Terrible blind the architect after its completion so that nothing similar would ever be built?"

Nuri nodded. "And Napoleon condemned its ugliness. Where you now stand church patriarchs blessed the crowds in one instant and Ivan tortured or beheaded his enemies the next."

Tina winced and looked around her. "You were joking about being married here, I trust?"

"It would be impossible; the structure is now a museum. But there are many other interesting places."

"May I suggest Yosemite, the Grand Canyon, or Niagara Falls?"

One of the policemen who guarded the square had seen the old woman place her candles and now came running up, shouting with anger. The *babushka* fled around the cathedral in the darkness. The militiaman stomped on the candles with his boots, extinguishing them before pursuing her.

Pulling Nuri to the steps, Tina retrieved one of the smoldering, bent forms. "In a high school play I memorized the words of Cavafy:

> "The days gone by remain behind us,
>   A mournful line of burnt-out candles
> The nearest still smoking
>   Old candles, melted and bent.
> I do not want to look at them
>   Their form saddens me.
> It saddens me to recall their first light
>   I look ahead to my lighted candles."

Holding hands, they strolled away from the cathedral and Red Square, south, toward the bridge and the Rossiya Hotel.

"Krasivy zhest!" Nuri said softly, playfully tapping the brim of her fur hat.

She smiled. "Meaning?"

"A fine gesture—your candles. The French would probably say *beau geste*." Nuri suddenly forgot that he was a dancer, and for a brief instant became a combination of all the leading men he'd ever seen on the silver screen. He kissed Tina again, softly, then firmly. When they finally separated, he whispered, "A wonderful finish to the scene, yes? In the film business it's proper to say 'fade out'?"

"*Zatemnemie*—I learned the Russian translation yesterday at Mosfilm Studios."

Nuri grinned as Tina's fur cap fell awkwardly over her eyes. He gently pushed it back in place.

She looked up at him, eyes twinkling. "If it's okay with you, let's forget all the fade-ins and fade-outs. Do whatever it takes for a *fast cut* back home."

ABOUT THE AUTHOR

Douglas Muir resides in southern California. He has degrees from the University of Washington and UCLA and was an award-winning film and television writer-director prior to turning his hand to full-time novel writing. His Hollywood credits include TV commercials, educational films, and several network documentary projects, among them the acclaimed *Undersea World of Jacques Cousteau.*

Muir's suspense novels include *American Reich, Tides of War,* and *Red Star Run.* He's currently writing a new thriller, *The Midnight Admirals,* about an errant captain aboard a Navy supercarrier. It will be published next year.